WHEN THE SI

Tom Barry's debut novel is the cri_
Calls, Book One of the Siren Calls Trilogy.

First published as a student, he spent twenty years as a management consultant and now writes full-time. Married with three children, he lives near London and counts Tuscany, the setting for this story, amongst his favourite places.

Contact him at: www.tombarrywrites.com

Praise for *When The Siren Calls*

See full list of independent reviews for this novel at www.youwriteon.com.

"Truly excellent writing and this is clearly a winning example of the genre: sultry and dangerous. The pacing is great – a roller coaster ride from the beginning, as the neglected Isobel goes from one reckless moment to another."

"The story drips with sexual tension, teasing you along with the promise of more to come. This is a book about craving and desire and the narrative has that in abundance."

"Grabs you by the throat from the start."

"The setting is vivid and alive. I could smell the mint tea and the bazaar spices and feel the oppressive sellers."

"It captured my attention immediately and kept me interested. It read well and rolled along nicely. Very readable, which is just what you want in this type of story."

"It flows easily. Attractive, lonely, neglected married woman discovers her own slumbering sexuality and finds it almost insatiable."

"The characters come across as real people with hopes and desires."

"A nicely stylized and provocative piece of writing, well paced with intelligently drawn characters and an excellent setting."

"I became totally engrossed in the story from the start. The build-up of tension is well paced and very real - my adrenaline flowed. This is likely not the book to read last thing at night if one has insomnia."

"This was fantastic. The pace was fabulous."

"There's a hint of menace and danger from the opening page. The author then skillfully toys with your expectations."

Praise for Tom Barry

"If 'humourotica' is a genre then Tom Barry is its king; if it does not yet exist then he is its creator."
                                        – Book Connisseur

"Tom Barry has a keen eye for detail, a strong sense of irony and a good nose for unearthing what lies beneath the civilised facades we present to the world. It's exciting to find a new writer who tells life like it is, but with a delectable twist of romance, sex and humour."
                      – Stephanie J. Hale, The Oxford Literacy Consultancy

"Tom Barry follows in the footsteps of the great Irish storytellers."
                                  – Ré Ó Laighléis, author, 'Hooked'

tombarrywrites.com

Matador
9 Priory Business Park
Kibworth Beauchamp
Leicestershire LE8 0RX, UK
Tel: (+44) 116 279 2299
Fax: (+44) 116 279 2277
Email: books@troubador.co.uk
Web: www.troubador.co.uk/matador

This book is a work of fiction and all characters and events are the product of the
author's imagination. Any resemblance to real persons, living or dead, is purely
coincidental. All rights reserved.

ISBN 978 1780883 106

British Library Cataloguing in Publication Data.
A catalogue record for this book is available from the British Library.

Typeset in Minion Pro by Troubador Publishing Ltd
Printed and bound in the UK by TJ International, Padstow, Cornwall

Matador is an imprint of Troubador Publishing Ltd

WHEN THE SIREN CALLS

Book One of the Siren Calls Trilogy

TOM BARRY

To my patient wife, Maysoon, for indulging my obsession over several revisions, despite claiming to have loved the first draft.

Foreword

What is this Maya we call Love? Why are we compelled to spend lifetimes in desperate pursuit of her, only to be left churning in her wake?

"Obstinate are the trammels, but my heart aches when I try to break them.
Freedom is all I want, but to hope for it I feel ashamed.
I am certain that priceless wealth is in thee, and that thou art my best friend, but I have not the heart to sweep away the tinsel that fills my room.
The shroud that covers me is a shroud of dust and death; I hate it, yet hug it in love.
My debts are large, my failures great, my shame secret and heavy; yet when I come to ask for my good, I quake in fear lest my prayer be granted."

— Rabindranath Tagore (1861-1941)

One

Grasping hands tore at Isobel's clothing and scraped her skin as she forced her way forward. She swung round to face the seething pack, the speed of her movement causing her handbag — too oversized, too glittering for these dusty lanes — to sweep with her in a defensive arc.

"Go away, allez, allez!" she shouted, trying to sound authoritative as the street urchins began to melt away.

Free from the pressing bodies, she wove deeper and deeper into the labyrinth of endless, identical alleyways, slipping between the sacks and the stalls with a serpentine ease that masked her increasing panic. She felt as if every eye were upon her, eyes shrouded by swathes of headgear or set within sun-dried faces, all disapproving, some accusing. Every turn revealed idle and cocky gangs of youths who straddled their cycles, observing her distress with knowing smirks.

Isobel looked for an opening, any way out that might lead her back to the square and return her to some kind of safety and normality. But every likely exit from this terrible maze was blocked with the knee-high beggars who had followed the scent of her like sharks, ever since she had taken pity on a tiny girl who, with swimming eyes, had pleaded for a dirham. But as they closed in to encircle her, there were no more pleas, only orders.

"You give dirhams!" they called at her, chanting their demand like a mantra.

"Yes, dirhams!" she cried in a sudden and reckless change of tack. "Dirhams for whoever can show me the way back to the square."

She pulled a single note from her purse and waved it before the outstretched hands. But the sight of money only fed the frenzy and the chorus of orphaned voices grew louder and more demanding, as ragged forms crashed against her legs and threatened to topple her with their combined force.

A barking voice cut through the chaos around her and her pursuers leapt back as if scalded. The sound of a wicker cane smacking against flesh was followed by shrieks of pain and the startled waifs scattered like stray cats. Isobel turned towards her saviour, overwhelmed with gratitude and close to tears. She guessed he was in his mid-forties, unmistakably Arabic, clean-shaven, and smartly dressed in Western clothes, his polo sporting one of the many designer labels that seemed to adorn even the cheapest t-shirts.

"They mean no harm, the children," said the man. "Do not think badly of them, perhaps they already saw you were a kind woman? The children, they see it in the face, if you are kind. So you must be very kind to attract so many children."

"Thank you," said Isobel, her racing pulse beginning to slow, "but I think it was the few coins I gave a little girl for sweets that was my mistake."

"A mistake perhaps, but also the sign of a good heart, no?"

Isobel smiled at the compliment.

"You wish to go to the square I think?" asked the man.

"Yes, yes, I do. Is it near?"

"If you know where it is, it is near, if not…" the man shrugged, "if not it can be very, very far. Perhaps you will let me show you the way. No one will bother you if you are not alone."

Isobel hesitated. "If you are sure you don't mind. I said I would meet my husband there."

The man motioned toward the space behind the open shutters.

"Please, wait inside for a few moments. I must get my son for he will mind the store. Please, this way, just a few moments."

Isobel idly perused the wares as she waited. Her appetite for shopping, if she ever had one, was exhausted. The glimmering trinkets in her bags were useless trifles, bought to justify her headstrong decision to come to the souk alone, a means to make her point to Peter when she returned. She checked her watch. It was clear that "a few moments" meant something other than what the words implied. Still, this was Marrakech, where life still seemed to follow the movement of the sun rather than the hands of the clock. She brushed her fingers along the reams of intricately adorned fabric with their brilliant shades of orange and blue, savouring the space around her and revelling in the silence broken only by the whining of moths around the turquoise lamp suspended from the ceiling.

Isobel noticed the lengthening shadows, and looked again at her wrist. There was a limit to how long a good deed could be considered a debt. She put aside the cloth she was admiring; she would just have to make her own way to the square. She was confident that her journey from the square had been upward, so the way back must be downward. As she pulled down her sunglasses like a visor to signal that no eye contact would be entertained, the silence was ruptured by the man's voice, he had returned — a twenty-year-old version of himself in tow.

"I am sorry to keep you, kind lady, but my son, he must close his shop, and before he can close it he must put away his fruit. This is my son, Sharif, and I am Ali."

Isobel turned to the young man. Putting away his fruit must also have involved boiling the kettle, as he carried a silver tray with a long, curve-spouted silver pot, and three glasses hardly bigger than egg cups.

"Please let me offer you a refreshment," said the older man, "it is our tradition and you are an honoured guest."

Sharif was dressed similarly to his father, except where the older man's shirt bore the emblem of a crocodile, his son's bore that of a prancing horse.

"You are in Marrakech for holiday?" asked Ali, who was clearly the talker of the two.

"Just the weekend."

"So short, so little time. You must not think that all of Marrakech is like the souk, that everyone is like the hungry children. You must return soon. We have much history, beautiful architecture, white sandy beaches. And you will find the Moroccan people very friendly, very welcoming. It is our tradition. I must give you something, a present, to remind you of Morocco."

"Really," said Isobel, keen to bring matters to a close, "you have been too kind already."

"Sharif, a little gift for the lovely lady."

Sharif seemed to have anticipated his father's command. He stepped forward, a ring-sized jewellery box between thumb and forefinger.

"It is only a trinket, of no real value to some, but precious to others."

Sharif opened the box to reveal a blue ceramic pendant on a silver chain. Isobel smiled and began to say thank you but was cut short by arms encircling her neck.

"Sharif will put it on for you, it is tradition," proclaimed the older man.

The young man's hands travelled swiftly behind Isobel's neck. For what seemed a long time, he stood in front of her, their bodies less than a foot apart, his forearms brushing her shoulders, as his fingers worked behind her neck to secure the clasp. Isobel felt the cool stone resting in her cleavage, visible at the opened top of her blouse. She fingered the pendant as she tried to ensure it rested on closed linen.

"I wish that my gift keeps you safe from the evil eye, and that it brings you back to Marrakech," said Ali, as Sharif retreated to the doorway. "But you must also choose something from my shop that you wish to have, something to wear perhaps. I have beautiful cotton and silk blouses. Kaftans also. You choose."

Isobel wanted to say that the rescue, the tea, the pendant, and the promised escort to the square were more than enough to bring her back to Morocco, but the need to repay a kindness weighed heavier than the need to get away.

"This way," said Ali, seizing on her hesitation and taking her arm, "you must see my special cloth, the cloth I must keep out of the sun and the dust." And with that she was whisked behind a draping curtain and her head then guided down through a low opening more like a metal cat-flap than a door, to emerge into a dimly lit and cluttered stockroom.

Cloth was no longer the prime commodity. Arranged around the walls and along parallel rows of shelves was a hypermarket-like selection of tourist ware: watches, jewellery, sunglasses, handbags, shoes, clothing, and the household contents of an entire village. All that was obviously missing was a live camel.

The absence of natural light, the confined space, the silence, and the realisation that she was with two strangers, one ahead, one behind, suddenly pressed in on Isobel. She bit down hard on her lower lip.

"Please, you pick something, it is for the memory, no?"

Despite the ambiguity in Ali's offer, Isobel was now expected to shop; that was clear. The opening she'd come through was closed, and Sharif was standing like a praetorian guard in front of it, his legs apart and arms folded. And for all Ali's geniality, the atmosphere changed as soon as the door closed behind her. Isobel's insides fluttered like caged birds. Did they want her money, or did they want more? In the dim light their eyes seemed red and never left her body.

"Do you have blouses?" she asked, desperate to keep the situation under control.

"Many, many. What colour you like?"

"Green. Or, or, maybe blue," she stammered, thinking about the pendant. Ali handed her a selection of cotton tops, each in a clear plastic wrapper.

Isobel sought to give her most positive eager shopper look. "Yes, maybe these, but I need to see them in the light."

"Here is light," said Ali, gesturing all around.

"No, I mean natural light."

"Green is green and blue is blue. Always same."

"No, I need to see them in natural light." Isobel held the half dozen blouses, and the question of price had yet to raise its ugly head. Ali looked off-balance.

"I can't buy without proper light," she repeated and with that, still clutching the blouses, she made for the door.

"Hold these, please." She thrust the merchandise toward Sharif. It was an order and he took them as Isobel pushed her way past and ducked through the opening.

She needed to get back into the front of the shop before the two men could recover from the shock of her assertiveness. She looked around but the exit was concealed somewhere behind the realms of hanging drapes. Where was the way out? She thrashed at a few of the curtains that were beginning to envelop her, but was finally through.

She resisted the urge to rush headlong into the street. She composed herself as the two men reappeared, their nostrils flaring in anger.

"My husband is waiting for me. I'm sorry, I need to go. I will come back tomorrow."

Ali held out his arm, stiff like a barrier. "Do you think you can rest from the heat of the day and drink tea in my shop for free? Can you drink tea in shop in London for free? Why you think you can do it here? You steal my time, you steal money. It is same. You buy now. No tomorrow."

It was the younger man that now grabbed her arm in a determined sandpaper grip.

"I'll come back tomorrow. Now let go of my arm."

"You must pay now."

"Let go of my arm, *now.*"

The older man stepped in between Isobel and the opening to the street. She jerked her arm free and pushed past him, fear closing around her like the Marrakech night.

"You steal my time, you are thief!" Ali shouted again, but louder, thrusting the blouses at her. Others were closing in, drawn by the commotion, and once more she found herself hemmed in. Stubbled faces with swarthy complexions were looking at her, joining in the melee. It felt like a hundred eyes were undressing her. She cursed her impetuosity in storming off from Peter, of not changing out of the revealing top and clinging slacks, both now wet from her own perspiration. A hand brushed the inside of her thigh and travelled upwards. She swung around and was met by a shrivelled face and a leering grin, a single black and yellow tooth behind the thin cracked lips. "Don't you dare touch me!" she shouted. But as she said it she felt more tugging, this time on her bag.

She clasped the bag to her chest with both arms but in doing so felt her body more exposed, more vulnerable. Her heart pounding, she steeled herself for a fight, but before she could swivel around again, she sensed the threat dissipating. The hand on her buttock was no longer there, bodies were backing off, parting like the Red Sea, and faces were turning away from her. The crowd shrank to the sides of the stalls and was disappearing; someone was pushing through from behind, shouting.

"Everything ok, darling?"

"Peter, thank god —"

6

But it was not Peter. She turned to see a tall, well-built man forcing his way towards her with the confident assurance of a native. She felt a protective arm around her shoulder, as he pulled her still shaking body close to his, his powerful presence both intimidating and reassuring. Only the storekeeper Ali remained in the confrontation.

"You pay now," he repeated, pushing his bundle of blouses forward.

The man grabbed the top-most garment; he spoke in Arabic to the storekeeper. From Ali's reaction, Isobel guessed it was something uncompromising.

"How much?" asked the man; the shopkeeper gave his price in Arabic. The man pulled some crumpled notes from his pocket and pressed them into Ali's hand. "Not the best time to bargain," he quipped.

With the exchange done, the hostile manner of the shopkeeper gave way to supplication. Ali returned to the smiling well-wisher Isobel had first encountered.

She let out a long, audible sigh, her breathing easier, as the stranger led her towards the fading light. "Where did you come from?" she asked.

"I don't know," said the man as they passed a stall of shining metal-ware, "someone must have made a wish, one minute I'm in this brass lamp and the next —"

She burst out laughing, the tension falling from her body. "So how do we leave this nightmare?" she asked.

"Come on, follow me, it's this way — or at least I think it's this way," he said, beckoning encouragement.

Was her rescuer all he seemed? It occurred to Isobel that she had already been deceived that afternoon by one smiling Samaritan. But she had little choice; the man took her by the hand and led her away with quick and purposeful strides, turning this way and that through the narrow alleys as if by instinct, into the spice market with its endless sacks of red saffron, golden curry, and bronze cumin, the aromas of mint and rose filling her senses and soothing away her fears, before they emerged into the square. The sky was darkening to a reddish brown, the orange veil which bathed the square now disappearing as the sun retreated beyond the horizon, along with the tourists and those who traded among them. From distant minarets came the wailing sound of the faithful being called to prayer.

The tension and seeming danger in the souk, the heroic intervention, the rapid escape, all made for a strange sense of elation in Isobel. She tried not to think of Peter back at the hotel waiting and, no doubt, worrying. Right now she wanted to enjoy the moment.

"Who do I have to thank for saving me from Ali and the forty thieves?" she asked, masking the strange importance she placed on knowing his name.

"Jay, Jay Brooke." He offered his hand and Isobel took it. His blue eyes bore into hers.

"Isobel," she offered in reply, unsure how to proceed.

"You were quite a fighter back there," he said.

"Fight or flight, I suppose. You must think me very foolish to have gotten myself into such a mess?"

"These things happen. Probably down to misunderstanding mostly. But a woman, an attractive Western woman, alone in the souk, maybe not the best idea."

Isobel blushed at the compliment but controlled her instinctive flirtatious response and settled for a simple request. "You must let me pay for the blouse."

"Don't be silly, you earned it," he replied before being cut short as a taxi broke from the rank, turned full circle, and pulled alongside them.

Jay opened the rear passenger door. "Where are you staying?"

"La Mamounia," she said.

Jay grinned. "Great taste. That's where I'm staying. How long are you there for?"

Isobel felt compelled to break the dream, to make it clear she was accompanied.

"We're just here for the weekend."

She expected him to seek clarification on who the "we" was, but he didn't.

"Me too. Maybe I can save you from drowning in the pool or something next time?"

He made no move to close the door and, taking the hint, Isobel slid across so he could join her.

He lowered his head to follow her movement. "I just need to get a couple of things before everything closes, lovely to have met you. Take care."

And with that he gave a final smile, before pushing the door closed. Was their brief acquaintance to be confined to and immortalised in one fleeting moment of chivalry? He hit the roof of the cab, signalling it to leave with the same confidence that seemed to permeate all his actions. And as the taxi drove away, all Isobel's feelings of elation evaporated, turning to embarrassment at her rejection and shock at her own forwardness. She huddled into a corner and willed herself home, perhaps not herself at all.

Two

Isobel stared at her reflection in the gilded reception mirror. She fancied it altered from the face in the bathroom that morning, somehow younger and brighter. Her eyes descended her figure and halted in alarm at the still damp linen blouse which revealed her nipples like roses in the mist. Fear and embarrassment flooded over her at the thought of her involuntary immodesty, although if the stranger noticed then he certainly concealed it well. She remembered the way his bright blue eyes held her own with an almost hypnotic gaze and was certain they did not stray to her body.

The concierge eyed her curiously as she turned from the mirror.

"Welcome back, madam. Your afternoon in the bazaar was pleasant I trust?"

Isobel forced a laugh. "Your sellers in the market are very persuasive."

The concierge simply returned a knowing smile. "Is there something I can help you with, madam?" She looked around the foyer and towards the bustling lobby bar with the golden statues at its entrance assuming poses of serenity that contrasted harshly with the harried staff that passed between them.

"Is my husband around, do you know?"

"Yes, madam. I believe he is in his suite. He rang down a short while ago."

"Looking for me?"

"If I remember correctly, it was to do with a courier delivery he was expecting. Some papers." Isobel feigned a look of surprise and nodded, turning her attention to a taxi that swept up outside. She watched in nervous expectation as a strong male figure, broad shouldered and straight-backed, emerged from the darkness of the interior. She craned her neck as the figure turned from her view and reached his hand into the taxi, helping an elderly lady from the vehicle and leading her into the hotel. Isobel blushed as he met her glance, his sandy hair and watery grey eyes worlds away from what she wished for.

She made her way back to the hotel room, choosing the staircase over the elevator, stepping on her anxiety and frustration with each firm footstep as she prepared to face Peter. The image of what this evening should have been — a night of dining under the stars with music, dancing, and horse riding across desert dunes — sat stubbornly before her eyes. Peter's words, his careless and thoughtless dismissal of her plans in favour of the hotel restaurant and its internet connection, still rang in her ears.

He was on the phone when she entered the room, papers and files arranged on the coffee table like place settings.

"We need to be in the lobby at six-thirty," she said, hovering by the bed to invite his apology, but he did not rise to greet her, just smiled and gave a thumbs up as he nodded assent.

"Six-thirty," she repeated, already pulling her blouse over her head as she made towards the bathroom, the beginnings of tears making spots like raindrops in its translucent fabric. She turned on the shower and tried to compose herself as the jet-stream cascaded down her body, allowing her emotions to evaporate as the heat of the water turned the shower door a milky white. She drew a tree on the glass, her finger etching paths through the moisture like a figure skater, as the trunk became branches with fingerprint leaves. As her fingers slid along the glass she followed the passage of time; through fifteen years of marriage, from Peter's growing infatuation with his work — a drug that fed his ego with a heady cocktail of success — to the missed anniversaries and interrupted holidays. As each year passed, things grew worse, and now she left the bathroom and Peter was asleep.

Isobel was running again through the winding alleys of Marrakech. Everywhere there were shopkeepers with many heads and many, many more hands. The square buildings grew rounder and rounder until they were crystal balls, filled with the sea and the sky, and great hands hovered above them covered in golden rings. Suddenly the rings started to fall, hitting against the glassy globes with a hollow knocking sound. The swirls of smoke became the damask pattern of the curtains in the half-light; it was 2am and the clicking was the whirring ceiling fan, the dullest of confirmations that she was back in the world of the living. Peter, she sensed, was also awake, his thoughts still no doubt consumed by the late night messages from Tokyo. They were as far apart in the king-size bed as it was possible to be, his straight, firm back repelling hers, and she felt sure that, if she edged closer, an invisible barrier would brush against her skin, so ingrained were the day's events.

"I'm sorry about this afternoon," she said, conciliation and warmth in her tone as once more she fought against what threatened to be nature's course.

He stayed quiet a few seconds before reaching out and pulling her to him, an increasingly unfamiliar gesture that made her jolt in surprise.

"It was my fault. And the evening too. I behaved unforgivably, sulking like that. I know how much you wanted it to be a success, to be a romantic evening. It was just..." His explanation trailed away. "I will make it up to you," he promised with a reassuring hug, his thoughts seeming to drift off with his words.

"Why don't we make it up now?" She slipped her hand inside his pyjamas. "It can still be a romantic evening." It had been many months, perhaps six, since she last prompted lovemaking, or since she last responded fully to his initiations. At times when the mood of martyrdom most gripped her, she would try to convince herself that she was content to lie beneath him and wait, until finally rolling away to let sleep envelop her.

She squeezed and massaged him, but he was slow to respond to her coaxing. As she stroked and caressed she pushed the guilt of her straying imagination aside, picturing herself the confused heroine in an epic romance. She felt again the adrenaline of the souk, and an unfamiliar lust coursing through her veins, her frustration rising at the lack of progress her efforts were instilling. At last she felt his readiness and rose to straddle him, gently helping him inside her with a mix of platonic affection and stifled fear.

His surprise at her initiation was almost comical, a jarring note of humour in her serious romantic drama. Yet she pursued her cravings nonetheless, strangely aroused by her experience with the man from the market and spurred on by fear, needing to reassure herself about her marriage. But his familiarity was crushing; she felt no possibility in Peter's embrace — only his inevitable climax and her seemingly eternal disappointment.

Three

Strange feelings of guilt surged and ebbed within Isobel as she sat with Peter at the breakfast table; she pushed her food round the plate with her fork, eyeing it listlessly and eating nothing. She had lost almost a stone in the past six months, the weight falling off as Peter's absorption in his latest client reached its peak. He, of course, failed to notice. Failed to feel her hip bones against his as they lay together, remained oblivious to the wedding ring that now slid loosely up her finger and back to the knuckle with a dull thud.

She studied him as he prodded his mushroom omelette, his attention temporarily distracted from the business section of the newspaper. His face and body were as lean and athletic as the day they met, but the vitality within him was so changed from the man she married. And without knowing why, she found herself resenting that he was the same, yet different.

"Peter, about yesterday…"

But her words were drowned by the quiet bleep of his phone, the 'please stay quiet bleep' as she once called it; it was late afternoon in Tokyo, and his eyes and mind went to the message on the screen instead of the anxiety on her face. She reached across and put her palm over the phone; he looked at her with impatience, perhaps even anger, in his eyes.

"I had quite a fright in the medina. At one point one of the sellers grabbed my arm, you know, really grabbed it, and a crowd gathered."

"Those guys don't take no for an answer. If you had just waited half an hour we could have gone together," he said, failing to sense any impending drama as he removed her hand from the screen. "Can I just deal with this, and then I'm all yours." But he was not and she feared never would be.

She rose and stood for a moment in exasperation. "I'm going to the room to pack, then I'm off to the pool."

He gestured to the phone pressed to his ear and batted off her words with a flick of his hand.

All guilt dissolved as she made the short walk to the elevator, her vision narrowed by rage she focused only on the shining doors ahead. A man leapt up from a chair to her left but she did not see him. He threw down his newspaper and ran up behind her, pressing his hand playfully to her back.

"Going my way," he said, as she almost jumped out of her skin, whirling round as the last of her tired nerves snapped.

"Oh my god, don't do that," she said, trying to disguise the contortion of emotions on her face.

He laughed a boyish laugh. "Sorry, I just can't seem to help myself jumping out of nowhere to rescue damsels in distress."

"I'm not in distress," she said smiling, "and the lift only goes one way."

The lift came and went as they exchanged pleasantries, Isobel offering her thanks once more for his heroics and he convivially dismissing them, his humour as pleasant and energetic as the day before. He seemed content to chat idly as the doors opened and closed, but Isobel found her eye straying to the breakfast room entrance. He seemed to sense her discomfort and stepped into the elevator at the next opportunity, silently beckoning her with his smile to follow him.

She looked at her watch.

"We're leaving in a couple of hours," she said, to which he muttered a nonchalant "uh um," obliging her to continue. "I thought I'd spend the last hour around the pool… just while Peter makes his calls."

"Sounds good, I was thinking about doing the same."

Isobel had to stop herself from running as she stepped out to the corridor and made for her room. Once there she threw her clothes haphazardly into the suitcase, rehearsing her reasoning as she went. "Why should I avoid someone who did such a chivalrous thing, if Peter's going to ignore me?"

She paused to consider her clothing options, dallying only seconds over the idea of travel clothes before opting for a swimming costume. Modesty and disquiet compelled her to choose the one-piece over a bikini but it was a striking black number, with a lace effect around the neck and midriff that allowed a veiled glimpse of both cleavage and waistline. She stood before the mirror touching up her lipstick; the woman looking back at her was strikingly attractive. Although her skin no longer shone with the dewy freshness of youth, it was firm and polished, taut across her fine bone structure. Taller than average, she was a sculpture of a woman, viewing herself in the mirror like looking at art behind glass. She subconsciously nodded her approval and moved to the door, grabbing a bathrobe as she went.

When she reached the pool, Jay was already there, his suit jacket draped over the lounger at his side. He looked effortlessly smart, his attractions in no way dulled by his unexposed flesh. Isobel broke her stride, now feeling foolish in her swimsuit and hating herself for her lack of subtlety. She pulled the bathrobe belt even tighter and made the walk across to him. She wanted to take the lounger next to his but her nerve failed her.

"Shall we talk at the table?" she suggested, as she hung her bag decisively on the nearest chair.

He was charming but professional as they chatted, and with every sentence struck another crack in her fragile, still almost unconscious, hopes and imaginings.

"Your husband not joining us then?" he asked.

"He's busy making calls to save the world," she said, reproaching herself for her bitterness.

"Ah yes, you said. What does he do, if you don't mind me asking?"

"He flies from boardroom to boardroom making fat cats look good." She tried to make her tone blasé, even amused, as she discreetly loosened the bathrobe. "You know, strategy. Buy this, sell that."

"So he travels a lot, I guess?"

"All the time. One luxury hotel to the next, like this place."

"That must be great for you." He smiled and raked his fingers through his hair before continuing. "The opportunity to travel with him, I mean."

"I used to think so. But after ten years it can get nauseating. Talking trivia with pampered spouses in the same bland function rooms all over the world."

"While the boys swig their brandy and swing their dicks?" His crudity should have shocked her and she blushed when it didn't.

"It sounds like you know the game he's in," she said, the bathrobe slipping from her shoulders as she put down her drink. His eyes lingered for a moment on her torso as curved black materialized from the soft, shapeless white.

"A little bit, maybe. But what brought you both to Marrakech, if he's so busy?"

She could not resist the invitation for disclosure. "My dreams, I suppose. You know, the romance of the place. But I did have to drag Peter here kicking and screaming."

"And your dreams were fulfilled?" His eyes burnt into her, seeming to see everything, to know everything.

"It hasn't been the right time, there's a lot going on."

She felt all of a sudden afraid of being quizzed further and drew herself up to become the questioner.

"And you, what brings you here?"

"Business. I'm checking out an investment possibility. A tourist development."

"And that's what you do all the time?"

"Some of the time. Right now I'm spending most of my time in Italy, in Tuscany; it's a new concept — a luxury hotel and spa, an idyllic retreat in the hills — somewhere for a romantic getaway, or just to get some 'me-time,' while being pampered like a princess. If you visit you'd love it, I'm sure, and if you didn't, then I'd know we were getting it wrong."

She smiled at the compliment. "Maybe I will," she said brazenly, taking a sip of iced tea through the straw, moulding her lips round it into a soft pink 'o'.

He laughed, and pulled a card from his wallet. "Here are my details, and there's a link on the back to a website; it will show you what we're up to much better than I can describe."

She tucked it away in the pocket of her robe as he stood up to say his goodbyes. As she rose to receive them, the bathrobe fell fully to the floor.

Four

Some eighteen months earlier, in an airport hotel, Lucy Baker basked in the familiar feeling of knowing she was turning every head as she entered the bar. A peek beneath her tight fitting outfit would have revealed a near perfect body, a breathtaking alliance of nature's gifts and a surgeon's steady hand. She had almost feline eyes; perfectly shaped, astonishingly green, and as angular and beautifully formed as the rest of her captivating face. They were restless eyes, full of energy and playfulness, but as she and her colleagues walked into the lounge of the airport hotel, her eyes rested on one man, and her thoughts stayed firmly on him for the remainder of the evening. He sat centre stage in the middle of the bar, nonchalantly straddling the back of a chair and holding half a dozen or so young men under his spell, their shoulders shaking with laughter, their faces exuding pure admiration.

"Let's sit over here, shall we ladies?" she volunteered, as the group behind her milled about in confusion. She led the way to the middle of the lounge, right behind the gathering and its enigmatic leader, and beckoned the others. Her movements were smooth and supple, exuding the sensuality that defined her appearance. Her skin glowed sunbed-brown and her hair was a carefully manufactured blonde. It had been every shade of this hue over the years — pearl white as an exotic dancer, sunflower yellow as a glamour model. Now she was an airhostess and this was reflected in the darker, and she fancied, more demure, honey tones that hung around her face like an unlikely halo.

As Lucy perched on her chair, luxuriously extending her long shapely legs to exhibit them to their best potential, she covertly returned her gaze to the man, watching with a hidden smile as he awarded a gangly but handsome man in his early thirties, attired in a ridiculous bow tie and plus fours, an award for his exceptionally bad play on the golf course.

"On one knee if you please, Eamon," he said, as the recipient came forward for his prize. He spoke with all the command and presence of a king, and as Lucy looked about her, it seemed the whole bar was watching and enjoying his showmanship. She was surprised that applause did not break out as, with a flourish, he produced a plastic funnel from beneath his chair and proceeded with much ceremony to concoct a punishment.

"The committee has decided," he proclaimed, obliging the now beaming Eamon to accept the funnel to his lips, "that your forfeit is a quad-vod, to be washed down with a half-pint of the vilest concoction of sangria and punch ever mixed at this fine hotel."

Lucy zoned out as the jovial Irishman took his punishment with pleasure, and willed herself to pay attention to the tortuous conversations of her colleagues, who were discussing at length the policies, practices, and pitfalls of a life in the skies. Her antenna tuned in as the discussion turned to sexual harassment at work, a continuation of one of the afternoon's topics. Lucy interjected boldly, "That was the problem at my last place - sexual harassment."

All heads turned as her colleagues focused on her, their faces expectant and hungry for a titillating personal disclosure. "Go on, Lucy," said one, "what was the problem?"

"There simply wasn't enough of it," she exclaimed, slapping her thighs with gusto as laughter broke out around her. She lowered her head in mock modesty and stole a sideways glance at the floorshow, but only the grinning Eamon, his eyes fixed on her, seemed to have heard.

The rounds of drinks came and went and her gaze was drawn back once again to the dashing compere. Her eyes travelled up his body, resting on the gold watch, the designer-buckled belt, the well-heeled suede loafers and, lastly, on the chunky platinum wedding ring - the only adornment to strong and animated hands. Three years ago that humble piece of jewellery would have been the end of Lucy's quest. But her career of late nights with her body wrapped around a silver pole taught her that the world, or at least one part of it, was stocked full of wealthy and generous men, married and otherwise, who were only too ready to spoil her. She attempted to engage him in eye contact as the spoof awards descended into bedlam but it seemed pointless; he was the one man in the room who didn't see her.

Even when his group settled down and struck up conversation across the two tables, merging the parties into one, he remained elusive, sitting at the furthest point away from her. Growing impatient, Lucy loudly excused herself to the bathroom and meandered her way towards the door, choosing a strategic route that took her between the man and one of his captivated courtiers. The gap was a narrow one and the man held his position, forcing Lucy to turn sideways to pass through, her crotch all but brushing his nose as she tried to make her way out. But he stopped her with a friendly hand on her thigh and, averting his eyes from the short skirt looked her straight in the eyes, grinned, and said, "It's all looking a bit tight isn't it?"

"Tighter than you might think," she replied, before making her way through to the bathroom.

Lucy lingered in the toilets at her leisure, reapplying makeup and fiddling with her hair as she contemplated what now inevitably lay before her. She could still feel his touch on her thigh and, imagining his hand sliding up under her skirt, wedding ring and luxury timepiece in close proximity against her skin, she left to claim what she hungered for.

Over the next hour the group was fluid, with people moving chairs as others came and went from the bar or the bathroom. The man, whose name she discovered to be Jay, remained elusive but Eamon — acting on his personal motto that 'faint heart never won fuck all' — eventually secured himself the seat next to her. He showered her with enraptured attention, stroking her crossed legs as he plied her with compliments and innuendos.

Lucy's concern was not the progress that Eamon's wandering hand was seeking to make on her anatomy, but the progress Georgia — her glamorous and worldly supervisor — was making a few feet away. She was probably close to Jay's age, and to Lucy's eye well enough preserved to merit the interest of even a discerning suitor. Worryingly, her advances seemed to be welcome and Lucy, powerless to intervene, had to resign herself to waiting for her superior to need the restroom.

Time passed with all the speed of a dull sermon but eventually, just when Lucy was concluding that Georgia must have the bladder of a bison, her rival took her turn to excuse herself.

"Don't go away now, will you," she instructed in her most seductive tone, before reinforcing her intention by placing her jacket over the back of the chair. But such signals were null and void in Lucy's world and with a seductive smile she turned to Jay, twisting her pole dancer's body with a graceful ease that threatened to make the most staunch and devoted husband want to rip off her clothes and devour her supple flesh.

"Oh Jay, while you have a second, you were talking earlier about your holiday in the Seychelles," she began, locking his eyes in a smouldering stare that said 'I don't need to introduce myself, because you've asked who I am already.'

"Maybe you could send me the details, if you still have them?"

"Sure," said Jay with a casual air, as if he had been expecting just such an enquiry, "I'd be pleased to. Do you have maybe an email address or something?"

Lucy reached down to the bag beside her chair, and took out her phone and her room key to search for a paper and pen.

"Here, put your email on this if it's easier," suggested Jay, offering his business card and his gold-tipped Mont Blanc ballpoint.

Lucy examined the pen with admiration. The movements of her fingers were deft and precise but languid, exuding raw sensuality. She scribbled on the card and handed it and the pen back to its owner, before turning back to reengage Eamon, the shrug of her shoulders deeming complete the tiresome chore of giving her email.

She watched him out of the corner of her eye as he replaced the pen and turned over the card, expecting to see an email address. Instead there were just two words:

"I'm Wet."

Five

As the cab pulled into Berkeley Square, Jay was chuckling. Lucy's latest photo message was on his screen, and it was x-rated material. He smiled as he wondered how she managed to get the blindfold and handcuffs on before the auto flash clicked. But then again with Lucy it was hard to tell; perhaps another girl was on the other side of the camera. If so, maybe he would be meeting her before long too. It was just a week since they met, and his aching body was already begging for respite from Lucy's voracious appetite. Tonight he was guaranteed that respite, at least from Lucy.

One floor below ground, with no natural light and scant attempt to replace it, Annabel's might have been designed for infidelity. It was a Tuesday evening and still early for the club's well-heeled and well-connected members. Jay and Andy, an old friend from university, had the Buddha Room — a sumptuously dressed, lounge-sized sanctuary, tucked away — all to themselves.

The two men spent dinner tentatively reminiscing over their exploits in their college days, cheerfully conversing as each tried to ascertain exactly what it was the other wanted. Back then the two were thrown together as flatmates and, as Jay was keen to remind him, Andy had been the studious nerd heading for a first class honours in computer science, and Jay was the slacker and all round cool guy heading for an attendance certificate. But an underhand and carefully executed deal between the two changed both their fates forever. Andy sold his brains for the tempting fruits of popularity, doing all of his friend's coursework in exchange for an acquaintance with the beautiful Simone — who took his virginity with all the care and mercy she could muster. Jay, in turn, surprised even his most ardent admirers, amongst whose ranks he could count several professors, and graduated with an upper second in economics and law. And now, nearly two decades later, reflected back in the large mirror opposite them they saw a big city dealmaker and a dot com millionaire — looking older but very much the same.

When they had exhausted their college anecdotes they moved carefully on to the present, starting with their spouses. "So you really hit the jackpot with Kate, didn't you?" said Jay, leaning back and spreading his arms.

"You've met Kate?" Andy asked in response, suspicion and a hint of dread clear in his voice. Jay wondered if his abrupt and unprecedented invitation caused Andy — with some justification — to worry this meeting might be in relation to his young socialite wife.

He laughed. "No, it is just that I saw the pictures in *Tatler*. She's quite a stunner."

"And that's what prompted the invitation?"

"Kind of, yes. It did remind me of the times we had together and that, frankly, the day might come when there might be something we could do together, that's all. But that's for another time, how about tonight we just enjoy ourselves?"

Jay sensed his friend was not quite ready to give up with his probing and moments later Andy began again.

"So there's nothing particular you are spending your time on right now?"

"Well, now that you mention it," said Jay, leaning forward, "right now I am spending a good deal of time in Italy, in Tuscany. It's a struggling tourist development. Quick in and quick out and a twenty to fifty million return on a modest investment. It's something I've conceived myself. My vision is for a five star luxury resort. There will be a boutique hotel at the centre, a spa, and one hundred condos owned by private buyers. It will be my job to turn the place around and complete the development."

"If you can only find the money?"

Jay laughed again. "You don't give up, do you? It's not a pitch, Andy — the financing is in place. I'm just sorting out the negotiations with the party in Italy. If we'd met up two months ago then there might have been a chance to do something together, and I really would have welcomed you in on the deal, but the investment window is now closed."

Jay watched his friend's eyes wander to the two elegantly dressed platinum blondes who had just materialised at the bar, looking over their shoulders and swiftly back at each other, the studied movement of their bodies inviting attention and approach.

"When you say enjoy ourselves, did you have those two in mind?" Andy asked with the same look of expectation that Jay elicited from him all those years ago.

Jay ran his eye over the two arrivals. "Gold diggers with six inch claws. Russians probably. You'll enjoy the night, but you could still be paying for it in ten years. If you do want some fun without any complications, this is not the place."

"But you know the place?"

Jay looked at his watch and discreetly rubbed a smidgen of lipstick off it with his thumb. "I think I just might."

A short taxi ride later and they drew to a halt outside a row of black railings in a side street off the Bayswater Road.

"A fun place I think you'll like," said Jay as he led them down a dark and inconspicuous flight of stairs to an unremarkable door with nothing to recommend it but a video entry phone. A cursory glance at the screen convinced the woman at the other end to let them in and Jay headed through the door, discreetly beckoning his friend to follow him. They made their way along a dimly lit passageway until a pumpkin of a woman in a flowing red dress, who seemed to fill the space like a London bus, firm and unassailable, blocked their progress. Jay leant forward and the two exchanged kisses to both cheeks, her body rigid and unmoving with one hand braced against the wall.

"Eva, this is Andy," said Jay. "He's a very dear friend of mine."

Andy stood to attention as if presenting himself for inspection before the school matron, aware he was being minutely assessed as her beady and heavy-lidded eyes ran over him like cold water. She nodded and turned without a word, opening a double locked door to reveal an expansive lounge area, devoid of windows and bathed in low-level mood lighting.

Andy took in the scene. A bar area, stools set around a dark wooden counter topped in an iridescent marble, was directly ahead of him and all around it sat beautiful young women, the light scattering upon the surface of the marble and creating strange symbols of shadow on their exposed skin. More sat in darker corners, lounging on sofas or draped over businessmen; they had smiles on their faces and eyes fixed on the new arrivals. Andy fancied their gazes lingered particularly long on him and he suppressed the tremble that longed to course through his body.

"This is what I think it is?" he asked, as Eva directed them towards one of the sofas.

"Relax," said Jay, "it's whatever we want it to be. There's no pressure. We can go or stay, but as we are here, how about a drink, a gin and tonic be ok?" he asked, gesturing for Eva's compliance whilst guiding Andy onto an empty sofa.

"Guess so," said Andy, the shrug of his shoulders far exaggerating the few remaining reservations that desire had not forced from his mind as he followed Eva's progress to the bar, the girls before her parting like silken curtains but returning to the same places and making no move to engage their new guests. Eva returned with a litre bottle of gin and two token bottles of tonic. Befitting an establishment that charged three hundred pounds for a bottle of spirits, an ashtray-sized silver platter of nuts and a terracotta bowl of olives accompanied the drinks. She poured the gin over the ice until the long glasses were almost full, leaving the tonic to their discretion. But the flow of liquor over ice did not long hold his attention as a slinking shadow at the doorway materialised into a woman more mesmerising than Andy had ever seen before.

He did not see her face, though it was an attractive one, but only the roundness of her ample derriere, the length of her smooth dark legs, and the irresistible line of her breasts against the clinging white fabric of her dress. Taking a long draught of his gin he returned his attention to Jay, now unsure of everything.

"The thing you mentioned in Tuscany," he said, "is the sort of thing that I might be interested in. Something you can feel and touch."

Not to mention the twenty to fifty million, thought Jay, remembering the involuntary glint in Andy's eye earlier. "It doesn't come more tangible than bricks and mortar, that's for sure," said Jay, a smile playing upon his lips as the white-clad vixen descended upon them.

"Hi," said the girl, her eyes fixed upon Andy, "my name is Britta, I am from the Czech Republic." She took a seat beside him, asking, "It is ok if I join you?" but without need for an answer. As she sank down into the cool leather, pressing against Andy's side as she shunned the available space, another girl, a brunette with a wanton smile and long tanned limbs, settled next to Jay as she leaned in to mouth her name. Eva returned with an offer of champagne and left smiling, averting her eyes with skill and precision from the beginnings of debauchery all about her.

Britta's soft left hand was fast causing Andy to forget the ring on his own as it stroked and caressed his neck, across his shoulders, down the front of his shirt, down, down to his trousers.

"Why you so tense," enquired Britta. "Your first time maybe?" she ventured, laughing at her own joke as she twiddled his wedding ring and pulled gently at his neck, pushing herself up and swinging herself onto his lap, revealing a glimpse of scarlet mesh panties against smooth brown skin.

Leaning forward, she whispered, "Britta help you relax, no?" pushing her breasts into his face, her perfume filling his nostrils and stirring his loins. Feeling hardness beneath her, she began to gyrate against him as she looked into his eyes with convincing excitement. He moved his hands, limp with pleasure at his sides, onto her knees and slid them up her thighs, reaching the tantalising scarlet and pulling it aside with his thumb. The girls that before kept him under close observation were no longer looking his way and he wondered just how far things might go on the sofa when Britta answered his unspoken question, and brought matters to a head.

"You going to fuck Britta right here, or take me upstairs?" she demanded, and without waiting for a reply, pushed herself to her feet, rearranged her skirt, leant forward, and took his hand.

"See you in a while then, and take your time," Jay said as he took a moment to extricate himself from his own distraction.

Six

Isobel and her friend Maria left their cab and walked towards the long queue for the Alpha Lounge. It was six months after Isobel's fateful meeting in Marrakech and the weather could not have been more different as London rain fell in sheets. Maria led Isobel past a close packed line of attractive girls, their hair extensions damp and long bronzed legs shivering from the cold. A heavy man dressed in black nodded in recognition and pulled aside the rope to let them in. The inside, so dark that it seemed inhabited only by shadows, broke into dimmed light as they wound their way into its heart. Isobel stood in bewilderment as they reached its centre, which swarmed with clones of the girls outside, amongst whom mingled dark, well-dressed men who soared above them like birds of prey. Maria tugged her gently by the hand and led to her to a high table by the wall, which gave a vantage point to view the posing and the pouting all around.

"How do you like the place?" Maria asked with a barely concealed smile.

"It's different," said Isobel, sipping her sparkling water as tension stiffened her shoulders and a feeling of nausea began to settle in her stomach. She looked around the room, her face full of disapproval. "These girls are all wannabe Wags."

"Oh Isobel, don't jump to judgment, they're only girls; girls who feel and cry, just like us." Isobel felt the reproach like a bee sting, and hated herself for wishing to seem holier than thou. She looked across at her friend who draped herself across her chair, her eyes on Isobel but her body advertised to the room. As Isobel did her best to shrink herself beneath the gaze of two men from the VIP section, she thought about their friendship. Maria, the Venezuelan trophy wife of an American business magnate, was her friend from design rather than choice or chance; their closeness was the result of one of Peter's business schemes, a carefully cultivated alliance that had in turn brought him closer to Arnie, Maria's husband. Isobel dwelt in amusement on how that alliance had run its course, but their strange friendship prevailed, hedonism and conservatism in unlikely harmony.

Maria loved to shock Isobel with her lifestyle and chose to now, sensing her friend's discomfort and seeking to alleviate it with her misdemeanours.

"I'm going back to Venezuela next week," she announced, the sparkle in her eye inviting a question that she did not wait for. "Arnie thinks I am just visiting the family, of course, and he won't notice anything different when I come back."

"Oh god, Maria, not more cosmetic surgery?" asked Isobel in exasperation. "What's the point of going to the trouble, and taking the risk, if Arnie isn't even going to notice?"

"Risk makes life worth living," grinned Maria, her dark almond-shaped eyes alight with laughter. "In Venezuela, cosmetic surgery is more common than it is in Hollywood, at least amongst those who can afford it. And as you know, I am not just doing it for Arnie."

"Ah yes, the lovely Angelo," said Isobel with disapproving laughter, referring to Maria's young Italian boyfriend, her latest distraction when she stayed in her villa outside of Lucca. "But surely Arnie will notice the difference when he sees you naked?" she asked in fascination, struggling to imagine how Maria must live.

"No, he does not examine me as closely as Angelo."

"So what exactly are you having done this time?" She leant in closer, her eyes widening as Maria gestured to her lap.

"Nothing major, just what you might call tidying up. Something to make me a little prettier. And maybe a little tighter." She giggled, revealing perfectly whitened teeth that could easily grace a toothpaste commercial.

"You don't mean what I think you mean?" Isobel whispered.

"Don't look so surprised," said Maria with mock indignation, "it is a very common procedure. Particularly if, like me, you have had children."

"Well, I can't say it's very common in my circle in Cobham," said Isobel, playing her role with as much delight as Maria played hers.

"Maybe it is more common than you think. I am told it is even available on the NHS, but by the time you get to the front of the queue your need for the tightening is well behind you." Both women burst out laughing; Maria threw her head back in dramatic style, exposing her bare brown neck like an antelope inviting a lion. The men in the VIP section shifted in interest.

"Have you told Angelo then?" Isobel asked, keen to block out the rest of the room.

"Of course not. First I want to see if he notices the difference. If I told him, he would say that it was better, because he would want me to believe so. Angelo is like that. He thinks all the time about my feelings, and what pleases me. He wants me to be happy, and will say what he thinks will make me happy. Even if sometimes it is not true."

Isobel pondered the intimacy of her words and their overt affection and, twisting her glass in her hands, asked, "Do you think it's all worth it? What if Arnie ever found out?"

Maria shrugged. "Better to lose a husband than waste a life."

"That is easy to say, until you lose him," said Isobel.

"You must understand I am twenty years younger than Arnie. That is a quite a difference, particularly if you are, like me, young at heart. And Arnie has not kept himself in great shape over the years, so sometimes the difference seems more than twenty years. So, yes, for me it is worth it." Isobel nodded as Maria continued. "I sometimes wonder if Arnie is happy to look the other way. That it is enough for him to have me on his arm, proof that he is not just successful in only his business. I know when we are together, he likes to know that other men are looking at me, and envying him. And I still take care of him in the bedroom. I do everything that he asks, which is in truth not very demanding. And mostly I do it without him asking. Maybe that is the price I pay for being what I am."

Isobel looked at her in undisguised fascination, feeling envy and repulsion in equal measure. "I sometimes wish I was more like you, Maria. You are so free to live your life the way you please. I have been feeling like that more and more lately."

"Just recently?" Maria leant in closer; Isobel rarely spoke of her emotions, let alone her insecurities.

"I don't know when I first had them. Maybe as long as five years ago, I really couldn't say exactly. All I know for sure is that I have them today."

"But Isobel, you are not saying you are unhappy with Peter, are you? You always seem to be the perfect couple, so content with each other, and you have such a fantastic lifestyle. Everyone would say the same." Isobel felt an edge or sarcasm, maybe even satisfaction, in her reply but she continued anyway, anxious to finally unburden herself.

"Maybe contentment is what most people settle for, whatever contentment is. But all I know is that whatever I have with Peter, it doesn't seem to be enough. Not for me anyway, not right now. Maybe I need to go out and buy a motorbike or something, I don't know. But I need to do *something*. I don't think I want to look back on my life and think that this was all it amounted to. That I...I wasted it." She stared at her friend in dejection, desperately seeking answers in her growing smile.

"So you are the spoiled woman who wants for nothing, but wants for everything?" said Maria with her normal sharp and irreverent incisiveness.

"Maria, I'm having this conversation with *you* because that's not what I want to hear."

"I am sorry. I am only teasing. So the problem is with Peter?"

"No, Peter is as he ever was, only now even more obsessed with his career," she said with a sigh. "And he would never be unfaithful to me, if that is what you're thinking."

"I would not dream of thinking such a thing. But never? That is a dangerous word."

"Not if you know Peter like I know him," said Isobel, letting out a derisory laugh, and immediately regretting it.

"I am sure you are right, Isobel, but sometimes it is the most innocent who are the most vulnerable, who are easy prey."

"Sex is not everything to Peter," said Isobel, "and anyway, he has everything he needs at home," she added hurriedly.

Maria sipped on her drink, eyeing her friend closely. "But it is not sex that a clever woman uses to turn a man's head; it is attention, it is flattery, the very things that no man can get enough of."

Isobel dismissed the notion out of hand. She was already Peter's wife, waitress, and mother; how much attention could one man need? "The problem is definitely not Peter," repeated Isobel.

Sudden realisation flashed in Maria's eyes.

"So something, or someone, must be bringing out these feelings in you now, making you more aware of them?"

"I'm not having an affair, if that's what you're asking." She said it quickly and indignantly, her mouth weak around the strong words.

"Completely sure?" Maria's eyes narrowed in knowing scepticism but Isobel grew in certainty as she spoke.

"Of course I am sure. I couldn't stand the lies, apart from anything else." Maria was silent, watching and waiting.

"Late last year I did meet someone," Isobel said. "But only briefly really, in the souk in Marrakech of all places."

Maria leant back in satisfaction, her movement pushing up her round and pert breasts for the examination of the VIPs, who watched their conversation like hawks.

"So how many times have you seen him since, and am I allowed to know his name?"

"Jay. And I only saw him by the pool. Not since. It was just one of those holiday things, you know. And anyway I seem to remember he lives somewhere in the wilds of Cheshire."

"So now you are, umm, pen friends?" asked Maria, biting her finger with highly charged nonchalance. The men in the roped off area shifted slightly and one beckoned their minder with the crook of his finger.

"He has some tourist project, near your place in Tuscany actually, and he is promoting it. He sent me some details and since then I've had a couple of invitations to attend events — with Peter. I couldn't make either and wouldn't have gone to them anyway. Except now he's doing an event in Cobham, so Peter and I might go along."

"So what's special about him?" asked Maria, her tone shorter and more demanding as she watched the minder cross the room to the velvet ropes.

"I'm not thinking along those lines, not for one minute," said Isobel. "But he *was* incredibly attentive, he really listened. The things I said in the souk, he played back around the pool like he had hung on every word."

"A player, if you ask me. You'd better watch out!" Maria said with a grin, her eyes now meeting those of the burly minder who strode up to them. Isobel laughed as Maria leant in towards her ears, touching her face for the benefit of the audience. She whispered, her lips exaggerated and sensual, brushing Isobel's cheek.

"Well, it sounds to me that you need cheering up. So come on, let's go have some fun."

"Mo and Safi," said the minder, now level with their table and pointing to the two Middle Eastern men who were watching their conversation, "would like you to join them for champagne…in the VIP area." He uttered the last words as if they were sacred, some Garden of Eden in this dark and sinful place.

"That is very generous," said Maria, "but you must tell your friends that, sweet as you may be, we do not accept invitations via intermediaries." Isobel exhaled in relief, glad, albeit shocked, that Maria refused them.

Maria returned to her probing. "So you would never just let yourself go, even for one night, even if you knew Peter could never find out?" she asked, locking eyes with Isobel so that she would not notice the tall man exit the roped area with purpose and lust in his eyes.

"No," said Isobel, feeling increasingly uncomfortable as the lounge filled and predators circled. "I have too much to lose; and anyway, sex without love is a bit meaningless, don't you think?"

"With love it is better, I agree, but sex without love is hardly meaningless, ask any man."

"Men are different. They can…can detach themselves from their emotions," said Isobel, not at all sure what she meant.

"And so can a woman," said Maria, aware that the man could now hear her perfectly. "I do not succumb to Angelo; I merely enjoy him, as I enjoy a fine wine. If it is good I may come back for more, but equally I do not want to sip from the same bottle every evening."

"Please, Maria, can we talk about something other than sex?" Isobel's voice was low; she could feel the shadow behind her.

It touched her shoulder and she stiffened; moments later they were behind the purple rope, with Maria coaxing her onwards.

Mo might have been a gold trader from the amount of the metal that adorned him. Isobel wondered that he could lift his arm given the size of the diamond encrusted watch on his wrist, which he flashed consciously to the room.

"It's a thousand pound per table minimum spend here," he told Isobel grandly, filling up her flute with Cristal as he edged into her. His body pressed in ever closer as he told her at length of his wealth and her beauty, alternating between the two in a calculated seduction. She shrank from him but he put his arm around her shoulder and pulled her closer, one hand straying to her thigh. Like a frightened rabbit, Isobel pushed him away, turning to Maria for help only to find her absorbed in Safi, whose platinum Rolex was slipping into his sleeve as he surreptitiously worked his hand under her dress.

"Now we'll go to my penthouse, ok?" said Mo, dissatisfied to be making less progress than his companion. He snapped his fingers and a minion appeared.

"Tell Toni to pull round the front." He put a reassuring hand on her thigh, his fingers edging their way towards her crotch. Isobel seized the offending hand and delivered it back to him with contempt, flinging him aside as she stood up.

"I'm going, Maria," she said, her voice loud with panic. Maria wiggled her fingers from behind Safi's bulk and Isobel turned to Mo, "You have been most generous, thank you."

He grabbed her arm and pulled her back into the seat, his breath hot with champagne. She dug her nails into his arm.

"I am leaving alone, if you don't mind, and my husband is waiting in the car outside. Thank you and goodnight."

He shrugged, "Your loss, Cinderella." With that last compliment to remember him by, she turned on her heels and fled as, behind her, Maria took Mo's hand and placed it on her thigh as Safi eyed his friend with expectation.

Seven

In their university years Jay and Andy tolerated each other for their own gain, maintaining a superficial camaraderie that only fooled the people that really mattered. But that was many years ago and as they sat in The Candle — London's top celebrity restaurant — celebrating their good fortune, not one of the C list actors or reality TV stars would have guessed tension ever festered beneath their surfaces. They sat like kings in their corner booth, selected by Jay for prime people watching opportunity, sprawled out as they luxuriated in fleeting fame.

"So tell me," said Jay, his mood particularly gregarious, "how come someone who cannot keep time to a beat made a fortune out of the music industry?"

"Luck," said Andy, batting away the compliment but beaming nonetheless, his eyes fixed on the back of a man who looked strikingly like John Travolta.

"Bullshit," said Jay, smiling. "Don't be so modest. I'm keen to know, really I am."

Andy leaned back, mirroring Jay's posture, while surveying his wine, deep red in a glass the size of a flowerpot. "Anyone could have done what I did, if you work hard enough that is."

"But there's a lot of hard-working guys who aren't rich, and never will be," said Jay, cheerful and matter-of-fact. "What was your secret?"

"No secret really. It just needed a thimbleful of insight into technology and one whole bucketful of perseverance." Jay nodded solemnly, restraining a snort of laughter at his metaphor. "Everyone at the top was so het up about the threat of the internet, you know, renegade students copying CD's in their dorms, that they gave no thought to the future of digital music."

"Well, whatever you did, you are looking mighty well on it." Jay smiled agreeably, about to change the topic, but Andy wanted to relive his glory days a while longer.

"The strange thing about the music business," he said serious and slow, leaning towards Jay, "is that hardly anyone in it has any talent. But the good news is you don't need it to make money. They are so crap at everything that there's plenty of opportunity."

Jay smiled but stayed silent; he had gained too many great things from letting a tipsy man ramble.

"What those guys need to do more is stay focused on what they know best — finding talent and selling records — and leave all that back office stuff to others."

Jay's attention was now sincere. "You mean they should give it to specialists who are experts with numbers, accountants maybe?"

"Yep, exactly."

"Are you still connected with the music guys, the ones at the top?" asked Jay, lowering his voice as if hoping to avoid spooking the other man.

"I've kept in touch," said Andy, his tone wary, as that low, soft voice of opportunity dragged him back to university, as if he was being asked again if he was interested in popping his cherry with the most beautiful girl in the medical faculty. "Why do you ask?" he said, his eyes narrowing.

"Oh, no reason," said Jay. "Anyway, what do you think of The Candle? Is it somewhere the lovely Kate would like?"

Andy bellowed with laughter; he had told Jay enough about Kate over the last few months for the answer to be an obvious one.

"Hmm, well let's see," he said, pausing in mock-thought, "it's famously hard to get into, always booked a month ahead, even though they don't take bookings a month in advance, it's notoriously expensive, and there's a chance she might see someone very famous."

Jay burst out laughing. "She'd be in heaven."

"She'd love it," said Andy, bonhomie washing over him, "and I was actually thinking of it for our anniversary. But anytime I've tried, it's been fully booked."

"When's your anniversary?"

"A week on Saturday," said Andy, his suspicion giving way to supplication. "At least that's when we're celebrating it. We're spending the weekend in London, taking in a show, you know, that sort of thing."

"Saturday night at The Candle," said Jay, rubbing his chin theatrically, as aware as Andy that such a request was considered impossible. "Before the show or after the show?"

"I'd take any," said Andy with a hapless smile.

"After would be better though," said Jay, still rubbing his chin. "You don't want to be presented with the bill when they serve the first course. I'll see what I can sort out."

"Thanks," said Andy, lulled by Jay's selflessness and by the wine.

Jay raised his palm, as if to wield off the gratitude, and refilled Andy's glass. After a respectable interval, he raised the topic that had brought him to the restaurant that night, now buried enough beneath friendship and alcohol to be almost innocuous.

"By the way, did you ever have a chance to look at the Tuscany pack?"

Andy nodded. In their late night cruising and bonding over the past two months, he had continued to make subtle enquiries into the progress of Jay's venture. His friend had been pleasant but business-like — it was an exceptional opportunity but there was simply no room for Andy. But things had changed unexpectedly, and perhaps wonderfully, two weeks ago when Jay's main backer withdrew, unable to come up with the money and Jay, in deference to his friend, magnanimously offered Andy the chance to step into the man's shoes, before someone else did.

"Yes, I did," said Andy, "So, the plan is, we renovate these properties, sell them at a fat profit, then the people who've bought them hand them straight back over to us so we can rent them out at another fat profit?"

"Right, they get to own a dream holiday property plus a guaranteed rental income. Everyone wins."

Andy leant back, as if a better view of Jay was an aid to judgement. "So the key to the whole scheme is really the rental income. That's the carrot to buy."

"And the carrot to give the property back to us to rent. It's a proven model in places like Dubai. It's just that no-one's done it in Tuscany."

"And the timeshare sales are the cream on the cake?"

"Right again. Though it beats me why anyone would part with good money to put a yoke around their neck, but that's the timeshare business, and who are we to argue with the customer?"

" But *if* I were to be interested, how could I be sure that the whole thing won't crash around me a few months later?"

Jay looked at him with overt and deliberate confusion.

"Andy, there's that risk with any business venture. You put your money in and take your chance, right? That's what you did with your music idea, you threw away a safe salary and invested in the future—"

Andy smiled at the compliment but cut him off nonetheless.

"Did you think I wouldn't have done my research, Jay? That failed timeshare venture in Malaga does not reflect well on you." He studied Jay as he continued. "The bank was left owed fifty million and plenty of other people are looking to get even. Do you want to tell me your side of it, the bits I couldn't read in the papers? And is the Tuscany thing totally legal? Is anyone going to get hurt?"

Jay put down his glass, and steepled his fingers under his chin. He expected this, though perhaps in less blunt a manner, and looked his friend confidently in the eye with all the seriousness of a man ready to bare his soul. "That could have been such a good story, and would have been a good story," he said, his eyes glazing with the memory, "but the ugly truth is that I got screwed by those banking bastards."

"How so?" said Andy, raising his eyebrows. "Didn't the banks put up all the money? The way I read it, the banks got fucked over, the punters got fucked over, the staff got fucked over, and you walked off with your pockets jingling."

Jay looked pained at his words and pushed his fingertips together until they were white.

"That's what the banks and their lackeys in the press might have you believe. But the thing is they were calling the shots from start to finish. They had full control."

"But I read you were the managing director, the guy in charge?" said Andy.

"The guy in charge?" cried Jay with a harsh laugh. "The fucking fall guy, more like. I offered them a great opportunity and they bought into it because the numbers stacked up, and that's all they were interested in, the numbers." He looked bitterly down at the table.

"But you were still the managing director, right up until the whole thing folded. If you were heading for a derailment, why didn't you jump train when the going was good?" Andy wasn't ready to drop it, his every iota wanting to be part of the Tuscan venture, but he had to be sure.

"A simple reason," said Jay, self-righteous indignation etched in his voice and lined in his face. "Someone had to try and look after the little guys. We had over five hundred salt of the earth people who had taken shares in the property. Some of them even invested their life savings. Someone had to try and protect those innocent poor sods, and the fucking banks weren't interested. All they wanted was their money out." Jay paused as if seeking to renew himself. His voice went lower still. "They went and sold the hotel from under my feet."

"So you didn't fuck up at all then?" said Andy. "It was all the banks' doing, have I got that right?"

"Listen Andy," said Jay, direct and assured, "he who pays the piper calls the tune, right? And you will be calling the tune in Tuscany, if you want to that is. Sure, I made some mistakes in Malaga, but I've learnt from them. In Tuscany we'll be working as partners, making the decisions together. We won't have any fucking banker with his hand up our arses, pulling all the strings."

"Would that be pulling them with the hand that's up our arse, or with the other one?" asked Andy with a smirk.

The two men lapsed briefly into laughter, the tension broken by unspoken agreement. Andy confirmed the peace with a broad smile and an unsubtle suggestion. "I wouldn't mind a drink somewhere else."

Jay nodded. Their evening excursions now invariably ended in one place — the capable and professional arms of Eva's finest.

He stopped by the maître d station as they left, signalling Andy to continue to the cloakroom. Jay was waiting when Andy returned and with a wide grin he slipped a card to his friend.

"Your anniversary dinner is all sorted. Any time you want to eat at The Candle, call the VIP number on the back of the card. Mention my name, just until they get to know you."

Andy beamed, buoyed that Jay had delivered on his first commitment.

"Come on, let's go and get that drink," said Jay, putting his arm round Andy's shoulder. They left The Candle as two brothers in arms, having for a second time silently agreed a deal that would shape their destiny.

Eight

Isobel awoke in a sweat; the smoke still on her skin from the Moroccan alleyways that once more filled her nightmares. She rarely dreamt of the souk since Marrakech, but each re-visitation seemed more terrifying than the last. The alarm clock ruptured the morning silence and she leant out and hit the snooze button, her fingers dragging on the embossed invitation card, still lying where she left it the night before. She picked it up again and studied it, dwelling on its ambiguity. Jay was inviting her to a marketing function. It was the third such invitation she had received since Marrakech — but this time the event was on her doorstep, in Cobham High Street no less. Whether he was attending was uncertain; the invitation was written in his hand, or so it appeared, but he was not the host. She flicked it from the table as self-loathing welled within her. Even if he would be there, why should she attend? Her brief flirtation in Marrakech was nothing more than that, and the mundane reality of daily life had long since displaced any foolish romantic notions stirred in a far off exotic location. No. She declined the two previous invitations, and she would decline the third.

She turned towards Peter's side of the bed, already empty. As her mind cleared, she could hear the sound of running water as he prepared once more to take on the world, and subjugate it to his will. She sank back into the bed and stayed lying down, collecting her thoughts and contemplating another day of nothing but emptiness. She nestled back into the rich cotton sheets, determined to fall back asleep so that, just maybe, she might be spared the chore of tending to Peter's domestic needs. It was her fault, the result of years of training him that he need not divert one microsecond of thought away from his obsession with the world of work and the insatiable needs of his clients.

"Are you awake, darling?" His words came sailing from the bathroom like a call to duty.

She scrambled out of bed and pulled on a dressing gown. As she rubbed the sleep from her eyes she stared at the wood and glass barrier now separating her from her husband; ten years ago it would have been annoying, inconvenient, perhaps even saddening. Now she rejoiced in the separation it gave her. "The car is coming at eleven and your case is ready in your dressing room. I'm taking Betsy out for a stroll."

She could hear more running water and his muffled reply was unclear; no doubt it was the result of a mouthful of toothpaste or a mind full of business, perhaps both.

Her lack of response drew Peter from behind the screen. He was still in his sweatshirt and shorts, his morning workout in the gym as sacrosanct as his low cholesterol diet.

"Sorry, I thought I told you I was coming back tonight. I'm taking the Eurostar."

"You didn't," she said with resignation, "but the case will keep for next time."

"And Rachel is coming over at ten, with some papers," he added. Isobel had yet to meet Peter's new assistant but she already knew he thought highly of her.

"Are the couriers on strike or is she just coming to nose?" she asked, and without waiting for an answer set out for her own bathroom, stooping to scoop up Peter's discarded underwear as she went.

She rode her horse hard along the bridleway that circled the farm, far harder than she knew she ought, as if physical exertion, if not a modicum of danger, could drive the feelings of restlessness from her body. But the rub of the saddle against her thighs only seemed to aggravate the aching within her. She pulled to a halt and jumped down from the panting mare, thinking perhaps that walking might offer respite. As she wandered along the path, she dwelt, as she often did these days, on her life and her marriage. Her mind drifted to the burgeoning career in the art world that she abandoned despite her passion for painting and sculpture. Was she to blame for sacrificing herself and her own ambitions for Peter's needs, or was he to blame for letting her? No doubt it was the right career decision, at least financially. In the last ten years Peter had accumulated more money than they would ever spend and, as he often graciously conceded, far more than he ever could have done without her to relieve him of every responsibility other than his own success. But what was success? What did it give her? What good were the money and the possessions, without life's true experiences, whatever they were? Perhaps they were what her privileged circle of friends believed: the things that money bought, the comfort of a first class cabin, the occasional private jet when the fancy took them, VIP status at the sought after social events of the English calendar.

But what good were such experiences if experienced alone, or without the possibility of sharing the pleasure with someone with the lust for life to live them, not simply attend them?

And such experiences must surely be enjoyed when one still has the vitality of youth, when the body still yearns excitement? Were not the old and the infirm, no matter how rich, content to see out their days close to hearth and home, with no more excitement than fresh air to breathe and a good book to read, and perhaps a tipple before bedtime? Isobel felt the ticking of her own clock keenly and did not like what she heard. How much longer would she be able to ride as she had this morning, with the wind gushing through her hair? How many more summers would her body retain the firmness of youth? Her mind went again to the invitation on her dresser and she hated it for its impossible possibilities. She looked at her watch; Peter would be expecting her back by now, no doubt searching for his passport or his train tickets or his shoelaces. She was needed elsewhere. She sprung onto Betsy and kicked her heels into her flanks, tearing off as if she wanted to cleave the air in two.

She arrived back breathless but with no sign of panic. Peter was in his study but not at his desk; through the window she saw him sitting at the low glass table with a brunette fifteen years his junior alongside him, leaning towards him with her head to one side, her immaculately groomed hair almost touching his cheek. Peter was looking at the girl with a bright intensity in his eyes, and she was looking back, Isobel fancied, with eyes wide in admiration.

Isobel easily recognised the glint in Peter's eye, but she was sure it was not a direct result of the shapely girl in the tight business suit sitting so close. His look was no longer ignited by her own naked body, or by any other tangible delight. It simply signaled the excitement that rose within Peter at work, when in his element. She saw it when he punched his fist in the air at the news of some big client success, or when he was seized by some great idea, some solution. And now the young brunette saw it, and perhaps thought it to be much more than it was.

Isobel framed herself in the study door, an imposing figure in her riding pants, knee high boots, and hard hat. She stood legs apart, with her hands on hips, still clutching her riding crop, the very picture of the lady of the manor. The young woman stood up and introduced herself, her eyes glowing with opportunism, her lipstick a bright, heavy red. She was perhaps three inches shorter than Isobel, and the older woman looked down without bending her head, wishing to assert her authority. Rachel did not shrink from Isobel's gaze, but held it with, it seemed to the older woman, a distinct lacking of due deference.

"We're just going through a presentation," she said, in explanation for her languid proximity to Peter. "For the meeting in Paris."

"I will leave you to it then," said Isobel with some aloofness. She looked across to Peter. "I'm taking a shower."

Isobel was in the kitchen when Rachel approached her again. Not to be outdone by the assistant, Isobel had applied her own make-up more thoroughly and carefully than normal, and, as she swiveled to receive the young woman, her beauty appeared more graceful than before.

"Peter would like a coffee," said Rachel, her voice powerful and demanding beneath a guise of submission.

Isobel looked her straight in the eye; a tray with crockery was already sitting ready. "The cups are there," she said, nodding towards the tray, "and the coffee machine is behind you. Anyone can work it. And make me one too… please."

"It's a beautiful kitchen," said Rachel as she went about her new duties. "I love the marble."

"It's granite," said Isobel. *And forget any idea you'll ever inherit it,* she thought.

As Rachel went on a crash course in coffee machines, Isobel weighed the girl up, noticing the trim figure so easily maintained with the advantage of youth, and resenting her for that advantage. She'd seen Rachel's type before at Peter's office — overdressed and over made-up for a mere delivery errand. She was pleasant and well-spoken enough and, if she played her hand well, in two years she would probably have her claws into some sad senior partner and, soon thereafter, her feet in his kitchen. But it wouldn't be this one, Isobel was sure of that.

"Simon's here!" shouted Isobel, as she saw the black Mercedes coming down the lane. She followed Rachel back to the study as the new maid delivered the coffee. Peter was already gathering up his papers.

"We'll finish the presentation on the train," said Peter. Rachel flashed a defiant look at Isobel, and as she took in the red valise by the table, it dawned on her that Rachel was going with him to Paris. She watched them leave, elbow to elbow, before separating and disappearing behind the rear blinds of the sleek black limousine. She stood and watched as the car pulled away, imagining them in eager conversation, their bodies leant in to each other across the thick armrest, and as the image played in her mind, she was unsure how to feel.

At seven that evening the phone rang, it was Peter. "The client wants to go to dinner, so I'm going to stay over." Peter never asked permission on such matters, and she never expected it of him.

"But you haven't got any things with you."

"That's ok. Rachel has popped out to get me a few bits and pieces."

"Ok, well call me when you set off for home tomorrow."

She hung up and dropped the phone onto the bed; stray feathers shot upwards from the duvet. One landed on the invitation and she brushed it aside with all her doubts, reaching for a pen with fire in her veins.

Nine

Isobel's footsteps echoed in the empty house as she walked over to the full-length mirror and appraised herself once more. The floor was covered in sad heaps of clothes; each garment carefully tried on and then flung aside in frustration as she attempted to find the perfect ensemble. She looked herself up and down, letting her eyes descend with growing satisfaction; finally, she had got things right.

She turned to the side and scrutinized her silhouette, running her hands over the smooth, slight curves that were highlighted to perfection in the otherwise demure Marc Jacobs dress.

Isobel fingered the invitation card as she checked the time, chewing her lower lip; another half an hour had to pass before she could leave. And, as the minutes edged across the face of her watch, nervous self-doubt began to impinge on her forced calm, and obliged her to wrestle with her motives. She felt sure that her flutter of fancy for Jay was over and that she was only accepting his invitation because it was at her doorstep, for she had after all, she reminded herself again, declined the previous two. Isobel walked again to the mirror and added a slim leather belt to her waist, tightening it to the point of pain as she stared blankly at her reflection and rehearsed the evening in her head. She would send clear signals of professionalism and disinterest, sticking closely to Peter and only engaging in the most trivial small talk. She looked at her waist, tiny and waspish in its leather fetters, and imagined his eyes resting there in desire as she stood chastely beside her husband like a caged bird. She shook the image from her head and grabbed the car keys. Maybe he would not be there, and perhaps it was better if he wasn't.

Isobel replaced her torments with a lesser evil as she drove to Cobham station to pick up Peter. She allowed her mind to return to her last evening out with Maria, to her resistance of another, albeit much less dangerous temptation, and drew strength from her decision. She was incapable of infidelity, she was sure of it. Still it was with relief that she saw Peter walking down the platform, his pace brisk and irascible.

"On time for once, darling, a first for everything," she said, stretching to kiss him in deliberate ignorance of his bad-temperedness.

He grunted in reply and swung himself into the passenger seat.

"A good day at the office, dear?" she said, knowing that Peter hated the Mayfair office and all its petty politics — he was at his happiest out in the action with his clients — but had for the last six months been obliged to spend more time there. The problem in Tokyo that first surfaced during their Marrakech break had festered and grown, and hung like a huge black cloud, casting a long and deepening shadow that was now threatening Peter's career, and absorbing him entirely. But to Isobel's frustration, he chose to share nothing of the seriousness of it with her. At least the grasping Rachel would be pleased that his troubles now kept him close to her desk, she thought.

"I have a call with Tokyo at ten, so we need to be home by then," he said, terse and unapologetic.

"That should be fine," said Isobel, determined not to begin the evening with an argument. "Two hours will be plenty."

"Two hours?" He looked at her with incredulity in his expression.

"This is not just a fly by and pick up a leaflet affair darling; there's food and wine, and even an Italian folk singer."

"A folk singer?"

"Ok, I lied about the singer," she said laughing, "but definitely music."

Muted strains of Italian folk music drifted into the still evening air as they approached Gateway Homes. Isobel ignored Peter's eye-rolling sigh as the door opened to reveal the offices transformed for the evening. Smartly dressed couples weaved in and out of the tables, pausing to examine the canapés or thumb through the glossy leaflets that graced every surface. The walls were bedecked with large plasma screens, which showed rolling slideshows of idyllic Tuscan scenes smattered with smiling, white-teethed Italians and their expensively dressed, and clearly discerning, guests. Isobel scanned the crowd as they entered, craning her neck to spot Jay. A man stood hidden amongst a crowd of rapt listeners, his charisma clear from the delighted coordination of their responses. Isobel raised herself fully on her toes, sure it must be him, but her vantage point revealed a beaming Irishman holding court, no doubt the Mr. Devlin on the invitation. But she could see no sign of Jay, and she could not hide her disappointment from herself, nor pretend it was relief.

"Isobel, Peter, I'm so pleased you could make it."

Isobel wheeled around, her heart leaping, but it was just David Knight, the regional manager for Gateway through whom they'd bought and sold several properties over the last ten years. He welcomed them like his closest friends, gripping Peter's hand as if he owed him his life and kissing Isobel on both cheeks, then talking away obsequiously as he led them into the melee. "What can I offer you to drink? We have a fine selection of Tuscan wines." Peter accepted a red with relief and Isobel opted for water, now feeling in no mood for Italy's pleasures. She looked around again as the sommelier engaged Peter in conversation and soon found herself watching an attractive blonde who sat alone at the back of the room, fiddling with her phone and looking decidedly bored. Above her a vast screen cycled a series of skiing images, their whiteness contrasting starkly with the sunflowers and rolling green hills that garnished the rest of the walls.

"I put that in as a conversation piece," said a low and inviting voice behind her.

Isobel turned to see Jay, smiling broadly. He took her hand, "I was so pleased when you accepted the invitation, but then my heart sank as it seemed you were a no-show."

Isobel beamed back at him, unable to suppress her joy that he was there after all. "I wasn't expecting you to be here," she said, "but it's my pleasure nevertheless."

"And you are fully dressed for the occasion, no troublesome robe to worry about this time," he said, grinning, "and most elegantly dressed too if I may say so."

"Why thank you," she said, her pulse slowing as her pleasure grew. "And what are you going to rescue me from this time?"

"Why, my silver-tongued Mr. Devlin, of course. You must allow me to show you around." Isobel nodded and turned to walk beside him. "Have you been keeping well since Marrakech?" he asked, seeming to span the months since they first met and reduce them to nothing with his words.

"Yes, if living one's everyday life can be called keeping well," said Isobel, trying to be jovial but feeling immediately embarrassed by her own pomposity.

"You were fascinated by the skiing scenes, I think?" he said, not seeming to notice her mistakes.

"Well, I just don't think of Tuscany and skiing as going together," Isobel admitted, "and isn't Capadelli in the middle of Tuscany, near San Miniato?"

"I'm impressed. It sounds like you know your geography of Tuscany very well."

"Enough to know there's no ski resort hidden in the vineyards," she replied.

He laughed. "A bit of poetic licence by my overly keen marketing people. I did wonder about the wisdom of it myself. But Capadelli is less than ninety minutes from Abetone, and I think their idea was that in the winter people can get there and back in a day and enjoy three or four hours skiing."

Isobel nodded, unsure of his reasoning but too lost in his easiness to care.

"So what do you like to do when you're not skiing, or shopping for magic carpets?" he asked, addressing her with the same studied interest that so characterised his speech in Marrakech.

"As far as holidays go, you mean? That depends on where we go. But we both like active holidays. Peter plays a good game of golf; I like the outdoors, as long as there are no greens and fairways involved." Isobel paused, pushing a stray strand of hair behind her ear, now fearing she was suggesting that she and Peter liked separate holidays, and attempted a recovery. "So often we try and find places where he can play golf and I can do other things." She cursed herself again, this time for failing to refer to her husband by name.

"And what would a dream holiday feel like, while Peter's on the golf course?" he asked. Every word was playful, teasing, a gentle mockery of their roles as guest and host. But Isobel couldn't bring herself to embrace his self-effacing honesty and avoided the true answer, that Peter's work schedule meant that she was used to organising for one.

"Horse-riding is something of a passion," she hedged, "but as long as I can find new and interesting things to do and places to visit then I'm generally happy."

Jay nodded. "Well, I expect this would be a good time to tell you what we have to offer at Capadelli, though I sense from what you said about skiing that you already know Tuscany quite well?"

Isobel smiled at his continual questions but before she could respond — before she could vocalise her happiness at talking to a man that actually listened — he gently took hold of her forearm.

"It will be quieter in the corner," he said, "and there's something I'd like to show you."

Isobel glanced around for Peter as they threaded their way through the guests. He seemed to be deep in conversation on wines, and they walked to the corner almost unnoticed — only the leggy blonde in the corner watched them, her eyes unblinkingly on Isobel as Jay guided her to the scale model in the corner.

Isobel looked at it in interest, an elegant construction, encased in a protective glass case with a discreet aluminium plate identifying it as a representation of 'Castello di Capadelli.'

"You were saying that you know Tuscany well?" asked Jay, looking into her eyes.

Did I say that? thought Isobel, feeling her lips a touch dry, and aware of a strange twisting in her stomach. "I'm lucky enough to get across two or three times a year," she said. "I have a friend that has a place near Lucca."

"Well, at Capadelli we are a little south of Lucca, maybe forty-five minutes," offered Jay. "About mid-way between Florence and Pisa."

Isobel felt more interested in Jay than Capadelli and, as he busied himself gingerly lifting the glass cover, she seized her moment to ask more.

"So the development is your baby?"

"If only," he said with a rueful smile. "No, I'm just the guy pulling it all together for the main investors. They call me the managing director, but I'm really a glorified project manager."

Isobel smiled at his modesty, seeing instantly through it with a practised eye; she had already noticed his watch, one of the lesser-known but more expensive Swiss brands and, as he leant forward over the display, Isobel could just see the Saville Row label inside his suit, and the discreet "silk and cashmere" tag beneath.

"So you spend most of your time on the development?" she asked, unwilling to tease him for so rare a virtue.

Jay held still considering the question, holding the glass cover rather than placing it on the table.

"I have for the last year or so. But I'm also involved in a project in London, which looks like it will need more of my time." He placed the glass lid down. "So when are you next in Tuscany?"

The question was casual, almost as if he read her mind and asked the very question she was holding back.

"I wouldn't want to miss your visit to Capadelli," he said, as her imagination jolted into overdrive.

Isobel pursed her lips to hide her happiness and assumed an expression of feigned affront. "Maybe you'd better tell me something about Capadelli first. Or Peter will be wondering what we have been doing in the corner all this time."

Jay laughed. "I suppose I'd better. But I guess you've a fairly good picture of the development from the brochure. So let me just point out a few things on the model."

He guided her to the far side of the display, pointing out where the new spa would be built as they squeezed into the narrow space between the model and the wall. Isobel asked a few questions about how it would all work, keen to monopolise him for as long as possible.

"I have something that will answer that question better than I can," he said. "I just need to get through here."

There was a second when Isobel might have moved from behind the model, the obvious thing to do. But something within her caused her to stay. Jay straightened his body, preparing to slide between her and the wall as she shrunk herself apologetically into the model. This surely was the moment for Isobel to move, the moment when it was

50

clear that there just wasn't quite enough space for him to comfortably get past. Yet still she stayed fixed to her spot. She felt the closeness of Jay's body as he eased his way through, his upper body for a moment against her back as he touched his hands lightly onto her hips, as if to ensure their lower bodies did not touch. Isobel felt a strange disappointment that they did not touch, that she had not felt his manhood, or imagined she could feel it, against her backside. As he strode across the room she was overwhelmed with a mixture of self-disgust and elation.

"Now, where was I?" asked Jay when he returned, clutching a limp, postcard-sized leaflet that hardly seemed worth the effort.

Pressed against my body was the answer that first came into Isobel's mind, but she held that one back.

"Talking about community. How you are creating a unique blend of Anglo-Saxon and Italian culture," she said, meaning to be matter of fact but aware of a hint of teasing in her delivery.

"I'm sure I could never have been quite that eloquent, Isobel," he replied. Isobel smiled at the compliment and let him continue as she bathed in his words. "The truth is the original concept was to create a cosmopolitan community, something very international. But it just hasn't worked out that way. And actually, I think in the end, it's for the better."

Isobel nodded, becoming even more enraptured as he forswore omnipotence and gave luck its due.

"So what went wrong with plan A?"

"I just never expected the level of interest we have had from the local Italian market; they've already snaffled over a third of the properties, so I probably won't be taking the marketing further than the UK."

"So what you're saying is that you've just done too good a job, is that it?" Isobel raised her eyebrows, teasing him again, craving his response.

"Maybe," he said, pushing back his hair with feigned arrogance.

Isobel laughed. "So anyone interested needs to get over to Tuscany pretty quick then?"

He laughed. "I think I need someone like you on my marketing team, Isobel. Someone that is an embodiment of the beauty, elegance, and serenity that is Castello di Capadelli." It was a light-hearted remark, delivered almost mockingly, but it did not match his eyes, which were deep with seriousness.

Isobel almost blushed, enjoying the jousting. "Do you say that to every girl?"

"Only if it's true." They were locked together in a moment of silence before he broke the spell. "But I must allow you to mingle. You must think very badly of me for monopolising your whole evening."

Isobel smiled, excitement running through her. "You have been the perfect host."

Seconds after Jay left, Peter appeared alongside her. "I thought you'd never stop talking," he said. "We need to go or I'll be late for Tokyo."

Isobel nodded and inched her way towards the door, willing Jay to break off his conversation with the three couples that had cornered him as he crossed the room.

They were making their apologies to David Knight when Jay, ever alert, smoothly disengaged from the group he was otherwise enthralled by.

"David," he said, "I hope you have been looking after our guests." He turned directly to Peter and extended his hand. "Jay Brooke. I'm afraid I need to apologise for being something of a poor host, and also for monopolising your charming wife. It's rare that I meet people on these evenings that know more about Tuscany than my own team."

"Take no notice, Peter, Mr. Brooke is just being polite," said Isobel, looking at Jay as she spoke.

"Isobel tells me you are a golfer," Jay continued. "Maybe we can play a round when you visit us in Tuscany?"

Isobel gripped Peter's arm as she felt him jolt in surprise, and shot him a threatening look that warned him to hold back any questions.

"Do you mind if we take a couple of brochures?" enquired Isobel, smiling widely over her husband's surly silence.

"Of course," said Jay, beckoning over the hovering blonde who sauntered up with a pile of information folders entwined in her slender brown arms. Isobel watched her as she rifled through the cardboard packs. She stood so close to Jay that their bodies were touching, her arm resting slightly on his as she supported the stack of paper. Isobel looked on indignantly; the girl was no wallflower, that was for sure, and she had to be at least ten years his junior. Isobel transferred her furtive gaze to Jay for clarity; she was familiar with the trophy wife syndrome, as there were enough of those around Cobham. But Jay had not struck her as the type who needed to compensate for deficiencies elsewhere by having a status symbol on his arm. Yet as she looked again, their bodies did not seem so close anymore. Jay had shifted his feet and a slither of light now split apart their silhouettes as they stood in the entranceway. Isobel thought she saw anger and disappointment in the girl's green eyes but quickly pulled herself out of her imaginings. What difference did it make who the girl was and what her relationship was with Jay?

Jay offered his hand again, first to Peter and then to Isobel, taking hold of her tapered fingers as she thanked him again.

"It has been my pleasure," responded Jay, and after what seemed an eternity to Isobel, he released her hand.

Isobel could have skipped along the pavement as they stepped out into the late spring evening and made their way to Peter's racing green Aston Martin parked directly across the road.

"You don't mind if I put the top down, do you darling?" she asked rhetorically as the roof glided away to reveal the beginnings of a starry sky. "It's such a lovely evening."

"That was a right royal waste of time," said Peter, fighting against her happiness as they pulled away.

"Nothing like an open mind, is there?" said Isobel, keeping her eyes firmly and deliberately on the road.

"Surely you aren't even considering what these guys are selling? You hardly spent any time in Provence last year as it is. How would you find time for Tuscany?"

"Time, time, time. Is that all you can ever think about?" said Isobel, her anger fed by the validity of his comments. "Well, maybe it's time you started thinking about how you spend your time."

"What's that supposed to mean?" snapped Peter, irritable from either too much wine or too little.

"We bought Provence for both of us," she said bitterly. "*You* cancelled out of the trip in May; *you* cancelled out of the trip in September. Well, *you* can't expect me to rattle around a rambling ruin in the middle of nowhere on my own. Tuscany is different. It's a resort, with other people, people who are not slaves to the great god of time. I would be perfectly happy there on my own, pampering myself in the spa."

"That guy Brooke must have addled your brain," said Peter with contempt.

"And what does that mean?"

"What does it mean? You spent the whole evening with him. I can't think what David Knight must have thought."

"To hell with David Knight and what he thought," said Isobel. "Someone was paying me some attention for a change and, quite frankly, I liked it. What is wrong with that?"

"If you can't see what's wrong with—"

"For God's sake, nothing was wrong with it!" she shouted. "I speak Italian, I like talking about Italy. I already spend time in Tuscany and, if you must know, I'm fed up with always imposing myself on Maria while you are selling your precious time here, there, and everywhere. So tonight was not a waste of time, not for me anyway."

Peter folded his arms, his face set against everything he was hearing. But Isobel refused to be intimidated into silence by his sullen look. "We've been invited to visit this place Capadelli, and I'm going just as soon as I can arrange it. So you can come and keep me company while I visit, because if you won't, maybe Jay Brooke will."

Ten

Jay stared out the window as the plane lurched into the first part of its descent, the sudden sensation of the drop adding to the nausea that had infringed on his mind and body since departing. Beneath him another plane seemed to slide across the sky, like a penny across a glass tabletop, and he pulled his gaze back into the cabin, painfully aware of his helplessness. He rarely looked out the window when flying but his company on the plane left him no choice. The two people he was most anxious to avoid were both just metres away and could approach at any moment; dread clutched his internal organs, twisting and knotting them until the sky seemed his only safe refuge. From the corner of his eye he could see Lucy's shapely arse, thrust very deliberately in his direction as she served a red-faced businessman his sixth flute of complimentary champagne. Jay half-sighed with nostalgia; if this was back when they first met, he mused, he would probably have already had her knickers off — if she was wearing any — and pleasured her behind the food trolley. But now, as she stood up, he turned quickly back to the window again, determined to avoid eye contact, fearing the power she held over him.

"Excuse me, sir? You were asking about transit arrangements in Pisa?" said a chirpy voice, professional precision slicing through his carefully created reverie. Jay looked up to find Lucy smiling down at him, a well-groomed picture of proficiency with immaculately coiled hair and devil-red lips.

"Actually—"

Before he could finish, she glided in next to him, pushing her gazelle-like legs beneath his as she leant towards him.

"I think you'll find everything you need in here, sir," she said, reaching one hand into the seat pocket and grabbing his crotch with the other — her smile fixed and precise.

"Really," said Jay, straining to keep the shock of the impact from his voice, "I'm ok with transit arrangements in Pisa. And, while we're at it, I don't remember booking the complimentary massage."

He tried to pull himself away but Lucy was not dissuaded and turned fully towards him, blocking off the view from the aisle with her back. Her grip tightened as her seductive smile vanished.

"Dream on, you smug bastard. It's what I'm planning on squeezing you need to be worried about."

"I don't know what the problem is, but this is a really bad time. I need you to get your arse out of that seat so I can collar that grumpy looking sod over there." He flicked his eyes agitatedly behind him, to where he could just make out the side of Andy's face, pressed submissively to his wife's lips as she whispered in his ear.

"My arse is staying where it is until I am good and ready to move it," hissed Lucy, "and so is my hand." She tightened her fingers around him as her lips trembled and formed themselves into a snarl.

"Why—"

"You know damn well why I'm here."

"Unfortunately, I do not," said Jay with as much cheerfulness as he could muster, his words short and breathy under her pressure. "Mind reading must only be a girl thing."

"Why haven't I been able to get hold of you for four weeks…until now?" Lucy squeezed harder.

"Squeezing my balls is not going to get us anywhere," said Jay, attempting to level his breathing.

"Pardon me, kind sir, if I beg to differ." Lucy wore her smile again, and mercilessly increased the pressure.

Pain shot through Jay's lower body, and he reached out and wrapped his fingers around Lucy's slender wrist.

"Lucy, I have been totally maxed out for the last four weeks; it's as simple as that."

"If you've had time to go to the loo in the last four weeks, then you've had time to call me. You need to do better than that," she said, tightening her grip.

"Ok, ok," he gasped, trying to push her from him. "I should have called you. I'm sorry. Ok?"

"No, it is not ok." She sat back and relaxed her grip, hurt now merging with the anger in her eyes. "And you have completely blanked me since you got on the flight."

"Working on my laptop is not blanking you," Jay sighed, "you are the only reason I am on this flight."

"The reason you are on this flight is because it's heading where you want to go. When it lands, you'd better get your butt over to the Tulip Hotel if you know what's good for you." Lucy as good as clenched her fist to reinforce the dire consequences that would befall Jay should he be foolish enough to spurn her invitation.

Jay said nothing as a torrent of contradictory thoughts ran through his mind; there were twenty good reasons why he didn't want to change his plans that evening. But if he didn't get rid of Lucy in the next five minutes then the repercussions could be terminal — he had to placate Andy before they landed. For the thousandth time in two years, lying was his only option, and he embraced it like an old friend.

"Believe me, as soon as I saw you at Gatwick I changed my plans."

"So you are booked into the Tulip?"

Jay faltered, caught in his lie. "Yes, my plans are to go over to the hotel from the airport. That is correct. I've already asked Eamon to meet me at the airport and take me there. But I'm also committed to meeting up with the team later. It's business. So I will have to get away promptly."

"You're supposed to be the big wheel; you've got the rest of your life for building your sand castles in the sky with a greasy cog like Eamon." Lucy tore at him with her hand as she said it until it seemed her nails would touch through his skin.

"Ok, you win!" he panted. "But you need to let go of that grip of yours and get out of here. Please?"

Lucy released him with a cheesy smile and rose to her feet before deftly twisting herself into the aisle, her body slender and pliant once more.

"Well, that seems to be all sorted, sir." Her voice was chirpy again, all sugar and sunshine. "If I can do anything else for you, don't hesitate to press the little button above your head." She flicked it on and off again with vigour before sauntering away, her heels clicking with applause.

Jay breathed a sigh of relief and tucked away his laptop, sure that any encounter with Andy would be simple in comparison, just so long as he got there fast enough.

"Are you operating an appointment system, or can anyone join you?" said a loud, grating voice. Jay almost jumped, the volume shattering his tense body like glass.

"Hi, Andy, I was just about to come over, but take a seat."

Jay looked furtively at Andy as he settled himself into the seat. His face was furrowed and thin, his sandy hair much coarser and thinner than Jay remembered. In the hills below them, Jay's team was burning through Andy's money faster than a forest fire and, if things down on the ground were really as bad as Jay had been told, if Andy truly was in danger of losing his fortune, then Jay knew only one person was to blame.

"I see you haven't lost your touch," said Andy, as Lucy strutted past again.

"She just wanted some information."

"Like your phone number?" He raised his eyebrows, unwilling to believe a word.

"I gave her yours. I hope that's ok."

"If only. Anyway, what brings you out on this flight? Weren't you coming tomorrow?"

"Eamon's got some concerns. I thought I'd better get across earlier, check things out before the board meeting."

"What sort of concerns?" asked Andy, his voice weary with disappointment and disquiet.

"The usual," said Jay, "too much to do and not enough money to do it with. I really can't say much more till I have assessed things in Capadelli."

"He must have given you more than that? Else why would you be coming out early?"

The weak blue of Andy's eyes glowed with the torment of not knowing, of not having known for two years. Jay felt sorry for him, but to save his own skin he had to be vague.

"Eamon doesn't have the big picture. He's mainly worried about the sales; that's the way he put it. As soon as I know the facts, I will update you."

He could feel Andy's eyes burning into him, looking past the words, but he took it no further, changing his line of attack to something more tangible.

"I was looking at the in-flight magazine. Nice piece you have in there."

"Thanks," said Jay, awaiting the blow.

"Though I thought we'd agreed to cut back on the marketing? To put what money is left where it's needed?"

Jay refrained from mentioning that there was no money left and simply watched fate take its course as Andy pulled out the magazine from the seat pocket and flicked through to the offending article.

"How much did this fairy story cost me?" he demanded, thrusting his finger into the face of the smiling policeman in the photograph.

"Twenty grand."

"And you think that's sensible, given the financial situation?" Andy's eyes bulged with disbelief as his finger bore a hole into the photo, tearing a black gulf in the smile.

"That article was commissioned six months ago," said Jay with a dismissive shrug, "things were different back then." Back then twenty grand seemed like loose change to a free spending marketer like Jay. But twenty grand would always be twenty grand to hard-nosed Andy, particularly when it was his twenty grand.

Andy snorted in bitter laughter. "And the couple in the article, the honest copper and his wife who are living the dream in the little piece of paradise we have created, do they even exist?"

"No, they do not," said Jay, determined to sound unashamed, "but that is not the point. They are intended to be illustrative of the type of people who are investing with us."

"And you are ok with that? Some people might think this article is misleading."

Jay sighed; they had debated the difference between spin and deception too many times now for him to care anymore.

"It was the writer who came up with that idea, not me, so I guess the technique is a standard one."

Jay did not meet Andy's eyes as he finished speaking, choosing instead to fiddle with the magazine in the hope that Andy would return to his wife, who had been watching intently, an irritating flash of blonde in Jay's peripheral vision.

"By the way, how's it going on the TMI deal?" asked Andy, seeing straight through his friend-turned-adversary. "You now part of the jet-set world of rock and rollers?"

Jay's mouth twitched into an involuntary smile but Andy beat him to his own answer. "I guess that as I haven't heard anything, it's still in play?"

Definite threat lined his voice; the knowledge that Andy could make or break the deal he facilitated festered on the edge of their relationship ever since the decline of the dream in Italy.

"No announcement as such," said Jay, "but everything we're hearing is that the decision has been made. It's just a question of the internal sign-off process. They have to make work for the bean counters."

"Better not take anything for granted," said Andy. "I hear it can be difficult to get a champagne cork back in the bottle."

Jay was in no mood for snide threats and gestured to where his antagonist's wife was straining her head above the seats to get a better view.

"Kate ok back there?" he asked.

"You in a hurry to make space for the hot hostess again?"

"It's a nice thought. But I was in the middle of something on my laptop. Maybe I can get back to it while the old creative juices are still flowing."

Andy laughed. "Ok, Julian, I will leave you to the hostess and your flowing juices."

Jay sunk into his seat, now left only with the dull and constant worry of his music deal. If he lost, then he would be slowly and agonizingly suffocated by his sins of the past two years, which already flitted like shadows in the corners of his life. But, if he won, they would be cast to the wind, blown away like dust to become the hate and tears of other people, and it didn't matter who those people were.

Eleven

Rain fell relentlessly on Florence, striking the ancient roofs and paving stones like heaven-flung spears as Peter and Isobel drove away from their hotel. They were heading for the Garfagnan area in northern Tuscany to hunt for their holiday home. They drove in silence, Isobel's brow as stormy as the weather whilst Peter clicked away at his emails in the passenger seat. A low and sullen argument in the hotel that morning determined the driver, Peter having blindly overridden Isobel's fears of driving abroad with his need to be constantly in contact with the office.

"I don't think you appreciate how serious things are," he said, referring to his work problems and ignoring his own failure to share them.

"But you are the star man," she said, in an attempt at conciliation.

"Star man or not, the client is threatening to sue."

"But that's Tokyo's problem, surely, not yours? And you've done nothing wrong."

But her curiosity only inflamed his agitation. "Right and wrong doesn't come into it. If the client sues then the firm will settle out of court. It will cost millions, and heads will roll. And the buck ultimately stops with me because they are my client."

"But what if—" she started to argue, but he cut her off.

"But what if nothing, now can we leave it, please."

She sat now, her knuckles white on the steering wheel, staring ahead as the events of the weekend played on her mind and his heavy breathing and restless shifting scraped at her skin like sandpaper.

Finally, Isobel could bear the silence and the tension no longer. Without warning, she jerked down on the wheel and across the oncoming traffic. The sudden change of direction threw Peter to one side and he grabbed instinctively for the handle above his ear, expecting an imminent collision, as the long and uninterrupted sound of a car horn blaring increased his fear for his life. The front wheel of the vehicle hit a low curb at twenty miles per hour, and Peter's head went upwards as the car came downwards, and collided painfully with the roof.

"I need a coffee," announced Isobel, braking hard and bringing the hire car to a jarring halt, and in the process throwing Peter's torso forward toward the dashboard, and his phone out of his hand. "You can stay here sulking like a spoilt child, or you can come inside. But don't come if you are going to bring that horse's face and self-righteous look with you." And having set her terms, Isobel got out and sent the car door crashing closed with all her force.

Peter had either sat to consider his options or to compose himself, because by the time he came through the café door, entering somewhat sheepishly, or so it seemed to Isobel, she was seated with a coffee before her. A second coffee sat in front of the seat opposite, under the saucer that Isobel, in spite of herself, was forced by habit and good nature to place over it.

"You have already ruined one day in Florence," said Isobel with a threatening look, "and now you seem determined to ruin another. It's bad enough driving on these roads in this weather, without having to listen to your silent disapproval."

Peter was not minded to apologise, but neither did he welcome the prospect of finding himself abandoned at a roadside café, which Isobel looked fully capable of arranging. "This is a fool's errand in this weather. We should have just cancelled. I'm not even sure the agent will be expecting us to show."

"Well, we are going to show, and we will look around Bagni di Lucca even if she doesn't."

"To what purpose?" asked Peter, "To buy a pig in a poke?"

"No, to enjoy it like normal people. Tourists come from all over the world to see the Garfagnan; it's famous for its natural beauty, and it's been a spa town for hundreds of years. Napoleon even had his court there at one time."

Peter let out a dismissive snort. "Look, Isobel, I am here because you asked me to come. And it's turned out to be the worst possible time, with everything that's going on at work."

"And when won't things be going on at work? Your clients can live without you, remember that."

"Yes, but can we live without them?"

"For three days? Yes, I think so. Now get yourself out of whatever doom and despair is gripping you, and let's give the exercise our best shot."

Isobel's assault was not a recipe for lifting his spirits, but Peter decided to show willing nevertheless. And he also had life and limb to think about. "I'll drive for a while if you like."

"I have started so I will finish. You can spend the rest of the journey on your precious machine, just be civil when we get there. Please."

Isobel's account of the previous day was true to the facts. Florence, in all its beauty and splendour, had been utterly ruined for her by his presence. As she sought to soak in the sun and the culture of her favourite city he scuffed along behind her, complaining about everything and rarely looking up from his hands. He trailed silently around art galleries — more concerned with his screensaver than the paintings — was sullen and introspective when they sat down for lunch, and accidentally dragged his feet through an artist's chalk painting as they walked along the Ponte Vecchio, leaving Isobel to apologise profusely and to offer a few coins in penitence as he slunk into the shadows to take a call.

Despite the attempt at an armistice in the roadside café, the rest of the journey continued as before. Each car that came too close, or bend that turned too sharply, pushed Isobel closer and closer to a new breaking point. Peter's eyes darkened and narrowed as the rain grew heavier, the rugged beauty of the Garfagnan obscured by raindrops that coated the windows, falling into one another in playful flirtation, growing and shrinking as they traversed the glass. When they arrived at their destination, the historic town of Bagni di Lucca, scant sign of life was visible; each swipe of the wipers revealing empty streets and dull, colourless rows of houses that bled watery dust into the gutters.

"The god forsaken place is deserted," announced Peter, indicating what giving it his best shot was going to involve. "Where are the bustling streets and the outside markets? Isn't that what you told me was a feature of every Italian city, large or small?"

"It's raining, Peter."

"I can see that. I suppose the locals have decided it's too bad to put out the dog, so they've decided to do what we should have done, and stay at home."

"We are here now," said Isobel, "and the rain seems to be easing." And as she said it they heard a dog barking.

They were due to meet Sophia, the estate agent that found Maria her villa, in the car park of the Marco Hotel in forty-five minutes, and they had intended to explore the town on foot to pass the time. But despite Isobel's optimistic forecast, the rain continued to pour and they were confined to the car, like two prisoners in isolation, Isobel watching the forlorn path of the raindrops as Peter glowed in the light of his phone screen.

Sophia was twenty minutes late when she finally arrived, and both Peter and Isobel jumped out of the car in relief at her coming, not even thinking to complain about her tardiness. Sophia was an uninspiring looking woman in her mid-twenties, with hawkish eyes and scraped back hair. She greeted the two warmly enough, but otherwise displayed all the enthusiasm of a funeral director for a cancer cure. The pace of her speech and the curt rapidity of her movements suggested that she viewed them as the worst type of timewasters, her eyes flitting between Peter's surly face and Isobel's anxious gaze suggestive of someone who wished she were somewhere else.

"How well do you know the area?" she asked, in a transparent attempt to establish whether the couple before her did have some genuine interest in a holiday home.

"We know several British people with homes here," said Isobel, feeling a white lie or two was justified. "And I've read quite a bit about the area, novels set here, and so on. And we've been told now is a good time to buy." In deference to Peter, Isobel spoke in English, while itching to show off her language skills.

Anytime would be a good time to buy, thought Peter, based on stories of the wholesale flight of Italy's youth from the hills to the civilisation in the cities below; but only so long as you were never expecting to sell what you bought.

Sophia gave a grudging nod of acknowledgement. "Yes, we have many British here. The weather reminds them of home." It was a half-hearted attempt at humour, and was greeted with the enthusiasm with which it was delivered.

She gave them a brief itinerary as they climbed into her Fiat Panda; they were to visit some of the scenic villages and hamlets in the spartan hills above Bagni di Lucca before descending back into the town itself to see two or three properties that "might be of interest." Her mood was polite but sour as they drove into the hills, and was made worse by the continuing drizzle, the only respite from which was the occasional bank of mist and fog encountered on the pot-holed and narrow winding roads.

"I don't think these roads have been repaired since the roman legions first trod them," said Peter, offering his own attempt at dry humour to contrast with the wet conditions. "And not much else has been repaired either." Isobel ignored the comment and strove to lighten the atmosphere, as she had been desperately attempting to do all weekend, making conversation as Peter sat silently staring at the rain.

"So, Sophia, do you live around Bagni di Lucca?"

"God, no," exclaimed Sophia, without further explanation, as none was needed given the sheeting rain and the spine juddering shocks from the road. But Isobel pressed on regardless, eventually switching to speaking Italian, given Peter's vacant look of resignation. Sophia took this familiarity to launch into a litany of complaints about everything from her sick mother to the decline of the local olive oil industry, all of which Isobel took to be an encouraging sign. "This country is finished," Sophia announced by way of conclusion, which Isobel thought was a curious observation from a woman whose livelihood depended on encouraging investment.

Peter's sullen silence continued largely unabated, but he became more vocal as they reached the villages, finding no charm in the consistently dark, damp, and dilapidated properties that Sophia showed them and, unlike Isobel, feeling more than happy to say so. He initially contented himself with grumbling to Isobel but snapped when Sophia led them into the fifth mildew-ridden apartment and suggested that, "this one might need a bit of doing up."

"Doing up? More like pulling down!" he responded in exasperation as Isobel hid her face in her hands in embarrassment, cursing herself for thinking this could ever have been a good idea.

Sophia responded with a derisive snort and led them back into the rain, turning to Isobel and saying, "I have more properties to show back down in the centre of the town, but I think perhaps they are not what you are looking for."

"Are they like these ones then?" Peter asked. "Falling down and inhabited by stray dogs, with neighbours who look like they belong in the village that time forgot?"

Isobel turned to Sophia in apology but she had already retaken her seat at the wheel, remaining silent for the entire journey back as Isobel and Peter argued with angry whispers in the back seat, he adamant that this fool's errand was her fault and she hating him for his blindness and arrogance.

The rain depleted to a drizzle when they arrived back in the town but this did not stop Sophia from limiting their exploration to just two properties, each, she assured them, boasting views over the River Lima.

Isobel nudged Peter from his phone as they approached the first apartment.

"The whole of Tuscany appears to be in a state of disrepair," he noted with sagging shoulders, glancing up at the tall blank building before returning to his messages. "I'm beginning to think that the only thing the Italians ever finish is their food." Isobel stormed inside after Sophia and, determined to like what she saw, scrutinised everything at careful length. Peter, after a perfunctory glance around the lounge and diner area, did not advance more than two steps beyond the apartment entrance and stood in the doorway like a petulant child.

"It is very relaxing to live beside a river," said Sophia, as the swollen waters crashed below them in the unseasonal rain.

"It would be quieter to live next to the motorway," snarled Peter.

"Shall we see the next one, Sophia?" asked Isobel with a quiet sigh, her tone flat and angry as she glared at her husband who stared back without repentance.

Sophia, seemingly equally anxious to bring the pain to an early end, signalled that they follow her, and led them back down to the overgrown garden area. As the three surveyed the view over the river, a dog howled miserably in the rain and a flock of bedraggled pigeons rose from the rooftops like sad little balloons. The last apartment, only a five-minute walk away, was more promising, larger and brighter, even in spite of the heavy French curtains that masked the balcony.

A deathly glare from Isobel ensured that they both ventured forth to view the property like serious buyers, encouraged, perhaps, that if time and money were no object, it may have potential. Sophia, briefly encouraged, gestured to the two to move towards the balcony, a miserable jutting stone that, if one was willing to toy with fate, provided a view of the river beneath. Peter exhaled loudly at the prospect and headed for the door, Isobel motioning apologetically in his wake like a mother at the supermarket. As they walked back towards the hotel where Sophia's car was parked alongside the hire car, it was difficult for either side to know how to bring proceedings to a close. Sophia, for her part, seemed to have already concluded that the Roberts were the last people likely to buy a place in Tuscany, and that the sooner they reached the car park and said *arrivederci*, the better. But one final hurdle now presented itself, as Isobel's attention was drawn to a balcony in the building alongside the hotel. Even from where they stood it seemed that it would enjoy direct sunlight, and offered a panoramic view down the Lima valley and over the river. "Maybe something like that apartment would be interesting?" she said, putting to one side the umbrella to point towards the balcony. "Somewhere with an outside terrace or balcony to enjoy the views from…"

Sophia's eyes pierced her like arrows, and her mouth curled in cynical mirth. "Such properties rarely come on the market; families hand them down through the generations." Isobel nodded in silence at the dismissive reply and they walked in black silence to the car park. "I hope today has been some value," said Sophia offering an extended hand before continuing, "it was a pity about the weather." She gave a limp shake of Isobel's hand, closed her umbrella, and lowered herself into the car. "I think maybe you have a problem with the tyre," she said with a barely concealed smile. And, without waiting for a reply or a request for assistance, she let out the clutch and pulled away, leaving Peter and Isobel to stare at the flat wheel, their tired and angry faces reflected in the endless purple puddles that licked their feet like flames.

Twelve

Jay switched on his phone as the plane descended, ignoring Lucy's scowl of disapproval. He found a text and email from Greg Johnson to say that he had been called in to a late meeting with TMI. He cursed the company for yet further dithering, but could do nothing but wait.

Eamon greeted Jay as he invariably did, with a smile and, "Hi, boss." Eamon rarely referred to Jay by name, preferring comedy to protocol. "Everything go ok on the flight? No problem with Andy?"

"I handled it," said Jay, not sure that he had.

"It seems there's no rest for the wicked, even up there in the skies close to the man himself. And no safe haven for the innocent either," said Eamon, referring to Andy, and dropping into his thickest Dublin accent. "You are surely like the Devil himself; you are there forever behind every man's shoulder and his Holiness the Pope himself could not resist your temptations."

"You had better get me his number then, because we need every sale we can get. At least if things are half as bad as you are telling me."

Eamon relieved Jay of his carry-on trolley case, like the obedient servant he was, before Jay continued. "There's a change of plan. I need you to run me to the Tulip, something's come up and I have meetings arranged there this evening."

"But what about the team in Capadelli? They are all expecting you. And Gina has arranged a bit of a welcome party, for the messiah's return."

"And look what happened to him," said Jay. "Let's leave the partying till the work is done."

As they approached the revolving doors of the Tulip hotel, Jay's phone rang and Greg's name appeared on the screen. "You go ahead and get us some drinks, I just need to get this," said Jay, his heart pounding. Greg was Jay's deal controller on the TMI bid. From Greg's tone, instinct born from experience told him it was not the news he wanted.

"The steering committee has made the decision," said Greg without drama, "and they good as told me the deal is ours."

"But," said Jay, half knowing what was coming.

"It has to be signed off in New York, by Rick Epstein himself. Until then, no white smoke. So we just need to stay calm and wait. No need to worry though, Epstein is just going to rubber stamp it."

Jay was not a man to leave his fate to chance. He'd been on the wrong end of mercurial decision-making before. He paced around the car park thinking, his phone pressed to his ear. Finally he spoke. "I can't take that risk; we need to get to Epstein."

"I wish," said Greg. "Ask me to get in to see Elvis; that might be easier. And we don't want to piss off the local procurement guys."

"Fuck the procurement guys, the decision is now out of their hands," said Jay, unable to contain his frustration.

"Cool it," said Greg, "we need to keep calm bodies and clear heads. The deal is ours."

Jay didn't want to end the conversation on a disagreement. "Sorry, Greg, you're right. How about you take the guys for a few beers, they're on me. Leave me to worry about Epstein."

He slipped the phone back into his pocket and made his way to where Eamon was sitting with the drinks. As he took his seat, a familiar figure walked through the revolving doors. Deep in animated conversation with a fellow flight attendant, Lucy strode across the lobby amidst the rest of the Anglo Airways flight crew. She passed him with only a cursory glance in his direction, the ring around his finger commanding discretion.

"Everything ok, boss?" asked Eamon, furrowing his own brow in empathy. The look of unease on Jay's face was a combination of his frustration with TMI and his still simmering anger with Lucy for putting him where he was. He watched her derriere disappear into the lift, cursing himself for his own weakness.

Eamon slapped his case full of papers down on the table with vigour, fully prepared to brief Jay on progress at Castello di Capadelli during his three-month absence. "Mind if I get a refill?" said Eamon, not waiting for an answer as Jay rifled through the papers.

"Start with the good news," said Jay as he slid the pile back over the table in exchange for a drink, holding back just one sheet of paper.

"That won't take long to go through, boss," replied Eamon with a further creasing of his brow. "Membership sales have been going gangbusters since you left, no connection, of course," he added with a self-satisfied chuckle. "I've now sold more memberships than we have room for."

Jay cut his mirth short as his eyebrows shot up into his hairline.

"Hold on, Eamon. We only have three hundred memberships to sell, no more and no less, even the Italians know that much."

"Technically, yes," Eamon replied, drawing out the vowels into a wheedling drawl, "but the punters want to stay in the apartments, not the Villa, so it's no problem going over the limit."

Jay sunk his head into his hands. "But it's not just a question of space, Eamon!" he exclaimed. "It's a question of legality. We have a Trust, lawyers involved and so on…" Jay's words trailed away. He knew he could not expect a chancer like Eamon to get his mind around the complexity which he had deliberately created so that only he could connect all the moving parts.

"Sorry, boss, but I thought maintaining cash flow was the priority, even if it means breaking a rule or two? We do whatever it takes to get the job done, isn't that what you told me?"

Jay looked around and hushed him with his hand.

"Things have changed. We still need to get the job done, but we also need to remember who pays the bills, and what they want." His voice was low and pointed, his eyes silently asking for discretion.

"You mean Andy?" asked Eamon leaning forwards. "When did we start worrying about how he wants things done?"

"Andy is a church-goer; he has his principles. Up until now he has been a passive investor, so we haven't needed to worry about how he wants things done," Jay replied, "but now he wants to get involved in day— "

"But we are selling timeshares here, boss, not lessons in Bible reading," interrupted Eamon in an uncharacteristic display of authority.

"If my hands are tied behind my back, then the selling is going to suffer. Now how does that help Andy?"

Jay feared that having his hands tied behind his back was what Andy might soon be worrying about; he rubbed his brow in thought while Eamon continued with his black reality. "We can't undo what's been done, boss, and a sheep and a lamb come to mind. So do I keep selling memberships or not?"

Jay nodded, his forehead crumpling into wrinkles as he weighed up the future in his mind. "Keep selling. I'll make sure we are covered." By which Jay meant he would make sure at the board meeting that it was not only his fingerprints on the gun Eamon was firing in all directions. "Anything else I need to know?" he inquired, making a show of looking at his watch.

"Just that trouble with the owners is definitely coming, there's rebellion in the air."

Jay took a long, calm draught of his gin as he took his time to think.

"Well, that's nothing new. Leave me to work out how we fix that. I've already got a few ideas. For the time being, keep feeding them a diet of good news. Negativity doesn't help us, and if those poor sods only realised it, it doesn't help them either."

"With respect, boss, it's not you who's been ducking and diving these last months, dodging the flak. We can't string 'em along much longer. The Barkers are on the warpath, they're trying to organise the owners into some sort of action group."

Jay let out a derisive laugh. "You are kidding me, aren't you? Geoff Barker would be out of his depth in a car park puddle, and his wife's organisational skills don't stretch beyond running the tombola at her church fete. Anything else?"

"I spoke to Davide yesterday and he said he needs another cash injection."

Jay blew out through his lips, an image of Andy's face with smoke coming out the ears in his mind's eye. "How much of an injection?"

"Two hundred grand...and this month."

Jay kept the look of a man being told the time of day. "No problem, Eamon, that's already sorted." He could see the look of incredulity on Eamon's face.

"But I thought—"

This time Jay cut him short. "I've told you before, Einstein, your job is selling, not thinking. Now how about another refill, and give me five minutes to look at Davide's figures." Eamon got up from the chair, his face far from sharing the confidence of his master.

Jay ran his expert eye down the columns of numbers. Cash injection or not, it was hard refuting the figures; anything he did now would only lessen the speed of his demise. Eamon dallied at the bar before returning, expecting to find Jay chastened by the merciless clarity of Davide's spreadsheet.

"Well, given all the doom and gloom this is a much better picture than I expected," he said to the returning Eamon. "The important thing now is that we look forward, not back. We just need to stay confident, stay focused, and do our job well over the next few days. Apartment sales could just be the silver bullet that saves all our hides, if you and the boys work your magic that is." He pushed a sheet across the table. "Get a couple of the guys to hit the phones in the morning. Call everyone on this list that has put down a deposit, and offer them a discount if they complete before the end of the month. Ok?"

"Offer a discount to punters already committed?" Again, incredulity was woven in every word.

"There you go again, doing the thinking. We need every penny we can get *this month*," said Jay, finally sharing the plight they were both in, "or there won't be a next month."

He glanced at his watch; Lucy was now half an hour late and he did not want Eamon around when she arrived.

"Leave the papers and I will go through them this evening. You've done good work here, Eamon. Any problems we've got are in spite of your efforts, not because of them." As Jay rose, signalling the meeting was over, Eamon remained seated.

"It's great to be appreciated, boss. It surely is," he said. "But as you've raised the subject of miracles, can I expect to see my last six months' commission this week, or will it be next? Last time we met I think you said I'd have it this month for sure."

"I expect to have some good news on that, but I can't say more till after the board meeting."

But this answer did not seem to satisfy Eamon. "That's fine by me, but I'm not the only one waiting on commission. I think you might get a lot of problems if the best I can tell the lads is that the cheque is in the post."

Jay bridled at the implied threat in Eamon's message, but did not show it. His sidekick had picked his moment well.

"Eamon, my good man, I've always seen you right, and that's not about to change." He pulled a wad of notes in a money clip from his pocket and peeled off ten fifty-pound notes. "Sterling be ok? I'm short on Euros."

Eamon nodded and tucked the notes into his pocket.

"That's just between you and me, a personal thank you. It won't be coming off your commission. You have a good time tonight with the boys, and let's see you bright eyed tomorrow morning and fired up to get these sales over the line."

"You can rely on me, boss. If it can be done, it will be done," he said, signalling the no holds barred philosophy with which he went about his work. Jay nodded the nod of a man who chose to look the other way at the sight of blood. Eamon gathered up the papers, sank the last of his gin, and all but skipped off, as if the money had miraculously unburdened him.

Jay looked at his watch for the umpteenth time. Still no sign of Lucy. "What in fuck's name is she up to now," he whispered as he flipped open the laptop to compose an email to Greg.

Thirteen

While Jay sat plotting with Eamon, three floors above him Lucy was similarly occupied. She sat cross-legged on a hotel bed looking up in admiration at the tall, hard-faced woman with the loud voice striding up and down the room. Tessa was a fellow flight attendant and newly appointed best friend; a battle-axe of a woman whose assertive views on the art of seduction had been absorbing Lucy's attention for the last five minutes. Even Jay's presence in the hotel bar was pushed to the back of her mind as Tessa praised her execution of their plan on the plane that afternoon and her subsequent reinvention as a woman in charge. Tessa expounded her views on this latter point with vigour, justifying every statement with a simple motto: "Men are bastards," a conviction that tainted every observation and each piece of advice.

"All they are interested in is getting into your knickers," she explained. "And your Jay looks to me the worst type of bastard. A smooth talking son of a bitch who uses money and good looks to turn an innocent girl's head." Her voice grew more ferocious as she fell headlong into her element, made huge and terrifying by her cynical derision. "Stringing you along, keeping your hopes up that he'll leave that skinny American wife of his, just so he can get what he can't get at home, and without even paying for it." She surfaced for breath then thundered on, worsening everything with an acutely graphic imagination. "How many other Lucys has he got out there? For all you know he's living the life of a fucking Pharaoh, shagging some olive-skinned tart right now in the next room."

Lucy considered these images before dismissing each in turn. She was not a home wrecker; Jay cared nothing for Rusty, and he was not fucking any Italians. He had assured her of all these things and she believed him entirely, or at least until recently, when Jay's elusiveness began to introduce the flames of doubt, doubts that her friend mercilessly fanned.

But Tessa continued, her tone rending Lucy's thoughts in two with its authority. "As long as you keep giving him everything he wants, he's going to keep taking it. Who wouldn't for fuck's sake? Before you know it you'll be menopausal, and you'll still be waiting for the bastard to do the right thing."

Lucy felt the need to offer the case for the defence. "To be fair to Jay, he never tried to hide his marriage from me, and he has never said he would leave Rusty. We are two consenting adults, and I entered into this willingly. So I suppose he might think he doesn't owe me anything?"

"Not owe you anything? Not owe you anything? The bastard's got you brainwashed. He's been *fucking* you; and when a man fucks you, he owes you. And forget that shit about two consenting adults. He's married and you're single. That is not what I call two consenting adults. One is a cheat, and the other is a victim. Jay's a fucking predator, pure and simple."

"Well, yes, maybe," Lucy hesitated, "but I wanted it as much as he did, at the time anyway."

Tessa looked positively offended. "Who wanted who more has fuck all to do with anything! You know what a meat market it is out there, but like in any market, you've got rules."

"Rules?"

"Yes, rules. Rules of supply…" She paused to convey the voice of authority, "…and fucking demand! You can get any man you want just by fluttering your eyelashes. Who can Jay get? A shrivelled up stick insect that's well past her sell-by date. You listen to me, girl; the bastard owes you, and owes you big time. The guy is nearly forty and going downhill fast. The only way he will ever get a woman like you again is by paying for her. He's been banging you for eighteen months, and what have you got out of it? Misery and heartache, as far as I can see. Has he ever bought you anything that cost more than a drink? No. Has he ever taken you on holiday? No."

Lucy stopped her there, standing up to stem the flow of legs and speech.

"Tess, Jay is very generous. We eat at the most incredible restaurants." Tess raised her eyebrow and dropped open her mouth in theatrical incredulity, the sight of her molars threatening another barrage of words.

"And we've stayed at such beautiful hotels," Lucy continued, "famous ones, you know, like the Dorchester."

Tess put a firm finger to her friend's lips and laughed.

"Give me a break, girl. Where's he ever taken you that he can't put through one of his companies? You are giving the bastard everything he wants for free, and you are just an item on his expense report."

"Look, Tess, I'm not sure where this is getting me. I could go back to my room and cry my heart out about all this but it won't take me anywhere."

"What you do with Jay and how you live your life is nothing to do with me. I'm happy to help but I'm the last person who would want to give you advice. All I am trying to do is to straighten your head out. To get you thinking right. You're his mistress, Lucy, and I hate to see it."

"Well, sort of, yes, except I am also going out with Rob," Lucy offered in some sort of mitigation for Jay's sins.

"Rob's got nothing to do with it," her friend declared as she cut her short. "He's a single guy, and you have every right to go out with him, or anyone else you want to. And, other than the fact he's fucking you, Rob doesn't owe you anything."

"So what does Jay owe me then, exactly?" Lucy inquired, intrigued as to what perks she was apparently due as a newly declared mistress.

"Anything you want," replied Tessa in triumph, "that is what he owes you. He wants to fuck you but keep you hidden away at the same time. Well, that comes at a price. Christ, girl, he should be keeping you, giving you an allowance, paying your rent, buying you stuff, and spoiling you at every turn. That's the way this mistress thing works. And in return you fuck him, and stay in the closet!"

But this fairy tale, this carefully crafted image of a satisfied woman's paradise, held little charm for Lucy.

"But that isn't what I want. I don't want his money, or to spend my life tucked away in his wardrobe or whatever. I want to enjoy myself, with Jay by my side, utterly and completely mine." She scowled as her friend rolled her eyes in reply but continued nonetheless, the tone of her voice rising as she imagined the dream. "You see, the thing is there's no sign of that happening any time soon, so things have to change. I know he's not happy at home, and one day he's going to have to make a choice, and I want that choice to be me."

"So why not put him on the spot?" Tessa replied, pounding her fist on the bed as she cried, "*Make* him choose you!"

"Because I'm not ready to take the risk," said Lucy, simply, "but the question is, how to get Jay to appreciate what he is going to be missing if he stays living a lie, to understand how much better his life would be if he were with someone he truly loved, and who truly loved him?"

The look of marked restraint in Tessa's eyes was telling and Lucy wondered if true love was an alien, even hilarious, concept to a woman who seemed to be made of iron. She imagined Tess must have read about love in books and seen it at the movies but dismissed it as a weak fabrication of a lesser human mind.

"What makes you think he loves you?" demanded her friend in a tone that was dangerously close to derision. "Any guy is going to spoil you and tell you what you want to hear. As I said, that's just about getting into your knickers."

"Oh please, give me some credit," said Lucy getting to her feet in exasperation. "I know a thing about men too. But Jay is different."

"How is he different?" said Tessa, more in scorn than in curiosity. "And let's not kid ourselves here. If Jay was a dustbin collector, would you have ever gone for him?"

An image of her mother, old and defeated before her fortieth birthday, cleaning up after a drunken slob, flashed before Lucy's eyes. "Maybe that is how it started, I don't mind admitting it," she replied with sudden conviction, "but things have changed. He is the only person in my life who has ever really believed in me. He tells me I can be anything I want to be, as long as I want it enough and work for it. He makes me feel like nothing is too far anymore." She did not tell her friend that it was Jay who, with understanding and patience, had helped her kick her cocaine habit; a habit she fell into when lap-dancing until it seemed to her that because of Jay she no longer needed it.

"Words are cheap," said Tess, ignorant of the debt and wiping away the romance with a gesture of dismissive disgust. "He's no different until he proves it."

"And how does he do that?"

"By changing his behaviour," she said, "and the only way you are going to get Jay to change is if you change your own behaviour first. What you need to understand is that he treats you the way he does for a very good reason." She fell silent, awaiting the question, relishing her advantage over the beauty before her.

"Which is?" said Lucy obligingly.

"Which is that it's the way you yourself have taught him to treat you. So now you have to start re-educating the shit. To teach him how you expect to be treated. How you *demand* to be treated."

"Do you have specific suggestions then?" asked Lucy with a smile, remembering her elation on the plane.

"Well, now that you ask, I do have a few," said Tess, mustering a grim smile in reply. "You need to introduce a few obstacles into the relationship. Things that make him sit up and take notice, things that give him pause for thought. You need to test him."

Lucy leant forward. "Test him? How?"

"Well, create situations that force him to start to step up to his responsibility to you. Obviously, you can't set the hurdles too high at first, but once you've got him to take the first steps, then you can raise the bar, and get him to make bigger leaps. Until you've got him where you want him."

"And where is that?" asked Lucy in mock innocence.

"Well, ideally, it's at the altar," Tessa grimaced, "if that's what you want. But it's small steps at first. What you are trying to do is move him out of his comfort zone with the lizard, until he's in a new comfort zone with you, and doesn't want to move back. That's when you've got him where you want him."

"And you've got the manual? That lists all the things I need to do and not do," said Lucy with scepticism bordering on sarcasm.

"I'm only trying to help. There's no recipe for this one. But maybe you need to start giving out a bit of what you've been taking, stop being such a pushover and make him do some waiting around for a change. Then you need to get him to do things, to go places, things that impact him and his married life. You need to start to show that you won't settle for being kept in the closet." She pulled at her ponytail before continuing, "And then there's also the sex of course, you'll probably need to scale that back, maybe even withhold it for a while."

"Oh, come on," Lucy exclaimed, her eyes filled with doubt, "let's be realistic here, I am still his mistress. If I start withholding favours, then I've got nothing left, nothing."

Tess slapped her back and squeezed her shoulder promising her, "There's no need to worry about that, believe me. Stand him up at the bar tonight and I guarantee you'll see how much power you have over him."

"After I've already forced him to change his plans this evening to be here?"

"He had that coming. He will have known there was a reasonable chance you would be working the flight today. So you've every right to make a last minute change."

Lucy sucked in her breath. "It's getting pretty last minute now. He's expecting to see me at eight."

"Well, wait half an hour and then let him know you have other plans."

"And you're certain about this?" questioned Lucy, unsure whether to put the future of her relationship into her friend's sharp, steely hands.

"Lucy, this is about power. If you really want him to ditch the lizard for you, then first he is going to have to respect you."

"And not keeping my appointments is going to make Jay respect me?" she replied with uncertainty.

"Yes, it is. It will show him you are a woman with your own mind. Who makes her own decisions. Someone to be reckoned with, not trifled with. A woman of substance, for Christ's sake."

Lucy was not sure if letting Tessa make decisions for her was evidence of a woman who made up her own mind, but she knew that she did need to do something; and in the absence of any other idea, Tessa's advice was worth trying. Lucy looked at her watch. She was now twenty minutes late for her evening tryst with Jay. She made her decision, and set out for the lobby bar to give him the bad news, striding from the room with a newly found purpose that made her dangerously beautiful.

Fourteen

Jay felt a shadow behind him and lifted his eyes from his laptop. He turned to look over his shoulder and found his face pressed against the sequins of a short, tight skirt. His focus on his work had taken his mind off Lucy's tardiness, and he was not inclined to jump straight to attention.

"I just need a few minutes," he said, asserting his authority while trying to ignore the smell of her perfume which, he guessed from the proximity of her crotch to his nose, had been applied liberally around the top of her thighs.

"That's convenient, as I'm not staying. I just came down to tell you that I'm going to have to postpone things for a few hours, a friend of mine is having a relationship crisis."

He turned to reply but she was already walking towards the staircase.

"Lucy—"

"And don't go anywhere in the meantime, I'll be finished at ten," she called back, her body illuminated by the soft lighting of the staircase which silhouetted her curves in its muted glow.

It was nearly eleven when Lucy promenaded in; he closed his laptop in anticipation and began to stand. But she walked straight past and threw herself onto one of the plush chairs that filled the lounge, ignoring him in favour of a willowy redhead with whom she was now in an earnest discussion, punctuated by surreptitious glances in his direction that never seemed to meet his eyes.

He took his place again and watched Lucy cavort with her colleagues from behind his laptop. He was tapping the keys harder and harder as anger welled up within him. This new game made him uneasy, like the calm before a storm, but after eighteen months, the thought of Lucy could still stir within him a desire he felt with no one else, and had not felt with anyone else for as long as he could remember. Resolving to get Lucy out of his life from afar was one thing; resisting her temptations when her flesh was within reach was something else. He could not let go, could not disentangle himself from her embraces; her long, lean thighs held him in a deadlock that threatened to continue forever.

The thought of eternity in any form was not one that Jay often allowed to cross his mind and he banished it by snapping his laptop closed and making for his room without a second glance at Lucy who was now acting out some earlier scene of hilarity to her friend, wiggling and twisting her body as she did so.

As he entered his sparse and depressing overnight billet he freed his mind from the snares of her body and congratulated himself on having insisted on booking separate rooms; there would be no confrontation, no eruption of whatever it was that was boiling inside her when she returned. He turned the deadlock with relief and picked up one of his mobile phones to call Rusty, who insisted on him checking in every night regardless of where he was. When no answer came, he flung the phone onto the bed. He flipped his laptop open but the stress of the day was taking its toll, and his tired mind was unable to pick up where he had left off. He found his eye straying to his second mobile phone and before long he could resist its allure no longer. He picked it up, entertaining himself with the concise erotica that Lucy texted him on a daily basis, as he waited for his wife to call back.

As he read the texts, one after the next, each becoming more graphic and more absorbing than its predecessor, he yearned for her body and half got up. He would go to her room and make her his again. But no sooner had he risen, than a knock on the door pre-empted his resolve. Lucy was posing in the corridor, standing legs apart, one hand on hip, and the other dangling two miniature bottles of in-flight champagne. Her blouse was loose outside her skirt, and fully unbuttoned, the cups of her lacy bra exposed above her bare midriff.

"Room service, sir?" she enquired. Jay stepped forward just enough to glance right and left, and hauled her through the door.

"Get in here, you slut," he commanded, kicking the door shut and pressing her against it. He could not fight the intense urgency that consumed him; even the glint of victorious elation in Lucy's eyes was not enough to quell his passion.

She managed to slip her wrists from the cuffs of her blouse as he was in the process of slipping the bra down her long tanned arms and both fell to the floor to be trampled by ardent, impassioned feet. The sight of her naked torso, bare of all but a nipple ring, aroused him yet further and he pushed her up the door, lifting her body from the floor until her breast was at head height. He proceeded to bite into and around the nipple ring as she pulled the back of his head into her breasts.

"No teeth marks now, there's Rob to think about."

Regardless, he sunk his teeth hard around her nipple.

"Ooh, what *has* gotten into you tonight, tiger?"

But he was hardly hearing what she was saying, and it was something other than pleasant conversation that he had on his mind at that exact moment. Without responding, he spiralled around, still holding her, and carried her to the bed. If she had not been attached to him in so unladylike a position, her legs wrapped around his waist, the manoeuvre might have counted as one of the more romantic gestures of their relationship. Just as bliss began to envelop, the shrill sound of his phone pierced the magic, cutting through his lust like a knife. It could only be Rusty at such a late hour.

"Answer that and you are dead meat," warned Lucy, pouncing on him like a kitten and holding him to the bed with fire in her eyes.

Jay's hand inched towards the phone, before he withdrew it; it was not yet so late that he would not be expected to be taking calls, and it was only a few minutes since he had left a message. He could only reasonably be in one place, his hotel room. But Lucy was proceeding at a whirlwind pace; yanking off his belt and tossing it behind her with all the regard she had for his marriage.

Yet she seemed to read his mind and to sense his dilemma. "She will just think you are in the bathroom," she said. "If it's important she'll ring back, and if I'm done with you by then, you can answer it. Right now, the only thing you need to be worrying about is how you hold out long enough till I'm good and satisfied. Because, in case you haven't noticed, you've already leaked half a pint of juice into your Calvin Klein's."

The phone fell silent and Jay looked down to verify her observation. But the top of Lucy's head blocked his view; he felt her tongue running over him, stimulating and teasing him with its path. He felt ready to explode and with no concern for Lucy's pleasure, lay back to allow her to finish him.

But with a yelp of pain, all the sensations in him shattered; she had taken her thumb and forefinger and pinched hard on his most sensitive part.

"What the hell was that for?" he demanded.

"For your own good, lover boy," she said, breathing hard and wiping her lips, "you just need chilling a bit that's all, you're so pumped up."

"Well, next time can you do it with ice cubes? And only after you've popped them in your mouth," he added for good measure.

"Ice cubes in the mouth? Won't be any room for your enormous python if I do that, Julian, will there?"

The treatment she'd administered, paired with her use of the name his parents had burdened him with, seemed to have the desired effect, and she leisurely searched one-handed in her bag for her condoms, while gently running her other hand up and down his upper body. Jay for his part was content to lie still, taking in the sight of the delicious curves above him, her perfectly enhanced pear-shaped breasts standing out, with her mouth-watering nipples hard and erect. Now naked, she moved around Jay's muscular body, pulling off his remaining clothes and exciting his skin with her fingertips. She sat back to survey her conquest with satisfaction, then rose, spread her legs across his body, rolled on the condom, and eased him inside her with an expert hand.

"That feel like how you like it, tiger, am I wet enough for you tonight?" she whispered in his ear. He could say nothing, Lucy was more than wet; she was hot and she was soaking.

"Now you be a good boy and make it last," she said, contracting her pelvic muscles and squeezing him as she tested his self-control. "We don't want any wham bam, thank you ma'am, do we now, just because your luscious Lucy has kept you waiting a teeny little bit?"

She gyrated on top of him as he played with her nipple in his mouth, curling his tongue around the ring. He could barely contain himself. But as he approached the point of no return she was giving every indication of being in full control of her senses.

"You are not going to shoot yet, are you, babes?" she enquired, nibbling and probing into his ear as she did so. "Sorry about tonight, darling," she continued, "it's just that I got some news today."

"Don't worry about it," Jay said, confused by her sudden desire for conversation.

"It's just that I have this wedding coming up." She gave another squeeze and held it. "And now Rob can't make it."

Jay merely grunted in reply, his capacity for speech rendered useless by her lovemaking.

"So you are ok to take me to the wedding, aren't you, Jay?" she continued, holding herself still to wait for his confirmation. He was at a point where he would agree to almost anything to achieve climax and replied with a simple "Sure, whatever."

"No, not whatever. You will take me to the wedding, won't you?" she persisted, suspending herself above him, her curves defined against the light.

"Yes, don't worry, I've said I will, haven't I?" he replied.

She smiled and sank down on him as far as she could go and he closed his eyes with a groan as she finally took him.

They lay next to each other, her head on his shoulder, and Jay felt the need to sleep washing over him. "What was that about a wedding?" he asked as he entered the twilight zone of semi-consciousness.

"We can talk about it later, try and get some sleep now," she whispered, stroking his chest. "You'll be needing your strength again a bit later."

Fifteen

After their trials in the hills of northern Tuscany, Isobel awoke back in their Florence hotel to glorious sunshine, and to the sound of Peter humming as his electric shaver whirred away. Perplexed, she made her way to the bathroom. She stood behind him, her arms around his waist, their faces reflected back at them in the mirror, his beaming, hers full of uncertainty.

"Well," she said, "are you going to tell me the good news?"

"I got a message overnight. The job in Texas looks like it could be on." Peter had not sat idle as his troubles over the Tokyo fallout mounted. He had called in a favour from an old client, Bill Rogers, the CEO of Reynolds Computer based in Dallas. It was a Board appointment as Strategy Director; if the worst came to pass, it was a position he could take with his head held high. "They want me to go across."

A sudden feeling of elation ran through Isobel, and she hated herself for it.

"When will you be going?"

"Sometime in the next week. I've already emailed Rachel to liaise with Bill's office."

Isobel bridled at the sound of Rachel's name, and she found herself tightening her hold on her husband's waist. But the strange feeling of insecurity passed as quickly as it came as she reflected on her good fortune that Peter's mood had been transformed for the day ahead.

The sun blazed through the windshield as they set off towards Capadelli along the scenic roads of the Arno valley, a convoluted route that they had decided on in high spirits at breakfast that morning, and a welcome relief from the flat, grey motorways that had loomed the evening before. It was a decision in keeping with their reinvigorated mood and the glorious weather. A greater contrast to the inclement climate of the previous day was hard to imagine and Peter was now conciliatory; he even offered to do the driving, allowing Isobel to relax and enjoy the journey.

They drove at a leisurely pace, stopping first in Vinci to visit the museum, which housed a number of models of the eponymous inventor's brilliant creations. Isobel hovered in the spacious cool rooms as Peter gazed at the great structures like a child, the enthusiastic engineering undergraduate of his youth resurfacing, as she had known it would. With pleasure, she watched his fascination, imagining him youthful again as the man she married long ago, when she was so much in love that it felt as if she was drowning.

After a full hour in the museum she suggested a coffee and as they left to seek out a café she stopped at the gift shop to buy Peter a book on the works of Leonardo da Vinci, her reminiscing having left her full of guilt and apology. But as he looked into her eyes and took it, she could not help but say, "Something for you in bed, darling, it might stimulate your inventive side." Her words were soft and affectionate, he saw nothing in them, and so they walked to the café, lightly holding hands.

The café was simple in the extreme, a few circular wooden tables with blue-checked plastic tablecloths. The sparse bar area was absent of any decorative effort and the simple white floor tiles and whitewashed walls would not have been out of place in a south London cab driver's retreat. Isobel took the simplicity in with a smile, sitting herself down in the knowledge that they had found the real rural Tuscany. Set upon a table in the middle of the café was a large leg of ham, next to a plate of assorted cheeses, covered by a large, clear plastic dome on which lazy flies briefly alighted. On the floor behind the bar was a crate with a dozen or so bottles with corks protruding from their necks. They were coated in a light film of dust, with no labels to declare their origin or vintage.

She chatted in Italian with the aging owner, a man whose eyes seemed to have fallen back into his skin over the years, now glinting out like coal from beneath the pleasant crinkles, and Peter ordered two coffees, his blank expression betraying his pitiful grasp of Italian. As another customer entered, Isobel turned her attentions to Peter, offering some unsolicited views on the contrasts between Tuscany and Provence, the site of their ill-fated holiday home.

"This is so refreshing after Provence, isn't it, Peter?" she said, sipping her coffee in satisfaction. "It's a much simpler environment. Less commercialised, and without all those Brits spoiling the ambience."

"I guess so, but I think you'll find plenty of them here too." He was unwilling to concede anything about Provence; even the dazzling sunshine was not enough to coax him into buying a house in Italy.

"Perhaps in the major tourist cities like Florence," she mused, "but it seems so unspoilt here. I mean, just look around. About as far as you could get from Starbucks without going to North Korea." She had picked up on one of his favourite gripes and waited expectantly for a positive reply.

"North Korea, darling?" he asked, more than willing to play her game. "I thought you were comparing Tuscany to Provence? I'm sure we'll find Starbucks in Pisa and Florence, just next to the McDonald's in all probability. And I'm betting they will be just like the Starbucks and the McDonald's in Cobham high street." He smiled as he shot her arguments back at her. "At least the French insist they make some concessions to Gallic language and culture."

Isobel smiled but rose to the bait nonetheless. "Peter, you haven't been in a McDonald's for at least twenty years, and the only time you go in Starbucks is when you are searching for a Wi-Fi connection for your penis."

He winced; she had titled his phone a penis when his email addiction was in its infancy, convinced that only something that gave sexual pleasure could be so frequently in his hand. He hated the nickname with a passion and twisted his mouth in discomfort.

"I think it would be polite to either pay or order another coffee," she said, aware of her victory, "and we have so much to do today. I'd like us to spend some time in San Miniato. That might also be an opportunity to draft a few of those power emails that I'm sure have been on your mind since this morning," she added, knowing the button she was pressing.

His face brightened at the reminder of his message from Dallas, validation of his importance, that he was still a man in demand, and he paid the two-euro bill with a five-euro note and left the change, throwing his face to the sun as they stepped back outside.

The countryside seemed to grow greener and richer as they drove through the valley and the hilltop town of San Miniato soon came into view, rising above the verdure like a citadel, magnificent and gold against the midday sky. Isobel had suggested their fleeting visit as it coincided with the annual crostini festival, a perfect opportunity to immerse themselves in the heart of Tuscan culture. They strolled into the labyrinthine centre with its narrow streets and tall buildings and the delicious aroma of food. The area of the festival was thronged with Italians, eating together in extended family groups, the tiny children darting in and out of the old people's legs, as the sun glanced off their leathery skin.

The place was buzzing with noise and with life, an abundance of food laid out on stalls for perusal and selection.

"How does this work?" asked Peter, who hated any form of disorganisation. "Do we try to secure some seating, and do I need to protect it while you order the food? Or do we just make a run for the food and take our chances we'll be able to get seats?"

"I expect the thing to do is to ask," she said, trying to disguise her impatience, "and as I'm the only one of us who speaks Italian, I guess on this occasion you have a valid reason for being reluctant to seek help."

She engaged a handsome young man wearing an apron, intent it seemed on some urgent task. He was all too happy to help, but offered his guidance at a pace that Isobel doubted Italians themselves could understand.

"Not as simple as forming an orderly line then?" Peter smirked, as the man melted into the crowd, leaving Isobel perplexed.

"Peter, this is Italy," she said in exasperation, "and anyway, forming a line is less fun than doing things the Italian way."

"And what is the Italian way, exactly, in these circumstances?"

"First we need to do a bit of a tour to decide what we might want to eat. Then we buy different coloured vouchers at different prices, then we go and spend those vouchers at the various food stalls, then sometime later someone will bring the food and drinks. But before we do all that, we need to select a table number." She folded her arms, daring him to contradict her understanding.

"They're all full, in case you hadn't noticed," he said.

"Yes, but you are the one in the solutions business, I believe. I've done all the research work, so figuring out how we get space on one of these benches is down to you." She had injured his weakest spot and he shrugged in assent.

"Well, we could just hover menacingly around someone who seems to be on the coffee course?"

Isobel burst out laughing. "I think maybe it's better if you leave me to sort out the solution bit too. This way."

Under her redoubtable leadership all the obstacles were quickly overcome, and the two found themselves seated alongside a family of Italians spanning four generations. A round woman with a nose like a potato turned to Isobel with a kindly smile and offered her some olive bread, entering freely and welcomingly into conversation once Isobel's fluency became apparent. All was going smoothly until Isobel indicated their destination. The mention of the word 'Capadelli' in an English accent drew the attention of everyone at the table, and they swivelled their heads round like owls.

"Capadelli? Inglese? You go to Capadelli to see the Inglese?" asked the woman's husband in broken and frantic English.

Isobel's fluent reply drew him back into his native tongue and he launched into what seemed to Peter to be an animated warning of the perils of travelling to see the Inglese in Capadelli. He watched Isobel in concern as she nodded and laughed along, the man waving his arms in wild gestures and yelling "PAZZO" at the top of his voice.

"Uh, what's a pazzo?" he asked his wife, as their food arrived and they were left to their own company. Isobel picked at her tagliatelle with dainty fingers and shrugged, her mouth full and her eyes unwilling.

"What was all that about?" he persisted. "Seems like he was giving us some kind of warning about the English, or about Capadelli, or about both. Have we stumbled into the Italian equivalent of Transylvania or something?"

"A bit melodramatic," she laughed, "and I think the tagliatelle is heavy on the garlic, so I'm sure we will be ok. But it does seem like Capadelli has achieved some kind of celebrity status with the locals."

"The locals? We are still ten kilometres from Capadelli, which is hard enough to find on a map as it is. Seems like there's more to it than celebrity status." His voice was ominous and she hated him for his automatic negativity.

"All he was saying is some English people a bit larger than life are living in Capadelli. Something like that. And, he also said that some famous Italian footballer from Sardinia is rumoured to be buying a house there, which I suppose would give it celebrity status around here."

Peter looked unconvinced. "So what is a pazzo?" he demanded again.

"It means crazy," she said, quickly continuing before he predicted their doom. "All sounds very exciting and quite intriguing, doesn't it? We've never met anyone famous in five years in Provence, and here we are on our first trip to Capadelli and it seems we might be in the company of the next best thing to Italian royalty, an Italian football star. I can hardly wait."

Peter made no reply, choosing instead to chew his pasta, and retreat into his own thoughts. Isobel gave an involuntary shudder, her eyes fixed on the distant hills.

Sixteen

Jay walked past the gleaming glass door of Castello di Capadelli's reception building, now kitted out with brass fittings and other high-end finishing touches. The development had been a construction site when he last visited. It was now a tourist complex, and a beautiful one at that. The apartments and communal buildings, dull stone on his last visit, were now plastered and painted. They glowed in the morning sun, warm yellows and oranges against the blueness of the Tuscan sky; their colours already faded enough to blend in with the architecture that dotted the neighbouring hills. Beautiful details had been sprinkled liberally across the structures by his exterior design team, from carved stone horses on the walls to vines that twisted their way around doorways in intricate natural arches. What had been dirt and rubble in the surrounding landscape was now verdurous and green with winding gravel walkways replacing the paths trod out haphazardly by heavy boots. He turned the corner to the pool, a monstrous concrete hole on his last visit that would now be a veritable oasis, suitable for the most discerning of holidaymakers. He froze in shock at what he saw in place of his vision. The pool sat in a field of mud; its clear blue waters topped with a layer of dust that floated in brown waves across the surface, revealing occasional strips of blue that flashed out of the muck like escaping sky. Around the pool were neat stacks of teak decking, decking Jay had been assured had been laid weeks ago.

"What is this then, Eamon?" he asked his genial bag carrier, who had been following him around and absorbing his praise like a dry sponge.

"Well, boss," Eamon replied, twisting his hands awkwardly in front of him, "those builders I told you about that we hadn't paid — they came in last night and tore up their work, and they say they won't redo it until they get all their money."

Jay turned to Eamon unfazed. "Get the maintenance guys to somehow make it useable, at least so people can get to and from the pool without sinking up to their arses in mud. I'll speak to Davide about settling the problem with the builder later." He made to move on, aware that the pile of bricks stacked by what should by now have been a vine-covered wall needed his attention too.

"Are you sure that's wise, boss?" asked Eamon, making no move to intercept his path but lacking too much of his normal jollity to be ignored. "If we do something quick and dirty it's hardly likely to be safe. What if someone breaks an ankle or something? A child even?"

Jay wheeled around and smacked the heel of his hand into his forehead in an exaggerated gesture of frustration. "Look around you. Do you see any lifeguards? Any safety belts? Any warning signs? I think we can take the risk of some kid twisting their ankle, seeing as we are clearly not too bothered about them drowning."

Eamon fought back a smile and nodded with his best impression of a devoted employee and a serious man. "I'll ask the maintenance guys to do what they can."

"Now if you'll excuse me, I need to catch up with Davide," said Jay, striding past the wall-turned-rubble with the jaunty steps of a man who couldn't care less.

Davide was at his desk in the poky studio apartment that was being used as the accounts office. Box files were stacked all around the floor and covering the surface of the desk, a sea of paper engulfing the room. But the accountant welcomed him warmly, clasping his palms around the hands of his visitor. Jay marvelled how the diligent and industrious Italian was so unruffled by the disorder in which he was working; when Jay asked for the paperwork he had requested the evening before, the man merrily sifted through the papers, tossing them over his shoulder like confetti as he attempted to find them.

Jay tucked the papers into his folder; reading them could wait. "Your presentation for the board meeting, how's that coming on?"

Davide beamed at the question, and from somewhere under the mountain of clutter he produced a professionally bound set of overhead slides, its pristine condition in contrast to the surrounding chaos. "Everything is ready," said Davide, eager to be stroked for his herculean efforts.

Jay began thumbing through the deck, each slide a wall of numbers like a bingo card, effusing praise as he went. "Excellent, Davide, excellent. Very thorough."

"I try my best, signor, I hope you agree it is complete," said Davide, unaware of the blow that was about to fall.

"It most certainly is," said Jay, "it most certainly is. But the thing is, Andy Skinner is not a numbers man. He likes to see the big picture. And also, these numbers are backward looking."

Mystification reigned on Davide's face. "But how else can I present the financial situation, if not from the past accounts?"

"What Andy has asked for," said Jay, authority and command in his voice, "is not a history of the past, but a view of the future, a sense of where the business is going. And that is a very healthy future, is it not?" continued Jay, with menace in his words. "Five or six slides, Davide, that is what we need, nothing more, without all these confusing numbers. We must believe in the future," said Jay, like some born again preacher, his body rising from his seat with his words. "Do I make myself clear?"

Davide nodded, his chin falling and his shoulders drooping. "Yes, signor," he affirmed as Jay held him with a laser-like gaze, before turning on his heels.

Jay set off for the car park at some speed, anxious to avoid anything or anyone that might delay him from meeting Andy in the village, the situation with the pool only adding to the urgency and importance of his mission. But as he turned the corner onto the long straight path to the car park, two figures came into view, two horribly familiar figures. He squinted into the sun as they approached, sure that fate could not have been so unkind as to send them his way today. But his eyes had not fooled him and it soon became clear that he was on a direct collision course with Geoff and Rosie Barker, the couple that Eamon had warned him about in the hotel and who he had been steadfastly avoiding for almost a year. They were closing in like two forlorn birds of prey and directly blocking the path to his car; he had no choice but to engage them.

"Geoff, Rosie, great to see you!" he called out, as he quickened his pace towards them. "I've just been looking around down by your apartment, hoping to catch you."

"Well, Mr. Brooke, you have caught us now," said Geoff, his wife close to his side and sharing his facial expression, one of unadulterated dislike.

"I was wondering if you were both free for lunch today?" he continued, smiling brightly. "I know you have some important matters to discuss, and there's someone very important on site today who is keen to meet with you."

Their faces lost their unity as they tried to process this turn of events. Rosie's had already broken into a smile as his charm took its toll and even Geoff, the stronger willed and less gullible of the two, was struggling to maintain his icy demeanour.

Jay continued, his acting buoyed by his success. "That's assuming you can do lunch today, of course? Needs to be a late one, at least by English standards. Can you be in your apartment at two today? I will have you picked up. Stay off the latte this morning, so you have a good appetite. It's somewhere special and it's on me, of course."

They both nodded, words failing them; like all honest and everyday people, they were simply no match for a master craftsman like Jay, and by the time they had collected their thoughts they were looking at the back of his car as it exited the car park.

As Jay turned out of his parking space he was already hitting the speed dial on his mobile to call Eamon.

"What do you have on this morning?" he asked as soon as Eamon had picked up, forgoing niceties in favour of a brutally quick exchange.

"Same as what we discussed earlier, boss," he replied, "why, do you want me to do something else?"

"What are your lunch plans?" came the reply, ignoring his question.

"Bit too busy for lunch," he sighed, "what with everything that's going on here today. I'm probably going to grab something quick in the wine bar around one o'clock. But I need to be ready for the Roberts' arrival around four-thirty, and I have other deals to close this weekend…" He tailed off.

Jay pushed these concerns aside with a dramatic exhaling of breath.

"Ok, here's what I need you to do. About two, go over to the Barkers' apartment and pick them up, take them out somewhere local, nothing too flash, and get as much house wine into them as you can. Enough to make them so ill tomorrow that they can't leave their apartment."

"I guess they are expecting to see you then?" said Eamon.

"Yes, they are. But there's no way I can do lunch. I have to see Andy today. But tell them I'll try and come for a coffee at the end of lunch."

"So assuming you don't make the tail end of lunch, which I expect is a safe bet, when can I now expect to see you? Will you be around to meet the Robertses?"

"I'll be back late afternoon. And remember that I want red carpet treatment for the Robertses."

"It will be as if Her Majesty herself was arriving."

"But without the smell of wet paint?"

"The Gardens of Babylon will seem like a farmer's field by comparison."

The attempt at humour sparked a thought in Jay. "Mrs. Roberts is into horses; it might be an idea to talk about the riding facilities we offer. The ones in the brochure."

Eamon laughed. "Which is the only place she'll find them."

Jay sighed. "Just get Gina working on it. And let the Robertses know I will be taking them to dinner at eight, if they are available."

"Dinner?" asked Eamon, surprise and shock manifest in his voice.

"Yes, Eamon, dinner," he replied with a smile, as he remembered his body pressed close against Isobel Roberts. "I have a feeling this might be our biggest opportunity yet, and I'm going to make the most of it."

Seventeen

Andy turned into the single street that ran through the village of Capadelli and under the narrow archway beneath the clock tower with mixed emotions. He needed nothing more than to believe in miracles. But he had little faith in the non-material world and less and less faith in Jay. He pulled into the only available space and sat in his car waiting for Jay to appear, determined to wrestle control from his tormentor.

Andy leapt out of his car the moment Jay arrived, anxious to get the meeting over with. "You want a coffee?" said Andy by way of good morning, and continued on into the galley-shaped café that offered counter only service.

Jay took a seat outside watching the scruffy brown children caper up and down the steps, chuckling in their invisible games. The few locals preferred the shade of the inside to the heat of the decking, leaving the sun to the foreigners and the crazy Englishmen who prowled the Castello battlements to prey on the unwary.

Andy returned from the counter with his purchases, his concern over his finances worsened by the experience. "Five fucking Euros for two coffees, do they think that's the Trevi fountain we're looking at?" he said, glancing at the trickle of water running down a crumbling wall from a broken outside tap. "Last time I was here it was less than half that."

"That's progress," said Jay, taking his coffee, "and it's your own doing. You've put the sleepy old village on the map; you can't blame the locals for cashing in."

"Too right I can," said Andy, decidedly low on generosity of spirit. "Anyway, why have you dragged me down here this morning? What's so urgent it can't wait till the board meeting? And what's wrong with meeting up the hill? The coffee's free there."

"Take it easy," said Jay, holding up the palms of his hands. "I'll pay for the coffee."

Andy's mood lightened at Jay's dry humour and he became more conciliatory. "It's just that this morning is not a good time. Kate's already chomping at the bit to get into Florence to go shopping."

"So the longer we sit here the more money I'm saving you, right?"

Andy was less than amused and his brusque manner returned as quickly as it had left him. "What's on your mind, Jay, because whatever it is, I'm guessing it's something other than saving me money?"

"Before we come to that, you had a chance to walk around the development yet? It's looking good, don't you think, now we are no longer trying to sell while up to our cobblers in concrete."

Andy's ten-minute tour of Castello di Capadelli had provided unexpected reassurance. The place was much busier than he'd seen it, and it no longer looked like a money pit. At least all the hard earned treasure he had invested was showing some results. But he was not minded to give Jay any credit.

"It could almost pass for the idyllic retreat that's described in your brochures," he said, sarcasm coating every syllable. But other than that Jay had cost him a lot of money, he still considered him a friend, so he pulled in the horns, his point made. "You still can't persuade Rusty to make it out here then?"

"I did ask. But she's kind of busy right now."

"Anything interesting?" asked Andy, unable to grasp what could be keeping the languorous socialite busy.

Jay rubbed his brow, opening his mouth and then closing it again before speaking.

"The thing is Rusty's been spending more time in Texas lately." He looked down at his lap for a moment before meeting Andy's eyes with resolve. "Her mother's on her own these days, and she's getting on."

Andy nodded, reading the sub-text in Jay's words, but unsure how to proceed, afraid of his pleasantries twisting themselves into soul-searching investigations.

"I'm sorry to hear it. Maybe—"

"Anyway, it all might work itself out," said Jay, forming his mouth into a straight smile that drew a firm line under the topic.

Jay moved the conversation back to the state of the development, cutting his usual upbeat tone. "Getting the building work complete was always the key. Just a pity it took six months longer than planned. We've still got to tidy up around the big pool, and finish off the fitting out of a few apartments, but the way the place looks now is more or less as good as it ever will be."

"Until phase two, the spa and everything," Andy reminded him.

Jay drained his cup and took a deep breath. "This may not be the best time to say this, but I think we need to re-think where we are going beyond this summer."

Andy set his coffee down with a bang, showering opaque drops over the table that rested on the wood like tiny globes of mud. This was the last thing he expected from Jay. But then again, was it what Kate had warned him about? Jay losing interest once the selling was done. Or half done.

"Cutting and running? You know how much I'm down on this. How is pulling out early going to give me time to get back what I've put in?" He glared at the man opposite him as anger and disbelief took over him, scorching through his veins and clouding his mind at his betrayal.

Jay stared back at him, his mouth twisting in frank humility.

"I don't have the answer to give you on that right now. What I do know is that my appetite for the holiday home and timeshare industry is about spent. And if I knew two years ago what I know now, I never would have gotten you into it."

"But you did get me into it. And what do you know now that you didn't know then? It's not like you didn't know what you were getting into, after the last escapade." Cold fingers of self-doubt now brushed at Andy's anger as he realised the fragility of what he had believed.

"Tuscany has proved totally different from Malaga," said Jay, his eyes imploring Andy to listen. "Maybe I should have done more checking on the location. The truth is I completely underestimated the complications involved in doing business in Italy, and the legal limitations on what you can actually do at a development like Capadelli. The place is a minefield of rules, regulations, and bureaucracy. And because of that, I've over-promised and under-delivered, and in the process cost you a lot of money. And for that I'm truly sorry."

Andy's eyes glazed over and he shook his head, unable to process this sudden abandonment of Jay's perpetual swaggering confidence. But he was not convinced that Jay's uncharacteristic humility was solely down to matters at home or to the hard lessons of doing business under the Tuscan sun.

"Come on, Jay, how much of this is really driven by the music deal, and the doors that are opening for you?"

"I'm not going to lie; the music industry opportunity has been a wake-up call, for which I thank you. And yes, it has made me question what I'm doing here, why I'm doing it. Grubbing around selling worthless timeshare certificates for a living, and all the hassle that comes with it."

"So what you are saying," said Andy, the sarcasm returning, "is that our modest venture is no longer worthy of a man of your undoubted expertise. Have I got that right?"

"No, what I'm saying is that whatever talents I do have can be put to better use, that's all. And maybe I just want to be somebody again. Someone the boys can be proud of."

Andy steeled himself against all emotion. "Before you get carried away by your come to Jesus moment, let's remember whose baby this whole show is. What happened to the vision you sold me on? You are the architect of the dream. And now you're saying that you want out? I'm disappointed, Jay. The one thing I never had you down as was a quitter."

"Well, maybe I've learnt that sometimes you do have to fold. But don't worry, I'm not quitting. We're in a hole but we can sell our way out."

Andy was not ready to recognise anything that might cut Jay some slack. "Maybe. But this hole you mention — and I'm still waiting for someone to let me know how deep it is — when we are out of it, what then?"

"We sell up. Leave it to someone else to run. Like we always planned to, but earlier." Jay placed every word on the table with delicate precision and Andy felt like bringing his fist down on each and every one.

"And continuing to pump in my money while we're doing it?" Andy held his eyes in challenge, daring him to pretend it wasn't true.

"Listen, Andy, I'm looking into the numbers. But right now I sincerely believe the worst is over." He returned the gaze with equal conviction but a softer, almost pleading, edge.

"And you reckon anyone will take it off our hands?" said Andy, caught between hope and disbelief.

"Sure, someone will. It is a perfect spot, and now it actually looks the part too."

"You got any evidence of interest to back that up?"

"I have some fresh investors lined up who are interested in taking a stake here. It's an opportunity for you to sell out your investment. Cash in. Not to get back what we first thought, but more than enough to recoup what you have put in."

It seemed to Andy this was classic Jay, pulling a rabbit out of his arse. "Who are these investors? Are they part of another jam tomorrow story?"

"Andy, I am currently bound by confidentiality. But these are real people, with real money. Right now they are looking at a draft proposal. If they like what they see, then it's game on. If that's the way you want to go, that is, because it would be your decision. So the last thing any of us should be doing right now is spreading doom and gloom. That's not how you talk up something when you are trying to sell it. "

"Why haven't I seen this proposal, if it exists that is, before you started touting it around?"

"Because, Andy, it would have been wrong to do that. I don't want you to think I am encouraging you to pull out."

If Jay is bluffing, thought Andy, *it is a high-risk strategy, given the knife-edge on which his music deal is sitting.* "Ok, let's say I'm interested in this proposal. But don't let anyone think I'm a pussycat who can be stalled by promises of some unknown white knight riding in to save us all. At the board meeting I want to know just how deep the shit I'm in is. Is that clear?"

"I want that as much as you do, Andy, trust me on that."

Andy nodded. "Ok then, I'll see you at the board meeting." He stood up and turned to leave.

"You ok for five minutes more?" asked Jay. Andy sat back down in his chair and folded his arms, with a good idea of what was coming.

"I need your help to get to Rick Epstein."

"No way. Impossible. I've never even met him."

"But you know people that have. I'm happy to meet wherever works for him. Failing that, I will settle for an introductory phone call. This is something I really need, and wouldn't ask if there was another way."

Andy could sense an air of desperation. Jay was close to pleading, and Andy couldn't recall him ever doing that.

"Tell me, Jay, why is this deal so important? And spare me the bullshit about rescuing you from timeshare and putting you back in the mainstream. Because something I'm puzzled about is whenever I read about this deal, your name is never mentioned?"

Jay leant forward, tension lining his face, his voice low and serious. "I had to take a back seat with the banks last year, given the Malaga malarkey. But everything I have is riding on the deal."

"So who *is* the guarantor to the banks?"

"Rusty."

"So you are using Rusty's money? I thought she was smarter than that."

"We did a sort of post-nuptial. If the deal goes down she's fine, and I'm skint." Jay held up his hands to signal he had done the best he could.

"I suppose that's what you get for marrying an American lawyer; you'd better not get caught with your trousers down, because she's got you by the balls," said Andy, laughing. But he could see Jay was not laughing. He leant forward across the table, his eyes fixed on Jay's. "*If* I could do something, why would Epstein take a call about you?"

"Because he's the decision-maker on the deal. He already knows who BB&T are but he won't know anything about my little outfit. So all I'm asking for is an opportunity to level the playing field a bit."

"I don't know. You're asking a lot."

"Just give it a shot, Andy. All I am asking is that you make a telephone call, nothing more. Making the call won't cost anything," said Jay, each word an imploration.

"But that's not a reason to do it, not after everything." Andy grew stronger and stronger, knowing his feelings as they materialised into sentences before him.

"We've known each other a long time, Andy."

It seemed to Andy that for the past year he'd had to vet every sentence that came from Jay's mouth, he was like a siren: beguiling, deceptive, maddening. But he wanted to believe this was sincerity, and he saw a new light in Jay's eyes that seemed to prove it.

"Spare me the old soldier routine. I'll think about how to get to Epstein, but no promises. That's the best I can offer. But if I find out you've not been playing straight with me, well, then I guess you can figure out the rest."

Eighteen

As Peter and Isobel approached the village of Capadelli it felt as if they were driving on the very edge of the earth. All signs of modernity seemed to have vanished as they wended their way across the very spine of the hill, a steep drop to either side giving breathtaking views across the countryside and into the valley below, its parched greenery broken only by the unnatural lines of the vineyards that snaked their way across the landscape.

Capadelli itself was simple and sleepy, a picturesque example of rural Tuscany at its most authentic. The only signs of life were cats draped over the dusty sunlit walls and a cluster of men, their working days far behind them, drinking espresso and idling the afternoon away.

As they left the village, Castello di Capadelli was visible before them, looming grandly above the settlement. The immediate impression was striking; large and intricately wrought iron gates opened up onto a tree-lined avenue that created a canopy of colour as shafts of sunlight streamed through the branches. At the end of the path, framed proudly by the branches of the trees, stood an imposing country mansion — the Villa Magda — majestically situated with the Apennine Mountains as its backdrop.

"Well at least the location is up to expectations," said Peter as he peered down the driveway.

"It's enchanting," said Isobel, ignoring his cynicism.

"Ok, well, let's say so far so good."

They stepped out of their car and were met by a glamorous young Italian woman elegantly dressed in a black trouser suit. She introduced herself as Gina and her companion, an athletic looking young man in a buttoned black jacket with lapels, as Paco, who would be taking their bags and parking their car.

"You will be staying in the Villa Magda," Gina announced as she ushered them to an electric golf buggy. "I will show you to your suite and you will have half an hour or so to freshen up before a tour of Castello di Capadelli."

Even Peter was rendered speechless by the splendour of the building's interior; the rooms they walked through were majestic, characterised by high vaulted ceilings and lavishly frescoed walls.

The suite itself was palatial; furnished and decorated in opulent style with the sort of sumptuously upholstered chairs and sofas more commonly seen in English stately homes. Cream-coloured concertina style curtains hung either side of eight foot glass doors, which provided an uninterrupted view across the gardens and down into the valley.

"I hope your stay here will be a pleasant one," Gina said with a smile. "I'll be back later to introduce you to Mr. Devlin." She closed the door gently and Isobel watched her through the window as she made her way back to reception, sharing her beauty and grace with the tall bending trees and the insects that danced on the air.

Isobel kicked off her shoes in contentment and settled down on the magnificent four-poster that formed the centrepiece of the bedroom.

"Well, Peter, now you've seen something of the place, how do you feel?"

"It's a bit early to be giving a summing up. A great spot, that's for sure, and everything seems very professionally done."

Isobel ran her hand across the Egyptian cotton sheets. "Nice bedding. And did you notice the Armani toiletries in the bathroom? And I believe I saw a bottle of champagne for us in the lounge."

"Champagne it is," confirmed Peter after an investigative foray back into the lounge. "No everyday prosecco here, it seems." He picked up the note beside the champagne bucket. "And complimentary too. The card here says we are invited to dinner at eight in the Il Paradiso restaurant. Guests of Mr. Jay Brooke."

Isobel arose from the bed to join him in the lounge, struggling to control her heart as trepidation took hold. She studied the card; dinner with Mr. Brooke, that was something she hadn't expected.

"Signed personally too," pointed out Peter. "I guess he thinks we are VIP guests then."

"Well, nothing wrong with being treated well. If only every hotel we stayed in tried this hard."

"True. But then again, how many hotels do we go to where they want us to buy the room we're staying in?"

For what seemed the millionth time that day, Isobel begrudged him his cynicism. "Well, I'm going to go freshen up. If they think we are VIP's then we may as well look the part."

Mr. Devlin was proving a charming and likeable host. Within moments of making Peter and Isobel's acquaintance he ushered them from their rooms and into the pleasant afternoon sun, chatting away like a born entertainer. As he did so he told them of the history of Castello di Capadelli, and how it was originally the ancestral home of the Visconti family, who were once lord and master of everything as far as the eye could see. "We have of course retained as much of the authenticity as possible, which naturally was a condition of being granted planning permission, and we have worked closely with the Italian arts authorities in the painstaking renovation of the buildings."

"Yes, we have been admiring the beautiful frescos," said Isobel, thoughts of an art career that might have been surfacing in her memory, as Peter knitted his brow and Eamon broadened his smile.

"It is such a glorious afternoon I'd like to take you around the resort and perhaps bring some of what you saw back in Cobham to life. Then we can spend some time discussing the different investment opportunities while watching the sunset and enjoying a cocktail. And at some point I have asked Gina," he gestured behind him to where Gina was standing with a stack of papers and brochures in hand, "to share with you the various activities and interests we are able to offer: Italian lessons, cooking classes, wine tasting and much, much more."

"I noticed you offer horse riding. I will be very interested to hear more about that," said Isobel as Peter frowned. "And I'd very much like to see the riding facilities."

Eamon gulped. "Well, I must leave that to Gina, but what type of horse-riding are you interested in? Your standard may be too advanced for the modest offerings we have here."

Isobel could not resist the temptation to reveal more of her interest and aptitude than was strictly necessary. "I used to ride competitively when I was younger, Hickstead, that sort of thing. But I gave up shows a long time ago. You really need to be dedicated. Now we just keep a few horses for pleasure, gentle strolls with friends around the farm. Nothing too ambitious…" She tailed off, Peter's increasingly contracting eyebrows warning her she was revealing too much.

"Horse riding is something we see as one of the great pleasures to be enjoyed at Castello di Capadelli," said Eamon, sharing Isobel's enthusiasm. "The riding trails are as good as any around Killarney, and have varying levels of challenge, particularly for novices. But for an experienced rider like yourself they are an absolute treat, as *Gina* will be explaining later." He looked at the girl intently as he emphasised her name. She smiled apologetically and hurried off, the dust rising in clouds around her heels as she did so.

Eamon took his guests round the development, pointing out detail after detail on the numerous and magnificent buildings which lined the pathways; each was a work of art with windows covered by stonework lattices and glass entrances secreted behind heavy wooden doors with elaborate iron hinges. He stopped at a limestone building with flaking walls and great wooden doors with a heavy padlock; only the stained glass windows, some cracked and broken, spoke of a more illustrious past.

"You noticed the church as you approached the entrance, I am sure. Well, here we are blessed with our own chapel. Next time you visit we will be able to see inside and, once it is fully renovated and re-consecrated of course, we will be able to host weddings right here. The perfect setting in which to exchange vows…or reaffirm them," said Eamon with a mischievous smile. Isobel couldn't stop herself squeezing Peter's hand, so lost was she in the romance of it all.

"What is over there?" she asked, pointing to an arched trellis with red and white bougainvillea adorning the latticework.

"Ah," said Eamon, "that is our modest vineyard. More a retreat than a serious attempt at viticulture, but I must confess one of my favourite spots." He beckoned them to follow and the three stood under the bougainvillea as Eamon motioned around. "Beautiful isn't it?"

Isobel skipped over to a weathered wooden bench that was strategically positioned to catch the sun, took a seat, and kicked up her heels in pleasure.

"It's just so quiet, so peaceful, so romantic," said Isobel, looking up to seek Peter's affirmation, but meeting only a look of incredulity at her girlish naivety. She pushed herself up off the bench, crestfallen at his total lack of connection with the inexplicable sensuality of the hideaway.

After an hour of demonstrating beauty upon beauty, Eamon signalled that the tour had run its course, and that real selling was about to start. "All that lies between now and a well-deserved cocktail is a view of a selection of the apartments we have here at Capadelli. I trust they will meet your expectations.

"What I really want to show you is apartment sixty nine," he confided as they exited the vineyard. "It's a great example of one of the best we can offer in the two-bedroom category. But just to manage your expectations, this particular apartment is sold, and the owner, Mrs. Carragher, is on site today, but she has kindly agreed we can show the apartment. Between you and me, I think she is very proud of it," he whispered.

A woman with perfect teeth and a penchant for brightly coloured eye shadow opened the apartment door and Eamon offered his apologies for the disturbance. But she brushed his niceties aside with a wave of a ringless hand and beckoned them inside, her advanced age — Isobel guessed her to be at least seventy — tempered with a disarming smile and a soft West Country accent.

"Don't worry about me," she reassured Peter and Isobel, "I am just enjoying a good book and a glass of prosecco. A bit early I know, but I blame Eamon." She shot a disapproving look in his direction. "I always find he has left a bottle waiting for me in the fridge."

"Away with you now, Eileen," said Eamon, exaggerating his broad Dublin accent, "the prosecco is meant purely for medicinal purposes."

She laughed and turned back to Peter and Isobel. "I would advise you not to believe everything Eamon tells you." And with that she returned to the easy chair by the large open window, through which the late afternoon sun was streaming. Just as she was settling herself down, a brash looking book with a leopard print cover in hand, Eamon's phone rang. The Irishman looked somewhat ruffled. "Excuse me while I pop out into the hall for a second to take this, I will be just a moment."

He shut the door behind him, leaving Peter and Isobel staring out over the valley, not wanting to interrupt their host's reading with questions or disturb her with their own conversation.

"That Eamon, he is such an old rogue," said Eileen, breaking the silence as if it was too much for her. "I expect he told you that this was my apartment, didn't he?"

Isobel turned to her husband and saw exactly what she expected, that horrible knowing glance that said, 'I told you so.'

"So you are a rental guest then?" asked Isobel diplomatically.

"You might say that, I suppose. But the apartment is actually owned by my son, Roger; he bought it as a present for me after my husband died last year. He keeps it in his name for tax purposes or something I think."

Isobel looked at Peter in triumph.

"Probably to avoid imminent death duties," Peter muttered under his breath as he stared out the window. Isobel pinched him hard on the back of his arm whilst assuming a sympathetic countenance. "Sorry to hear about your husband."

"No need for that, I was glad to be rid of the skinflint. If it had been left to him I'd be in some home for geriatrics in Truro by now, waiting for the call from above, not frolicking here in Tuscany."

"So you like it here?" enquired Isobel.

"Oh, much more than that. It's like I have a new lease of life. Last summer I came out here as often as I could; it's the perfect place to relax and get away from all those tourists in Devon. And now I even speak a bit of Italian, enough to get by that is, thanks to the classes Gina runs."

"And your son uses it too?" asked Peter.

"Only when I let him," said the older lady. "He tells me it's the best investment he's made in years, so I reckon he's not doing too badly out of it. Pity for him is I love it here so much I now think I might be around for a lot longer than he thought I would when he bought it."

"It is certainly a beautiful apartment, and very tastefully decorated too," said Isobel, keen to avoid any further talk of death.

"Oh, thank you so much. But I'm afraid I have Eamon to thank for that. Roger wanted to be part of Eamon's rental scheme. I think he was worried that if he didn't join it I might take root here for good. So all the furnishings are Eamon's work; at least that is what he tells me, but I've a suspicion it might well be Gina that chose the furnishings. Are you thinking of buying here too?"

"Well, we are having a look around. It is a beautiful spot. And I think Peter likes it too."

Peter gave a non-committal grunt and resumed his vigil out the window.

"Well, if you do decide to buy, I have a secret to share with you. Eamon is ok, everyone likes him, but he has a job to do you know. And some apartments are easier to sell than others. Roger says, looking back, he felt Eamon pushed him towards a standard two bedroom, because he had more of those on his books than the better deluxe apartments."

"Did Roger remember how he felt he was encouraged towards the smaller apartment," asked Isobel quietly, sure that if they were duped in any way it would be the last time that Peter would give her the reins on anything larger than grocery shopping. But Mrs. Carragher had no time to answer as a knock at the door signalled Eamon's re-entry.

"Thanks for your patience. The call took a shade longer than I expected. And, Eileen, thanks a million for your indulgence. Next time you visit I will have a bottle of French champagne waiting for you instead of the prosecco."

"Well, Eamon, that's very kind of you. But no need to put off until tomorrow what you can do today. I seem to have finished the prosecco, so you may as well drop that French bubbly round this evening."

Eamon laughed heartily. "I'll have one sent down from the restaurant, ready chilled for you. But make sure you don't drink it all in one go now."

Eamon turned to Isobel and Peter, the remnants of a grin still painted on his features. "One last hurdle and then we are done. The last apartment we are going to view is known unofficially as the Visconti suite; I'm sure the old Count would be flattered, if he were not occupied fertilising the olive trees. I think you may like it. Thank you again, Eileen, and say all the best to Roger for me."

As soon as Isobel entered the Visconti suite she was conscious of the need to suppress her enthusiasm. She felt immediate wow factor from the open plan arrangement that filled the elegantly furnished space with air and light, its ceilings perhaps twice the height of any other apartments. Unlike the other units which stood in lines — so charming at first but now no longer good enough — the Visconti apartment stood in its own private garden with open views in three directions. Eamon was subdued and matter of fact in his description, without labouring any of the most distinctive features, until he led them out through the kitchen onto a secluded outside terrace.

"Quite a view, isn't it?" he burst out as he looked over the hills towards the distant mountaintops and into the beginnings of a red Tuscan sunset. "It's been a busy day and I hope a worthwhile use of your time. I think we have all earned something to refresh us and, as I see it's past six, perhaps I can persuade you to a glass of fine Tuscan wine?"

"Lead us to it," said Peter with relief.

"No need for that, I have it on ice in the fridge right here, take a seat and I'll be right back out."

As soon as the door clicked shut behind him Isobel turned to her husband.

"We have to have it," she said, "it's perfect, so, so perfect!"

"For god's sake, Isobel," whispered Peter, "can you calm your enthusiasm till we are alone? You are worse than a bouncing puppy."

Eamon returned with three glasses and a bottle of wine on a silver tray. "I expect you both have many questions, and there has been a lot for you to digest this afternoon. But now, I'd like to suggest, is a time for you to relax, enjoy the beautiful sunset, take the evening to think about things, and for us to talk more in the morning about the choices you have."

Peter nodded and reached for the fullest glass.

"Apart from Mrs. Carragher's apartment, are all the apartments we have seen today available?" Isobel asked, unable to restrain herself.

"To answer your question very specifically and very candidly, this has been a busy week for my team here at Capadelli. I think I am right in saying that over the past two days we have seen a record number of people visit us. Not all will invest of course, but yesterday we received several strong commitments on a number of apartments, though I think none of the ones you've seen today."

Isobel reached for the wine in relief but tensed as he spoke again.

"However," he said, "I do need to make you aware that the Visconti suite is something of a special case. The directors of Tyneside Holdings identified it as one to be held back for their personal use. Originally this was until the end of phase one, which is only two weeks away, so it may not be an issue."

Isobel exhaled in relief and Peter's hand went to her knee in warning. Eamon did not appear to notice and continued talking.

"One possible complication is that one of the directors, a Mr. Andy Skinner, may, I understand, have an interest in purchasing it outright for his own family's private use. I guess you can appreciate why he would want this particular suite," he said with a smile. "What I would like to suggest, if I may, and if the Visconti suite was one of those you are considering, that this is something you may wish to raise over dinner this evening. I'm told Mr. Brooke will normally guide Andy. And it may be that because apartment sales are running ahead of plan that he'll be ready to let the Visconti suite go."

Isobel opened her mouth to speak but was silenced by the hand tightening like a vice on her knee.

"As regards to the other apartments we have looked at today, I could take a holding deposit if that is something you wanted to do, maybe on one of the standard two bedroom apartments?"

Isobel smiled as the old lady's words became reality, and dug her nails into Peter's hand so that he removed it with a barely suppressed yelp. She had one up on Eamon now and she was not going to waste her advantage.

"Obviously, price is a consideration, and Peter and I need to discuss things more, but based on what we have seen today, if we were to be interested, I think it would very likely be in this apartment, in the Visconti suite."

While Peter busied himself with plans for his trip to Dallas, Isobel strolled around the grounds, and found herself drawn back by some compulsion to the secluded vineyard. She took her place on the bench and luxuriated in the stillness as the evening sun cast its long shadow, and bathed her face in a warm glow; she closed her eyes and imagined herself already owning the Visconti suite. And as she imagined it, she again became the heroine in a great romance, a free spirit forced by tragic circumstance to deny herself the passion she craved, the passion she deserved. And soon her thoughts took her to the very centre of her existence: was she to live her whole life having known only one man, what purpose was her faithfulness to Peter actually serving, she asked herself. And why should she not pursue passion if Peter would not even notice, if he would never know, not even suspect?

A light evening breeze rustled through the vineyard and pulled Isobel from her introspection. As she rose from the bench she felt herself somehow calmer, more certain, as her thoughts turned to the evening ahead.

Nineteen

As Jay drove, field after field streamed past, punctuated by tall sparse trees, dried by the heat and standing out against the cerulean sky. But they had lost any charm they once held for him, as the world closed in around him and day by the day the threats against him loomed nearer.

The ringing of his mobile interrupted his thoughts. It was an unknown number, perhaps Andy on a hotel line, with news he had relented. He hit the green tab on the screen to take the call.

"Hi, big boy, it's me," purred a female voice, "don't worry though, I just need a quickie again."

His annoyance at Andy's continued silence disappeared with her words, their raw sexuality drawing him in like honey.

"Over the phone? I'm driving, Lucy, it will have to wait."

"Not that sort of quickie," she said with a laugh. "I just need to check something about the wedding."

Jay's heart skipped a beat. "The wedding?" he asked, unable to suppress his excitement, knowing in his gut that Rob must have finally proposed, and Lucy mercifully accepted.

"Yes, Jay, the wedding to which you are escorting me, or have you forgotten that already?"

With a jolt his mind returned to the events of the previous night and everything within him deadened. "No, Lucy, of course I haven't forgotten," he said, forcing indignation into his voice. "But I don't have time to discuss it now, I'm running tight for time."

"Don't worry, tiger, there's nothing to discuss, I just want to let you know that I've gone ahead this morning and confirmed a few things to do with the wedding, that's all," she said, her voice growing higher as if she was about to hang up.

"Hold on a second, this is something we need to talk through. You know weekends are difficult for me; Rusty expects me to be around, for the kids and stuff," he said, quickening the pace of his speech in fear that she would drop the call.

"When you are not in Tuscany," she retorted with such delight that he could hear the glee in her voice.

"Of course when I'm not in Tuscany. What has Tuscany got to do with anything?" he replied, anxious to end whatever charade she had constructed this time.

"Well, that's why it's so perfect!" she exclaimed.

"What is so perfect?" he demanded, feverishly trying to put the pieces, the convoluted segments, into place in his head, panicked by the euphoria in her voice.

"The wedding of course, didn't I tell you? It's in Tuscany. In some cathedral in Florence."

"*Some cathedral* in Florence?" said Jay in transparent disbelief as an image of the iconic church, the Dome of which dominated the skyline of the great Renaissance city, flashed before his eyes. A knees-up in the Croydon Holiday Inn sounded more up Lucy's street. His anxiety began to ease.

"Ok, maybe not *the* cathedral," said Lucy laughing, "but definitely in Florence, the Church of San Marco to be precise."

Lucy's precision made the wedding all too real. Italy continued to soar past the windows and Jay could not have hated it more. He despised its beauty, its culture, its architecture; he heaped contempt upon anything that could have drawn Lucy's friend to have her wedding there.

"So it couldn't be better," she continued. "You don't need an alibi or anything, or to worry about being seen with me in daylight. Don't you think that's so romantic? I mean Italy is famous for weddings, isn't it? People go there from all over the world to tie the knot in Tuscany. Hollywood celebs even."

Shit, thought Jay, *shit, shit, shit*. How had simple Lucy anticipated his escape route? But all was not lost; in his nearly forty years he had never truly been brought to account for any of his promises and he did not intend this to be the first time. He decided the best option was prevarication, particularly as he was now about to turn into the grand tree-lined avenue that led up to Castello di Capadelli.

"Let's talk more about it later," he suggested, "right now I'm late and I need to get into my meeting."

Lucy was conciliatory. Jay had a horrible feeling that this was because she knew she had him where she wanted him but he pushed this to the back of his mind.

"Of course, you being the hot-shot that you are, don't let little old me keep you," she said, her voice sugar sweet. "And anyway, I still have to sort out my outfit and some naughty new lingerie for you."

"I don't wear lingerie," he said, "and anyway I prefer you with nothing on...except maybe that nun's outfit." In his mind he was reliving one of the many bedroom scenes Lucy liked to stage. He pulled into his parking space outside reception and as a slender, dark female emerged from the doorway before him.

But Lucy ploughed on as if she hadn't heard him, and Jay was obliged to dismiss the young lady with a wave of his hand.

"And maybe you can give some thought to a wedding present, there's a list, in Harrods I think. But you run along now and do your moving and shaking, and you can call me back when you've got more time to talk. Ok, big boy?"

"Harrods? Come off it, Lucy. Who do you know that shops at Harrods?"

"Well, I know you, don't I?" she said coolly. "Anyway, I'll let you go. But call me soon, babe, you know I don't last long without you."

Jay got out of the car in a daze and made his way to reception. He realised that she had not only cornered him, but that he had recklessly given her the weapons she needed to do it. The thought that Lucy had outsmarted him, that she had planned and connived how to trap him, made him uneasy, uneasy at what more she was capable of. Maybe he had underestimated her. And as he thought it, the resolve to get Lucy out of his life one way or another strengthened within him.

Twenty

Cicadas hummed in the olive trees as Peter and Isobel made their way through the balmy Tuscan night to Il Paradiso restaurant. Isobel was silent, her mind on Jay; his image transforming and mutating as she flicked between the dashing stranger from Marrakech and the suave professional at the estate agents. Peter raised his eyes from his phone and broke her introspection, noticing neither her glazed eyes nor half smile.

"Amex has sent through the options for my flight to Dallas. Looks like we need to cut short our stay here, and head to London Sunday afternoon."

Isobel flinched as reality flooded back in, the world of husbands, airports, and business. "But I've arranged dinner with Maria. Can't we take the early flight to London the next day?"

Peter shook his head. "The connections are tight, and you know how I hate dashing for flights. We need to go back early. You can have dinner with Maria some other time."

Isobel kept her eyes downwards, avoiding his gaze.

"I don't know, the dinner has been arranged a long time."

"Dallas is more important than Maria," he said. "We need to get back Sunday."

"So business over friendship?"

"I'd prefer to call it common sense."

"Maybe I could stay over," Isobel suggested, as an argument threatened. "You could drop me at Lucca and continue onto the airport, and Maria can drop me off on Monday?"

Peter glanced at Isobel, and then shrugged. "If that's what you want to do, sure, no big deal either way."

They continued the rest of the walk in silence, only assuming smiles and forcing conversation as they came into view of Il Paradiso, from which calm music and polite conversation emanated, dissolving into the buzz of the cicadas.

As they entered the high arched doors of the restaurant, an immaculate waiter ushered them to a circular corner table at which Jay was already sat, the warm and roughly hewn red brick of the walls tinting his brown hair a shade of auburn in the low light. He stood up immediately and shook Peter's hand first as Isobel's mind processed the seating options; the three places were set so all were looking away from the wall, into the restaurant, and Jay, curiously, had not secured the centre setting. Even before Jay offered his hand, she placed her bag to secure the centre seat.

"Ah Peter, I'm so glad you made it," he said. "You're probably the first real expert on wines to grace this fine establishment."

"I'm sure that's not true," said Peter, in no mood for toady flattery.

Isobel observed her husband's wry smile and the knowing glint that never left his eye and it made her heart fall into the pit of her stomach. It felt like many years now since Peter had truly lived life, lived it as an emotional experience and not as a series of business transactions. Jay turned his eyes to her as Peter busied himself with the prosecco.

"Isobel," he said, his voice low, "it's so lovely to see you again." He reached out to shake her hand and held it in his for what seemed like hours. She glanced at Peter but all that was manifest in his eyes was that same glint again; no jealousy, no fear, just arrogant assumption that it was all a sales technique. She stubbornly ignored it as she turned her gaze back to Jay and, fuelled by passion and rebellion, allowed herself to be lost in his eyes. She barely saw the sommelier as Jay beckoned him over and asked for his recommendation for the evening, seeing only the strong hand that demanded his attention and the perfect lips that formed his words. A brief discussion between her husband and their host decided the meal and it arrived in seven courses, all well presented on square earthenware plates.

It seemed to Isobel that Peter was determined from the outset to lock horns with Jay like a rutting stag as he assumed the role of inquisitor, whereas Jay was equally determined to make light of every loaded question.

"You are a chartered accountant, I notice, and you qualified with BB&T, but now you don't practice," said Peter, challenging Jay to explain his career choices.

"It seems to be the way more and more," said Jay with a disarming wave of his hands. "Lawyers, doctors, accountants, they qualify and then they run off and pursue their real passion. We must all pursue our passion sooner or later, must we not?" Isobel fancied Jay threw her a furtive glance at the mention of passion.

Peter was not so easily thrown off the scent. "But BB&T are the biggest show in town. And you were with them, how long was it, over ten years, so you must have left when close to partnership?"

Isobel could feel her anger rising at Peter's rudeness and his ingratitude for the food and wine before him, and she feared the rising tension. "Must we talk history all night," she interjected, "when we should be talking about this absolutely unforgettable food and wine? Your chef and sommelier are to be congratulated," she concluded, her attention directed at Jay.

"I must apologise, Isobel, we are forgetting our manners. How is the wine, Peter? I know Marco will value your expert opinion."

Peter held the wine to the light before burying his nose in the glass, and to Isobel's relief, nodded his appreciation. The wine continued to flow with Peter drinking most of it; inevitably his phone bleeped and he became distracted, paying no heed to Isobel's growing absorption in the man opposite her, which, as the wine took hold, was clearly visible on her face in the candlelight. Had Peter glanced up from the screen he would have seen happiness melt into confusion and then disappointment, Jay's careful sentences and professional manner crushing her secret hopes. He turned to Peter with just as much, if not more, interest and struck up a conversation about his work and quickly latched on to his mention of an opportunity in Dallas.

"In Texas, the lone star state? You may need to go carefully there. You've seen the 'Don't Mess With Texas' car stickers, I guess? Well I reckon they should say 'Don't Mess With Texans.' I found that out the hard way. I went and married one." His eyes flicked from Isobel to Peter and then back again, resting on her face.

"And you are still married to Texas then?" Isobel asked, cutting into the wild boar and careful to keep her tone casual as she pushed back her hope.

"I can't afford not to be. Rusty is a trained lawyer and a US citizen. So you can probably imagine the damage she could do if she ever needed to," said Jay, smiling as if speaking in jest but his eyes serious.

Isobel ran her hand up and down the table leg, scraping it with her nails as she did so. "Well, you know, it can be difficult for us wives with you men globe-trotting. Being left on our own so much. And when you are around, your mind is elsewhere half the time. And it is also difficult for the kids too I should imagine?"

"The boys seem to manage ok. I inherited them from Rusty's first marriage. And to be fair, they still see a lot of their natural father. Holidays in the States and all that."

"So you were married in Texas then?"

"No, Rusty didn't want a re-run of the first time around, and she didn't want to be surrounded by rednecks. Her family have roots in the highlands, so we tied the knot in Scotland. Pipers and kilts and all those shenanigans. Damn near bankrupted me."

Isobel smiled apologetically as Peter lifted his eyes back up from his phone at the word 'bankrupt' and she moved the conversation into less personal territory, concerned not by Peter's lack of discretion, but her own.

"I expect Eamon has updated you on our discussions today, and in particular the situation with the Visconti suite?"

"Yes, he gave me a quick debrief earlier on how things were going. And one of the things he did mention was that you might want to talk about the Visconti suite in particular. I hope I've got that right. I will be happy to see if I can help in any way."

"Eamon believes that the suite is still reserved for one of the directors, but he wasn't certain on the exact status."

Jay leant towards her and lowered his voice. "I think Eamon might be being a touch diplomatic. Andy Skinner has indeed reserved the Visconti suite, but that was some time ago now. It may be that his thinking has changed; he certainly hasn't mentioned anything about keeping it, to me at least, for some time. He may even have forgotten he put down the reservation. I would need to check."

Isobel nodded, her eyes in her lap, as she tried to stop herself inhaling his breath that reached her in mint and champagne waves. She raised her face but not her eyes as she spoke again. "If we were to make an investment here, I think it would most likely be in the Visconti suite, assuming we could come to a fair agreement."

"It may well be that we are discussing a problem that doesn't exist," he said, staring straight at her until she met his gaze again. "What I might suggest, if you are happy to wait a few days, is that I discuss it with Andy. I will be speaking to him on Monday anyway, or I can call him tomorrow if necessary."

"No need to bother him at the weekend, next week is fine," Peter said, "let's not harass the poor man."

"Actually, there may be something we could do to hurry this along that won't risk a restraining order," said Jay. "Something that could definitely help Andy come to the right decision on the Visconti suite." He did not even glance at Isobel but locked his eyes on Peter. "Andy is looking to his next project. He's already eyeing an investment opportunity in Capetown. I do know he has prepared a short prospectus with a view to selling his interest here at Capadelli. Maybe, if you wouldn't mind, Peter, it's something you might run your eye over on the flight to Dallas? With your background, and as someone who has seen what has been developed here, I think Andy would find your input very helpful."

Peter shrugged, but Isobel sensed the compliment had hit home. He glanced at her before replying, her eyes wide in encouragement. "Sure, I'd be happy to have a look at whatever he's put together."

"That's very kind of you, thank you." Jay's eyes returned to Isobel and his voice became measured and formal. "I really appreciate you making the time to join me this evening, and trust you have enjoyed what the team has put together here in Il Paradiso. This area is blessed with many excellent restaurants, which I very much hope you will be discovering in the future. And we are determined that Il Paradiso will be amongst the best of them."

"It's been our pleasure," said Peter. "Thank you for your hospitality. It's been a lovely evening." They shook hands and said their goodbyes, taking deep breaths as they entered into the fragrant night air. Jay seemed to have forgotten Isobel was even there as he turned towards the car park.

The lure of soft music carried across the courtyard as they passed the enoteca. But Jay was gone and there seemed no point to prolong the evening. Nevertheless, she could not keep mention of Jay from her lips. "That was very generous of him, wasn't it? With the wine and everything."

Peter scoffed at her naivety. "Don't confuse generosity with inducement."

"What do you mean?" she said, feeling compelled to defend their host, and risk her husband's wrath.

"What I mean is I felt no sincerity in anything tonight. Everything he said and did tonight was cold calculation."

"Like when you entertain your clients?"

"That's different. I have a long-term relationship with my clients. Brooke is only interested in a transaction."

Isobel wanted to scream at Peter's double standards, but held her tongue. He would be off to Dallas in two days, and all of a sudden she felt those two days could not pass quickly enough. But Peter was not finished with his character assassination.

"And I don't buy for a minute all that tosh about following your passion; no-one walks away from a winning lottery ticket."

"I'm sure you're right, dear," said Isobel craving nothing more than silence and pulling her pashmina around her shoulders, now too exasperated to care what Peter thought.

They returned to their suite to find two bottles of wine in a wooden presentation box, with a card signed by Jay thanking them for their company. "How very thoughtful," said Isobel.

"He's a smooth operator, I'll give him that," said Peter with a distinct lack of bonhomie.

It had been a tiring day, and Peter tossed aside the card and announced he was turning in. By the time Isobel finished her bedtime routine he was already asleep, his breathing deep and heavy. She picked up the card as if it were precious to her before slipping into the bed — so wide that she could have been alone — and reached for her book on the side table, tucking the card in between the pages. It was a thriller she had been engrossed in but tonight she was unable to concentrate, the conflicts in her head screaming their arguments over the pages until they turned black and the words swarmed like flies. She looked at the card again, her finger running back and forth along Jay's signature. She put the book aside and tossed and turned as the sound of the pulse within her head reverberated off the pillow, until she found herself staring at the ceiling. She tried deepening her breathing as she fidgeted and fumbled, and then began drawing circles around her belly button with her finger as if zoning in on a target. Peter contorted in his sleep as her hand moved itself lower and rested in the warm area between her legs, its fingers beginning to twirl themselves into the soft triangle of hair. They touched wetness and began to shake.

Isobel moved them slowly, but her body was quick to tense, and she soon found herself biting down on her lower lip to hold back any sound that might betray her rising emotions. As the intensity neared its height she turned her head to the side and sought to press her face into the soft whiteness of the pillow. The sensations ran hotter and faster through her body; when the climax was at its most intense, she forced the pillow hard against her mouth, absorbing the sounds of a woman releasing all of the tensions within her body.

Twenty-one

The pink evening sun of the next day gave a rosy hue to the inner courtyard as Isobel aimlessly wandered across its smooth grey stones, their dullness cast into featherlike shades of dove and pigeon in the muted glow of the afternoon's end. The scraping of chalk broke the silence as the waiter from the enoteca wrote up the evening specials on a blackboard. She stopped to read the list, unsure if Peter had decided on where they would dine that evening.

"How is the white?" she asked in Italian as the man smiled and cocked his head, seeming to welcome the interest of such an elegant guest.

"It is excellent I believe, like your accent. But then I did choose it."

Isobel laughed; he could not be more than twenty and his youthful vivacity was welcome respite from the grey solitude of her day.

"Please, let me offer you a taste," he said. "It would be my pleasure."

Isobel assented graciously, in no hurry to get back to Peter who was deep in preparation for his departure the next day. She sat down at a circular, dark wood table and accepted the long stemmed glass, filled with considerably more than a mere mouthful. She took a sip and pressed the glass to her face, relishing the coolness against her skin. The waiter held her eye in expectation.

"It's every bit as good as you promised," she said, looking away to avoid further discussion — the coolness of the room and the stillness in the air eliciting a reflective mood within her that did not invite conversation.

She stared into the mirror on the opposite wall but did not see her own face, only the coming and going of people in the courtyard behind.

For the most part they were older couples, walking out for dinner or straggling home after a long day in the heat and sun. They drifted past in varying states of dress; some formal and tailored, others loose and billowing, but all with the same drooping faces that looked straight ahead. They reminded her of fish in a tank, with their bright colours and burnt-red skin, and for a while she amused herself with the idea that if she turned around and walked towards the courtyard, an invisible pane of glass would obstruct her path, and she would press herself against it like a child and watch them walk past, their mouths opening and closing without a sound.

As she swirled the last of the wine around the glass, her attention was caught by a familiar figure passing in the background, a male figure, and her heart jumped a beat or two. It was Peter, the motion in her chest inspired not by feeling but almost automatically — as instinctive as flight to a bird. For a split second she was tempted to let him drift past like all the others, carried on the tide of pebbles out through the courtyard archway and away from her forever. But as she glanced down at the empty glass, at her smooth, tanned hands, the bright yellow wedding band, at the dark surface of the table and the deep red tiles beneath it, she was pulled back to reality, back to the mundane side of the mirror. She turned to face the world and called out, "Peter, over here." He did not want to hear her and headed resolutely in the direction of reception, his laptop frantically blinking a red light beneath his arm. She turned away from the mirror, all she saw through it saddening her and embittering her heart.

"Deep in thought, or drowning your sorrows?" asked a low, amused voice from the shadow of the entranceway.

She turned towards him, already knowing who it was, his arrival seeming inevitable. "Can I tempt you to another glass, but a warm red perhaps?" She extended her hand in greeting and Jay pulled her towards him, kissing her on the cheek.

"Only if I can pay this time; I still owe you for a blouse," she said, reverting back to the safety of their first meeting as his kiss burnt on her cheek. He laughed at her offer and accepted, already sliding into a seat close beside her.

She sipped the red. "Perfect," she said, trying to keep the happiness from her face.

"I didn't get the chance to say it at dinner last night, but it's great that you have made it here, it really is." His face was sincere and she forgave him everything without question. "After our brush in the estate agents, I was so much hoping that we would see each other again."

She met his eyes in confusion, unsure of everything all over again.

"And few women would have been brave enough to venture where you did in the souk. Which left me intrigued." She sipped her wine and smiled, wanting to maintain some air of mystery but also at a complete loss for what to say. He took her silence in his stride and continued.

"So there we go, I'm fascinated," he said. "Unveil yourself and solve the mysteries for me. The things you didn't tell me that day around the pool. I want all your secrets."

"Well, as for the souk, there's not much to tell. I just stayed out a bit too late and walked a little too far."

"Don't be so modest, Isobel, you were incredibly brave that afternoon."

She laughed and began to deny it but he interrupted her and clasped her hands in his in mock-supplication. "Please, don't ruin the memory for me! I have my dreams too, you know. You must tell me more about yourself."

He dropped her hands as she assented. She was enthralled by his playfulness and, relaxed now, began to share more about herself, touching on her own feelings, uncovering them for herself and for him.

It was perhaps an hour later when he coaxed her from her introspection. "And so far," he said, "you like what you've seen here?"

"Yes, very much, I love it."

"And Peter?"

"He's not much of a romantic I'm afraid."

Isobel felt herself blush from her forwardness and returned to looking at her glass in embarrassment. He continued talking, not, she thought, oblivious to her discomfort but attempting to heal it.

"I noticed you looking at my ring. Maybe I shouldn't say it, but Rusty and I are barely married anymore; we've grown apart so much, I'm all but waiting for her to serve me the papers."

"Oh, I'm so sorry."

He looked her directly in the eyes and said, "Don't be, sometimes it's best to move on."

She sometimes wished she could do the same, but despised herself for thinking so.

"I guess every marriage has its problems," he said in reply to her silence, "but it's easy to get carried along on emotion alone, don't you think?"

Isobel imagined Peter getting carried along on his emotions and almost laughed aloud.

"Yes, I suppose it is."

He looked puzzled as she held back her smile. "This is the most relaxed I've been in a long time," she admitted by way of apology, banishing all thoughts of her husband from her head. "This place is so beautiful, so authentic."

"That's exactly why I love it here!" he exclaimed, looking around at the whitewashed walls and the lamps tarnished by age and use. "It's living, isn't it? It's the real world in all its splendour." He stood up, still looking around in pleasure. "I have to go, I'm afraid, I have a meeting with Eamon that started ten minutes ago." He dipped his head in playful apology. "And by the way, I'm paying for the wine, just try and stop me!"

She watched as he strode off across the courtyard. The sky had turned dark and the leafy trellises were strewn with twinkling white lights. Two patches of white leapt and bounced in the dark as a black cat with snowy paws batted at a butterfly which flapped its frail yellow wings in the last throes of its short and graceful life.

Twenty-two

Isobel was subdued in the back of Eamon's car watching the Tuscan landscape bounce up and down as they navigated the winding side roads. Peter too kept his own counsel, preferring to let Eamon monologue as they trundled through the countryside.

"We are fortunate to have so many horse riding options around, that at first it was difficult to know where to start." He sounded upbeat and cheerful, unfazed by the silence of his audience. "And what I have found is somewhere that miraculously is a short walk from the resort. When I discovered it I knew it was the right location but its facilities are a trifle primitive." He glanced round for a reaction before returning his gaze to the road. "In the end we struck a compromise. The directors agreed to support the location I found, as long as we would be able to bring the place up to the Castello di Capadelli standard. So what I am going to show you now is the site in its raw state, but I am sure you will see the potential."

Isobel was propelled from her stupor as they turned sharply onto a dirt track and hurtled down a steep hill.

"Could be a bit difficult getting in and out in snow and ice," remarked Peter as the car became almost perpendicular, his flat tone revealing the extent of the pleasure he took from the excursion.

Isobel looked straight ahead, allowing a few words through her pursed lips. "You rarely get snow in this part of Tuscany, Peter."

Eamon pulled into a muddy field and hastened them from the car, a slight red tinge to his cheeks as he greeted Gina who was talking to a large sun-crinkled man with a generous stomach that stretched his woollen jumper to breaking point. She stood in the muddy field lacking her usual ease, and Isobel was puzzled that she had not thought to change out of her high heels. Gina turned to

Eamon and the two exchanged brief and hushed words. Isobel could feel their eyes on her as she took in the stables, their walls crumbling into dust beneath haphazard and cracked roof tiles; their proprietor smiled broadly to reveal black gaps between yellowing teeth and greeted Isobel with a thunderous "Buongiorno!" and a kiss on the cheek.

"I'm afraid he doesn't speak any English, Signora," said Gina, "but he does seem to like you."

The man beckoned Isobel to follow him to the horses, his booming voice echoing about the yard as he talked jovially of the weather, the horses, and his farming, with Gina trotting behind to translate. Isobel's face lit up as they reached the animals. The horses, despite the lack of obvious facilities, were fine, well-kept animals in excellent condition. She began to complement each as she stroked their noses and admired the lustrous sheen of their skin, dropping into Italian as Gina struggled to keep up with the quantity and pace of her raptures. The man's face radiated delight at this revelation and he led her off to another stable block, chattering at twice the previous pace.

Peter shifted from foot to foot in agitation as they walked off, soundlessly cursing the valley for dipping so low that he could not receive a signal, and his wife for charming yet another stranger and wasting his valuable time. Two feet beside him, Eamon echoed his actions, straining his neck to watch them and flapping his hands at Gina to try and make her follow them.

When Isobel returned, Eamon tried to steer her into the car as quickly as possible, beads of sweat forming on his brow as the old man blocked the door to say goodbye.

"Are you all right, Eamon?" asked Peter in concern as his wife nodded along to the stream of Italian in the background.

"Yes, yes, it's fine. Just been out in the sun a bit too long I think."

Isobel turned to him in sympathy as her host ambled back to the stables, and with a reluctant sigh got into the car.

"I'm sorry to delay us so long, Eamon. He really was a fascinating man though." Eamon loosened his collar and flicked on the air conditioning.

"He seemed a very genuine type, what was all that about at the end?" asked Peter.

"He was just saying that it was a pity that I could not spend more time with him and the horses this morning. He said it would be his pleasure to introduce me to the trails around Capadelli, as his guest. He's obviously passionate about horses and loves riding the trails."

"He's got an animal that can take his weight, then?" asked Peter.

Eamon burst out laughing as Isobel directed a fine scowl into the overhead mirror, his face transforming in seconds as the worry ran off like water.

"Now, now, behave you two," said Eamon. "Let's keep the arguments to which of the apartments is right for you, shall we?"

Isobel swelled with elation as they drove back to Capadelli and walked through the twisted vineyard — brighter and greener today — towards the marketing suite. She could still smell the horses on her skin and feel the admiring eyes on her back.

"You definitely made a good choice, Eamon. Those horses are in amazing condition. Your man down there knows how to select a good animal, and how to look after one. That's much more important than the stabling."

"To be fair, most of the credit needs to go to Gina. She has done the leg work over the last months." He gestured towards Gina who was standing by a giant model of Capadelli; her arms were folded and she seemed to be scowling in Eamon's direction. Isobel turned to her with warmth. "Thanks, Gina, you really are to be congratulated."

"You are too kind, Mrs. Roberts," she responded with a shy smile. "If you do ever want to go horse riding, then please call me directly, and I will be happy to accompany you, if you would like a riding companion."

"Thank you again, Gina. I think that will be all for the moment," Eamon said, beckoning Isobel away from her to the table at which Peter was already seated.

He placed the price and availability list before them once more and Isobel noted with alarm that four new apartments had been crossed off since their last viewing. Eamon reached out and crossed through a fifth. "I just need to update this. One of the existing investors here at Capadelli has asked to take out an option to upgrade to a larger apartment." Isobel nodded and swallowed her last reservations.

"Eamon, we like what we have seen here and we think we would like to make a reservation. But our preference is the Visconti suite."

He rubbed his chin and furrowed his brow but allowed himself an optimistic smile.

"Mr. Brooke did seem quite hopeful when I spoke to him this morning; if I might suggest—"

Peter cut him short with a cough and placed a restraining hand on his wife's arm. "What we wish to do is to put a deposit on apartment forty-two, which is a one bedroom apartment. And if the Visconti suite becomes available, we would intend to transfer the deposit."

"And if the Visconti suite does not become available you will, I expect, wish to choose one of the other two—?"

Peter again stopped him short. "At the moment that is not the way we are thinking. We will simply stick with apartment forty-two, and primarily see it as an investment. On those occasions we visit, we would either stay in the Villa or a larger apartment."

"The Visconti apartment, of course," added Isobel.

"A very shrewd approach," said Eamon, his voice congratulatory but business-like. "But for this to work you'll need to pay the deposit for both apartments at the same time. If I cannot secure the Visconti suite, then of course that part of the deposit will be refundable."

Peter opened his mouth to speak, his eyebrows set in refusal, but it was Isobel's voice that broke the silence.

"Of course, we'd be happy to," she said with a smile.

Twenty-three

Peter dropped Isobel off at the end of Maria's sweeping driveway and did not glance back as he headed for the airport, his eyes on the road and his mind already in Texas. Had he thought to look back, he would have seen his wife fall into her friend's arms in desperation, confusion and loneliness set like gemstones in her eyes.

"Maria, I have to talk to you," she cried, her face half-buried in her friend's shoulder. "I have made the most terrible mistake, which I still can't believe, and I am so scared, I am so afraid." Her face was fragile and beseeching, and Maria could not help but smile as she looked at it, finding it full of human frailty after all.

"So you are pregnant, but you are not sure who the father is?" she asked.

"Please don't taunt me, my nerves are in pieces already."

"Because of your new friend, Jay, yes?" Isobel nodded like a mute, as if afraid to repeat the name.

"Get your coat. We are going into Lucca right now, because if you start to tell me here, we will be here all night, and we have nothing to eat." She headed for her car, leaving Isobel no choice but to follow her.

Maria's driving was fast and sporadic but for once Isobel was too occupied to complain and, as they zipped round the winding hill roads, she set out her dilemma.

"Today I left him a note with my phone number on, giving him an excuse to call me about the apartment. I tried not to be too obvious, but I really had no need to do it, and he will know that. I can't believe I did it. I don't know what he will think of me. And I am out of my wits that he actually might call."

Maria grimaced into the mirror, disappointed at the slightness of her sins. "You did the right thing, if you are sure you want to see him,

131

that is. Men cannot read our minds, however much we like to think they should be able to. Even if he wanted to make a pass at you, he's going to be very hesitant to do it. You are a wealthy woman, you are married; he's going to need some sort of a clear signal before he risks making a fool of himself."

"Like I made a fool of myself?" Isobel asked, hesitant and tragic.

"No. You had to make the first move. And you have done it very cleverly. If he calls then you know that he wants to at least explore the possibility of taking things forward. And if he doesn't call, there is no loss of face all round."

"So now I just wait to see if he does call?" asked Isobel, so out of her depth she was unwilling to even think without instruction.

"No, you are going to eat," said Maria, pinching Isobel's increasingly slim arms as she pulled the car to a halt outside the grey city walls. "And you are going to forget about it and enjoy yourself here in Tuscany with me. If he calls, he calls. If he doesn't, it wasn't meant to be."

"But now I'm not sure I want him to call; I'm afraid I will make the most enormous fool of myself. Peter is the only man I've ever known."

Maria blew the air from her mouth in exasperation. "Do not tell me another thing until we are in the restaurant. Some wine will calm you, and I want you to talk me through everything that has happened."

She led Isobel to a typical osteria hidden away in a narrow side street. It was crowded with Italians, all conversing and laughing in the evening's quiet, the soft street lighting dyeing their smiles orange with its invasive hue.

"I'm sorry about running off that night in London," Isobel began, as they waited for the wine. They had not seen each other since and she was conscious of the void it had left between them.

"Think nothing of it," said Maria, shooting her a broad smile, "it was fine. Everyone had a good time. All three of us."

"So he wasn't disappointed?" said Isobel, shuddering in the warm night at the memory of Mo's persistent touch.

Maria laughed. "Oh Isobel, you can be so innocent sometimes. The three of us went back to the penthouse and had a party." She looked at Isobel's bewilderment with pleasure and beckoned her closer, her eyes aflame in the candlelight. "You cannot imagine how it feels to have two men inside you at the same time."

Isobel stared at her in open-mouthed disbelief that gave way to morbid curiosity. "But surely no pleasure is to be had from it, not for the woman, anyway?"

"The pleasure is in the thrill of it," Maria replied. "Of course you must relax, and use something to help things along. You should try it sometime." Her last words were purely for her own entertainment; she was not a natural confidante and had no need to ask Isobel's advice, gaining amusement rather than solace from their conversations.

"But we must talk about you, and your new man," she declared as the wine arrived. "What has happened, Isobel, that you are now leaving love letters? The last time we spoke you were certain that this man Jay was just a memory?"

Isobel squirmed at the recollection of her own arrogance.

"I really did think that at the time. But then I met him again, at the Italian evening in Cobham, and ever since I can't stop myself thinking about him. I even wonder that he might be the real reason that I am in Tuscany, buying a property."

She waited for Maria to express some kind of astonishment but none was forthcoming and she was subdued by her transparent predictability.

"It sounds crazy, I know, to buy a property in the hope of seeing more of someone you hardly know, but I think that is what is happening. When I came out of that estate agents' it was as if my mind was made up."

"Is it that Jay is someone special, or is it that he is someone in the right place at the right time, who can help you deal with the feelings you are having?"

"I'm not sure. But what I do know is that he is very different to Peter."

Their waiter arrived with the antipasti and they fell silent, both reflecting on what had been said as he topped up their glasses.

"How is he different from Peter?" said Maria, breaking the silence with genuine curiosity.

Isobel contemplated the question for a while as she fiddled with her bruschetta. "He picks up on what I'm thinking and takes my thoughts somewhere else, somewhere that feels better," she said, learning as she spoke.

"What you are describing could just be a very slick operator. Have you thought about that? That he is just somebody else that wants something from you? And maybe you are a little vulnerable because you feel something is missing in your life?" Maria bit into the centre of Isobel's fears with precision, and she halted her questioning with humanity as agony contorted her friend's mouth.

"Yes, I have thought about that. But I can normally tell when someone is sincere or not."

Maria nodded like a sage. "Tell me more about him."

They had eaten their first course by the time Isobel finished; she covered everything she knew of him as she tried to piece him together.

"So it sounds like he's definitely not some bottom feeding low life type," concluded Maria with typical frankness, "which are the worst kind. But then I never thought for a moment a man like that would interest you. And he does not sound like your typical gigolo, like Angelo; he's too old for that. And he's probably not looking for a simple meal ticket, because he seems well able to make his own way in life. But he is trying to sell you a property," she concluded, pressing again on to Isobel's deepest fears.

"If all he wants is to sell me something, then I suppose I don't have too much to worry about other than making a clown of myself," she conceded, tired of her own uneasiness.

"I think, Isobel, the most important thing is that he is married. The last thing he is going to want is some psycho stalker on his hands. He has as much to lose as you. Which is a good thing, unless you are thinking of leaving Peter, that is?"

Isobel shook her head in certainty. "Maybe if someone like Jay had come along ten years ago, and had evoked these feelings earlier, then who knows what might have happened. But these needs, these feelings, they aren't enough to turn my life upside down for, not now. I couldn't imagine life without the horses for one thing. "

"Did you not tell me that you were happy with Peter in the bedroom, or at least not unhappy?" asked Maria, seeing straight through her euphemisms.

The waiter interrupted with the main course and they barely heard his approach; every table was now taken and the osteria was bustling with noise and movement. Isobel felt private enough to be frank with her friend.

"Maybe I just see things clearer now. We haven't made love in three months," she admitted, hating herself for her previous conceit.

"And you haven't tried to initiate it?"

"Not for a long time, maybe not since Marrakech."

"Why ever not?" exclaimed Maria, genuinely appalled.

"Because I don't feel anything. Not anymore. For the last year I have just lain there and let him take me, giving my body but not myself. I hold him of course, even encourage him sometimes to get it over quicker, but I still don't feel anything."

"And you thought this would be enough for you, forever? A life with no physical satisfaction?" laughed Maria, now satisfied her friend was intent on infidelity.

Isobel shrugged in embarrassment under her friend's piercing gaze, her silence confirming her foolishness and her intentions.

"So," said Maria with finality, "let us speak nothing more of Jay, we must—" She froze as Isobel's bag vibrated against the table and a pealing ring fractured the night with the sound of beginnings.

Twenty-four

As she wandered across Piccadilly Circus, her hands raw from the cord handles of a collection of designer store bags, Lucy's gentle pace slowed further. The afternoon had been an expensive one but, as Tessa told her, the price tag is the last thing a well-dressed woman should look at. Particles of London dust and grime floated in the air around her, rendered star-like by the low afternoon sun that fell over the buildings and hung in the streets. Everything seemed slow as she drifted along with the foot traffic — now fifteen minutes late for her meeting with Rob but not caring, her eyes on the more distant future.

A wiry young man drew up next to her on a bicycle drawn buggy, blocking her route.

"Can I interest you in a ride, luv?"

Lucy considered smiling and just going on her way, but she liked the cheeky grin enough to dally. "I'm not a tourist."

"Did I say you was? Anyway, no crime being a tourist, not in my business. Come on, gal, do a bloke a favour?" He nodded towards the shopping. "I reckon you can spare a shilling."

"You can drop the Oliver Twist routine. I'm from Croydon, and I'm only going to Covent Garden."

"With those bags? Well, you're lucky you got this far, all sorts of terrible things might 'appen to a luvly girl like you between 'ere and Covent Garden."

"I'll take the risk."

"Well, as it 'appens, I was moving up Long Acre anyway. So the ride's free… as long as you give me your number."

"So it's not free then," said Lucy with a grin as she hopped into the back, lolling fearlessly over the ripped and discoloured seat like it was velvet.

"You don't have to give me the right number." He smiled back at her, weaving through the traffic like lightning, twisting so instinctively through the taxis and buses that they seemed static in his wake.

"Why wouldn't I? I've always wanted a guy with his own transport." She lurched to one side as they tipped almost horizontal, rounding the corner.

The first hints of evening threatened and Rob was sitting at an outside table. He was a mountain of a man, a great wall of muscle, dressed in black and leant over a pint; his breath smelt of mint and his skin of plaster — the pleasant dry scent a constant reminder of his profession. The strength of his physique was echoed in his handsome face, with a defined jaw and a heavy brow. Yet the granite features were paired with a pleasant countenance; he had a soft voice and gentle eyes, which flitted between impatience and excitement as he waited for Lucy.

He sprang to his feet as she came into sight, dangling her shopping bags in the air by way of apology. He ran forward and caught her in a bear hug, lifting her off her feet and planting a kiss full on her lips.

"Steady, Tarzan, this body's got to last a lifetime, even if the lipstick doesn't." She pushed playfully at his face and he delivered her gently to the floor as if afraid she would break against the Covent Garden cobblestones.

"We need to move," he said as he gallantly sank the remainder of his pint, "we're late already."

"Uh, what's wrong with here?" She looked puzzled, the attractive café at which he had been sat already proving beyond her expectations of his taste.

"I thought we'd eat Italian." He betrayed an excited eagerness in his tone, tempered by a fear of rebuke.

"Italian? Not Indian, not Chinese?"

"I thought we'd celebrate, something different. But if you want Indian or—"

"Italian's fine. But what are we celebrating?"

"A couple of things. You'll see." He tugged her by the hand and led her down the street and along a side alley to Luigi's Restaurant; a quiet and leafy place with white tablecloths, rustic frescoes adorning its walls, and legs of cured hams hanging from the ceiling. By Rob's standards, they were eating in the stratosphere. Lucy studied the menu with apprehension as the waiter ran through the specials of the day, offering no indication of their price. She was used to Jay being in control in restaurants, asking questions, authoritative and decisive. Rob seemed limp and emasculated in comparison. She spared him any discomfort and pointed to the menu.

"Asparagus to start, please. And the sea bass for main."

"And for you, sir?"

"I'll have a pint of lager to start." Lucy buried her nose in the menu, fearing the worst. "And the fish." He faltered for a second before adding, "With chips."

"And the wine, sir?" The waiter's expression was almost a leer, his lips curling up at the sides either in derision or amusement.

"Actually, Rob, if you're ok with your beer I will just have a water." She looked up at the waiter. "Sparkling, please," she said and thrust the menu towards him as she had often seen Jay do in a clear signal of dismissal.

"So what you been shopping for?" Rob asked.

"Nothing that would interest you," she said, although quite aware that crotchless panties fell well within the scope of his interests. "Some shoes and a few things for the thing in Tuscany."

"What thing?"

"The thing with Tessa. One of the girls at work is having a hen night in Florence." Manipulating the truth was so simple, so easy, but she tried hard not to enjoy it.

"A hen night in Florance?"

"No, Flo-RENCE."

He laughed off her teasing. "You gonna show me what you got then?"

"Of course I'm going to show you," she said, her words soothing. "But not now. Besides, I can't bear the suspense any longer. What's the celebration for? You been asked to plaster the big wall or something?"

Before Rob could answer, the food arrived.

"French fries for the gentleman," said the waiter, as if to emphasise that this was an establishment that did not stoop to serve chips. Rob picked up the half lemon that sat at the side of his plate, and he examined it as if valuing a delicate antique. He picked awkwardly at the gauze with his heavy fingers, as Lucy watched. She was reminded how a year before she'd made the same mistake when dining with Jay, and how he caressed away her embarrassment, saying he did it all the time.

"I think you are supposed to leave it on," she said, as Rob looked blankly back, "to hold the pips." It was not intended to sound patronizing, but it did.

"You want to know something," said Rob with sudden irritation, "since you've got your job up in the skies you've become proper high and mighty." He gave a self-satisfied grin, surprised with his own unintended wit. "You reckon you are too good for me now?"

"No one could be too good for you, babe."

"Now you *are* just taking the pips," said Rob. They both laughed and he leant across and gave her cheek a playful stroke with his rough hand.

"You were just about to tell me what we're celebrating," she reminded him.

"Better than tell you, I'll show you!" He grinned like a child as he pushed his left sleeve up to his bulging bicep. "Wait for it."

Lucy put her hand to her mouth in dread as Rob forced his sleeve over the taut mound of flesh.

The words "oh my god" fell from her mouth like a stone as the sleeve began to reveal red, raw, inky skin.

"What do you think?"

"What do I think? About having my name forever engraved on your skin?" Lucy didn't know what to think but she could see the needy look in his eyes. She reached across the white tablecloth and put her hands on his. Finally, words came to her. "Rob, I'm touched, I really am." She chewed at her lower lip and squeezed his hands. "But I think that's the sort of thing we should talk about before we do it. You know, about our feelings and stuff."

"But that's just it. It is about how I feel. And putting your name on my arm shows how I feel about you." He looked at her intently with hurt in his eyes.

Lucy pulled his hands towards her and leant forward to kiss each one. "It's a very sweet thing to do, and I really, really like you, but we

139

are just going out, seeing each other." She hesitated. "You don't— we don't — own each other."

His lip quivered as he recovered his composure. "Of course we don't. I know that. I'm just proud of you, that's all." His voice was gruff and stilted and he rammed his hands into his pockets as they fell into awkward silence. Lucy lowered her gaze in shame and self-loathing, her eyes coming to rest on his pocket, which revealed the outline of what seemed to be a small square box, pushed into sharp relief by his still, gentle hands.

Twenty-five

After the highs and lows of the weekend, the last meeting Jay would have chosen to start the new week was one with Franco Mancini, the ageing lawyer who had been a thorn bush in his backside since they first met two years ago. And as he pulled into the Castello di Capadelli car park and emerged from the air-conditioned interior of his car into the fierce mid-morning heat, he was oppressed by his own foresight as he imagined how the day would proceed. Previous meetings between Mancini and himself followed a familiar and unfaltering pattern and he feared that today would be no different unless he did something drastic. He strolled to the entrance, ideas and plots spinning in his mind as he felt the sun soak into his skin, imbuing him with fire. And by the time he reached the tall glass doors of reception he had steeled himself to rid his mind of Mancini forever.

"Good morning, Signor Jay. Another lovely morning, is it not?" called Gina, throwing the doors wide so that the archway framed her slender body like a portrait in a gallery.

"Good morning, Gina," he replied as she rushed to walk alongside him. "Right now it certainly is, and your presence brightens it up for me even more. What can I do for you?"

"I would like to go through this week's booking schedule for the Taste of Tuscany programme," she said, handing over a modest-sized list for his appraisal.

"Let's go over it together later with a coffee," he suggested, brushing the paper away and quickening his pace for fear of angering Mancini.

Gina continued walking alongside him, matching his strides with ease as her athletic body kept pace with his. "Signor Mancini has already arrived. I welcomed him earlier. He has his granddaughter with him this morning."

"His granddaughter?

"Yes, Signore, but she is almost a woman," replied Gina, looking him straight in the eyes as she did so. But he hardly heard her, so intent was he on staring into every window they walked past.

"Is Eamon around?" he asked in answer to her inquisitive glance.

"Yes, Signore, he arrived a while ago," she replied, "although maybe a little, how do you say it in English, the worse for the wear after last night." She was referring to Eamon's team celebration in the bar in Capadelli village.

"And how was last night, Gina? I hope you left before things got too ugly."

"Yes, Signore. I left early. I picked up a pizza on the way home and spent the evening watching an old film in English. It was called *Brief Encounter*, very romantic but also sad."

"A good film," said Jay, with some vague recollection that he had heard of it. "Did you enjoy it?"

"It was, I think, complicated in parts to follow, listening in English. I thought perhaps I would have enjoyed it better if I had not been alone."

"Yes, perhaps," agreed Jay as they drew level with Mancini's apartment. "I'm sure Eamon would oblige; he loves a good pizza with his pint." And with that he knocked on the door, Gina's crestfallen face reflecting back at him in the highly polished glass.

Franco Mancini welcomed him in like he was the returning prodigal son. "Benvenuto, Signor Brooke, benvenuto. Please come in! May I introduce my granddaughter, Carla?"

He moved his portly form aside to reveal a petite girl dressed in black with a face like a film star's and eyes like daggers.

"It is my pleasure, Signorina," said Jay with sincerity, turning to Mancini to add, "she is a beautiful young lady, Signor, you must be very proud of her."

"Please, Signor Brooke," said the lawyer smiling, "today I am Franco; I prefer it if we are informal. I think we know each other well enough, no?"

"As you wish, Franco. My friends call me Jay."

"Then let me do the same if I may. For I think it is possible for us to think of ourselves as friends." He turned to his granddaughter. "Bella, I am sure Jay would be interested to learn something about what you are up to."

Unusually for Jay where a pretty girl was concerned, he had no particular interest in hearing what kept Signor Mancini's granddaughter occupied, and was bemused why the retired gentleman might think otherwise.

"Please do, Carla. I am always keen to learn how beautiful young ladies in Italy spend their time."

"You are very kind, Signor Jay," she said, her voice suggesting a blush but her face betraying nothing. "I am now completing my first year at the university in Firenze. The course I am studying is marketing. My grandfather has told me that you are an expert on the subject of marketing."

Jay stayed silent, bewildered at her presence, as she elaborated on every detail, from her modules to her desire to know him and his strategies better. "Anyway, Signor," she concluded at last, "I hope I have not bored you. But when my grandfather told me such a guru as yourself was here in Capadelli, it was my great desire to meet with you. Now let me say *arrivederci*, as I know my grandfather and you have business to discuss." And with that she exited into the kitchen, her gait graceful and her perfume filling the close air.

Jay shifted uncomfortably in the hard, straight-backed chair and waited to hear what Mancini so urgently needed to tell him. Past experience suggested it would be a problem, a large problem, that Franco alone could resolve, and that he would want some extortionate recompense as a result. As the old man leafed through the stack of papers on the wooden table, Jay cast his mind back to their first meeting. His adversary had appeared with open arms, cordially requesting the immediate construction of a porch outside his apartment, in return for his silence on Castello di Capadelli's lack of planning permissions; the thought that erecting a porch on a protected building also required permission seemed to escape the learned gentleman. Six months later and he was back again with a smile wider than his arms requesting a new kitchen for his silence about Villa Magda's missing fire escapes.

But that had been almost a year ago now and his long silence did not bode well. Yet the old man continued to thumb through the paper, extending it minute by minute as if drawing strength from the silence.

"I am sure, Franco that you have not asked me here just to have your eloquent granddaughter flatter me on my marketing credentials. What can I do for you this morning?" said Jay, unable to bear the silence any longer.

"I have asked for this meeting," began the older man with slow deliberation, "because I wish to help you on a serious matter. A matter on which I believe you are facing a most serious threat to your business."

Jay could think of myriads of such matters but was not going to reveal his hand just yet, opting instead for a humour-clad defence.

"You imply that this threat is more serious than the possibility of the guests in the Villa being turned to ashes for want of a fire escape?"

"That is all in the past, Jay. Now we are friends, things are different," he replied, brushing off the accusations like flies. "No, the reason I wish to talk with you is to alert you that several of your creditors are planning to seek an order against you that will shut down your company."

"Against Quayside?"

"Yes, that is the company you have registered here in Italy, I believe. The creditors believe that your business may be insolvent, which is very serious in Italy," he said, sticking out his chin and daring Jay to contradict him.

"My company is perfectly solvent, and these creditors, if they exist, have no way of knowing otherwise without access to our accounts," responded Jay with a shrug, maintaining his cool as he had done thousands of times before.

Mancini threw his arms up in the air. "Say what you will, Mr. Jay! But the issue is that the suppliers have not been paid, and they are owed a substantial sum. And if you do not settle it they will put you in the courts."

But Jay was not ready to roll over easily on the question of disgruntled creditors. To have such burdens was the normal situation of his business affairs and he cared little for it. Perhaps Mancini saw this in his eyes, for he ploughed on with his speech without waiting for an answer.

"So, Jay, even if your business is solvent, which it may or may not be, you cannot afford to have your creditors petition to close down your company. And that is what I am here to help you with!" he concluded, resting his hands in satisfaction on his large stomach.

It was one of the times in his life that Jay wished he was a smoker. So that he could hold his adversary in expectation as he nonchalantly lit up a cigarette, like Humphrey Bogart in some film noir or other. By way of substitute, he transferred his phone from one pocket to another, glancing at the screen as he did so. Mancini, well versed in courtroom theatrics, scowled at the posturing arrogance of his opponent.

"So, while we are in this hypothetical world, where I assume you can pull your usual strings and silence the usual voices, what would you seek in return for your kindness?" Jay inquired, his voice laced with sarcasm.

"Only a small thing, and not a very expensive one," he replied. "You have met my granddaughter Carla. As you have seen, she is a very beautiful girl, very bright and very intelligent. And she speaks excellent English."

Jay could see where the conversation was leading. "All that is true, Signor Mancini, but I must tell you that I am already married."

"You have much humour, Jay," he assented, his face deadpan, "which is why I understand you are so good at what you do. And I am sure Carla could learn great things from working alongside you. You do not speak Italian and have, I suspect, no plans to learn it. I believe an excellent role would be as your personal assistant."

Jay opened his mouth to refute this wholeheartedly, unable to imagine anything worse than a Mancini under his tutelage. But Mancini continued before he could formulate an excuse.

"Carla would be a great asset to you, Jay. She does not require a permanent position. Six months might be sufficient, so that she has the experience on her resume. And also, when she returns to university, she must submit a marketing case study as part of her course work. What better than a glowing account of what you have achieved here, and how you have achieved it. You might even be famous."

Jay waved these temptations aside with a sweep of his hand and leant forward across the table to fix his eyes on Franco's. "So, if I understand you, you would like me to hire Carla for six months?"

"Yes, Jay, starting next week. I will leave the salary decision to you, but something on the same level as your other sales people would seem fair. But that is, of course, not for me to dictate." He started to stand up, signalling their audience at an end. But his rival was far from done and his fixed gaze brought Mancini back into the seat of his chair with a thump.

"Unfortunately," Jay said, "it is not my decision. Much as I would like to help, the company that Carla would be working for is not my own but that of Mr. Andrew Skinner. And whilst I am happy to ask him to employ her, I can tell you now that he will refuse. Only yesterday he was insisting on staff cuts to the operation here. I am sorry about that." He rose from his chair as he concluded, pressing his hands into the arm rests until they creaked from the force. Mancini was visibly taken aback and all but leapt from his chair, moving his bulk with surprising speed in front of the door.

"Mr. Brooke, maybe I have not made myself fully clear. What I am asking is for my granddaughter, not myself. But it is very, very important to me. Much more important than any of the things we have discussed in the past. If you know what is good for your business, then I urge you to reconsider." He grasped Jay by the forearm and stared him straight in the eyes, his lips quivering and nostrils flaring with ill-concealed rage. "I will give you twenty-four hours to reflect. Tomorrow I expect you to come back to me with the right decision. If you do not, then it is you who will be responsible for the consequences." He gave one final withering stare and moved away from the door, bidding Jay a loud and disingenuous 'arrivederci.'

As the recently anointed marketing maestro stepped out into the Tuscan breeze, Jay felt renewed and free, the freedom of a man whose execution has been rearranged for a later date.

As he wandered back to reception, a welcome figure turned the corner of the old stone villa, the gold of the brick glowing against her skin like honey.

"The guest list, Signor Jay," Gina reminded him. "I thought perhaps we could review it here."

"Sure, Gina, let me take up a seat." He pulled up wooden chairs for both of them.

"I think, Signor, this is not a good time? Perhaps your mind is still on the meeting with Signor Mancini?" she asked, her face full of interest and compassion.

"Yes," he admitted, "but what better way to take my mind off it than sitting here with you. And going through the guest list, of course." He gave her one of his broadest smiles, and moved his chair around to her side of the table. Today he would live like a free man. "Gina, the dinner you mentioned, is that offer still available?" he asked, his hand inches from hers.

"But of course, Signor Jay, but I thought perhaps you were too busy?"

"Hmm, yes, I do have a lot going on, and I need to get back to England later this week. And next week is going to be very difficult too," he remembered aloud as he ran his fingers through his hair.

He looked into her dark brown eyes, looking back at him so familiarly, so openly, so ready to give him everything that they could have been Lucy's. An idea struck him like lightning and lit up his whole countenance. "But it so happens, Gina, if it is not too short notice, I have no commitments this evening. And I can think of nothing better than dinner with a stunning young lady. Will this evening work for you?"

She nodded automatically and he covered her smooth, tapered fingers with his hand, his wedding ring cool against her warm skin.

Twenty-six

The phone call that Isobel received over dinner in Lucca was neither a declaration of love nor a frank admission of sexual desire; it was a short and business-like message. Jay informed her warmly but otherwise without emotion that a decision might have been made on the Visconti suite, and issued a polite invitation that she come to Castello di Capadelli to find out.

The conflicting possibilities of secrecy or rejection battled in her mind, trampling across her brain and marauding through her heart. Maria's judgement favoured secrecy, convinced that he was simply exercising caution, and it was with her forceful urgency that Isobel was driven to Castello di Capadelli.

A smiling Gina met them at reception, her eyes jet black with birdlike limpidity. "Good afternoon, Signora Roberts, Signor Brooke has asked me to greet you and to show your friend around if she wishes it," she acknowledged Maria with a quick and unyielding smile, "as he is currently with a client."

"I think a long cool drink is what I need right now," said Maria, determined to meet the mysterious Jay and see for herself the chemistry between him and her friend.

"As you wish, Signora."

They followed her to the wine bar in the inner courtyard as she led them to a table spotlighted by the sun and called for some sparkling water, bidding them goodbye as the bottles arrived with a smiling waiter.

"Just one thing, Gina," said Isobel, as the girl turned away. "Maria and I would like to go horse riding tomorrow afternoon. Is that something you can arrange for us?"

Gina twirled back to meet her gaze.

"Yes, I think I can arrange that, Signora. Is there anything special you need?"

"Maria is able to lend me everything, except the riding boots. Would it be possible for you to find a pair for me, size thirty-nine?"

Gina nodded in acquiescence. "That, Signora, is also my size. If you are happy to use my boots, it will be my pleasure."

"Thank you, Gina, you are very kind." The girl smiled and walked away, her movement poised and delicate.

The two friends basked in the sun and the silence as her footsteps faded, Isobel closing her eyes like a cat whilst Maria looked around in interest at the place that had captured so sensible a heart.

"Do you like it then?" Isobel asked, her eyes still shut, her eyelids faint blue in the sunlight.

"I can see why *you* like it," Maria said, wrinkling her perfect ski-slope nose. "The views are stunning, the staff are obliging, and the whole place glows with money."

"B-u-u-t?" said Isobel, opening one eye in cheeky acknowledgement of Maria's notoriously candid opinions.

"But," Maria grinned, "it's not quite the same as having your own place. For me and for Angelo, we like to swim and to lie naked by the pool. They probably have a rule here against that sort of thing."

"Splashing in the pool naked is not quite mine and Peter's thing," she replied with a laugh. "The last time we were in a spa we were the only people wearing anything. It was in Austria and someone asked Peter to close the door to the sauna when we went in. The woman spoke English in a German accent, and Peter couldn't understand how she knew our nationality."

Maria snorted with laughter. "Well, let's just hope your new friend doesn't want to do things with the lights on. Have you thought about that, Isobel? And talking of new friends, is that hunk coming towards us Jay?"

It was, and he strode across the courtyard like a king, tall and magnificent, imbued with strength by his kingdom. Isobel stood to greet him, filled with a sense of pride at his powerful presence, and introduced Maria who, with typical disregard for inhibition, launched into conversation.

"An interesting spot you have here, a hideaway on top of the hill," she said with a smile.

"Thank you. Yes, it was quite a find," he said, turning to Isobel, seemingly to escape Maria's eyes. "Isobel mentioned she is staying with you in Lucca?"

"Just outside Lucca, a converted farmhouse. We love it there," said Maria.

"So how much time are you able to spend here?" he asked.

"As much as I can, at least in the summer, it depends of course on when my boyfriend can join me."

Jay nodded, his eyes resting on her wedding ring. Her openness did not surprise him; everything in her manner seemed an infidelity. Seeing Isobel next to her, innocent and contained, made him doubt everything he had supposed.

"And I hope that we will be seeing you here often, Isobel?" he asked, seeking answers in her face. "Everyone who met you yesterday was quite struck by you, particularly the Italians. It's quite rare for our English clients to speak such fluent Italian and, Gina tells me, with almost no trace of an accent. You must have spent quite some time in Italy?"

She smiled, her face alight from the compliment. "Thank you, but I'm a little rusty. Though getting my Italian back up to speed is something I'm looking forward to."

He agreed with enthusiasm, trying not to watch her with too much intensity.

"You said you might have an update from Andy Skinner?" she asked, unable to read him.

"Yes, I spoke with Andy again earlier. He isn't quite decided I'm afraid; he has to talk things over with his wife Kate. But I should be able to let you know in the next few days." He crinkled his eyes in apology and changed the subject, turning the conversation to their plans for the next few days.

"Tomorrow we thought it might be nice to spend a couple of hours in the morning by the sea. And then maybe to come horse riding here," said Isobel, buoyed by his interest.

"Yes, Gina told me about your visit to the paddock yesterday. Do you think you might use the local facility? Gina says the old boy there took quite a shine to you." He looked at her as if waiting for a reason to like her more.

"I don't know about that, I think he was just a very sweet man. But, yes, we hope we can go back there. Gina is seeing what she can sort out for us." Her words trailed off, she was unsure what else to say and happy to end the subject, which she thought was probably a boring one for a man with so much.

Maria, however, was unrelenting in her curiosity.

"Is horse-riding something you have done much of, Jay?"

"The last time I was on a horse was on a beach in Thailand. It was quite a few years ago. I thought I did ok..." He ruffled his hair in thought.

"Well, perhaps you can join us tomorrow. Isobel is an excellent horsewoman, much more experienced than me, so I am sure you will be in safe hands."

Jay murmured in thought before replying. "That sounds fun, and tomorrow I have a quiet day. But I wouldn't want to slow you down."

"But that is exactly what I need tomorrow," Maria exclaimed, "someone to slow Isobel down, so she doesn't race ahead as if she is at Aintree. I think it's a super idea, if you are able to join us."

"And you promise you won't laugh when I make a fool of myself?"

"Of course we will, that is half the fun of having you along," said Maria, as Isobel looked on in awe.

"I would hate to disappoint you," he said with a grin. His laugh was deep and genuine as he pledged his agreement and he watched Maria in admiration as the two women walked back to the car.

"Maria, that was somewhat forward of you, don't you think?" whispered Isobel as they walked away.

"Maybe yes, but once you mentioned horse-riding, I think your man Jay was playing for the invitation to join us."

Isobel nodded in defeat. "Well, I suppose I'd better stop at reception and let Gina know we need three horses now."

Maria held her gaze for a split second, the knowledge of all womankind behind her eyes.

"Don't worry, Isobel. You will only need the two horses."

Twenty-seven

Jay walked to Gina's place in Capadelli, a bottle of the finest red wine he could lay his hands on in the cellar of Il Paradiso under his arm. The evening was cool and refreshing, the sky pink and blue with endless stars that pierced the colours like pinpricks. Her apartment teetered on the fourth floor of a great square building, dyed honey orange by the dust and the heat with its stucco flaking away like wafers.

He had not known whether to come, his mind and body near ripped him apart as they pulled for command of his fate. To entangle himself with Gina would be an additional complication, another fine line in the web he was weaving around himself. Isobel played heavily on his consciousness, stirring within him desires that not even Lucy awoke in him. Yet how could any man resist Gina? Innocent and fresh, her beauty was undeniable and she seemed to offer herself to him, how could he not take it? Nothing, no logic or sense, could stop him from doing so.

As he stepped into the apartment any doubt of her intentions vaporised into the candle-lit air. The room was bathed in a reddish glow, tables and corners illuminated by flame-like shrines, and mellow music played in the background. It looked quite magical in its own way and when Gina stood there in the doorway, the softness of her curves traced in the darkness, Jay wafted in, a slave to his senses. They shared a delicious dinner, the air between them thick and aromatic, full of satisfaction and dissatisfaction.

After they had eaten, Gina suggested they watch a film on the sofa, and so they lounged with a half-body of space between them whilst Audrey Hepburn ran around Rome, the black and white of the screen projecting strange shapes into the darkness of the room. Jay shifted his position to make himself more comfortable, inching closer as he sunk into the cushions. Gina echoed his movements like a marionette, leaning towards him as he put an arm round her shoulder and pulled his legs up onto the sofa. She mimicked him again, her lissom form melting into his firm bulk as they lay together like sculptures.

"You are comfortable in this position, Jay?" she asked, looking into his eyes, as the film became mere noise and light.

He shifted again to pull her closer, pressing his hardness against her in silent answer.

"Are you happy with my work?" she asked, stroking his chest with the slightness and vulnerability of a child.

"Very happy," he replied, his bemusement lost to her in the dark.

"Then perhaps you will now allow me to help you in your work; I have many skills and I fear I do not use these skills, and I would so much like to be closer to you…in your work." The words came out in a torrent of repressed hopefulness and she pushed herself closer until even the tremble of her breathing gave him pleasure.

"We are not looking for additional staff right now. What do you have in mind?" Jay asked.

"Well, you have your meeting soon, no?" She ran her hand up his chest like electricity. "And I can translate and type and even take dictation."

He shifted beneath her again and she fell between his body and the sofa.

"Please, Jay, it would mean a lot for me to do these things for you at the meeting." He shifted again until she was beneath him, stroking his neck in submission. He pondered the suggestion as she caressed him. A striking girl like Gina in the room would be a distraction to Andy and her presence would help to keep tempers from flaring if things became difficult.

"It might be possible, Gina, but I will need to speak to Andy. He's very stressed at the moment—"

"I could smile at him and tell him how handsome and virile a man he is," she interrupted with a mischievous grin.

Jay imagined her tempting Andy, who held such power over him; dangling herself teasingly before him to never be had, after he, Jay, had owned her with his body.

"Then you must dress in your best outfit, Gina, to show Andy how important he is," he declared, his arousal now almost unbearable. She radiated pleasure at his words and pushed herself yet closer, fitting into every contour of his body.

"I think, Jay, that you must have been with many women in your life, no?" Damp and hot against him, she nuzzled at his neck.

"Not so many. I have a wife and a girlfriend," he admitted, stroking her hair, "but I do not love either of them. My wife knows this and we are together for convenience but the girl…" he hesitated, "it has been very difficult to break with the girl. Although I do not love her, I do not want to hurt her."

"This girl, then she loves you, no?"

"Well, that's the strange part," he murmured, half to himself. "I don't think she loves me. It's more that she thinks she needs me. She has her own boyfriend, but she won't let me go."

"Then she must be very selfish."

He stroked her in assent, silent for a moment with his thoughts.

"How about you, Gina? A girl like you, you must have every man around chasing after you?" She pushed herself up beneath him and held his gaze, her lips quivering with truth.

"At the moment I think of no one special, Jay, only perhaps you. I look out for you every day, but it seems that you do not notice me. You do not look at me." He said nothing, just stared back as she continued. "Let us not talk any more about these things. I am sorry I asked you about your girlfriends. Now you have made me feel a little foolish."

Jay shook his head, sliding a hand onto her chest as if to keep the words within her. But she interlocked her fingers in his, trapping him until she could find solace.

"I have another great worry, but you will think it silly."

"Not at all, Gina, but I can assure you it's not that big." He laughed at his joke but it was lost on Gina, and she continued.

"But it is a big worry, for me. You do not learn our language, and it seems Castello di Capadelli is nearly finished. So perhaps you will be leaving here very soon?"

"Not at all, Gina," he said, as if such a thought had never occurred to him.

But she persisted. "If you do wish to leave here, you will tell me first? For it would be terrible for me to hear it from others."

Jay cupped her face in his hand and kissed her in answer, hoping that it would say everything she wanted it to. She let his tongue breach her lips in response, offering no resistance as he began to massage her breasts through her blouse, and kept her arms locked around his neck. He travelled his hand down to her waist but froze from the burst of tension in her body, running through her bones like ice until he moved his hand back up again.

Jay kissed her more ardently now, wanting to convince her of his sincerity, and slipped his hand beneath her blouse and over her warm satiny skin.

He was starting to ache for Gina to explore his own body; he pressed harder against her so that she could have no doubt of his excitement. But the most that he seemed to be encouraging was the movement of Gina's hands up and down his back in a panacean rhythm.

She gasped as he pushed his fingers into her mouth, but she licked them like a kitten and shuddered and murmured as they rubbed against her hard, erect nipple. He travelled his hand slowly southward again, hungry for her, but as it passed the waistline a swift motion from Gina's hand intercepted it.

"I am sorry, Jay, tonight I am not ready. It is too early for me." She stared up at him, afraid but resolute, her eyes swimming with a black that could not be pierced.

"It is me who should be sorry, Gina," he sighed. "I did not mean to pressure you."

"No, it is my fault. I should not have encouraged you. It was just that I was enjoying the evening with you so much and I did not want it to finish. And also I was enjoying what we were doing. But I just need a little more time. It is silly I know, but that is the way I am." She sat up, refastened her blouse and pulled down her bra. "I think we have missed the end of the film. Should I rewind it?"

"We can finish it next time, Gina, it's getting late anyway." He stood up to leave, drained of everything and feeling strangely lost.

"Tomorrow you will not ignore me again, Jay? You will not punish me because I was without courage tonight? Because then I will be very sad."

He cupped her chin in his hand and smiled, her words reminding him of his plans for the next day. "You have had a very busy weekend, Gina, and you must be tired." She shook her head automatically. "But you worked this weekend, and the last weekend. When did you last have a day off work?"

"I cannot remember. It has been very busy. Maybe a month ago." She cocked her head like a bird, her eyes questioning him.

"They are working you far too hard. Everybody else gets a break. Eamon and the boys pop home for a few days every month. I don't think they are being very fair on you."

"It is nice that you tell me that I work so much. Perhaps it's for you that I do it—"

He cut her off, mercy and kindness held to his face like a mask.

"Well, tomorrow you must have the day off. You have earned it."

"It is not possible, Jay. Tomorrow I have promised Signora Roberts that she may use my riding boots. So I must go in tomorrow."

"Nonsense, Gina. Give me the boots and I will take them in, and I will leave them in reception for Mrs. Roberts."

"It is very kind of you. But only if you are sure, Jay?"

He held her waist and looked long and deeply at her.

"I insist on it. You have a lie in, and take yourself shopping or something in the afternoon. I will be very disappointed if I see you anywhere around Castello di Capadelli tomorrow."

Twenty-eight

Isobel mounted her horse in one swift movement and watched in amusement as Jay scrambled on to his, eliciting a furtive leg up from the round-bellied owner. They were back at the dilapidated stables and she sat tall and dignified on her steed, clad in Gina's riding boots and haloed by the fierce sun.

"This way, pardner," she instructed, swinging round to face a narrow, dusty track that led deep into the trees.

"Would this be a good time for you to let me into the secret of how to do this?"

"Practice, Jay, lots of practice," she said, trotting a few paces ahead and directing her words to the sky.

"Any other useful advice?" he shouted as she pulled further away.

"Wear a helmet!"

He feigned shock as he patted his bare head and made to follow her. But his horse insisted on stopping every few steps to peruse the grass, snaffling at the longest and most tender stalks with unconcealed indifference for her rider. He kicked at her sides, then tried again with more force, but she was immovable.

"What's going on here then? Do I need to shout giddy up or something?" He arranged his face in grotesque puzzlement, so confident in his attractiveness that it mattered to neither of them.

"The problem is not the horse, Jay," she joked, looking back as she cantered ahead of him. "A mare requires a firm hand, everyone knows that."

She seemed to him at one with the horse, their forms merging and separating in an elegant dance that was at once savage and refined, animalistic and spiritual.

They followed the trail for about an hour, meandering through abandoned olive groves — the trees gnarled and twisted from age and freedom, no longer bearing fruit — and shady woodland paths, where lizards spread themselves in the blotches of sun and hoverflies bobbed up and down on invisible strings. Isobel stayed tantalisingly ahead of Jay, pausing to tease him only to pull ahead again, half in play and half in fear. He enjoyed her games and clowned around on his patient horse, clinging to its neck as if for dear life and pretending to be falling out of his saddle.

"For someone who has only ever been on a horse on a beach in Thailand, you seem to be doing pretty well," she told him with a smile, finally allowing him to draw level with her. They were approaching a stream and the ground rose steeply on the other side.

"I don't think my newly discovered talents are up to that though." He gestured to the bank and Isobel nodded in amused agreement. "Maybe we can take a break for five minutes?" he continued. "I'm feeling a bit saddle sore."

They dismounted and tethered their horses beside the stream. A large tree on the cusp of the water provided an ideal seat. Its long, fingered branches spread out over the water like a canopy and it had a strangely concave trunk like a natural arbour.

Jay turned to her as they nestled into the shady alcove. "I can't remember the last time I had so much fun, Isobel."

"Me neither," she admitted in return, gazing out across the water, which seemed a thousand colours in the afternoon sun. They looked at the stream for a long time without speaking; Isobel dared not look at him and the air seemed heavy with soundless words. He leant across and kissed her, parting the air with his lips and holding them to hers as her face quivered beneath his. She pulled away and looked through him expressionless, not knowing which emotion to show.

"Did you like that, me kissing you?" His voice was low and anxious but wonderfully unafraid.

"Yes, you know I did." She looked into his eyes but his face blurred and swirled into pieces as tears distorted her vision.

He put his hand slowly to her neck, gently pushing her head upwards so that the tears ran symmetrically down her cheeks, dividing her face into three.

"Are you ok?"

"I'm sorry. I don't know whether I can go through with this." She couldn't look at him.

"Through with what, Isobel?" He pulled her face to look at his. "It's just a kiss."

"But it's a beginning," she said, needing him to know what it was, to reassure her that he felt the same.

"If we don't do anything more, it will still have been a great day," he said, his eyes growing in an intensity not shared by his voice.

"But one with a disappointing end," she conceded, her self-loathing clear through her pallid skin.

"What's holding you back?" he asked, his hand light on her arm.

"I'm sure you can guess," she said, sadness in her eyes, "a rush of guilt. And fear too. When you've been with only one person in twenty years it feels like the first time all over again. And I don't want to hurt Peter, or put my marriage at risk." Her body sank into itself as he watched her. "How's that for a stack of good reasons to get up, get on that horse, and go back?"

"Isobel, if you get back on that horse now I won't think any more or any less of you." He stroked her back and pulled her closer. "You will still be a wonderful woman to me. It's because you're the person you are that you have those fears." She stirred as if to get up and Jay pressed his hand on hers, holding her to earth.

"The thing is," he continued, his voice soft and reassuring, "fear and doubt are perfectly normal feelings. And some people lead a miserable life because they are ruled by fear; always looking back on what they might have done, or wished they had done, but let fear stop them. If you are too scared, if the risk is too high then we can go back now, as friends instead of lovers. But if it helps, anything that happens today is our secret. No one but us need ever know." Isobel felt herself falling forwards as she gravitated towards his words, which spoke such sense and comfort to her heart. He squeezed her hand in his, and she felt again the security of his protective embrace, the way she remembered it in the souk, how he had taken control in the melee and the feeling it instilled in her, the feeling that she must obey him. "But you have to want to."

"I *do* want to." It was said and she could never go back.

His hand travelled to her blouse and she was powerless to stop it as he kissed her passionately, melting her last defences, which slipped from her as her bra fell to the leaf-strewn floor.

His voice was mellow and soothing, low and beguiling, his words rising and falling, the pace of his speech slowing further as her breathing slowed, as he coaxed her to "just let go." She heard his words without hearing them, her limbs feeling heavy against the earth, as if she could not lift them. He put his fingers to her eyebrows and dragged them downwards, her eyelids closing in unison; his hand slid to her waist and rested awhile, as if waiting for her breathing to ease, then onwards, into the velvety softness of her French knickers. For an instant she wanted to open her eyes, to clasp his hand in hers and hold it fast. But she could not; if she did then she would have to tell him to stop. And she did not want him to stop, not yet. It was so much easier to lie there, to let her mind follow his enticing words, to let him slip off her riding breeches, to pretend that she was not aware of his tongue, of the sensations travelling up her legs, so much stronger and more intense than they'd ever been before. She knew now that she was not going to stop. She knew that she was going to let Jay do anything he wanted to do to her. Instinctively, she pulled his body towards her own, tugging at his waistband in the heated urgency of all-consuming lust.

She felt a rush of pleasure at his hardness to her touch and whatever fears or misgivings she took into the woods that day were no longer with her. It was she who now took charge, pulling at his belt feverishly and pushing her hands inside his jeans.

He pressed his mouth to her ear, his hotness on her skin pushing her to breaking point.

"Easy, Isobel, there's no rush, let's take this slow, ok?"

She could not bear it and pushed her mouth to his until he tasted her breath, until he knew how much her body cried for his.

"Fuck me, Jay. Please. I just need you to fuck me."

Twenty-nine

The pure whiteness of Jay's bathroom, with its gleaming tiles and snowy, fluffy towels, made Isobel's head ache. She had shut herself in, seeking solace from his tormenting presence, wanting to lose the aching desire to have him again. She had believed so ardently that once would be enough and yet here she was waiting for him to claim her. The purity of the white hurt her eyes. She had not washed since their lovemaking in the woods and now closed her eyes as she remembered how she groaned in frustration at his last second withdrawal, how she tried to pull him back into her even as his seed spurted onto her thrilling skin. She could still smell his musty odour, the way she smelt him when she wiped her fingers across her belly and furtively brought them to her nostrils. She had wanted to taste him, but was afraid he would notice even as he lay beside her, his eyes closed and body spent.

As she stood in the white, alone with her thoughts, the fear that had gripped her in the woods subsided and a shiver went down her spine; want trembled within her like a bird, hitting her with its feathers until she burnt for his touch. She let her clothes fall to the floor and stood naked of all but her wedding ring. She tugged it off and looked again at her reflection; she expected satisfaction but it was now too bare, too exposed and she crammed the ring back on, her knuckle aflame with red as she hid deep in a towel.

Three gentle taps at the door pulled her from herself and she braced her body against the sink's edge as it swung open. Jay entered with a swaggering confidence. He was naked, and fully erect; Isobel cowered in anticipation as he strode towards her. He reached out and grasped the towel, pulling her to him as she clutched it, and tearing it from her. His mouth was on hers and he kissed her hungrily as she felt him against her. She pressed the hardness of her nipples into his chest, needing him to feel her pleasure and to know that she was unquestioningly his. He was stiff with passion against her and pulled his mouth away to look into her eyes. It seemed to Isobel that at the moment he saw everything and she craved his reciprocation.

"You didn't come this afternoon, did you?" he murmured in her ear.

She shook her head into his flesh like a child. "Are you disappointed?"

"Was it my fault?" he asked in return, his eyes penetrating hers, strong and inquisitive.

Isobel looked back into them, scared of his strength and his confidence.

"I was nervous," she whispered, hoping to satisfy him as she yearned for him to satisfy her. His hand went between her thighs and he shuddered at her heat and her wetness.

"Do you usually come?"

"Please, Jay," she protested, terrified of the growing numbness of recent years, at her blind and docile acceptance of mundanity. She pressed her hands onto his, pushing his fingers inside her.

He lifted up her chin and spoke into her neck, etching each word into her skin with his lips. "Just promise that you won't ever fake it for me."

"I promise."

He kissed her with satisfaction, his hands drifting up to her shoulders as she fell into him, giving herself entirely.

She felt the pressure of his strong hands on her shoulders, encouraging her downwards, urging her downwards, forcing her downwards, and she dropped to her knees in obedience before him, trailing her tongue down his torso as she descended, knowing what he wanted, and knowing that she was powerless to deny him.

She rubbed his member against her cheeks, seeking him out with her tongue, before taking him into her mouth. He pulled her to her feet and kissed her, tasting them both, and his hands went to the back of her trembling thighs. He pressed her hard against the wall, pushing her up the shining whiteness of the tiles and lowering her onto him. She locked her ankles behind his back as she tensed around him, the coldness of the wall and the electricity of his skin convulsing her body with pleasure.

He carried her to the bed and laid her down upon it and stood at her feet. She quivered as he feasted his eyes on her nakedness, seeming to sense the aching between her legs from the imploring, pleading look in her eyes. She felt a craven, wanton desire to have him take her, and pulled her knees upwards towards her body, letting them fall wide apart, exposing her full sex to his gaze.

He approached her from the foot of the bed, inching forward on his knees. She felt the brush of his evening stubble first on one thigh, then the other. She closed her eyes and lay back, waiting for him to find her. He ran his tongue up her thighs, but his mouth passed the burning centre of her desire, until she felt it on her midriff, licking slow circles around her belly button, before continuing to mark its trail upwards towards her nipples. She could bear it no longer and now her hands went to his shoulders. She forced the heels of her hands into him, feeling his resistance, then feeling it ebb as he moved lower. She quivered as he rubbed into her with the hard part of his nose, seeking out her most sensitive spot, before his tongue found her wetness. She pulled his head into her, wrapping her legs over his shoulders, wanting his mouth to devour her. As she felt the shudder of orgasm she was oblivious to the low cries of ecstasy crossing her lips, but he heard them and he knew her, he knew all her weaknesses.

Thirty

Andy leant back in his seat with pointed disdain as Jay strode theatrically into the meeting and thumped his files down on the table with exaggerated authority, beaming around him at the faces transfixed by his aura. Andy allowed himself a slight sigh of anticipated derision and watched Jay assume his seat at the side of the table, following his movements with narrowed eyes and folded arms, sure this time that he knew the man behind the mask. Still, he couldn't deny his adversary had style; his presence and charisma made the men and women around the table — sharp suited lawyers and accountants alongside soberly clad Capadelli employees — seem dull and lifeless. The only other light in the room was Gina, resplendent and virginal in her flowing summer dress, a white swan amongst grey geese, glowing with soft and tactile beauty against the stone of Il Paradiso's private dining room.

The occasion was the grandly titled board meeting of Tyneside Holdings, the umbrella under which Jay created the bewildering web of companies in which Andy was now enmeshed, if not fully ensnared. The quiet, almost reverent, atmosphere made him uneasy; he felt as if he could almost feel the spiders circling around him as one by one the faces at the table acknowledged Jay with warm smiles and meaningful eyes.

"We are all waiting for you," said Andy with deliberate gravity, tapping his fingers against the table as Jay circled the room to reach his seat. Andy watched him stop to greet Gina and for a split second allowed his hawk-like gaze to falter as she rose to pass him his notes and her lithe form cut through the air, filling his nostrils with her perfume.

Jay placed down his papers and marched to the front of the room, the sound of his heavy footsteps on the dark red terracotta floor tiles echoing around the room and ascending to its whitewashed vaulted ceiling, as he marched to the front, a picture of cool confidence.

"Just checking the connections," said Jay with a smile as the presentation screen refused to turn on. Andy fidgeted with agitation in his seat, his finger tapping reverberating like drumbeats as a tangle of nerves obscured his senses; he needed to be in control and this was not a good way to start. But as weakness began to needle in his bones, the screen flashed on, illuminating the room with an image of the bikini-clad beauty that was Jay's screensaver.

"I was worried there for a second," said Andy, surreptitiously wiping the sheen of sweat from his brow, "that we hadn't paid the electricity bill."

Jay ignored the slight and busied himself with nonchalantly arranging the onscreen information. Andy took up his drumming again, frustrated that his adversary could be so calm and unflustered in the face of his insistence that this meeting would be Andy's, not the usual stage-managed affair that Jay relied on.

Andy's eyes strayed once more to Gina as she swung her long brown legs playfully beneath her and deliberately caught his eye, her low cut dress revealing the roundness of her breasts above her notebook as she sucked her pen and peeked over at Jay's notes. Andy's eyes lingered as she reached down to her bag, the light cotton falling forward and allowing him to steal a tantalising glimpse of her dark brown nipples.

Only necessity drew his eyes away as Jay finally stood to address the room, kicking off the formal part of the meeting with a summary of the status of the business, confident and upbeat with a flintiness in his eye that forbade any contradiction from his followers.

"The past has been difficult and challenging as we all know," he began, "but I truly believe that we have reached a tipping point. As recently as a month ago I was concerned that our venture here in Tuscany might be at risk. Today, I am delighted to report that this last week we have turned the corner; timeshare membership sales are ahead of plan. Even more gratifying, this last week we have taken record enquiries for new apartment sales. By the end of today I expect to be able to confirm additional sales, including the sale of the Visconti suite."

Andy listened intently, the edge of Gina's hand brushing against his arm and his senses.

"I know one or two in the room might have thought it impossible to sell the Visconti suite at the price point we have set," Jay continued, looking pointedly at Andy. "That we are able to do so, and may I add at full list price, is tremendous validation of our business strategies."

Andy stirred beneath his gaze and retorted, "If this is a sales update, I think I'd rather hear it from the Irishman. He's the one that should be getting the credit for selling, while you've been frolicking around music city."

Jay seemed to welcome the dig, as if it made his point for him, and continued as if addressing some great auditorium.

"None of us are indispensable. But unfortunately, Eamon is unable to be with us this morning. He is fully engaged on closing those apartment sales. I hope we can all agree that this needs to be Eamon's priority today." Jay looked around the room, daring anyone to contradict such perfect logic. "Therefore, if I may, I will continue with an update on sales. Alberto and Davide will give individual updates from their areas, as you requested."

"Jay, can you please get on with it?" said Andy. "We can all see the agenda… for once, and I've got a few questions I want to get to," he added ominously.

"'There will be ample time for questions and discussions," said Jay, unruffled. "I suggest that after the coffee break, we continue with director only business, with Gina too of course."

Jay smiled at Gina, as Andy too was drawn to her face by the mention of her name. She met his eyes with barely concealed appetite, brushing her foot against his under the table as Jay began an itemised update on each agenda item, covering every significant matter. He focused overwhelmingly on the positive and Andy was forced to concede he recognised some substance to Jay's optimism, which reinforced the evidence he had seen with his own eyes as he toured the development.

"I have one request from the board, if I may," said Jay, causing suspicion to well up within Andy. "I should like permission to begin taking reservations on phase two membership sales. We are getting many enquiries, and I don't want to disappoint anyone."

Andy's mind processed the request, but he could find no ulterior motive in it. But still he probed. "Since when did you start asking permission on operational matters?"

"It is purely a matter of timing, Andy. Normally I would just make an executive decision and go ahead, but seeing as the directors were meeting, it only seemed respectful to check before giving Eamon authorisation."

Andy looked around the room, but saw no sign of dissent, so nodded his agreement, unaware of the feel of cold gunmetal against his fingertips.

"Gina, can you please make a note for the minutes," said Jay, beaming with pleasure and relief, before Andy cut him short.

"This is enormously encouraging, and I'm sure down to fine work by all," he declared, allowing the room a few cruel seconds of hope before he continued, "but perhaps we can now move on to Alberto?"

Alberto was Jay's Geometra, a man who performed the combined roles of a surveyor, planner, and estate agent from the safety and influence of Jay's palm. He rose and gave Jay a nervous glance as he stepped into the spotlight. His clear discomfort bolstered Andy's confidence in his own position and Andy allowed himself a satisfied, almost predatory, smile as the short, wiry man with a shock of silver-grey hair like a scouring pad, began to speak. He gave a buoyant overview of building progress, as Jay nodded and smiled encouragement. He flicked through slide after slide, with a green tide slowly rolling across the screen to indicate progress, building by building.

"I am pleased to say that our difficulties, particularly with the builders, are now behind us," he concluded. "All one hundred apartments are close to complete, and will be completed within a month." He folded his notes precisely in half and made to flee for his seat but Andy held up a hand, firm and flat against the air, to stop him.

"So all the planning permissions and permits are in place?" he asked, raising his eyebrows. "No danger of anyone coming along and trying to close us down, or knock the place down?"

"I am more in consultation with the planning authorities than with my own children," said Alberto, beads of perspiration dotting his brow.

Andy laughed with hollow dismissal. "Is that yes or no?"

"In Italy things are not so straightforward, Mr. Skinner," Alberto replied, twisting his hands together in unease. "Palms must be greased and so on. And it is often the way that permissions are withheld, but it is nothing more than a negotiation."

Andy could have argued the point for hours, but time was limited with too much else to discuss.

"There's something else I'm curious about," he said, running his fingers down the columns of figures as Gina leant her body into him as if following the movement of his hand. "The sales prices that we have realised on similar apartments vary enormously. Why is that?"

"It is a complicated matter," said Alberto, as if this alone was sufficient explanation.

"Well, speak slowly and I will do my best to follow you," said Andy. "Why do we sell some apartments at less than half the list price?"

Alberto shifted on his feet for several moments before offering the answer. "We sell at one price to the Italians, and a different price to the British."

"Why exactly?" asked Andy, with cold logic, careful to keep emotion and injustice from his tone.

"It is a very unusual arrangement, I admit, but it is a necessary one, and it is legal, we have been assured of that," Alberto replied, pushing his needle-like fingers through his hair until Jay intervened.

"The Italians are buying bricks and mortar; the British are buying a lifestyle. Everything is perfectly legitimate, Andy. What the Brits are investing into is their own little dream of a home in Tuscany. And we incur heavy marketing costs to promote that dream. And for all that, they are prepared to pay a premium over what an Italian is prepared to pay. So—"

"How much of a premium?" asked Andy, cutting him off. "And let Alberto answer, if you don't mind."

Alberto did not need to check his notes. He dined out in Florence too often on this particular anecdote. "The price we market the property to the UK is never less than twice that we sell to an Italian, sometimes much more."

"And what, Alberto," asked Andy, "what happens when the British come to sell, and find their apartment is worth only half what they paid for it?"

"All we are doing is charging what the UK market will bear," answered Jay in his stead. "No one is forced to buy."

Andy laughed with derision, having been only too recently berated with a tearful account of high pressure selling by Eamon and his team of arm twisters. "If you say so, Jay, but before Alberto sits down, I have another question. I spoke with one of the owners here yesterday, an English couple, the Barkers, you may know them, Alberto?"

"Yes, I think I do," responded Alberto.

"The Barkers tell me that some owners on site have paid for kitchens to be fitted, for which they have been waiting over six months. They say that each owner has paid you twenty-five thousand Euros. Twenty-five thousand Euros for a few cupboards and appliances?"

"Only four such owners are in that position, Mr. Skinner," said Alberto, caressing the razor sharp fold of his paper.

"Only four? Why are there any at all?"

Much to Andy's chagrin Jay intervened again. "It is a complicated story, Andy, and not at all appropriate for this part of the meeting. The point is that the end-user is paying. You are not subsidising anything."

"I'll decide what's appropriate," said Andy jerking his thumb towards his own chest. "And that is not how I see it. They are people, clients, and we are cheating them."

Jay flinched as the accusation echoed about the room. "Ok, Andy, maybe what was done was not properly thought through. I'm sure no wrong was intended."

Andy sighed, his frustration not so much at Jay's methods, but that the man genuinely seemed to see no wrong in them.

"Well, maybe this is a good time for Davide to give us a financial update," he said in concession, unwilling to desert the figures in favour of philosophic discussion.

Jay nodded in apparent relief as Davide stepped forwards, striding into the foreground with the confident air of a man who had rehearsed his presentation carefully.

Before Davide could launch into his bird's eye view of the land of plenty just over the horizon, Andy shot a pre-emptive missile. "So, right now, how much is owed to owners?"

Davide floundered under his directness. "That information would need time to put together."

Andy tried to keep his temper. "Davide, what are the numbers?"

"These I do not have exactly today."

Andy's temper rose. "What is this, Jay? An accounting presentation with no numbers? This meeting has been scheduled for over a month. Where are the numbers?" He slammed his notepad down in exasperation.

Alberto attempted to continue. "This is not that easy to answer—"

"Well, answer it as best you fucking can."

Jay shot a glance at Gina and she put her hand to her mouth in a loud and obvious gesture of shock. Andy touched her arm in apology.

"Excuse my language, no need to put that in the minutes."

Gina somehow managed to recover her composure, and rewarded him with a look of undiluted admiration, as befitted a man of such authority, pushed to his limits.

"Davide, watch my lips," Andy said, low and measured. "How much do we owe to owners who have bought property here?"

Davide quivered as he eyed Jay's threatening look, but he was cornered. "Over a million Euros is owed."

"A million," said Andy, throwing down his pen, "so that explains why the Barkers are banging on my door like demented bailiffs."

"The Barkers are in a special situation," said Jay.

"Fuck all is special about having your home repossessed," said Andy, standing in fury. "Take fifteen, everyone, I need some fresh air."

While Jay was on the defensive in the board meeting, Geoff and Rosie Barker were on the offensive in an Internet café in the industrial town of Pontedera. They were huddled conspiratorially around a computer screen as they waited nervously to access their email account, unsure whether Gina would have fulfilled her promises and well aware of the damning financial implications of their helplessness if she had not. Rosie's hands trembled as she typed in her password with deliberate single-fingered jabs. The Barkers were infrequent computer users but after several unsuccessful attempts, Geoff suggested Rosie might need to be typing in lower case, or upper case, or whatever the other case was to the one she was currently in. Half an hour later, by a process of trial and error, Rosie somehow managed to enter the right sequence of letters.

The Barkers did not send many emails, so they did not receive many, other than junk mail. The mail they were looking for was sitting unopened in the top of their inbox, directly above the one offering Rosie discounted penis-enlargement cream. Rosie jerked the mouse like a joystick till, by as much luck as judgment, the cursor was where she wanted it, shrinking back as the link glowed blue. She looked at Geoff, who nodded, and she clicked the mail open, to find it blank. Their immediate reaction was that Gina had played some cruel joke. But after some thought, Geoff suggested that Rosie click on the paperclip on the mail.

Before them was a long list of email addresses. They scanned the list, recognising a few names. It was two hours later, and only after the help of the patient café owner that they managed to get the email addresses in the attachment into the address field of the email they wished to send. And it was another hour before they were happy with the mail they had composed, and felt ready to send it.

"You are sure we should be doing this, aren't you?" asked Rosie.

"It's now or never, dear."

Rosie girded her loins, moved the cursor to the send button, closed her eyes, and clicked on the mouse. A cyber second later, and a group of some sixty investors at Castello di Capadelli were to learn that they were invited to the first ever meeting of the "UK Capadelli Owners' Action Group."

Andy strode back into the room last, almost five minutes after even Jay resumed his seat. He smiled with confidence as he sat down, well aware that his anger had left the ghostlike men and women desperate to pacify him. He changed the point of attack to money wasting, highlighting every extravagance, of which there were many, and proceeding to impress the stupidity of every item of over-expenditure for the next half an hour.

As he began to deride the Armani toiletries, Jay interrupted him with a sigh.

"Andy, this item-by-item nit picking is a poor use of everyone's time. No one wants to waste money, and I as much as anyone want us to run lean and mean. But we need to focus on the bigger picture."

Andy raised himself up full of confidence and vindication as he launched his carefully formulated argument.

"Many of the costs you are incurring, Jay, are around intangibles. I am talking about things that do not impact the product that is delivered. Expenditure that does not affect the actual holiday experience on site. And isn't that the important thing?"

"No, Andy, it is not!" retorted Jay, all of a sudden passionate and vehement. "It's the intangibles that people value."

Andy threw a brochure across the table. "Look at that; you could print bank notes on paper that quality. All I can see is cost."

Jay heaved another heavy breath. "Andy, that is a very fancy watch you are wearing. A Hublex, I believe. The Timemaster model if I'm not mistaken. How much did you pay for that?"

"It was an anniversary present from Kate," said Andy, narrowing his gaze.

"Well, just so you know, last time I looked that particular model cost the same as a small family car. That is for a few ounces of pressed steel, weighing no more than one of the wheel nuts on your little hire car. And, by the way, the car comes with a clock too."

Andy did not welcome the digression, but felt obliged to defend his wife's generosity. "This watch has one of the finest Swiss movements. It is a masterpiece of craftsmanship."

"You read that on the box I suppose?" said Jay. "The fact is that you are wearing that watch because it makes you feel good, not because it keeps good time. *That* is intangible value. That is why we have freshly squeezed orange juice, why we have Egyptian cotton sheets, and why we have brochures made with parchment paper, not toilet paper. Because we are selling a luxury product, just like your Hublex. Surely you can see that?"

Andy's instincts conflicted as he stared down at the outrageously priced glistening steel on his wrist. On the one hand his decision to put Jay and his team on the spot had been vindicated; he now knew that Jay had been stringing him along for over a year, and that the operation was on a knife-edge. On the other hand perhaps they were about to turn the corner, as Jay was seeking to assure him. And for all his growing doubts about Jay's methods, and possibly motives, he recognised that Jay knew his stuff, and that he could sell. If anyone could get him out of the hole that Jay had put him in then, ironically, that man was Jay. But somehow he was going to have to reconcile Jay's practices with his own principles.

"Davide, I want a full financial picture on my desk in the morning, the numbers, or your next pay cheque will be your last. Apart from that, I think we've covered all we need to, unless there are any more questions?"

His eyes twinkled with morbid amusement as everyone looked down at their laps, far from keen to prolong the agony.

"There's transport outside to take everyone to lunch; Jay and I will catch up with you after we've gone through a few things," he announced.

"I will return to my duties, then," said Gina. "I do not want to impose more on the discussions of such busy and important people."

Andy put his hand on her arm, excited by the touch of her skin and encouraged by the submissive look in her eye. "You have earned your lunch like the rest of us, Gina. And I insist you join us." Gina smiled, emanating humility and gratitude, while not knowing whether she, Mancini, or Jay should be most pleased. She hurried out with the rest of the chastened gathering a few steps behind.

As she disappeared across the courtyard, Jay turned to Andy.

"You had no need to dress Davide down like that; he's only a book-keeper."

Andy twitched but stood firm. "I can only take so much smoke and mirrors. I want to know exactly where I stand in the morning. And if I don't get what I want…" His voiced trailed away.

Jay raised his hands in surrender. "The bottom line is like I said it. The sales coming through at the end of the month will see us right."

"And until the end of the month?"

Jay offered his open palms. "We won't be able to meet the payroll run without another cash injection. But from next month, we'll be accumulating cash. You can start taking out instead of putting in."

"How much of an injection?" asked Andy, bracing himself for bad news.

"A quarter of a million."

"For fucks sake, Jay," said Andy, throwing his head into his hands, "the business is supposed to keep me, not the other way round." He raised his head and met Jay's eyes. "Kate will go ape-shit."

"Then don't tell her," said Jay with comradely mischief. "I said I'd sell us out of this mess and that's what I'm doing. The Visconti sale alone will more than cover it."

"Forever the pragmatist, hey?"

"It's just business, Andy. You do what you have to do."

The last sentence hung ominously in the air, blackening the sky as Andy's spirits and expectations plummeted afresh.

"What does that mean exactly?" he asked. "I didn't sign up to defraud anyone."

"What it means is sailing close to the wind. I've got enough to contend with already with all the red tape these Italians keep winding me up in. For better or worse, we are in the timeshare world, and it isn't a kid glove business."

Andy pondered a while before responding, his mind dwelling on the human cost of Jay's pragmatism, on the tearful face of Rosie Barker. "So Jay, let me see if I understood why people might be upset. We sell apartments in paradise to overseas buyers at a hugely inflated price on the promise that they'll receive a generous guaranteed income, an income that knocks the socks off bank interest and more than covers any mortgage they take out. And our management company will take care of everything, so they don't need to worry about anything?"

"Yes Andy. The same deal you'll see in other major tourist developments. Like I said back in The Candle. It's totally legit."

"Except we have no intention of paying them a rental income. And we're going to do a runner as soon as our coffers are full, leaving everyone high and dry, with apartments they can't give away let alone sell."

"That Andy, is most certainly not what the intention was. And it is intent that is what is important. Everything was well intended, we've just run into difficulties. It happens all the time in business, as you well know. It's unfortunate, but it's not a scam and, frankly, I resent the suggestion that it might be."

"Then what *is* the future for the scheme now?"

"There isn't one. It will be closed down, and replaced with another that does not rely on tour operator contracts. The guaranteed rental scheme is, or rather was, essentially a marketing device to attract investors and make sales. It was not necessarily viable in its own right."

"In other words, a sort of 'buy to let' scam, then?"

"No, not a scam at all, as I said, everything was well intended."

"Come off it," snapped Andy. "You are not telling me the people buying this week are not being partly induced by a guaranteed rental scheme? It's trumpeted in all the literature. That is deception."

"First, none of us want to be in this situation. It has been forced upon us. Second, it is not deception. Yes, it may be manipulation; that I grant you, but manipulation is very different from deception."

"Help me understand that, in case I ever need to explain it to a man in a blue uniform."

"It is not semantics. Everyone in life is manipulating those around them all the time. Trying to get things done their way. You manipulate Kate and Kate manipulates you. Businesses and newspapers and governments are manipulating people en masse all the time. They just tell you that part of the story that they want you to know. They leave out the stuff that doesn't fit with their agenda. It's how things work. Some people are just better at it than others."

"Sorry, Jay, I'm not buying it. There is such a thing as integrity. Or at least I thought there was."

Jay mustered every ounce of sincerity within him, looking Andy squarely in the eye. "Maybe some of the people who bought here have been naïve. And whoever said gullibility was finite probably didn't sell timeshare. But it is not our job to protect people from their own naivety. Our job is to run a business and make a profit."

Andy nodded in silent resignation, his eyes gloomy with the thought of Kate's wrath. "Let's just make sure everything we do is legal; losing money is one thing, we don't want to lose our liberty."

Jay put his arm round Andy. "Come on, let's have some lunch. Unless my eyes were deceiving me, there's a young woman with hazel eyes and raven hair who will be mightily disappointed if you stand her up."

Thirty-one

Lucy kicked off her shoes and spread her long legs across the bench seat of the café at Gatwick's North terminal, and settled down to wait for Tessa to come through arrivals. She was soon lost in her own world, like any literary genius in the throes of creation, as her imagination ran wild and her thumbs worked feverishly to keep up with it.

"Caught you," said a familiar booming voice, as two hands slapped down on Lucy's shoulders, startling her and causing her to guiltily snap her phone shut over the graphic text she had just composed.

"About time too," she said with a smile, leisurely flipping her phone open again and reading over her masterpiece with satisfaction. "What do you think," she asked, offering the screen to Tessa for her literary critique, as her friend settled herself in the seat opposite.

"Very good, very good," said Tessa, marvelling at Lucy's inventiveness and her capacity to dangle and tease through cyberspace. "I really think you are beginning to get the idea of this guy thing and how it works."

"I suppose you mean that Jay thinks with his dick?"

Tess drew herself up on the seat to embark on her unique brand of moralising. "A standing cock has no conscience," she declared, "and you proved that by getting him to commit to going to the wedding, which you could never have done otherwise." The two middle-aged ladies on the neighbouring table tut tutted their disapproval before falling silent, eager it seemed to have their ears offended further by Tessa's vulgarity.

Lucy hated to dampen the look of victory on her friend's face but she could not pretend any more that all was going to plan. "But he's trying to back out of it, Tess. I'm in danger of being no better off than

176

before, except that in the process I have given him the shag of his life. So he wins again."

Tessa scowled and drew herself even higher. "Wrong! He only wins if you let him. Let's go over how it works one more time shall we?"

Lucy almost felt she should take notes at what was fast becoming a regular lecture. She settled instead for a look of attentiveness, one that she convinced herself was feigned but often proved all too real.

"Jay, like all bastards, will say anything he has to in order to get you to spread those thighs, or get you to swallow when you don't want to," Tessa continued.

Lucy suppressed a smile and said, "I know I don't have to Tess, but I like to swallow."

"Then, Lucy, you are an exception," she replied, her voice growing higher as she tried to understand how one woman could be so perfectly constructed to satisfy male desire. "And Jay is one lucky fucker. But what you need to understand is that you need to make everything a negotiation. Swallowing is a big thing and you need to take advantage of that. There's no way that Texan tart will still be doing it, if she ever did in the first place. She'll be spitting it into a Kleenex, and only then on his fucking birthday."

"Still, I think it may be a little late to make that aspect of our relationship negotiable," said Lucy, twisting a strand of hair around a slender finger as last week's lovemaking replayed itself behind her sparkling eyes.

"But it's the wider point I'm making that you need to get your head around, instead of mooning over what you've been getting your mouth around," continued Tessa, whose eyes were lit up by the chance to reiterate her principles.

"Jay has things that you want, and you have things that he wants. So what you did the other night was exactly right, and it worked. You held out giving him want he wanted, until he gave you what you wanted."

Lucy dug her nails into the arm of the chair in frustration. "And as I said, now he wants to back out. He can't leave Rusty over the weekend and he says that's that."

"Bullshit," said Tessa, pounding her fist into her palm, "we know the bastard spends half his weekends in Tuscany anyway, so his wife's needs on a Saturday afternoon are hardly his top priority, are they?"

"But if he won't come to the wedding then there's not really much I can do about it…"

Tessa shook her head vigorously, lashing her glossy ponytail like a whip. "The man has made a firm commitment, and you need to hold him to it. For fuck's sake, girl, it's damn near an issue of morality, and right is on your side. He's made a promise, and he needs to stick to, it's as simple as that."

Lucy rolled her eyes. "So I just tell him that, the morality bit, and he will realise that he's in the wrong, and it will all be sorted? Sorry, Tess, but I don't think so."

"True," she acknowledged, "telling an arsehole like Jay what he should or shouldn't do is completely useless. You have two weapons you should be reaching for and neither of them involve common sense — the carrot and the stick."

"The carrot and the stick?" Lucy echoed as she slumped back into the chair in preparation for a simile the length of a blockbuster.

"It works like this," Tessa began, "think of the carrot as Jay's dick." Lucy could have written a book on phallic metaphors — her text earlier proved that — and she sat even straighter as her colleague continued with considerable gusto.

"That's what you reached for the other night, and you got him to commit to being your escort at a wedding. Now all you need to do now is reach out those magic hands of yours for the stick."

"And what is my stick?" asked Lucy.

Her friend let out a hint of a snort. "Some things you need to figure out for yourself. I can only help; I can't tell you what you should be doing. But, if I were in your shoes, I'd be thinking about what it is that really scares Jay. Get him focused on consequences; the consequences if he doesn't honour his solemn commitment to take you to this fucking wedding."

She took a sip at her latte, studying Lucy across the rim of the glass and watching the wheels go round behind the soft emerald green eyes.

"You don't mean threatening to call Rusty, or something like that?" she asked in a hushed tone, fear of the very idea of such a conversation written bold across her features.

"Well, maybe tone that idea down just a notch or two, Luce," said

Tessa, everything in her body language promising an idea that she wouldn't share.

Lucy's patience with her friend was waning. "Listen, we can play twenty questions here or you can help me out. What are you thinking about?"

Tessa shrugged. "That has to be up to you. But I don't think we should be thinking about threatening anything, not least unless you are prepared to follow through on that threat if necessary. And if I recall last time we spoke on this, bringing things to a head with the Lizard was something you didn't want to do, right?"

"Not yet anyway."

"Ok, so think about something you could do that would put the fear of God into him. You've got a while to think about it anyway because you aren't seeing him for a couple of weeks now, are you?"

Lucy nodded. "He's tied up in Tuscany apart from next weekend, and he has to be home then, something to do with Rusty needing him to be at the kids' end of term sports day."

Tessa burst out laughing. "That's the shittiest excuse I've ever heard."

"Well," said Lucy, glad of the chance to take some of the initiative from her friend, "from what I gather, it seems like things are a bit different up in Cheshire from where I went to school in Croydon. I got the impression from Jay that the school sports day is something else. The mums all dress up and try to outdo one another. It's more competitive a day for the parents than it is for the kids. A big social get together."

Tessa imagined what a sports day at an exclusive private school must be like. The enclosure at Royal Ascot came to mind, except with spoilt brats running around instead of preened horses.

"Perfect, Lucy, just perfect!" Tessa shouted, making the women at the next table shake their heads and finally pick up their cups and leave. "The last place anyone would want to see his mistress, right? Just imagine it for a minute; a possible scene in front of the kids, all those stuck up parents just lapping it up, teachers in their frilly cotton dresses gossiping. And it's less than a week away as well."

"So you reckon I should threaten Jay that I'll turn up and make a scene at the sports day?"

"Better than that," said Tessa, knocking the menu off the table with a gesture of triumph. "You do turn up. But you don't tell Jay what you are planning. They don't hand out printed invitations to the kids' sports day, and there'll be no security or anything at the school gates. He'll be bricking himself from the moment he first sees you, which you need to make sure is when he is tied up with Rusty and her friends."

"And make a scene?" asked Lucy, looking apprehensive.

"No need for that. In fact it's almost better if you can arrange it so you don't give Jay a chance to talk to you. Once he's seen you, the job's done. Then get the hell out of there, which will leave Jay shitting himself for the rest of the day that you will return and show up in the egg and spoon race."

Lucy was warming to the idea. "Or the sack race, he's used to seeing me in that."

"You will need to look your best, like a proper tart; a see through blouse and legs showing right up to your arse. Just so you get noticed. Think about it —all those dads with their eyes out on sticks wanting to fuck you. And the mums trying to figure out whether you're bonking their husband or one of the six formers."

"He'll go ballistic," whispered Lucy in tentative glee.

"Yes, he will. And then he will go to the wedding. But that's not where the game ends; it's where it starts."

Thirty-two

The view from Maria's porch was the very picture of serenity, the gentle incline of the driveway falling away into olive groves and vineyards, stretching into the horizon like an ocean of green. Isobel felt a part of it as she enjoyed a light breakfast with Maria, the near-permanent tension in her body eased by the knowledge that Peter was three thousand miles away. The silence was only interrupted by her own gentle humming, an almost unconscious noise that seemed to throb from the very centre of her body, resonating happiness into the morning air.

"So all is well in the world this morning, despite the cat having taken your tongue?" Maria asked with a smirk, unable to restrain herself any longer.

Isobel looked up from her toast. "I'm sorry, I was miles away."

"I know where you were," said her friend with a smile, "now are you going to tell me what happened there?" She looked almost wicked in the morning sun, her eyes sparkling in anticipation of Isobel's fall from grace.

Isobel held back her laughter at Maria's transparency. "I'm sorry about not coming back here yesterday; it was very selfish of me. I hope you aren't too mad at me."

"Don't be silly, Isobel; it's not as if you left me in some bar while you made off with your catch for the evening. And if it helps your guilt, let me tell you that while you were with Jay, I was catching up on lost time with Angelo. So we both did ok." Even though Maria wasn't asking any questions her voice was laden with expectation and Isobel had only to lean back and wait for her patience to exhaust itself once more.

"Now come on, I want all the juicy bits," Maria burst out, bouncing on her chair in anticipation. "Nothing too graphic..." she added, grinning so widely her face threatened to tear in two, "unless you feel you must, of course."

Isobel kept her expression blank as she appeased her, giving a matter of fact account of the events of the day before; how she and Jay made love in the open, and then spent the rest of the evening and the night in his flat.

"And everything went ok?" asked Maria with a suggestive lifting of her eyebrows.

"Yes, I think so. For me, anyway. And I think for him too."

"So he is not just a charmer with a big smile and good looks, he also knows how to make a girl feel good in bed?"

Isobel frowned, hating how Maria turned everything beautiful into a cliché.

"Yes, he does," said Isobel, stiff and emphatic, as if Jay's sexual prowess was testament to her own discerning tastes, an area too sacred to mock.

Maria allowed herself a quiet smile of vindication. "So, it was once in the wood and then about twelve hours straight in his bedroom?" Isobel nodded, bracing herself for further questions. "So more than once in the bedroom then?"

"Yes, Maria, more than once." Her words came out as a series of sighs.

"So twice, three times, four times? Come on, Isobel, you've got to let me have some fun here too."

Isobel acknowledged her excitement with slight displeasure but indulged her nonetheless. "Three times, I think."

"And lots of different ways in the process?" Maria reached over and flicked her arm, the answers not coming fast enough for her voraciousness.

"A few different ways."

"What sort of different ways?" Her hand now grasped Isobel's arm, tightening with suspense.

Isobel opened her mouth to speak but somehow couldn't; she wanted the night to remain inviolate, untouched by Maria's interrogation.

"You know, different positions, that's all," she said, her words lacking conviction as she turned back to her toast.

"Oh please, stop being so coy, we are grown up girls. For all you are telling me you might as well be describing a night with Peter. And I know that deep down you are longing to tell me how it was different."

Maria's final words stirred Isobel and she steeled herself to reveal the details, happy in the belief that her initial reticence had established her as different from Maria, shown that they still sat at the breakfast table, an angel and devil in alliance. She took a deep breath and revealed everything, hesitant at first but then lost in the memory of it all.

"What was strange," she said, "was that in the wood he was so tender. As if it was my first time, which in a way it felt like it was. But then in the bedroom it was different. The things he did. The things he encouraged me to do. I did things I haven't done with Peter in ten years."

"And how did you feel about all that?" Maria asked, the words of a counsellor falling from her seductive mouth.

"I don't know, my mind is all mixed up about it. On the one hand I felt like I was being his whore, doing those things. And at the same time I knew I wanted to do them. He didn't make me. It felt like I wanted to try everything, do everything, all the things I've never done before, the things I've just read about." She was tentative and anxious, looking to Maria to pierce the dream with her claw-like nails.

"Wow, this is more like it," said Maria, leaning in closer. "Do tell more. And can you please be a bit more specific?"

Isobel twisted her fingers in her lap, wrenching them apart and forcing them together again and again. "Well, at one point he was running his tongue all around my belly button, and the next thing I knew I was pushing his head lower."

"So lots of oral?" Maria was almost salivating at the mouth as Isobel nodded, her face tinged a cherubic pink. "And not just one way of course?" Again Isobel nodded, the pink darkening to red.

"He likes me to do it on my knees, in front of him." She blushed deep scarlet. "And I've never done that before."

"On your knees?"

Isobel looked at her desperately, seeming simultaneously young and old as she shook her head.

"No?" exclaimed Maria. "Surely you must have at some time, for Peter, at least at first?"

Isobel shook her head again, and her eyes glazed over with memory, too distant and unreal now to be painful.

"On our honeymoon, we did a stopover in Bangkok. We went to the red light district, like everyone does, and we came across this sex show. I was curious, and persuaded Peter that we should give it a try, you know, just for a laugh. He was surprised, I think, it was so out of character for me. I was painfully shy in those days." She halted, unsure if she could continue.

"Go on," said Maria, rapt with fascination, and more than familiar with Bangkok sex shows.

"Well, it was everything you'd expect. Lots of ping pong balls flying through the air. And at one point an attractive Thai girl came and sat with us, and asked if it was ok if she had a drink with us. I was getting a bit uncomfortable because, well, she was paying me just as much attention as Peter. I suppose we'd both drunk too much wine by this time. She wore one of those kimono type dresses and it was slit up to her hip, and it was all quite erotic, to say nothing of what was happening on stage. After a while she asked if we wanted to go to a side room with her. She rubbed my thigh as she said it, but she was looking at Peter. We refused of course," she said, wistfully. "Peter just gave her a few baht and we got up and left." Maria nodded, afraid to break the trance of recollection.

"But when we got back to the hotel we were both still excited and we made love, and at one point he tried to put it in my mouth, to force it almost. But I just couldn't. It had already been inside me and, I don't know, it was just the thought of how unhygienic it was." Isobel's eyes came back into focus. "And he's never asked me since."

"And you've never just done it, without him asking? In all your years of marriage?" There was undisguised incredulity in Maria's voice. Again Isobel shook her now bowed head.

"But you wanted to do it with Jay?"

"Yes, I wanted to. Even if he hadn't encouraged me to, I know I would have. I can't explain why and why not with Peter. It's just that I wanted to with Jay."

The revelation brought them to silence, but Maria's appetite for disclosure was yet to be sated and she refilled Isobel's cup before continuing.

"So Jay didn't try to make you do anything you didn't want to do? Something even more sinful than oral?"

"I have absolutely no idea what you might have in mind," said Isobel, pausing to sip her tea, "but no." She spoke with a touch of defiance in her voice, as if it was Jay's reputation as a gentleman that was at stake, let alone her own morality. Maria remained silent as Isobel fell back into her memories, hypocrisy taunting her as she remembered his hand straying behind her, seeking to explore her, even as she pushed it away. It was almost apologetically that she continued with her revelations. "Well, there was something he did ask. It was early this morning, just before we got up. We were just lying there, naked in bed talking, and he was idly stroking me, you know where. And he asked if I had ever been completely shaved."

"You mean a Hollywood?"

"If that's the term," she said primly. "Anyway, I said no. I mean I have the occasional bikini waxes, but nothing more. It's not like I've got Sherwood Forest or something down there."

"And he asked you to have one?"

"No, not really. He just said I might find it quite erotic, being completely shaven." Maria's brows contracted and she became still.

"So you are going to have it done then? Like some lap dancer?" she asked. Her condescension was cruel rather than concerned. She seemed to be enjoying the discomfort she was causing her often prudish friend, as if pulling the legs off a spider.

"No, I certainly am not," she replied, her voice strong with indignation. "Apart from anything else, Peter might notice. How would I explain that?"

"You could tell him it's been itching down there. Which it seems it has been," Maria said, her eyes mischievous. "But the interesting thing is why he asked you…"

"Because he prefers it that way, I suppose." Isobel's forehead creased in confusion; Maria was an enigma as soon as she became indirect, and it worried her exceedingly.

"Well, that's hardly surprising," said Maria, throwing her head back in laughter, "given all the oral that's going on." Isobel's face returned to its earlier redness. "I'm just having fun because you are making me jealous," said Maria, with a comforting caress to her friend's arm, before her look became serious. "But maybe it's also about power and control. You said he likes you on your knees?"

"Only one time, in the bathroom," stammered Isobel, feeling the need to jump to her lover's defence, and to preserve her own pride, as she saw the image conjured behind Maria's eyes.

"Have you thought that perhaps he wants to establish that he's the dominant partner?" Maria asked, now visibly inflamed by the intrigue of it all. "That he wants to find a boundary that you don't want to cross, and then to see if you do cross that boundary, just to please him?"

Isobel shrank from her imagination. "Well, if so, I'm afraid he's going to be disappointed. He will just have to come up with a different boundary."

"Although he already exhausted quite a few yesterday," said Maria.

"Remind me never to tell you anything ever again," Isobel laughed, now feeling light and free, as if her disclosures had relieved her guilt.

Exorcised of her desire for titillation, Maria now lapsed into contemplation. "What's wrong?" asked Isobel.

"I'm just wondering about what else Jay might want," said Maria. "In between the steamy passion does he ever talk about the apartment, or this proposal Peter is looking at, or anything, well, pecuniary?"

"He hasn't asked me to pay for his services if that's what you mean," said Isobel with a dismissive laugh. But then she thought for a while before adding, "Yes, I suppose he does bring those sorts of things up. But in an oblique way. He never asks me outright what we plan to do, or tells me what he thinks we, Peter and me, I mean, should or shouldn't do. He just probes about how I'm feeling about things."

"Do you think perhaps that is all deliberate?" asked Maria. "That he works on appealing to your emotions, not to your logical reasoning?"

"You're over analysing things," Isobel snapped, rising from the table to take her plate inside.

"So when are you next seeing him?" Maria called after her as she disappeared inside.

"I said I'd call him this morning," Isobel answered as she reappeared. "He did ask if I wanted to take a few days to think about it, to make sure I could handle things. So we didn't arrange anything there and then. But with Peter away and everything—"

"And do you want to see him again, now you've had time to think?" asked Maria, keen to show her support.

Isobel hesitated, and then spoke, her voice heavy with realisation. "I do want to see him again."

"But he didn't actually suggest anything, even though he knows you're kicking your heels in Lucca, and that Peter is on the other side of the world? And he didn't even take responsibility for the next step, calling you I mean, so there's a chance that he doesn't really want there to be a next time."

Isobel knew Maria didn't mean to be cruel; she simply spoke and thought in unison.

Isobel sought assurance in the memory of their lovemaking, in the urgency with which Jay had wanted her, how he had taken her with an intensity she could never remember from Peter. "I know he wants me," she said, bowing her head, unable to explain more. But for the first time since her lovemaking in his flat Isobel felt the knots of anxiety return to her stomach, tighter and more threatening than before.

Thirty-three

Lucy had to raise her hand to shield her eyes from the blinding midday sun as she entered through the imposing iron gates of the school. She struggled to contain her nerves as she followed the signs directing parents to the sports fields behind the main school building. The very atmosphere of this bastion of privilege compromised her normal cool indifference, with its sports fields seeming to stretch endlessly into the distance as they merged with the vast, open countryside. Yet she was here to be noticed and she drew confidence from the beautiful weather; the scorching heat facilitating an outfit that made her look capable of bringing a blind monk to orgasm. Her legs were smooth, bare and bronzed, her feet encased in four-inch heels. She had paired a tiny, skin-tight and high-waisted black skirt with a loose white blouse which, when allowed to rest against her skin, clearly revealed through its almost sheer fabric the shape and colour of her fulsome pink nipples, hidden from the public only by the folds of a soft leather jacket which, when she chose to let it fall open, made the need for imagination redundant.

She practised her strut as she passed the last of the mock Gothic school buildings, and made her way on down a tree-lined path. The dappled, shady cover of the oaks allowed her to survey the area before her nubile presence shattered the genteel setting of the privileged at play. The verdant field, perfectly mown into undulating strips, was surrounded with pure white marquees adorned with colourful bunting, each housing a variety of foods and beverages. Above these tents rose two gently sloping banks, each melting into the running track as it reached the ground. Both sides were populated with couples, families or groups of kids in summer uniforms, sat on blankets with picnics spread out around them. The very top of the bank, the prime viewing position, was lined by a row of vehicles, mainly estate cars, people carriers, or brash four-wheel drive executive saloons, and in front of each the owners had erected what seemed might almost be permanent structures. Folding tables and chairs, marquee style canopies, and even the occasional barbecue were in evidence.

Lucy had no difficulty guessing where Jay would be and ran her eye along the row, her gaze coming to rest on the largest and most centrally located marquee. If Jay had been privy to his own family crest, she thought, it would surely have been flying from a flag above the tent. She could not see Jay himself but his familiar black Range Rover with its darkly tinted windows was parked alongside. The last time she had seen that vehicle was close up, very close up, her nose pressed against the bonnet while Jay took her from behind.

The thought of that encounter, the urgent passion, the trembling simultaneous orgasms, instilled confidence in her and she took her place in the line for Pimms; she was now breathing more easily and relishing the attention she was receiving. Boys were openly ogling her while their fathers tried their best to disguise their blatant interest. She did not need to wait in line for long. Within two minutes a short, grey-haired man with a kindly face stopped beside her as he returned from the front of the queue.

"I assume you are in need of one of these?" The man was beaming up at Lucy like a cocker spaniel puppy, offering her a glass with an umbrella sticking out.

She accepted with a gracious "thank you," and turned and walked alongside her admirer to the outside of the tent, sipping her drink as she went.

"I'm Roy, by the way. And you must be one of the pre-school mums?"

"No, I'm Lucy. And I'm not a mum. I'm here looking for a husband. Somebody else's husband actually."

The man laughed. "You've come to the right place then, because an awful lot of husbands here will be looking for a girl like you."

"Why thank you, Roy," she said, with a bashful flutter of her eyelids, "but I am looking for one particular husband."

"So that rules me out then?" he asked, a rueful look in his eyes.

"Are you available?"

"I can be. In fact I have just decided to make myself available."

Roy looked her directly in the eye, or as directly as someone can from five inches below.

Lucy pouted as she sipped on her straw. "So who do I have to worry about scratching my eyes out?" she asked.

"About half the women here, I should think," he said with a grin, "but not by my wife, she's over there with her boyfriend." He gestured towards a short but well-formed woman with a sharp face and regimented posture who had a bouffant-haired man half her age beside her, absentmindedly playing with her hair.

"And you are ok with that? In front of everyone here?"

Roy shrugged. "No choice really. Either put up with it or miss the kids' sports day."

Lucy gave his upper arm a reassuring caress, stirred by the injustice inflicted on her new-found beau. "Maybe you should introduce me. Give *her* something to worry about," said Lucy with a mischievous giggle.

Roy had the disbelieving look of a man unexpectedly asked if it would be all right if he were upgraded to first class on a flight to New Zealand; he was for a moment dumbstruck. Another caress to the shoulder speeded his recovery. "That might be fun. Come this way, Lucy, if you don't mind that is." He held out a crooked arm and Lucy slipped her own through it, in the way she might have done had they been walking back down the aisle.

Roy's wife and her pre-pubescent looking boyfriend were now huddled together in conversation, their body language indicating that they did not wish to be disturbed. "Excuse me, you two love birds. You don't mind if I just say hello do you?" asked Roy, with a smile as wide as the running track. His wife looked awestruck at the sight of Lucy, statuesque and adoring on the arm of her diminutive and pot-bellied husband; her mouth opened and closed like a goldfish as she struggled to compose herself.

"I don't think you have met Lucy, have you? Lucy, this is Helen and, um, Greg."

"Graham."

"Sorry, Helen, of course, Graham. I'm afraid I've already sipped a few of these," said Roy merrily, taking a sip from his glass.

"Roy has told me so much about you; it's a pleasure to finally meet you. I hope I am not intruding or anything," said Lucy, as she slid her hand over Roy's shoulder and stroked his chest.

"No, no, not at all," stammered Helen, turning to Graham with the imploring look of someone seeking explanation or inspiration.

Lucy turned to Roy, gave him her most submissive of looks, adjusted his collar and ran her fingers through his hair. Graham asked the question that Helen seemed currently incapable of verbalizing. "So how long have you and Roy known each other?"

"Quite a while now, I expect you remember the date better than I do, Roy."

"September, darling, early September."

"But, but that's since before—" stuttered his wife, her body now limp and her mood deflated.

"Before I learnt about you and Greg, you mean? Don't be silly, I heard about that months before you told me. I thought you knew that?"

While Roy was having fun, Lucy was under close observation from the hill above, her every move being followed by two men with binoculars.

"You are not going to believe what I am looking at, Doug," exclaimed the first as he focused in on Lucy's breasts. "Roy Chambers, the sly old bastard, has got the hottest tottie you've ever seen at sports day hanging on his sleeve. Legs that go up to her armpits and jugs to knock your eyes out."

"No way," replied the second, grabbing the binoculars from his companion's outstretched hands, "you are having us on. Roy Chambers is about ready for his free bus pass." He peered intently into the binoculars and scanned the field as his friend continued, "I'm telling you. She's a complete stunner and she's more draped than a friggin' curtain over Roy, in front of his ex and her toy-boy. There's no way Roy pulled that, she's got to be on a meter."

"Yeah, wait, got her!" interrupted Doug as he finally managed to locate the pair, "Whoa, you weren't lying!"

"Give me those glasses," said another man, appearing from the depths of the marquee to join them. "If this is a wind up, the next bottle of bubbly is on you." He took the glasses and scanned the crowd.

"To the left of the drinks marquee, Jay, you can't miss them," said Doug, itching to get the binoculars back.

At first Jay could not believe his eyes. The sunglasses offered some disguise but you would be hard pressed to find another pair of legs like those in a Miss World contest; it could only be Lucy.

"I'm going to need these for a while," he said, knocking away the eager hand of his companion and striding off along the embankment to where his wife was sitting with some friends.

Meanwhile, Lucy was gazing into her compact mirror, causing its mirrored diamante to reflect the sun right into the binoculars that she could see fixed upon her from the cusp of the hill. She carefully tucked some stray tendrils of hair behind her rhinestone bejewelled ear before being interrupted by the ringing of her phone.

"Excuse me while I take this, babes," she said to Roy as she retrieved the phone from her clutch bag before looking at the name on the screen and jabbing her finger into the red decline button. She glanced up to see the binoculars had disappeared from the hilltop.

She turned to Helen. "Just my agent. I've told him not to call me at weekends. You know how it is." The older woman nodded, her face full of confusion. She turned to her boyfriend for reassurance only to find his gaze fixed on Lucy's jacket, which was mercilessly falling open in tandem to the man's mouth, as she bent over Roy to whisper in his ear.

"Now, honey-bun, how about you show me around. I'm sure we don't want to overstay our welcome," said Lucy, all but licking his ear with her tongue. And with that she intertwined her fingers with his and led him off, leaving Helen silent and bewildered.

They wandered around the field and then set course for the embankment as Roy struggled to contain his delight. "Things are never going to be the same for me again at this school, Lucy," he told her, his voice low and excited. "I don't think I will have any more trouble getting an appointment with the headmaster, not if he thinks you might be joining me."

"You are such a sweetie," said Lucy, putting her arm around his waist and pulling him closer as they ascended the slope towards Jay, who had just come into view. He was hovering near Rusty, looking right and left, his fingers tearing at his scalp.

Lucy and Roy strolled along with all the care of lovers on a riverbank and came to a halt half a dozen paces in front of the area that Rusty had meticulously staked out as the private space for her party. The two were standing directly in front of the semi-circle of chairs ostentatiously occupied by Rusty and her friends and blocking their view of the track. It could surely only be moments before the uppity Texan rose to assert her territorial rights.

Lucy bent forwards to whisper into Roy's ear, her skirt rising to reveal the curved lines of her derriere. "If you feel the need to touch my arse, babe, that is perfectly ok," she said, her breath hot and inviting in his ear. "I think you will find it a lot more solid than Helen's. And we don't want to disappoint the audience behind us, do we?"

Roy's hand tentatively brushed the curve of Lucy's back as she willed it lower; to her delight he continued downward, seeming to want to savour every inch of the journey until it came to rest on a cheek as round and firm as an oversized snooker ball. "Now squeeze!" she mouthed, as Jay, his armpits drenched with the cold sweat of fear and sounding considerably more high-pitched than normal, broke the stunned silence behind them with a frantic announcement.

"I'm going for ice creams. Anyone want ice creams? Rusty, can I get you anything from the ice cream van?"

"We have chocolate ices in the cool box, honey," came the reply in a lazy Dixieland drawl. Lucy was desperate to turn around and at long last match a face to the voice that left such formal and unemotional answer phone messages but she resisted — she was causing just enough trouble already.

"Well, I fancy an ice cream," said Jay's voice again, "and I think the boys do too. You coming, Rusty?"

"You go ahead, honey, the next race is about to start."

While Jay was distracting Rusty, Lucy turned and glanced towards him. She felt that she saw a plea for mercy in his eyes and held his look for the briefest of moments before gently pulling at Roy's arm and starting to move away. Rusty's two boys were making a dash for the ice cream van and she very deliberately walked between them and Jay, daring him to follow her with the hypnotising sway of her hips. She thought she heard the word "slut" being exclaimed with a harsh Texan twang and turned round to return the compliment. But Jay's face was pale as a shroud, so full of panic and despair that compassion dissuaded her, and she returned to her previous path — faster and more purposefully than before. She promenaded along the top of the embankment, the slight breeze pushing her blouse into her flesh and revealing the outline of her breasts, turning every head that she walked past. She joined the queue for the ice cream van and gently tapped the shoulders of the twin boys in front of her. As they gazed up at her she turned her head slightly, just enough to see Rusty rise angrily from her seat and Jay start forward in alarm, his phone to his ear. She surprised herself with her own composure, and playfully patted one of the boys on the head before proceeding to pay for their ice creams, bending over to bestow them to willing hands as she created an almost pornographic silhouette against the deep blue sky, her phone vibrating in her hand.

Lucy was at the school gate working her tongue around the last of an ice cream cone when the Range Rover with the personal number plate and blacked out windows screeched to a halt beside her. The passenger door opened and she climbed up onto the running board and pulled herself in as the powerful machine accelerated away, forcing the door to slam shut dangerously close to her ankle. She glanced across at Jay and saw a man fighting a battle with himself, breathing deeply, his mouth a hard, thin line that clamped the air like a vice. He pulled into the first side road and slammed on the brakes.

"Lucy, great as it is to see you," he said, measuring his words, "why the hell are you here?"

"To see you, of course," she replied with a wide smile, reciting her lines like an actress.

"Well, here I am," he said, his eyes boring into her until she had no choice but to close her cupid's lips over her dazzling white teeth.

"I haven't heard from you for over a week," she said, her tone now sharp and unforgiving, her fingers lightly on the door handle in silent threat.

"And you haven't called me for over a week," he replied by way of apology, lowering his gaze in submission.

"I called you a few hours after you last stuck your cock in my mouth," she said, ignoring his humility, "you were going to call me back, about the wedding, remember? It's only a week away now. So I've come here to make sure that you are still coming." It was a well-rehearsed summing up of the situation, an ultimatum that threatened all-out war should it be spurned.

"For Christ's sake, Lucy, of course I am still coming. What do you take me for? I said I was coming and I am coming. I've already bought the flight tickets."

She widened her eyes in shock and lowered her voice yet further. "So why haven't I heard anything from you?"

"Because I am dealing with a major crisis over in Tuscany right now," he said in exasperation, "and you know I never want to bother you with my business problems. But I have hardly had a minute to draw breath this last week. That's all."

She faltered and played with her fingers, everything she'd imagined assaulted and cowed by the truth. "So, so, you weren't just ignoring me, hoping that I would get someone else to take me to the wedding?"

He reached out for her hands. "Lucy, that is the last thing in the world I would want. I'm looking forward to the wedding. It will be a great weekend. I've even bought a new suit for the occasion."

"And you've already bought the flight tickets?" she asked, it all seeming too good to be true.

"Yes, I have, we are flying from Gatwick on Friday. I thought maybe we could meet up in London Thursday night. You always said you wanted to stay at the Savoy, so I have booked us a nice room there. It's a suite overlooking the Thames." He lowered his head and looked down at his lap, saying quietly, "But it was all meant to be a surprise."

The anger and fight was seeping out of Lucy and she glanced upwards, her heavily made up eyes brimming with tears. This all seemed so unlikely but she could not argue with cold, hard facts. He was telling the truth and she had done a terrible thing in doubting him, perhaps ruining everything forever.

He glanced at her tears and gave her thigh a squeeze. "Lucy," he said, his eyes full of compassion, "I need to get back. Rusty thinks I just popped out to get more bubbly. Can I drop you somewhere? The railway station?"

"Roy is expecting me back. I said I was just going to powder my nose."

He gave a hollow laugh. "You can't go back to the school. You've damn near caused a riot already. You came here to see me and sort things out and you've done that now."

"And you won't change your mind about Tuscany?"

"It's all arranged, Lucy. I promise you."

"And when we are in Tuscany, I want to talk about you and me, and our future together. I want us to talk about everything. I'm not going to put up with things going back to the way they were before. I am not getting any younger, and I do want to have children." She looked Jay directly in the eye. "Our children."

His facial expression stayed fixed and unreadable. "I understand all that, I absolutely do. And just because of Rusty and the boys doesn't mean I don't have similar thoughts. About you and me and everything." He took her hand. "I only want what's best for you. Up to now the time hasn't seemed right to talk about the future. But I was thinking that next weekend could be the right time. But right now I need to get back, or there might not be any next weekend."

Lucy smiled with a mixture of relief and guilt, leaning across and putting her arms around his neck and holding him tightly, like a lost child reunited with its mother.

"I'm sorry, Jay, I didn't mean to doubt you. It's just that I haven't known what to think these last few weeks. I was feeling almost like you didn't want me around. And then this last week, with you not calling or anything. I couldn't bear the thought of not seeing you anymore. Please don't think badly of me. I didn't want to cause you any trouble. I would never have spoken to Rusty today, you know that. It was just that I had these horrible feelings and I so needed to see you." Her voice was pleading, her head buried into his neck in supplication, her hand grabbing at his crotch in a desperate reminder of her value to him.

"Let me drop you at the station," he suggested again. "I will call you when you are on the train."

Lucy took a deep intake of breath in an effort to compose herself. "Not straight away. I have come all this way. Please. Can we go somewhere quiet for a while?"

She embraced him again, her hand now playing with the waistband of his trousers.

"I do need to get back," he repeated, but this time with less certainty.

"Only for a little while," she said, squeezing him gently and pressing her breasts into his solid chest whilst fumbling with his zipper. Her hand found its quarry. "I'm not letting you go back to Rusty with that."

Thirty-four

Isobel's thoughts went back to the previous day, how she and Jay ran through the great broad streets and winding alleys of Siena, skipping over the cobblestones like the wind itself, squealing and laughing, going so fast it seemed as if they would never fall, would never stop. They had arrived for dinner panting and wheezing as they fell against the vine-clad wall, rapidly breathing in each other with the air.

Her stomach squirmed with pleasure at the memory, at Jay's wonderful abandon, at his free-spirit that contrasted so terribly with Peter's slow and upright life, so bound by rules and convention.

It was nearly seven and impatience ate away at Isobel like a monster, as she lay luxuriating in the middle of the vast white bed. Jay should have finished at six but was still at the office; he had been there since nine and she could not understand, nor bear, the length of his absence, which seemed so unnecessary if Castello di Capadelli was the smooth running engine he assured her it was.

She pushed her naked limbs into the folds of the sheets, feeling clean and new in the whiteness. She flipped over in restlessness and pressed her face in the pillow and imagined herself blindfolded, his hands running up her smooth, lean thighs. She cast her eyes to the ceiling, quivering in excitement, and buried her face deeper into the fabric, brilliantly and awfully aware of an aching within her, a deep, physical yearning, as she imagined it was Jay's hands and not her own that were exploring her.

Isobel leapt from the bed. She could not bear to wait for him a second longer and the urges that coursed through her veins were suddenly stronger than the need for discretion. She resolved to go to his office; ignoring all their plans and ruses of secrecy, she threw away safety for pleasure.

It was all she could do to stop her hands from shaking as she slid open the lowest drawer of the dresser, revealing a kaleidoscope selection of lingerie, almost entirely purchased in the last month; mesh, lace and silk piled like glimmering fish scales in the darkness of the mahogany.

She held a pair of sheer white stockings to the light and they hung like icicles in its glow. It was ten years since she had worn suspenders, an ill-fated fancy dress choice that had brought a gently disappointed reprimand from Peter, and months of teasing. She pulled them on now with pleasure, imagining Jay's thumbs dragging them to her ankles, his teeth pulling at her, his body crushing her to the wall. A matching pair of skimpy briefs and transparent bra completed her ensemble. She could have been a bride in all her snowiness, and, as she pulled on a short white mackintosh that barely covered the top of her thighs, she imagined them married, Peter banished forever as a ghost of the insignificant past.

Even in Isobel's fantasies, the outfit was not suitable for the street and she dropped the coat to the floor and pulled on a pencil skirt, throwing off the bra and pulling on a pale, silky blouse in its place. She turned and admired her own derriere, running her hands over it as Jay so often did, firm and full and round, and she smiled as she thought about how he was fascinated with it, always touching it and complimenting her on it. More than satisfied, she donned the Mac once more and headed for the courtyard, her head going lower as she reached open air, in sudden realisation of her foolishness.

She was forced to hide behind a barrel as Gina passed with a trio of guests, her heart beating against her chest in terrified excitement at the very idea of being seen. She almost sprinted up the stone stairs to Jay's office as adrenaline propelled her forwards, each step revealing a strip of silk-clad flesh beneath her coat. The air electrified her skin and she threw open his door without knocking, streaming in like some pale, voluptuous demon.

A few seconds of silence followed as the two stood within touching distance in front of Jay's desk. "I couldn't wait," Isobel said, by way of brazen invitation.

"And I'm almost done," said Jay, picking up his pen as if to continue.

"You're done," she said, with a tone that dared him to dispute it, and she took the pen from his fingers and put it to her lips, circling the tip of her tongue around it.

She shut the door with her heel and pushed him to the wall on his swivel chair, her eyes full of the hunger she felt for him.

He watched in excitement as she rested her palms on the desk and spread her legs, leaning back to show him everything. Jay hesitated, though his loins ached with excitement. He was, after all, in his office, and the hamlet was by no means deserted. Eamon, if not Davide, was still around somewhere.

But Isobel's head was now back, her hair hanging clear of her shoulders. He looked at what was before him; the tight skirt pinstriped, almost business-like, against her thighs, the blouse hung from her hard nipples like cascading water. Sensing some hesitation, Isobel brought her knee up, her skirt riding north with it, revealing the decidedly un-business-like delights beneath. She closed her eyes, and moved her hand across her chest, undoing the top button of her blouse as she did so and continuing, in one uninterrupted movement, until her hand was lost inside the silk. She held her left breast, her fingers tensing and easing again and again until finding her nipple and pinching it hard; she let out a muffled sound as pleasure and pain ran through her, before she brought her head forward and opened her eyes to look fully into Jay's.

He skated forward, still on his swivel chair, his hands reaching to the hem of her skirt, and he inched his palms up the back of her thighs, the movement alone sending bolts of sensation through her body. He pushed her skirt up onto her hips, his wrists trapped in its tightness as he breathed into the silk of her panties, his hot breath against her wetness making her murmur with delight and anticipation.

She pushed him away, loving the thrill of denying herself.

"You better make sure we can't be disturbed," she said coolly, stepping back from the desk to watch him. He moved to the door and turned the key, then went to the venetian blinds, which shuttered closed, blocking them from the outside world.

"Ok if I leave the light on?" he asked without caring for any answer; she did not reply, as it was of no consequence to her.

By the time Jay turned from the window, she had left the desk, discarded the blouse, and was slouched across the dark leather sofa, one knee flung across the heavy studded armrest.

"Will this go on my appraisal, sir?" she asked.

Jay advanced stealthily as a hungry lion across the office, loosening his tie as he went. "Give me your wrists, Miss Roberts," he commanded, now stretching the tie wound around his fists.

She offered her wrists. "You won't hurt me, will you, sir?"

"No promises, Miss Roberts, no promises," he replied as he bound her hands together, her flesh fluttering under his touch.

Thirty-five

As Isobel meandered past the tall fir trees that lined the drive, shading her eyes from the spears of sunlight in their branches, Gina bounced out of reception, bursting into conversation before Isobel had a chance to say hello.

"Perhaps you would like to go riding again today, Isobel?"

The two women were fast becoming friends, bonding over their shared love of the outdoors, of riding, and of art.

"I think it will be much too warm for that," said Isobel, already feeling a trickle of perspiration on her spine; the temperature was already touching thirty and it was only a few minutes after ten.

"But much pleasure is to be had in the woods, no? One does not only have fun in the saddle."

Isobel looked at the girl, wondering if she detected some innuendo in her question, but dismissed it immediately as a clumsy translation.

"I think not, Gina," she said apologetically, "a cool drink and a good book by the pool feels more like it today."

"Then I will walk with you to the courtyard," said the younger woman, looping her arm through Isobel's in happy familiarity. "You may have something in the enoteca; they will still be serving breakfast, and we have many visitors here. So you will not be short of company, if you wish it, that is."

Gina was almost skipping along in her joy at her friendship with such a refined and elegant guest as Isobel — and someone who it seemed was so important too, given the attention that she merited from all the staff, and of course from Mr. Brooke himself.

"I was wondering if you have somewhere I could change into my costume later?" asked Isobel. "An empty room perhaps?"

"But Isobel, no one at Capadelli today is more important than you," said Gina, pulling her closer and dropping her voice to a whisper, "except perhaps the handsome Mr. Brooke." She giggled like a schoolgirl before continuing. "I will have housekeeping prepare a suite for you in the Villa; you may change, and rest there too, at your leisure. I will ensure everything you might need is available for you."

Isobel took a seat outside the enoteca, and, despite the heat, ordered an English breakfast tea. She took out her book and sat back, watching the world go by and hoping that Jay would come with it. Even in her loneliness she could not ever remember such happiness, such expectation. Her husband was on the other side of the planet and her lover was somewhere close by. She was so content that she resolved not to distract Jay from his duties; she would spend the day independently, in his midst but not in his way. She could enjoy herself perfectly well without his presence. And yet her eyes came up from her book at the sound of each approaching voice, and her head turned at every crackle of footsteps on the gravel behind.

As she drained the last of the tea, Gina reappeared, dancing towards her and looking very pleased with herself.

"It will be busy around the pool today, Isobel. Already I see many people putting out the towels."

"The Germans?" said Isobel, smiling.

Gina laughed, "Yes, the Germans of course, but also the English, because today is very hot and they wish to be very red. So I have reserved you a place, everything is set out for you; you have a nice quiet spot with your own parasol. You may come and go as you wish from it."

Isobel smiled and thanked her, watching her running off across the courtyard with perplexed affection. Gina's mood seemed to echo her own and Isobel mused with delight that she might be in love too. A stray black cat that fed off the kitchen scraps settled at her feet, and she luxuriated in the feel of its coat as it rubbed against her ankles, and she leant down to stroke it, running her fingers through the fur, a now familiar restless ache stirring within her.

She shook herself out of her thoughts and tucked away her novel in preparation for her poolside paradise, but as she looked about for a waiter her eye again caught the elderly couple sitting two tables away that, she noticed, were throwing regular glances in her direction, as if summoning up the courage to approach her. She saw a sadness about them that embarrassed her, as if her own happiness must somehow aggravate whatever plight had befallen the sorrowful pair.

"It's a beautiful morning, isn't it," she called over, giving them her most encouraging smile, and dropping some coins on a saucer as she rose to leave. But the lady lifted her cup and made her way across, now smiling, with her partner gathering up their bits and pieces to join her.

They introduced themselves as Rosie and Geoff Barker, a retired couple from Derby.

"We were wondering if you were British," said Rosie, a tiny woman with a pink lined face and glum brown eyes, "because we heard you ordering in Italian, but noticed your novel is in English."

The couple seemed anxious to establish Isobel's credentials, whether she was a visitor, an owner, or connected to the developers. Her delicate answers seemed to reassure them, and they moved onto the business at hand.

"We want to arrange a meeting amongst all the owners," said Geoff, who had the kind face of a tippler, with a bloated nose and cracked veins, "to discuss the situation."

"What situation?" said Isobel, perturbed by their earnest looks and conspiratorial manner and feeling the pull of the pool with increasing intensity.

"Well, we can't be sure of anything," said Rosie, "you never can be in this place, and people only tell you what they want you to hear. But what we do know is we are owed some money, and we think there might be other people in our situation."

"Oh," said Isobel, already feeling some disloyalty to Jay for even listening to such tittle-tattle. "I'm sure it must be a misunderstanding."

"But we are so worried," said Rosie, "we have put all our savings into buying our dream holiday home, and we've taken a mortgage on our cottage in England."

This was all too much for Isobel, for whom the concept of a budget was an alien one. She decided she had indulged the old couple enough.

"I'm afraid I must dash," she said, scribbling a note on a piece of paper. "My email address is here; perhaps you can send me details of the meeting when you have arranged it?"

As Isobel lounged by the pool, applying a further layer of sunscreen, something about the ambience was puzzling her. She had noticed it before though thought nothing of it, but now as she looked around at the groups of people, they all seemed to be huddled in the same guarded way, as if sharing dark secrets and fearing being overheard. She dwelt again on the hapless Barkers. A naïve but harmless old couple who had bought a home in Italy, and now found they could not afford it. They were not the first, and would not be the last, she thought with a sigh. Nevertheless, she decided she would talk about it to Jay; maybe he could help in some way. But still she saw no sign of him. She debated going inside; the anxious faces round the pool made her nervous. She had felt them watching her ever since she'd arrived and she sensed that it was not her appearance that attracted them, but rather her position; a mysterious lone woman who seemed to command the deference of every employee who passed her way.

But the midday sun was merciless and she could not resist the subtle sheen of the water. She dived in and swam the length of the pool underwater, exhilarated by how it cleansed the heat from her body. She broke the surface like a salmon, throwing her shining body from the water and pulling her wet hair into a ponytail. But as she did so she was struck by horror, where was her wedding ring? She dropped down in panic, searching the area around her feet, but seeing only water and tiles. She surfaced, a thousand thoughts flashing through her mind. How could she possibly explain it to Peter? He would surely think she had removed it in the act of betrayal. She filled her lungs and dived, working back along the bottom, her hands desperately sweeping left and right. Just as she felt her insides would burst, a finger brushed metal, and she surfaced with the ring in the palm of her hand.

She filled her lungs, the relief overwhelming. But as she stood looking at the gold band she hesitated. What if she did not put the ring back on? What if she never put it on again? She closed her eyes and nibbled her lip. What if she never went back to Cobham, to her life of emptiness? Who would really miss her? Peter could devote his energies with more vigour to his work, and her fickle and superficial friends could entertain themselves with gossip about the lady of the manor who fled to Tuscany for the pleasures of the flesh. And she would be sad for Peter, but she would be living her own life, for herself, for the first time.

When she pulled herself from her self-indulgence and opened her eyes, her ring still poised at the nail of her wedding finger, she looked up to the terracing above the pool. Her eyes met Jay's, and she knew he was watching her, studying her. He waved, as if to hide his thoughts, and she slipped the ring along her finger, the sunscreen aiding its easy progress, hoping he would not notice. When she looked up again he was gone, and she felt a shiver of fear run through her, afraid of what he might know.

After her morning in the sun, Isobel chose the coolness of the enoteca for lunch, rather than the shade outside in the courtyard. She sat at the same table where Jay first signalled his interest in exploring romance. She felt a warm contentment as she replayed the scene in her mind, remembering every look and every phrase with which he enchanted her and, as she now realised, seduced her. The sight of Eamon peering in, his scraggy neck extended like a wary heron, interrupted her thoughts, and she gave an encouraging wave, frustrated that Jay had not appeared instead of the genial Irishman, but glad of his company nevertheless.

They exchanged pleasantries but Eamon refused her hospitality with a polite "not while I'm working," as if alcohol were the only option for refreshment. He asked her about her morning.

"I met a couple, they seemed to be in some distress," said Isobel, without specifying who the couple were. Eamon could have pondered a long list of suspects, but had spied the conversation from the lofty vantage point of Jay's office.

"Oh, you must mean Hansel and Gretel," said Eamon, grinning at Isobel's bewilderment. "Geoff and Rosie Barker?"

"Yes," said Isobel, relieved that the affliction from which the two unfortunates suffered was not widespread. "I think at one point Rosie was almost in tears."

"Wine can sometimes do that to women," said Eamon, but his chauvinistic humour was not appreciated, so he quickly continued. "I expect they were still agonizing over the rental scheme?" Isobel nodded. "I did my best for them," said the garrulous Dubliner, his eyes mournful and voice heavy. "They have a very hard to let apartment. A broom cupboard of a place with no view up in the eaves. I advised them against the purchase, but they were insistent." He lowered his voice, "Strictly between the two of us, I think it was the only one within their price range. I took it on as a rental proposition more in sympathy than anticipation."

"But they said they were owed money?"

Eamon was forthright, and given to indignation by her doubt. "That is not the case, and unfortunately, they have only themselves to blame. I did manage to rent the apartment to some, shall we say, less discerning visitors. But Rosie, bless her, was unhappy that they were not people of the church like themselves. I'm afraid Rosie and Geoff seem to believe they are nailed to the cross which they carry on their shoulders, but lovely people all the same. They insisted I move the rental couple out, even though the wife was invalided, as I recall. To be truthful, I half expected Rosie to demand I call in a priest to perform an exorcism. I tried to explain that it was not going to work if Rosie insisted on dictating who I could and could not allow to use the apartment. I even referred her to the rental agreement, but she was adamant that God came before profit. Something about the good lord throwing the moneychangers out of the temple. So, sad as I am to say it, she effectively cancelled our agreement. I know I should have charged her for the rental furniture package, and I would have lost my job if Andy Skinner had found out, but I just didn't have the heart."

Isobel was reassured by the account, though she thought with an almost fond smile it was rather likely he had embellished it somewhat. She thought to tell Eamon about the meeting the Barkers were planning, and might have done had he not risen to take his leave, anxious, it seemed, to get back to his good works and the cause of humanity. Isobel raised the glass to her lips as he left, in a silent toast to her new life.

She did not want to return to the pool in the scorching sun, or suffer the inquisitive glances of those around it, so decided to stroll through the shade of the olive grove, and from there onto the vineyard which so captivated her on her first visit. As she approached she could hear the ringing of bells from the church outside the entrance to Castello di Capadelli, and a horse and buggy was drawn up beside the vineyard. A couple were posing for posterity at the arched trellis of flowers that led into the vineyard, and she stopped to watch the photo shoot, stroking the horse as she did so. It was an idyllic setting, with so many of the elements she had often pictured in her own dreams of romance, and she imagined herself as the woman in the white dress, radiant in her happiness.

She passed by the young couple with a furtive wave and entered the vineyard, seeking out the comfort of the sun-warmed bench to be alone with her thoughts. A gardener, stooped from age and toil, in corduroy breeches too heavy for the heat was tending the vines, his back bent to his labours. He rose from his work as he heard Isobel approach, and smiled kindly at her, his face as reddish brown as the earth beneath his boots. Isobel sat and watched him, his back still supple despite his years, the sinews on his arms suggesting the strength of his prime. She marvelled at the care with which this simple man of the land went about his work, a cutting tool in one hand, a vine in the other, the calloused hands so tender in their touch. Tears rose within her as she thought about her marriage, and its emptiness. The labourer looked up from his work and saw her distress, and went over to her.

"You must not be sad to see an old man toil," he said, touching her arm and looking into her eyes with the warmth that she remembered in her own father's gaze. He stroked the vine with the back of his hand. "My work is my pleasure and I rise to it every day thankful that I can do so. For one day the sun will rise, but I will not." He gave an ironic laugh, and took her hand gently in his palms, and she rose from the bench. "Let us walk the vineyard and it will reveal its treasure." He held onto her hand as they walked between the rows, she a step behind because it was too narrow to walk comfortably beside him. He stopped and held a cane, offering it to her, and she held it, stiff and naked in her hand, as his words soothed her. "Every vine is different," he said, "but each must receive the same care if it is to flourish. The vine is like a young woman, it must be cherished, and then it will grow tall and strong, and the fruit will be plentiful. The vine will give back only what is put in, and if it is given everything it needs, it can give untold pleasure."

The old man's soft voice and his love for his vineyard had taken Isobel's thoughts away from her own sadness, and she smiled up at him, squeezed his hand, and gave him a kiss on the cheek. And she saw he was pleased at her happiness. "If you ever feel hurt in your heart you must come here to the vineyard, and the vines will soak up your sadness, I promise you, and your presence too will cheer me."

Isobel felt reinvigorated as she raced back to the Villa Magda, remembering that Peter was due to phone. She ran up the stone steps two at a time to the sumptuous suite that Gina had reserved, which was cool and inviting in the afternoon heat.

Peter called and she lied to him without shame, wishing the call to end, but desperately trying to disguise it. She sat listlessly on the bed, letting him talk but willing him to finish, until three gentle knocks on the door interrupted the dullness of his voice. Thinking it must be Gina, she readied herself to interrupt him.

"Someone's at the door, darling," she said, but he kept speaking regardless, telling her how murderously hot it was in Dallas, and similarly uninteresting trivia. But it was Jay at the door, wearing an apron and a maid's cap, and she had to stop herself laughing as she pulled him inside, silently mouthing "Peter" and pointing to the phone, and putting her finger to her lips.

"Just the housekeeper," she said, looking menacingly at Jay, "here to turn down the bed."

She sat back on the cushions and continued listening to Peter, but Jay knelt at the foot of the bed and took off her bathroom slippers, grinning up at her as he began to suck her toes, each one in turn, and to tickle the soles of her feet until she silently writhed before him. She kicked him playfully away, gratifying Peter with yes's and no's.

But Jay stood up and took her ankles, and dragged her body towards him until her sarong rode up to her waist. He reached for the wine cooler and took some ice cubes. She shook her head frantically, laughing mutely with anticipation, as he began slowly sliding them up her thighs. She tried to bat him away with a pillow, but Peter kept demanding her attention and ruining her aim. Jay deftly slipped the ice inside her panties and pressed the coldness into her with his chin, holding her gaze as she grabbed the vase beside her and lifted it as if to strike him, but it only encouraged him. He pulled her panties to her ankles and took an ice cube between his teeth, trying to work it inside her with his tongue as she attempted to thrash her legs. But he held her ankles in his strong hands and she had to submit to the invasion, mouthing, "Just you wait" as he laughed silently and started to lick her. Soon she stopped struggling and just lay there while Peter was talking until eventually she could stand it no longer and told him Maria was trying to get through and that she would call him back later. She felt quivers run through her as the phone fell from her hand and she buried her head in the pillow, fearing she would call his name as her excitement washed over her, and not wanting him to know how completely she was his.

It was past midnight when the taxi dropped them at the back entrance to Castello di Capadelli. It was a moonless night and the blackness was entrancing with its infinite possibilities. They did not need to concern themselves with night security; Andy had stopped it to save money, but they kept up their subterfuge in necessity and excitement. They were both pleasantly lightheaded from their dinner together, the romance and the wine hung around them in the night air. Jay fumbled for the master key to open the forbidding padlock that held the two heavy wrought iron gates together. He sent her ahead, saying that he would follow her, but as she crept obediently forth a thought struck her, and she seized his hand, pulling him after her away from the main buildings. He tripped along after her and she capered along swinging his hand in hers and gently humming over the cicadas. She led him towards the vineyard and she stopped in the darkness before it, at the trellised archway where earlier the bridal couple had stood. And she pulled him under the archway like it was mistletoe and kissed him passionately, and he held her waist securely, so she kicked her heels up behind her, delighting in the feeling of him holding her, as her arms locked behind his neck.

As the clock ticked on and only stillness and darkness surrounded them he took her by the hand to lead her back. She followed him starry-eyed up the stone steps to the upper pool, which glowed with ethereal blueness in the black. He kissed her slowly by the light of the pool, looking into her eyes with such intensity that for a second she thought he was going to say that he loved her.

"This is the perfect time for a midnight swim," he said, his voice low and enticing.

"It's long gone midnight," she said, teasing him, before kissing him again.

"Come on, let's do it," he said, already undoing the buttons of her blouse.

"But what if someone comes?" she whispered.

"No one has any reason to come up here this time of night, and they'd risk breaking an ankle on that decking if they did."

"Let me go and get a costume," she asked, although she didn't mean to, as she was caught in the grip of modesty and fear.

"It will spoil the moment," he said, slipping off her blouse, "and what's the point of swimming at midnight if we're not naked? Come on, let's live young and free for once!" And he took the decision away from her by pulling off his underwear. Isobel tore at her own clothes to catch up with him until he took her by the hand, putting his finger to his lips and slipping into the water as smoothly as an otter. She stole after him, sliding into the water as her nakedness shone blue in the darkness. They swam soundlessly back and forth and she loved the water against her skin, the feeling of exhilaration at her own body; she felt light, almost fluid, utterly without care. He swam ahead and stood in the shallows, calling her to him with his eyes, and she swam up to him, cutting gracefully through the water, and kissed his chest. He kissed her nipples in return and she wondered for a second if he would take her in the water, but he pressed his lips to hers and led her up the steps, drying her tenderly as he savoured her body. She wrapped herself in the towel and Jay led her back to their clothes, forlornly strewn by the water's edge. He scooped up his trousers and looked out over the hills where the faintest of sunrises seemed to threaten, even though it was not yet two.

"We'd better go inside," he said.

She pulled him to her and let the towel fall from her and put her mouth to his ear and said, "You can go inside here if you want to."

He looked into her eyes but said nothing, so she took his towel and stooped to lay it out next to the pool, falling into its softness and sprawling out like a starfish. He looked down at her and threw away his trousers, dropping to his knees beside her. And she could feel the thrill of him even before his hands were upon her.

Thirty-six

Isobel sat, upright and bored, in the back of the plush limousine, patiently waiting for her husband's call to finish, her thoughts miles away. The countryside was vanishing behind them with worrying speed; Peter was on his way to the airport and Isobel was anxious to discuss the situation in Tuscany before he left. Eamon had called her earlier to confirm that the Visconti suite was now theirs — they had only to sign the papers and hand over the rest of the money.

"Everything ok?" she asked as Peter tucked his phone away, his brow furrowed and mouth taut.

He shrugged. "They are planning to announce a reorganisation on Monday. They said it would be simpler if I didn't come in to the office when I get back from Dallas. I was expecting it really. It just saves everyone embarrassment."

Isobel touched his arm; it was the end of an era, but he was bearing it well. She looked at him, admiring his stoicism and his strength in adversity. "You don't need them," she said with genuine empathy, and in the comforting knowledge that after ten years at the top, her husband did indeed not need them, except perhaps for his ego. But she could not dwell, she needed to move on to matters closer to her heart than Peter's business problems, which she now lived with every day. She was still smarting that it had not been Jay that called with the good news about the apartments.

"Sorry to raise it now, but before you get on the flight, I need a decision. Eamon is waiting for a call back. If we are going ahead, he wants me to go to a solicitor this week and sign the papers."

Peter knotted his fingers into his hair. "Well, the Visconti suite we are agreed on. So what do we want to do with the second apartment?"

"That's up to you, darling. It's just an investment after all, moving money from one place to another."

"If I remember," said Peter, "the deal on both works out at over a thirty percent reduction on the cheaper one. So let's buy both. It's a better return than we're getting from the bank."

Isobel smiled to herself at the thought of how pleased Jay would be, a second holiday home a small price to please her lover.

"Well, ok, if you think that's right," she said, trying to sound as indifferent as Peter. "I will call Eamon later and let him know."

She sank back into the leather in satisfaction, appearing appeased but still not finished with her efforts.

"By the way, that thing that Jay Brooke asked you to look at…" she said, filling her voice with false hesitance.

"The prospectus?"

"Yes, did you have a look at it?"

"A brief one. The phrase too good to be true comes to mind. And you know I have my reservations about our friend Brooke and his integrity." Isobel flinched in indignation and worry but let him continue. "But it's too good to ignore as well. So I've got some people running the rule over it."

"So it could be something worth considering?" she asked, full of nonchalance, yet uttering the same question that Jay had whispered in her ear the last time they lay together, their bodies mingled and wet from the sweat of their lovemaking.

Peter looked at Isobel quizzically, surprised by her interest.

"Much too early to be thinking like that."

Isobel nodded and stared out the window, now willing the airport closer.

She began to imagine a game she might play, teasing Jay that she had good news for him, but would only tell him if he could make her really, really scream. The heat of her excitement flowed to her face, illuminating her like a beacon.

"Do you want me to open a window?" asked Peter, looking at his wife with even more puzzlement.

As soon as Peter went through the departure gate, Isobel took out her phone to call Jay. She had been consumed by an almost itching nervousness since the call from Eamon, unable to understand why he hadn't called and with a million awful possibilities circling round her head. It took her eight attempts and nearly an hour to get through, in which time doubt turned into suspicion and then into fear.

"It's Isobel," she said the second the phone was answered.

"Isobel, great to hear from you. Is everything ok?" His voice sounded false and exaggerated and she had to hold back the words with all her might.

"Yes, I, I'm just ringing about the apartments; I haven't been able to get through to Eamon, so I thought I would call you. Peter wants to go ahead." She rattled out the words like a machine gun, afraid to let him speak and confirm her fears.

"With the Visconti suite? That's excellent news. Do you want me to get Eamon to call you?"

"Peter wants to go ahead with both."

"I'm really pleased for you. And Peter, of course."

"Please, Jay," Isobel burst out, his business-like tone pushing her to the very edge of her panic. "You know I am not just calling about the apartments. I want to see you. Why are you making this so difficult for me?"

"I'm sorry; it's just that I had someone here with me. So I needed to be professional. But it's ok to speak now."

"I want to see you; why haven't you called me?" She tried to hide everything, to be calm and measured, but she could hear the desperation spilling over the words.

"I have wanted to call you every day. Ten times a day. But I don't want you to feel I am putting any pressure on you. And remember, we said that when you were back in England you were going to take some more time to think about things, away from me, away from Tuscany and everything; to think whether it was still all a good idea or not. So that's what I have been letting you do."

Isobel shuddered with relief. "I have thought about it. I've hardly thought about anything else these last five days. When can I see you?"

"Well, when are you next in Tuscany?"

"Why does it have to be when we are in Tuscany? And anyway, when I am next in Tuscany, and I don't know when that will be, Peter will probably be with me. I thought maybe we could meet up in London this week. Peter's in Dallas till Saturday, so this week I don't need to explain anything." She could hear her own eagerness but did not care, so sure that he would share it, even exacerbate it.

"I can't get to London before Thursday at the earliest. And then I am only passing through on my way to the airport."

"Thursday in London is good for me," she said, before he could change his mind.

"Not so good for me," he said firmly. "I'm tied up in the morning, and I have a flight to catch in the evening."

She said nothing, bewildered by his evasion. He seemed to sense it and relented. "How about a late lunch Thursday?"

"Jay, I want to spend the night with you. It won't always be as easy for me to get away. Please can you get down Wednesday, or stay over till Friday morning. Or I could come to you, if you wanted me to." Again Isobel's words poured out uncontrollably; she heard the neediness in her voice and immediately regretted the suggestion that she travel to him.

"Let's see," said Jay, "I would love to do London, but this week I really can't do an overnight. But I can get down early Thursday, and book us in somewhere. We can spend all afternoon together. And if anything changes we can stay longer. How does that sound?"

"Thursday morning I'm going to the solicitor in London to finalise the purchase of the apartments. We can meet right after that, at about eleven. It is something for us to celebrate. It is not every day you buy two holiday homes abroad."

"That works perfectly," he said with enthusiasm. "Let's meet in the foyer of the Savoy at eleven thirty then, if that's ok with you?"

"Eleven thirty at the Savoy. I'll bring an overnight bag, just in case."

Thirty-seven

Isobel's emotions were tangled in impenetrable knots as she left the solicitor's office. She knew she should be celebrating. But as she had signed over the money, Peter's money, the hands of doubt had clasped her in a deathly grip. She had wrestled with many doubts over the period of her infatuation with Jay; she had questioned her values, her self-esteem, her morality, her emotional worth, everything — but money's gruesome head had never reared itself. It had been too exterior, too superfluous for her attention, readily available and seemingly unlimited. But as she put pen to paper on Peter's behalf — etching her signature under his name — she felt as if she was buying a lover. She knew deep in her heart that she only wanted to be with Jay, to please Jay, not to drink or to uncoil herself in the Tuscan sun. Peter was paying for his own betrayal and the very thought of it made her feel sick. As she walked past St. James Palace and along the expansive pavements of Pall Mall, past imposing buildings that were home to several of the exclusive London business clubs of which Peter was a member, she tried to justify herself, saying over and over that he could afford it, that the money was nothing to him.

But the principle stabbed at her heart like a dagger as she reflected on the woman she had thought she was. Did she really have the principles and the strength of character that she supposed? Or was she in reality no different from all the thousands of other women in London, who met their lovers in seedy, pay by the hour motels? Yes, she could at least console herself that she would be doing it in the comfort of a luxury hotel, but that was a bitter consolation that poisoned her integrity like arsenic. She could not hide from herself the knowledge of her own wanton urges; that every day she was apart from him she craved his touch, burnt for the feeling of him exploding within her.

Jay was waiting for her in the foyer when she arrived. It was a few minutes after eleven thirty and every step towards him seemed too long, like a waste of their precious time. She wanted to go straight to the room, to run upstairs like light itself and make him hers again and again. But she restrained herself; lunch first would make her feel more civilised and perhaps somehow less debauched.

He embraced her warmly and kissed her on the lips, gently and politely. They walked hand in hand to the bar like the lovers they were, and secreted themselves at a corner table.

"Everything go ok with the solicitor?"

"Yes, I am now the owner of two properties in Tuscany that I probably didn't need," Isobel replied with a weak smile, almost wanting him to judge her.

"But you are happy with the purchase? I know Eamon goes over the top sometimes. Tells people want he thinks they want to hear."

"Yes, I'm happy. As long as it means we can see each other, then I'm very happy. I don't think Peter will have much interest in coming out to Tuscany, so hopefully I can lead the kind of life that Maria has enjoyed, only with you on my arm." She sounded almost cynical, although her smile was saccharine.

He looked at her hard, as if trying to place the wistful distance in her manner.

"So no regrets? You are sure this is the right thing for you. You and me I mean?"

"Yes, I'm sure," she said with decisiveness, as much for herself as for him. "As long as you don't hurt me."

She affected a self-effacing humour in her tone, but her expression was serious, as Jay searched her face.

"Why should I want to hurt you?"

Isobel lowered her gaze, afraid of what he could see. "I don't know. I don't plan to give you any reason to hurt me. But Maria thinks you might be the kind of man that…you know, has their fun and then moves on."

He laughed at the suggestion. "And *you* think I am like that?"

She summoned her strength and held his eyes with some force.

"I think you have probably done that sometimes in the past." She spoke slowly and earnestly, beseeching him with every fibre of her being not to hate her. "I just hope you don't do it to me, because I don't want to hold back with you. And if I give everything, then, well—" She lowered her head. "Then I will be very vulnerable."

"Maybe you should spend less time with Maria," said Jay with an agreeable smile. "I think she might be a girl that has attracted the wrong kind of guy. And I think you are very different from Maria. Much softer, much gentler."

Isobel looked at him, her head cocked in amusement as he stroked her arm with the backs of his fingers.

"Maybe Maria gets what she deserves," he concluded, bringing his hand up to her chin and cupping it in affection.

"Sounds like you didn't warm to her?" Isobel tried to be cross but couldn't hold back a smile.

"I thought she was a great girl, right up to a minute ago when you told me what silly thoughts she was planting in your head."

Isobel laughed, filled once more with the heady desire that he always awoke in her, that banished all doubt and guilt until he left again and the shadows crept back in.

Jay put his palm to his breast in mock sincerity. "It would take a very stony hearted man to hurt you. And I do not think I am that kind of man. At least I hope not. And anyway, I can feel it beating, so it can't be all stone." He checked his watch. "Are you hungry?"

"Maybe a little."

"I have booked us a table here in the Savoy Grill, if that's ok? Maybe we can just order a glass of champagne and some oysters. They're very good here."

Isobel simply smiled and allowed herself to be led away, her fingers safe in his.

The maître d' welcomed Jay with friendly familiarity and he responded in kind, immediately likable and instantly charming. Isobel watched him in admiration, the fluidity of his speech and movement, the utter absence of airs and graces, endearing him to her even more.

"Your usual table is waiting for you Mr. Brooke," said the maître d', walking ahead and beckoning them to follow.

"Looks like you're a regular here, not everyone has their own table in the Savoy Grill," she said.

"Don't be fooled. I tipped the maître d' to say that. Normally he sticks me by the door to the kitchen with the tourists." Isobel laughed again, feeling lighter and freer with each burst of mirth.

When they were seated she plucked a rose from the centre glass and sniffed its freshness, looking furtively around for anyone she might know. Peter did not lunch in the Savoy and Isobel was confident she would not be recognised, but she scanned the room nonetheless, determined not to become complacent. As her eyes lingered on the tables she noticed that each had a single white flower in its centre. Only Jay's table had the five red roses. Her fingers went back to the vase and she again inhaled its perfume, somehow sweeter now. She felt a rush of warmth in her veins that he had made such a gesture. "Are you always this romantic?"

"Of course. It comes with the stony heart."

She felt an urge to kiss him, refraining momentarily for fear that he might think her heart could be bought for a single rose. But she leaned across anyway, knowing it to be already lost.

When the champagne stood empty and the oyster shells were piled up, beautiful and forlorn in their iridescence, Isobel and Jay made their way back to the foyer, discussing what to do next.

"It's a beautiful afternoon, we could take a stroll along the Strand, or we could go out the back and walk along the Thames, stretch our legs a while," Jay suggested, always in charge of the decision making.

"We could."

"Maybe go as far as the Ritz and have afternoon tea?"

"We could."

Isobel smiled at him coyly, inching her body closer to his until they touched, becoming one unified shadow in the light of the revolving doors.

"Maybe later then," he said, pulling her to him.

He took her by the hand and led her to the lifts as she almost skipped alongside him in perfect happiness.

When she entered the suite her ecstasy intensified yet further: all London stood before them in its majesty. Isobel resisted the urge to throw herself on the bed and inspected the suite, revelling in every aspect of it.

"A walk-in shower, very nice. Do you mind if I take five minutes to freshen up?"

"Be my guest, as long as you don't mind me catching up on a few emails while you do it?" Isobel laughed, wondering if maybe there were some similarities between the two men who shared her bed after all.

She took her case into the bathroom and re-emerged shyly in a short black silk top, buttoned at the front that revealed her midriff, and matching French knickers. Black stockings clung to her lean, shapely legs and high heels exaggerated her lithe body to supermodel proportions. She twirled herself around for Jay's inspection as he sat on the bed, his eyes hungry and triumphant.

"Is this ok for you? I bought them especially for the occasion." She twirled herself again, knowing it was but wanting so much to hear him say it.

"You look sensational," he said, rising from the bed to hold her.

Isobel backed away tantalisingly. "I thought maybe if you really liked it, you might stay for the night?"

"If I only could, but I must be out of here by six." He smiled briefly and apologetically before striding purposefully across the floor to take what was his.

He pulled her towards him as she melted into his arms and he held her tightly, his hands pressing into her buttocks.

"This is going to be good, Isobel, this is going to be so very good," he whispered into her ear.

Isobel stretched up and kissed him, delighted at the ease of it with her heels on. She clasped her hands on his as they held her buttocks and pressed them there firmly, not wanting him to explore her as he normally did. They kissed, absorbed in one another for a long time before Isobel pulled away.

"I want to undress you, Jay," she whispered, her fingers already at his collar. "But you have to stand still. You mustn't move; that's an order."

He stood there as she undressed him slowly from the top downwards, until he was naked of all but his socks.

"No moving now, not till I tell you," she murmured, running her fingers through his chest hair and then dropping slowly to her knees, because she knew it pleased him more than anything. He was not ready and she stayed on her knees before him until he was engorged inside her, as he ran his fingers through her hair and murmured with pleasure, powerful and guiding above her.

"Now your turn," she said, rising to her feet and trying to appear commanding. "I want you to undress me the same way, but very slowly."

Jay meticulously undid each button of her silk camisole, working down from the top as she arched backwards and let him put his mouth to each breast and nibble her nipples. He pushed the top from her form and it fell to the floor, unveiling her like a statue. He dropped to his knees and kissed her stomach. Isobel could feel the wetness between her legs and hoped it had soaked into the blue silk because she wanted him to see her excitement.

She felt him kiss her around her belly button, his lips gentle as a butterfly on her skin, and he put his hands on her hips and slid them down to the top of the panties. She shivered with pleasure as he rolled the silk downwards inch by slow inch, closing her eyes in delight as the light tan of her own skin gave way to snowy white as Jay slipped her panties lower. And as he did so he revealed a little more smooth white skin, and more white skin, and more white skin, until Isobel was fully exposed.

Jay admired what was in front of him, as he sat back on his heels. She looked down at him, pleased at his pleasure. "I did it for you, Jay. I hope you're not disappointed."

He kissed her and rubbed his chin against her smoothness and pushed his nose into her, teasing and arousing her with its hardness. He touched her smooth mound lightly with his fingers and traced patterns over it before his tongue explored her in the way she craved, that he knew she craved. He continued to kneel before her until she felt her knees buckle with pleasure and then he rose to his feet and pressed his hardness into her belly. When he stepped back from her she looked down and saw the fluid he had left on her, twisted like a symbol on her stomach. She scooped it off herself as if it were honey and put her finger to her lips. He stood and watched her glide it across the redness; she looked into his eyes and he ran the tip of his tongue back and forth along her lips.

As they stood, locked together, he swept her up, her stockings and panties still at her ankles. He put her on the bed and took them from her, throwing them aside and standing over her nakedness, deciding how best to take her. Isobel gazed up at him, holding his eyes and daring him to do anything. He grabbed her by the ankles and lifted her legs to his shoulders; she saw the fire in his eyes and knew he would be forceful but she did not care. She wanted him to take her with the same abandon that she gave herself, but he did not. He pressed the weight of his body down on her legs until she felt him deep within her, but he did not lose himself in the excitement as she did; he watched her as he took her in a steady, controlled rhythm until she could not bear his gaze. He continued with no rush to fulfil himself and he stayed inside her, shuddering from the sensation of her pleasure, as she reached her climax. When she was still he asked her if he could finish on her breasts, so that she could watch it, and she nodded assent as he rose and straddled her and she took him between her breasts. This time she watched him and they held each other's gaze as he built to his own peak. But she sensed from the flame in his look that he did not want to come on her breasts, so when his breathing told her that he was near the end she released her hands from her breasts and closed her eyes, feeling him rise up from her and put himself lightly to her lips. She parted them for him so he could let his flood into her, and when he was spent she gently pulled him from her, and held his gaze as she swallowed because she wanted him to see her take him completely. Then he lay beside her and pulled her close into his body and, safe and contented, they drifted into sleep.

As they awoke some hours later, Isobel turned to him, made unsure and vulnerable by sleep.

"If anything happened, you'd look after me, wouldn't you, Jay?"

He pulled her tighter and kissed her brow.

"Nothing's going to happen," he said, brushing her cheek, "it's our secret, remember."

She reached for his hand and intertwined her fingers in his, staring resolutely at the wall as she continued.

"Apart from Rusty, there isn't anyone else, is there?"

"Why do you ask?" he said in a matter of fact tone.

"Well, the way you said things were at home, you know, I would understand if you had needed someone…"

"Let's not spoil things by talking about home," he said, playing with the creases of her ear, "we've got each other, and that's what matters."

But Isobel persisted, desperate for his reassurance.

"There was a striking young blonde woman with you in Cobham."

"A blonde woman?" he replied vaguely, nuzzling his nose into her neck.

"Yes, you must remember, quite statuesque, she gave me the brochures."

"Oh, the girl from the marketing agency, you mean." He laughed and squeezed her hand, his touch full of affection. "I really only had eyes for you that night."

"But now we're together, it's just you and me isn't it? Because I couldn't bear you touching someone else — like you touch me."

He pulled her closer still, in silent answer, as she sank back into his calmness and warmth.

Eventually, Isobel pulled herself from the safety of his embrace and went into the bathroom, returning with a towel and a bottle of coconut oil.

"I want to give you a massage," she told him, laying the towel down and cajoling him onto his front. She took the oil as he watched her and rubbed it into her hands and into her smoothness, and she straddled him and rubbed herself up and down his backside, feeling excitement rising within her. Then she put more oil on her hands and let her fingers dance along the inside of his thighs as he quivered in pleasure. As he pushed himself towards her in want, craving her touch, she tapped his side, encouraging him to turn over; she put more oil on her hands, massaging him tenderly and kissing him as she felt his blood rising within her palms.

"Now me," she said, pushing her mouth into his ear as she spoke. Jay rose, shining and rippling beneath the oil. She lay on her stomach and he straddled her legs, oiling the inside of her thighs, his fingers inching upwards as she trembled beneath him. He poured the oil directly onto her and eased her legs wider apart, his fingers gliding around her most intimate of places as she murmured with pleasure to encourage him. He dropped his head to the pillow to look at her while he drew circles around it, gazing into her eyes and asking her silently, as his finger continued to draw circles, but more slowly.

She held the gaze wantonly, saying nothing but saying everything, and turned her face from him so he knew all of her body was his. And she lay quiet and still as he took her because she did not want any pleasure from it, only needing him to know that she was his in a way she had been no other man's.

They lay silent for a long time before he spoke. "Was that ok with you?"

She said nothing for a moment, not knowing if it was.

"It was different," she said.

But her answer did not seem to satisfy him, so he pressed her. "Does that mean you would do it again?"

"Not every time."

"But sometimes?"

"If that's what you wanted."

Later, Jay's movement awoke Isobel as he sought to disentangle himself from her body. As he noticed her stir, he playfully slapped her twice on the bottom. "Chop, chop, it's getting late; we need to be making a move."

And before she could object or suggest an alternative, he freed himself and was heading for the bathroom; Isobel had hardly collected her thoughts before she heard the shower running. She followed him into the bathroom, saddened and feeling cheapened by his abruptness, and went into the shower. She opened the hotel shampoo and began to wash and caress him although she sensed that his business-like manner was intended as a signal that he did indeed need to make tracks. But nevertheless, as she used the shampoo to help glide her hands around Jay's lower body she again asked him if he could stay, by now in hope rather than expectation.

"Can't you take a flight in the morning; surely a few hours can't make that much difference?"

"Sorry, I'd love to but I have appointments," he said briskly, kissing her on the top of the head and walking out of the shower. Isobel remained a couple more minutes, letting the force of the shower beat down on her head and the water cascade down her body. When she emerged from the bathroom, her hair still dripping wet, wrapped up in the heavy cotton Savoy bathrobe, Jay was already dressed and seemingly ready to go. He was clearly waiting for her.

"If you need to rush off, then I'll stay on here for a while and sort myself out," she said, running her fingers through her hair, her posture languid.

"Unfortunately, the room is only booked till six. So we need to go. And anyway, I feel responsible to make sure you get away safely."

"I'll just call down and extend the booking. I'm sure that won't be a problem, particularly as they know you so well here. And anyway, I've arranged to meet Maria here at seven."

"At the Savoy? So you couldn't have stayed over with me anyway?" He didn't sound hurt but she felt a confusing sort of accusation in his voice.

"Yes, I could, and I still can if you want me to. Maria knows the situation. If I call her now there will be no problem." Isobel stood in front of him, her hair scattering droplets of water on the carpet. She could see anxiety in his face. "It's not the bill is it, Jay? You don't need to worry about that. I'll take care of it in the morning." She headed towards the hotel phone.

"Isobel, I wouldn't dream of letting you pick up the bill," he said, moving quickly between her and the phone. "By all means, stay on here for an hour, I'll sort it out with reception when I go down."

"Well, actually, I thought, as I'm in town already, I would stay over. Peter's half expecting me to anyway. So I'll need the room for the night. That's ok, isn't it?" Again she saw him hesitate. "If you think there might be some problem, I'll go down to reception after you've gone and I won't take no for an answer."

Jay shrugged. "That sounds great. And I'm sure there will be no problem with reception. You take as much time as you need. And it's my turn to call you next, right?"

"That would be nice," she said with a smile.

Jay grabbed his bag, gave her a passing kiss, and was through the door. If Isobel had looked down the corridor she would have seen him break into a run as he reached the corner.

Thirty-eight

Jay almost flung himself onto the reception desk, panting with breathlessness as he stared desperately at the young blonde who watched him from behind the marbled counter.

"Is everything ok, Mr. Brooke?" she inquired.

"I would like to settle the bill." Jay looked around, his face full of worry, and tried to regain his breath.

"Of course, sir," she said, her expression suggesting concern. "Has everything been satisfactory?"

"Yes, everything was first class." He forced his mouth into a smile and tried to focus on her as she printed the bill, too panicked to look around again.

"I will need to charge you for the night."

"No, no, I am not checking out." He waited several agonising seconds for a response but she merely stared at him in confusion. "I have booked the room for the night and I am staying the night. But I will be in a hurry in the morning, so I want to settle my account now."

"But it is not necessary, Mr. Brooke," she replied with a bright smile. "We have your credit card details. You can leave in the morning at your leisure and everything will be taken care of."

Jay shook his head frantically. "I'm sorry..." He leant forward to read her badge, "Kaisa, I know that. But I would still like to settle my account now, if that doesn't screw up your system, that is."

Kaisa looked at him shrewdly for a moment and nodded. "As you wish, Mr. Brooke. Any additional charges will be added to your account."

Jay gestured his consent and snatched the bill from the desk. It took all his self-control to remain in the building and he walked business-like to a quiet corner to call Lucy, formulating a plan beneath the soothing light of the chandeliers. The phone rang for what seemed an eternity but yielded no answer. Jay checked his watch and saw that it was now six-thirty.

"Fuck," he mouthed with a wary eye on the door, his panic increasing with the realisation that if he did not do something in five minutes, he and Lucy would run into Isobel and Maria in the foyer. He backed into the corner, although it couldn't hide him, and called Lucy again but still he could get no answer. Was she ignoring him, fearing with foresight he would seek to change their plans? He wheeled to face the wall in despair, pushing the phone into his forehead as he screwed up his face in hopelessness.

"Are you all right, sir?" asked a voice behind him.

"Yes, yes, fine," he snapped, waving away the bellboy with uncharacteristic rudeness.

A dark female silhouette loomed at the doorway and Jay closed his eyes slowly, sure it was over. But no cry of recognition pierced his fear and he opened them again, letting the light flood back in, to see an unknown woman conversing with the bellboy. Jay's heart raced and he made the rash decision to break his own rule, the first commandment of adultery; he took out his phone and sent Lucy a text.

"Urgent. Call me now."

He fired off the text, and waited for what seemed an age, yet despite his prayers, his phone remained still and silent. He called again, each ring sounding like a death toll. No answer; he composed a second text.

"Urgent, change of plan. Go directly to Ritz. Do not go to Savoy. I am waiting for you in Ritz. J."

Jay knew he could no longer stay in the foyer of the Savoy; every second he remained pushed him closer to the end of everything. He briefly debated concealing himself outside, somewhere near the entrance, and intercepting Lucy as she arrived. But as six-forty heralded another stream of guests, he remembered that there were two entrances, and Lucy could use either. He agonised for a few moments, unsure what to do, and glanced at his watch again, ten to seven, Isobel would probably be leaving the room now, on her way down to collect Maria.

Jay sprinted for the concierge desk, slamming his hands down on it with relief and staring wildly up at the concierge, a tall, slick-haired rake of a man with a nose like a beak.

"Yes, Mr. Brooke, how can I help you this evening?" He looked at Jay blankly, battling to remain professional and keep the gloating amusement from his face.

"I need you to do two things for me, right now."

The man allowed himself a smile; he loved urgent requests, they were by far the most profitable. "If it is possible, Mr. Brooke."

"I need you to post a man at the Embankment entrance this second, and to intercept the arrival of a young lady. She's in her late twenties, tall, attractive, and blonde. You know the type. Her name is Lucy Baker. When she arrives, direct her straight to the Ritz. She must under no circumstances come in to the Savoy. Understand?"

Jay handed over two fifty-pound notes, and the concierge nodded to the man beside him who sped off through the foyer in the direction of the back entrance. Jay glanced quickly from his watch to the lifts, knowing Isobel might appear at any moment.

The concierge held his chin as he watched the beads of sweat form on Jay's brow.

"And the *second* request, Mr. Brooke?" he asked with a knowing delicateness.

"The same thing, but at the main door," said Jay, already holding out the money.

The concierge looked at him with the faintest trace of a sneer and did not move. "Unfortunately, Mr. Brooke, as you can see, we are very busy this evening. And my colleague, much as he might like to, cannot be at two entrances at the same time. And I myself am required to remain here," he spread his arms wide, "at the desk."

"I only need you to cover the door for five minutes, ten at the most."

"That is very difficult, Mr. Brooke," he said, looking pointedly at his pocket.

Jay peeled off another four fifty-pound notes.

"Does that make it easier?"

The concierge signalled across the foyer and a bell boy sprinted over. "Cover this desk for the next ten minutes." He turned to Jay. "I believe I have your number, Mr. Brooke. When the young lady arrives we will put her in a taxi, and let you know when we have done so. Now sir, perhaps you would like to slip out through the porter's entrance?"

The Ritz was illuminated in imposing grandeur, seeming to extend forever into the early evening sky, as Jay's taxi pulled up beside it. A royal blue Rolls Royce embellished with the hotel number plate stood proudly outside, reinforcing that only the discerning and deep pocketed need cross the threshold. A man in a top hat and coat below his knees materialised from nowhere and held the door open, allowing him to step out onto the pristine pavement like some sort of king. Jay nodded his thanks as he crossed his palm, and all but ran inside, slowing only on the approach to the desk. He scanned the lobby as he walked through, but he saw no sign of Lucy, and had given up on any message from the concierge. The receptionist, uncannily similar to the blonde from the Savoy, smiled an empty smile as he reached the counter.

"Welcome to the Ritz Hotel, sir. How may I serve you this evening?"

"I may need a room for the night, what do you have available?"

"We are very full this evening, sir. I will need to check for any non-arrivals. Were you thinking of a single room, a double room, or a suite?"

Jay tore his fingers back and forth across his brow, instinct and habit called for the suite but he had already paid for one outrageously expensive room that evening.

"A double."

"Twin beds, double, or king size, sir?"

Jay was beginning to feel like he was at a fast food restaurant; he drew himself up to full height and spoke with stern assertiveness.

"If the hotel is as full as you say it is, how about you just check what you've got, and I'll make the decisions?"

"As you wish, sir, just a moment please." She tapped away at lightning speed as Jay's eyes wandered apprehensively to the doors once more. "I can offer you a double room with a king size bed, or a penthouse suite overlooking Green Park?"

"How much for the suite?"

"Three thousand pounds, sir."

"And the double?"

"Let me see, that would be twelve hundred pounds, sir."

Again, routine called for the suite but Jay had a horrible feeling, from the way Andy had been talking, that his next set of expenses might be on his own tab. The blonde glanced at her watch and back at her computer screen as if watching the last second bids of an online auction.

"I'll take the double."

Jay only just had time to arrange himself comfortably in a chair before Lucy arrived, feasting on the opulence around her with wide, hungry eyes.

"Sorry I'm late," she said lightly, kissing him on the cheek. "I got held up at Clapham Junction. I got your texts so I came straight here. Is there a problem?"

Jay laughed to himself as he thought of the two concierges outside the Savoy, waiting for a blonde that would never arrive, but it was a brief and bitter sound — it was shaping up to be an expensive evening.

"No problem," he said with a casual wave of the hand, "I just wasn't happy with the room in the Savoy. I think someone had been smoking cigars around the clock in it. So I thought I'd treat you to the Ritz."

Lucy's eyes swept the foyer, resting on the fine jewellery outlet with approval. "The Ritz is great."

"I thought we'd go to dinner first, if that's ok, maybe the Caprice next door?" Jay volunteered, physically and emotionally exhausted by the afternoon's exertions and resigned to further five-star expense.

Lucy shook her head apologetically. "I'm sorry, Jay; I grabbed something at the station, I was famished. So it's not food I'm hungry for. I vote for enjoying the hotel. Maybe you can order up."

She bounced into the room like a child, inspecting everything with glee. Jay watched her in amusement as he lounged on the bed, only thinking to speak as she began to take her clothes off. For all her beauty and outward confidence, Jay was often struck by Lucy's contradictions;

she never sought to deny her cosmetic enhancements, and as he drooled at the perfection of her breasts, blessed with nipples he could hang his umbrella on, his mind went to the night he first asked her why she had invested in implants. "So the boys can tell the front from the back," she had told him with endearing and self-effacing honesty.

"We're not going anywhere then?" he asked.

"First things first, lover boy," she said, wiggling off the last layer to reveal a fetish-like combination of tight red underwear and stockings.

"Nearly ready for you now, tiger," she purred as she delved into her bag, retrieving a large tub of plain yogurt from its depths. She glanced at Jay's puzzled face and burst into attractive laughter. "I think you said you prefer organic?"

Jay did not say anything as she again rummaged through her things, emerging with a set of steel handcuffs dangling tantalisingly from her fingertip. They were no novelty store toy, suggesting industrial strength, perhaps even Metropolitan police issue.

"You going to pull a blue uniform out of that bag next?" asked Jay, greedy hope manifest in his voice.

"Dream on, soldier," she said with a wicked grin. "Just be thankful there's no truncheon in here, then you'd really have something to worry about. And the 'cuffs are for me. So you need to be working out what you're going to do with the yogurt."

It was ten-thirty when Jay finally collapsed on the bed, a slippery and satisfied Lucy pressed against him. She fiddled with his watch, stroking the metal and pushing its coldness to her face.

"It's still early," she said softly, pushing against his face with her nose, "are you going to show me around the hotel now? And then can we check out a club or something?"

"What type of club do you fancy?" he asked.

"I don't know. One that's difficult to get into I suppose," she replied, sitting up abruptly with excitement. "We have plenty around here to choose from. You got any preference?"

"I did speak to the concierge earlier," said Jay, also now sitting up and nuzzling into her neck. "He recommended somewhere not far away. Very exclusive, very expensive."

"Is it one I would have heard of?"

"Hopefully not, I asked him for somewhere a bit different, where there's definite action, somewhere a bit racy. He said it was a fun place. A bit kinky."

"Kinky?" She ran her hands up his thighs again, as if the word itself aroused her.

"Yep, that's what he said. Do you want to give it a try? We can just check it out. If we don't like it, we can go somewhere else."

"Ok, let's give it a whirl," she said, pulling his arms to get him up, "but if I want to leave, we leave, right?"

Jay led Lucy down the unlit corridor of the club; she held his hand, needing to feel secure in the darkness. At the end of the corridor, illuminated by the ridges of light that outlined a door, stood Eva.

"You must be Mr. Brooke?" she said, looking him up and down as if assessing him for the first time.

"And you must be the lady I spoke to, Eva wasn't it? This is my friend Lucy. We just want to have a drink and see if it is what we were expecting."

She nodded and led them through the door. Jay strode in and Lucy followed, squinting in the light and surveying the scene around her. Ten girls stared back at her, draped around in various levels of undress, like strange porcelain figures bathed in a soft red glow.

"Jay, this is a knocking shop," she whispered, looking around in astonishment.

"Let's give it a chance," he replied, "I think she said the shows go on upstairs."

Jay led her to a sofa and a bottle of champagne arrived before them within moments, proffered by a girl in a tiny black mesh dress.

"Did you order that, Jay?" Lucy whispered, not wanting to raise her voice.

"No, I think it's sort of compulsory, instead of paying at the door."

Lucy continued to gaze around, stealing surreptitious glances at the women arrayed all about her.

As she did so a petite girl, perched at the centre of the bar, sought her eye contact and held it. Lucy looked away unsure what to do and the girl slipped off her stool and walked over. She wore only a bra and a wrap that barely joined around her hips. She addressed Jay, perhaps sensing Lucy's unease.

"Is it I ok if I give your friend a lap dance?" she asked him.

Jay looked at Lucy. "You ok with that?"

"Sure, babe, why not."

The girl turned to Lucy, her mouth pink and sugary as she spoke.

"My name is Camila, I'm from Argentina. The first dance is free."

The business-like nature of her words contrasted sharply with the sensual, erotic shapes of her lips and Lucy almost laughed but, aware of Jay's fantasises and expectations, she decided that she was going to play along.

"Will you let me touch?" she asked.

"Maybe, if I like you."

Camila whirled, twisted and gyrated around Lucy, forming strange and alluring shapes in the air as she pushed and rubbed against her body, tantalising and pulsating against her skin. Lucy encouraged her, letting her fingertips brush against her skin as she dropped to her knees, twirling her hair around her as she buried her head in Lucy's crotch. Lucy let out an encouraging sigh of assent and Camila rose again, looking her in the eyes as she spread her thighs across her and pushed her breasts forwards, tempting her, daring her to take them. Lucy reached out and stroked them, holding them in her hands as Jay looked on.

Camila moaned and moved Lucy's hands to her lean brown stomach, rubbing her crotch up and down Lucy's thigh as she unfastened her bra. She leant forwards, circling and gyrating against Lucy, offering her breast to Lucy's deep red lips. Lucy moved in, tentative but purposeful, one eye on Jay who smiled with satisfaction. But as she opened her mouth, Camila sprung up and refastened her bra, bobbing in a perverse curtsy as the show came to a close.

Jay gave a brief clap of appreciation.

"Would you like to stay for a drink, Camila?"

"Thank you," she said with the well-honed reflex of her trade, "a champagne, please."

"You still ok with this?" Jay asked as another girl, all but naked except for two strategically positioned strips of fabric, joined them on the sofa, sitting herself on the arm next to Jay.

"I'm ok." Lucy smiled widely as if to prove it. "It's fun. If you want a dance, you go ahead."

"I'm told it gets even more fun upstairs. You up for that?"

"I might be," she said, as she considered her options, "but only with one girl, ok?"

"Which girl?" he asked magnanimously.

"You choose, big boy, you'll be the one that's watching."

His smile faded slightly but he nodded, "Let's go upstairs and have a look around."

"What about Camila?" asked Lucy, feeling strangely guilty at not following through on such meticulous foreplay.

Jay laughed. "She isn't going anywhere, are you, Camila? Let's just have a look upstairs." He walked over to Eva and talked briefly with her in the corner, low and inaudible.

She beckoned to Lucy, "Follow me."

At the top of the stairs Eva stopped and turned to them, her voice hushed, almost secretive.

"You are very lucky to come now. I have a girl here who is very special, only eighteen. She is from Siberia. She has just arrived seven days ago. Very beautiful Russian girl, with the smoothest, whitest skin I have ever seen. I do not let her work downstairs, not yet, she is too precious to me. You would like to meet her?"

"Can't hurt to just say hello," said Jay with a shrug, as if they were calling on a neighbour, while Lucy stood in silence behind him, happy to just let things unfold.

Eva rapped at the door with her knuckles and opened it without waiting for a reply. The girl in the room was sat on the bed reading, her knees pulled up to her chin with blonde hair cascading down her back. She looked over and smiled but did not get up. Eva stepped back out and pulled the door until it was almost closed.

"Like a beautiful white flower, isn't she? Her name is Katrina, but the girls call her Rapunzel. You must be gentle with her. She may need a little coaxing. She is different from the girls downstairs. So fresh. So innocent. And she speaks only Russian."

"No English at all?" asked Lucy, feeling strangely sorry for her.

"Only one word, which is yes. I think she can say yes in five languages."

"Not bad for seven days!" said Jay with a laugh. "I think we'd like to get to know Rapunzel a little better."

Eva ushered them back into the room and exchanged a few sentences with the girl in brusque Russian. The girl stood up, lithe and sylphlike and in a short pale dress; Eva walked quietly out and left them in her hands.

The second the door was closed Lucy turned to Jay, fierce and fiery.

"Before we go any further, I want to get the rules straight. This is just going to be a show. You can watch, but you can't touch. Not Snow White over there, anyway."

"Come on, Lucy. You can't expect me to stand here holding my hands while you get it off with Miss Siberia. Be fair."

Lucy was nothing if not fair. "Ok, I'm going to allow touching, but only with your hands, and only then on the outsides. No penetration, you got that? Not with your hands, or anything else. Nothing of yours goes inside her, not the mouth, not anywhere else."

Thirty-nine

Isobel left the Savoy with a spring in her step as she and Maria emerged into the tepid warmness of the grey-blue morning, refreshed and elated by the air of peaceful contentment that had pervaded their evening together. They waited together in the Savoy courtyard for Peter's driver, who was to pick them up and take them to Gatwick for Maria's impending flight to Pisa. They sat in serene silence in the car and arrived with two hours to spare.

"I'll come in and see you off, Maria, I'm ready for a coffee anyway."

"Call me ten minutes before you need picking up, Ma'am," said the driver, more than used to hanging round airports, "and I'll see you back here."

They lounged together in the café, sipping coffees with one eye on the departure gate for queues.

"So what happens next, Isobel?" asked Maria, her curiosity getting the better of her. "Can you see yourself repeating what you did yesterday when Peter is around? Have you thought about all the lies you'll need to tell?"

"I really don't know," replied her friend with a sigh. "I'm not very good at lies. But right now I don't think I can stop seeing Jay. It's like I'm a different person when I'm with him. The way he makes me feel…I just can't give that up, not yet."

"And you think he feels the same way?"

Isobel shook her head. "I know men are different, but yesterday he did say that what we had was something special for him, something that he couldn't remember feeling before."

"You mean, he sort of said that he was actually in love with you?" Maria looked sceptical, even shocked.

"No, of course not. I know that's not possible. We're not teenagers and there hasn't been enough time. But I do believe there's something there, something he feels with me that he isn't feeling at home, or has felt with other women. Not for a long time at least."

"So he wasn't put out that you hadn't passed his little test with the Hollywood?" asked Maria, annoyance flickering across her face at the wrongness of her predictions.

Isobel looked away, unable to answer.

"Oh my god, Isobel, you didn't?"

"It's not illegal!" Isobel exclaimed. "What is so wrong about *me* doing it?"

"What's wrong is that you might as well tattoo *I am besotted with you* on your forehead!"

"Is doing what he wants me to do so bad, if we both like it?" asked Isobel dreamily, wanting nothing to encroach on her bliss.

"So I suppose now he has he asked you to get a stud in your clit or something?"

Isobel laughed, unwilling to rise to the bait. "No, Maria, he hasn't asked me to do anything else. Nothing like that anyway."

"So he has asked something?" Maria latched onto her instantly, immediately knowing. Isobel hesitated, unwilling to expose herself.

"Come on, Isobel, what hurdle has he asked you to jump over next?"

"It's not a hurdle or anything. He just asked me when was the last time I masturbated, that's all."

"When was the *last* time! Quite a supposition there. Not something you can answer yes or no to, is it?"

"Anyway, I didn't tell him," said Isobel, sipping her coffee to end it.

"And he just left it at that?" asked Maria, her voice etched with disbelief. "He popped the question out there, and then forgot about it?"

"No, he asked me if I'd ever let anyone watch me do it, and I told him the truth, which is no. And what he then said was that he would like to watch me do it. And if you must have the gory details, he then asked if I owned a vibrator, and I said no because I don't, and never have."

"So that's when he pulled one out of his backside?" cried Maria, cold and frenzied.

238

"No, he just said it's something he'd like to see me do, with a vibrator."

"Did he specify the model? A black, twelve inch corrugated monster perhaps?"

Isobel started to answer, but Maria was no longer listening; she was staring down the concourse towards the departure gate.

"Have I lost you at the interesting bit, Maria?"

"Sorry. Did you say Jay shot off at six last night to catch a flight?" Maria glanced at her, her whole face blunted and saddened.

"Yes, yes he did; he was coming straight here."

Isobel looked into Maria's face, at the eyes that were looking right past her. She stood up and followed their gaze, letting out a strange, strangled squeak as she saw Jay standing alone next to the gate.

"Something must have happened," she blurted out with bewilderment in her eyes. "I need to speak to him."

Maria grabbed her friend by the arm. "No, Isobel." It was an order, not a statement, and she pulled her close to her body.

Isobel tried to push her away. "I must, I need to know what's happened."

Maria tightened her grip. "No, Isobel, not yet. Just wait one minute."

The two stood there looking down the concourse; the people that milled about blurred together in Isobel's vision, a dark rainbow of colour that swirled around the image of him alone, expectant, at the gate. He lifted his head and they followed his gaze as a long legged blonde in a black beret approached him. Isobel watched as they embraced, sharing a kiss, before linking arms and disappearing through the gate. Maria held her friend as she felt her body go weak, her grip tightening as Isobel started to shake and her tears started to flow.

"It's better this way, Isobel. It's better to know now."

As Isobel shuddered in anguish, Peter sat calmly on the other side of the Atlantic, waiting patiently in Dallas International Airport for a call from Massimo Pitsone, an old colleague from the Milan branch of his previous job. He straightened himself with confidence as the first peal of the phone rang out in the silence of the first class lounge. They had barely exchanged pleasantries before Massimo, who sounded strained and anxious, broke into the reason for the call — the prospectus for Castello di Capadelli.

"Peter, my assessment of the proposal is similar to the one you have from the guys in London. But there's something more I think you should consider. Whoever has written this document is either a complete fantasist, or is simply ignorant of the laws and regulations here in Italy. Or maybe both. The numbers are attractive, but what is proposed is impossible to do at this place Capadelli."

"How can you be so sure?" asked Peter, taken aback.

"Because in this matter the law, for once, is black and white — your so-called resort is an illegal tourist complex. "

"But there's already a hotel and restaurant operating on the site; how can it be illegal?"

"Yes, I noticed that. But I can find no reference to any licences being granted for hotel and restaurant operations at Castello di Capadelli, which I think would be very difficult to obtain."

"So what about the spa and all the other developments that are in phase two?" asked Peter, his voice steadily rising as unease turned to foreboding.

"All these are, and I hate to use the word, impossible. No one in the business of operating tourist facilities would buy into the development, that I can guarantee you."

"I'm sorry to sound like a broken record, Massimo, but from the very outset the place has been promoted as a tourist complex, as a resort."

Peter could almost hear Massimo shaking his head. "I saw that too, but my view is that all these promises are nothing more than inducements, hooks to sell property. It never has been, nor ever will be, a tourist resort. You see, I can give you a thousand reasons why it can't b—"

"Massimo, you have been most helpful. I owe you one."

The Italian did not take offence at his brusqueness; he knew a chastened man when he heard one, and thus carefully laced his apocalyptic words with a soothing tone.

"It has been my pleasure. I am sorry to have not been able to be more encouraging. I have just one other incidental point. I think you said you were thinking of buying an apartment at Capadelli, irrespective of the wider investment. If so, I very much recommend you seek an independent valuation. I say this because the prices I see on the Capadelli website for apartments are strange." He hesitated, seeming uncertain whether to heap further bad news on his old friend; in the short silence Peter could hear the tapping of computer keys somewhere at the other end of the line. "Perhaps I am not understanding something, but even in the centre of Milano I would not pay so much as these prices."

Forty

Jay and Lucy sped from Pisa to Capadelli in a pearl white cabriolet, the top down and the wind in their hair, resplendent together in symbiotic beauty. Her sultry, youthful allure complimenting his mature and magnetic presence, they seemed to sail along the road as if propelled by their own power. The cool breeze rendered the sun-beaten landscape no more than a vast and beautiful painting, an idyllic backdrop for their perfection. She fiddled with his hair in playful affection as he drove, her eyes fixed on him.

"Jay?"

"Yes, Lucy?"

"Did you like what I did for you last night?"

He threw her a glance. "I will send you a thank you note," he said, smiling at the memory.

"Jay?" She looked at him unblinkingly now, her gaze almost predatory in its attentiveness.

"Hmm?"

"You remember at the sports day, when I said I wanted to talk about us and the future?"

He held back a sigh. "Darling, I'm driving, let's discuss it later."

She shook her head, flailing strands of gold through the wind as she did so.

"No, if you can handle me giving you a blowjob while you're driving, then I think you can manage to talk and steer at the same time. And if you can't do that you are just going to have to listen."

Jay looked at her, weariness clear on his face. "What's on your mind?"

"You know perfectly well," she replied. "We've been going out together for nearly two years now. That's how long it's been since you first told me that you weren't happy with Rusty."

"I'm not sure I said that exactly." Jay did not mean to bait her but couldn't quite banish the blitheness from his tone.

"So are you now saying you *are* happy with her?" she asked, in no mood for games and well aware that she had less than an hour before they reached Capadelli.

"Lucy, this is all a bit heavy. We're here to enjoy ourselves, not to talk about Rusty." She tried to interrupt but he powered on, "and anyway, from everything you've been saying about Rob lately, it hardly matters what either of us said two years ago."

"I only have Rob because I need someone when you're not around," she retorted. "If you were around more, then things would be different."

"But you live in London, and Rob lives in London, and I live in Cheshire, so he's always going to be around a lot more than me."

Jay took his eyes from the road and flashed her a quick smile, by all appearances reconciliatory but confident he had trumped her.

"Well, that's what I want to discuss," said Lucy, reflecting back the smile like a mirror but with danger in her eyes.

"You mean you and Rob are moving to Cheshire?" He widened his eyes in playful shock, determined not to let the conversation become real.

"Jay, I'm serious."

"Serious about what?"

"I want to come and live with you."

He turned sharply onto a side road, swinging his body into hers with the force of the manoeuvre.

"Do we have to do this now? I live with Rusty and have two twelve-year-old boys. Now can we just leave it?"

She ignored him and continued, placing each well-rehearsed word after the next with calculated rigour.

"Most of the time you don't live with Rusty. Most of the time you are somewhere else — here in Tuscany — living by yourself in your own flat. So if I lived here with you, then there wouldn't be any problem."

She stressed her final word in premature elation but Jay made no reply, keeping his eyes firmly on the sharply winding road.

"So what I'm saying," she continued, "is that I am not asking you to leave Rusty right away, but I am asking to come and live with you here. I've been thinking a lot about it, and there's no reason why it can't work."

"Except you have a job in London," he reminded her, still not meeting her gaze.

"I only fly fourteen days a month. And if I want to I can do the London to Pisa run permanently. I know it can be made to work because other girls do it. I really don't know why I didn't think of it before."

"Just because it works for other people doesn't mean it will work for you. And what about Rob's feelings?"

"When have *you* ever cared about Rob's feelings?" she said, her tone derisive.

"Probably more often than you have." He met her eyes now and would not release them. "Anyway, this is too big a thing to unload on me now and expect me to discuss it sensibly, let alone give you an answer."

"If you love me, Jay, as you say you do, then there's really not much to think about. We can be together here and you don't have to change anything at home, not yet anyway."

"Where is all this coming from?" he asked, fearing he would drown in the sheer volume of her words. "Things have been working fine the way they are."

"Not for me. At least not anymore. Anyway, now you know what I want, you'd also better know that I've asked for a transfer to Pisa, and I've given notice on my flat. So while we're here I'll be taking notes in your place. Measuring curtains and all that sort of thing. Deciding what bits and pieces I want to bring over."

She met his eyes once more, challenging their indifference. "I'm moving in with you, Jay."

Forty-one

Soft white clouds blanketed the Surrey sky as Peter Roberts wandered late down to breakfast, still in his dressing gown as his gym kit lay untouched on the dressing room floor. For the first time he could remember, there had been no particular reason to get out of bed on a workday. Powerless frustration lingered on him like a stale odour. As he wandered aimlessly into the lounge-sized kitchen, its granite surfaces refracting the light into emblems on the walls, he found Isobel sitting listlessly at the breakfast table. She was nursing a cup of coffee and staring intently at a single piece of paper, her eyes flicking frenetically back and forth as she read and reread the cold black words.

"There's a letter here that you might want to read," she said, looking up at him and folding the paper in two. "It's from Andy Skinner, about the rental scheme and what's happening at Capadelli."

Peter took the letter from her and paced about reading it in silence, his face reddening bit by bit as his eyes descended the paper. Isobel could not watch him and distracted herself as best she could in the murky depths of her latte.

Peter scrunched up the letter and threw the ball at the wall, the sounds resonating like artillery fire in the intense quiet of the room. He moved to the window and looked into the distance, out across the fields, and said nothing for a long time as Isobel watched, tense and anxious. Several minutes passed before he spoke.

"The bastards," he said, his voice low and emphatic. "But it's not Skinner that's the villain, you know, it's smooth talking Brooke, he's the one that screwed us."

Isobel flinched beneath his words and said nothing, opting for sitting motionlessly and staring once more at the still surface of her drink. Peter approached his wife and leant over the table, his weight supported by two clenched fists.

"Isobel, did you hear what I said?"

"Yes, I heard you," she said quietly. "But all the letter says is they are reviewing the rental scheme."

"It's not what it says. It's what it doesn't say. We've been cheated. It's not just about being turned over on the apartments. Or being screwed on the rental deal. If I'd bought into the project, in six months, we'd be looking down the barrel of a £30 million loss."

"Save the melodrama," said Isobel with a sigh, "he only asked you to look at something for Skinner, he never asked you to invest."

"But he was hoping I would."

"Was he, really? He must have known you'd check things out. Maybe he was just trying to buy himself some time, to keep Skinner off his back." Isobel looked away, conscious she had said too much, and shocked to hear herself seeking to make excuses for the man who had so recently betrayed her

Peter ignored her words of mitigation, and ploughed on with his tirade. "He can't be allowed to get away with this. And, for better or worse, we are the only people who can make sure he pays for his sins."

Isobel gulped at his words; was she now to pay for her sins every bit as much as Jay? She looked up at him unsteadily.

"Well, we need to do something," he declared, pacing away in frustration.

Isobel blew through her lips in exasperation. "For god's sake, stop talking like a boy scout. There's nothing we can do."

"The hell there isn't. We can get even, that's what we can do."

"I don't see how," she said, "and getting even won't get us our money back."

"It's not about money, it's about satisfaction." He thumped his fist down with the last word and silent tremors crossed the surface of Isobel's coffee.

She put her hand over Peter's closed fist. "How about we just let it go?" she suggested gently, as much for her own sake as his. "Save ourselves any more grief."

"Grief? Giving out grief is what we need to be doing, not saving ourselves from it." Peter paced back to the window, a slight spring developing with every step.

"An hour ago I woke up thinking I had nothing to do. Well, this letter just changed that. I'm going to make that smug bastard rue the day he ever met me."

"Good money after bad?" she asked, with sarcasm etched into her voice.

Peter returned to the table and sat opposite his wife, wrapping his hands around hers so that they held the cup together. "Listen, no one's going to fuck me over and get away with it, especially not when I've got the time to do something about it. And certainly not a failed bean counter like Brooke."

He pressed her hands into the cup with determination, until her palms felt raw and blistered from the heat. She looked up at him and felt a strange mixture of apprehension and awe; she knew there must have been times when her outwardly mild mannered husband had been ruthless; after all, his work was fiercely competitive, a world where survival of the fittest was the name of the game, and the weak went to the wall. But she had yet to witness his ruthless side in their daily life, to see it burn through her cotton wool existence. But fear again gripped her.

"What's gotten into you?" she demanded, pulling her hands from him. "Be serious for a moment. This is not the City, and it's not the Wild West either. We made a mistake, that's all. At worst it was a poor investment. It isn't the first, and it won't be the last. Maybe we just need to take our medicine and move on."

Peter laughed bitterly. "Over my dead job prospects we will! Now are you going to sit there spooning your coffee, or are you going to get involved?" Isobel stared up at him quizzically as he loomed over her in his dressing gown, speaking like some great warlord or propagandist. He should have been a comical figure but he instilled respect in her; she knew how easily he could have lashed out at her and blamed her for their troubles, but she sensed only determination in his voice.

"I think I'm already involved, aren't I?" she asked, her feet shuffling nervously beneath the table. "But I still don't see what we can do. What I can do."

Peter smiled at her, his determination almost manic. "We need to entrap Brooke, that's what we need to do. And to do that what we need now is information."

"What sort of information?" she asked, knitting her eyebrows in genuine puzzlement.

"That's what we need to work out. But it's often that way — that you don't know what you need to know until you start asking questions. The thing we mustn't do is put them on their guard. If we do that, the best we'll get out of them is more bullshit."

Isobel's lack of enthusiasm was almost manifest, it stood between their minds like a wall.

"I'm no detective," she said, "and I'm not sure I've got the skills for whatever it is you're thinking about. I wouldn't even know where to start."

"Where we start, where you start, is over in Tuscany."

"Go back to Tuscany? Now?" Isobel shook her head automatically as her whole body screamed no.

"Where else?" said Peter, as he beamed at her. "We can't wait till they've done a runner! You need to get over there and get them to open up. Use your charms if you need to." Isobel shifted awkwardly in her chair. "Make them believe we are still fat and happy."

"Or rich and stupid?" she offered, but without humour, thinking she'd like to engrave those words on her tombstone.

"All the better if they think that!"

As Peter looked across at her, his jaw set hard, Isobel sought frantically for an excuse, any excuse that would change his mind.

"But Peter, why do you need me to dig around. What can I find out that accountants can't?"

"Accountants are not the police. They look at ledgers and public records. We need to see the real dirty linen, the stuff crooks hide from the accountants...and the taxman."

"But what if it all turns out to be a fool's errand?" she asked. "What if there's nothing to find out, except what we already know? And why would they open up to me, charms or no charms?"

"Just trust my instincts on this. Their whole operation is a bag of worms; I already found that out from Massimo. I've been mulling over what he told me all weekend, trying to think like they think, trying to make sense of it all."

"And when we've found out what is to be found out, what then?" asked Isobel, for whom the idea of truth grew larger and more terrible by the day.

Peter leant forward in theatrical secrecy, fuelled by a sudden boyish enthusiasm.

"I've already been thinking around a few ideas. And they all involve Brooke's balls."

Isobel closed her eyes at the phrase; an agonising image of her on her knees, her red lips caressing them, delighting in them, flashed before her.

She felt Peter sense her discomfort; he reached out and gave her arm a reassuring squeeze.

"We need to act quickly. So get on that phone and get your flight booked."

"Peter, please, I really don't want to go back to Tuscany...not right now." A heavy silence hung in the air, as Peter seemed to wait for an explanation. "It's just the letter, I feel so awful, that it's all my fault."

Isobel could feel his stare, could see the look of puzzlement in his eyes; she pressed her fingers onto her eyelids to suppress the tears as he gently touched her shoulder.

"Peter, I'm really, really, sorry."

Forty-two

Peter had suggested that Isobel stay at Castello di Capadelli whilst she was in Tuscany, setting out the many advantages of being so close to her target. But even the idea of closeness was now an unbearable one to Isobel and she had protested without conviction, saying that it would be better to stay elsewhere until the furnishings she had ordered arrived. Eamon had plied her with a stay at the Villa Magda over the phone, his voice silky and tantalising. But the memory of her wantonness in Villa Magda came back to haunt her, and her imagination was seized by a vision of a rapacious Jay coming to her suite in the dead of night, engorged and hungry for her, ready to take what little that was left.

She stayed instead with Maria, nestled safely away in the hills, obliged only to explain her situation to her friend — a far pleasanter prospect than explaining her elusiveness to her lover. Nevertheless, she did her best to delay conversation of any kind, languishing in her room, deep between the sheets, too listless to eat or drink until Maria could suffer her suffering no longer.

She burst into the bedroom without knocking, pulled back the heavy curtains and threw open the windows, letting light and life back into the room.

"It is a beautiful day and Mia needs the sheets to wash, so you must get up out of your bed as well as your stupor," she said, cheerful and brisk, as she set down a tray on the bedside table.

Isobel shielded her eyes from the sun and blinked in the unforgiving light. She pushed herself weakly up against the pillows, a shaft of light revealing the tear tracks that spidered over her face like ink, polluted by her make-up.

"Breakfast is on the table," continued Maria, "though it is nearly lunch-time. And you need to be ready to go in thirty minutes. So up!"

"Go where?" asked Isobel feebly, sinking back into the covers.

"You can come with me to enjoy an afternoon on the beach at Forte di Marmi, or I can drop you at Pisa airport where you may continue to wallow in self-pity, the choice is yours." Maria looked down at her sternly. "And by the way, you look awful."

Isobel's mood brightened noticeably as she helped pack all the picnic things into the car; the sun imbued her with warmth and feeling again after two days in the terrible cold stillness of the air conditioning. Maria made a pact with her not to talk about Jay or Angelo before they were comfortably on the beach, and they travelled to Forte di Marmi mostly in silence, Isobel lost in thought as Maria concentrated on navigating the hazardous roads.

The resort was a haven for the rich, with boutiques and jewellery shops to rival their Milanese counterparts and an abundance of beautiful young things, browning their lithe bodies in the white-hot sun. The two friends caused a stir as they walked onto the beach; Maria paid a man to carry their picnic baskets and bags and another to lie out their towels on loungers. She walked confidently in her bright bikini, her eyes hidden behind butterfly sunglasses, and Isobel walked thankfully in her shadow, wishing to share its impalpability. She found solace in the crowds that filled the sandy stretch, pleased to watch the holidaymakers playing with their beach balls and buckets and remember that life continued as it always had. For a time she watched the young and the vain walk along the sea's edge, splashing their feet but keeping their designer costumes dry, envying their youthful assurance and their futures.

Maria poured them each a glass of chilled prosecco from the cool box, narrowing her eyes in impatient concern as Isobel's introspection continued.

"To men, may they all rot in hell," she said, raising her drink.

"But then what would we girls talk about?" said Isobel in a poor attempt to be blasé, and they tapped the plastic flutes as they laughed.

"So, have you heard from him?" asked Maria.

"I haven't spoken to him, but he has left text messages. He knows I'm in Tuscany, but thinks Peter might be with me, so he's waiting for me to call."

"So you must call him and meet him," said Maria, more as an instruction than a suggestion.

Isobel took off her sunglasses in shock. "I never want to see him or speak to him, ever again." She said it hurriedly, taking a frantic mouthful of wine as if her statement were a resolution to be toasted.

"But if you do not see him, there will be no closure. You must confront him and denounce him, or have him explain himself."

"What is there to explain?" Isobel said, anger in her voice. "You saw what I saw at the airport."

"So, he has a girlfriend," countered Maria dismissively. "And a wife, like you have a husband. So he is a cheat…"

The inference was not lost on Isobel and she rose up in indignation. "But, Maria, there is a difference. I have not lied to *him*. Everything he told me in London was a lie. He was lying while I was giving everything, doing everything. It was all lies."

The fire seeped out of her with the words, and she shrank back into the towel in sadness. Maria touched her friend's arm in response.

"We all lie, every day. If we were truthful all the time we would live our lives in perpetual conflict. Sometimes it is perhaps better to seek to understand first. Who knows, maybe he has an explanation, not one you will like of course, but maybe one you can live with."

"If it were only that simple," she said, pressing her temples, "to shout and scream and slap his face and have it done with. But I can't. Peter *wants* me to see Jay. It's why I'm here. To be some spy in the camp," she said, spitting out the last words, unsure what to do or who to dislike.

"So that is what you must do. And in the process you will have your own answers too. It is perfect," replied Maria, flopping back into the sunbed with gratuitous satisfaction.

"It is not perfect, and you know it." Isobel fell back onto her sunbed too, directing her words into the endless blue of the sky. "Peter's idea of charming Jay is not the same as Jay's idea of being charmed. If I see him I will have to sleep with him."

"And what is so difficult about that? Did you not say you 'give your body but not yourself' to Peter? Well, do the same with Jay. And let it be the 'meaningless sex without love' that you are such an expert on."

She flinched from the venom in Maria's words as she recalled the platitudes of their conversation in the Alpha Lounge. Isobel turned her head away in submission.

"I'm sorry. When I said those things I wasn't judging anyone. It just seemed a clever thing to say."

Maria could not resist seizing the moment. "But you thought you were different from others, maybe better." She threw back her head, seeming to relish her victory before sympathy quelled it into benevolence. "But it does not matter. Now it is about what you must do."

"But I have a conscience," said Isobel, unwisely ascending to her pedestal.

"And where was your conscience when you knelt before the king with —"

"Maria! Please. Whatever I've done or said, I can't bring myself to sleep with Jay again. It would be so humiliating."

Maria took her friend's hands. "But you must see Jay, or confess to Peter. Which is the greater humiliation?"

Isobel lowered her gaze, imagining the scene with Peter, as she had so often since her betrayal. She could not confess, she could not even imagine confessing, and as Maria looked into her eyes, she knew it too.

"You do not need to destroy your marriage. You must see Jay and do what Peter wants."

Isobel opened her mouth to contradict her, already formulating a hopeless excuse, but Maria hushed her with a gentle touch.

"If you must take Jay to your bed, do it with a cold heart but a warm smile. Detach yourself from the act and rise above it. You will not be subjugating yourself to Jay's will, not like before. No. You will be subjugating him to your will, to Peter's will. It will be a victory for both of you. A victory over Jay."

"I don't know," said Isobel, devoid of hope. "Peter may be the victor, but Jay will not be vanquished. He is too strong, too... indomitable. He might hit back, lash out, and who knows what damage he could do."

"But he is married. He has as much to lose as you," Maria said.

"He says his marriage is a sham."

"But of course he does. It is what every cheat says, that their marriage is meaningless." Isobel squirmed once more beneath her words. "And why is that not another lie? And even if there was some truth in it, he is too clever to lash out, because it achieves nothing for him." Maria threw her arms out as she said it, dashing half a glass of prosecco into the sand.

"You can do it, Isobel. And Peter need never know."

Isobel was silent for a moment, hesitating to convey her largest and most unfounded fear.

"Maybe Peter already knows," she whispered, her head down.

"About Jay? What has he said?" asked Maria, turning in sharp consternation.

"That's just it. He hasn't said anything. But I have given him so much cause to that I don't see how he can't know."

Maria shrugged. "You are safe for now, I think. What husband does not confront his cheating wife? But you must see Jay and do what you have to do, or Peter will surely ask why you didn't. And then he *will* know."

Isobel nodded and lay lifelessly on the lounger, falling back into herself at the prospect of what was ahead.

Maria stood up, stretching and scanning around to ensure she was noticed before lying down to pose seductively on her towel, enjoying the feeling of being watched and desired, and of being envied. Half an hour passed before she tired of displaying her beauty and turned to her friend again.

"Now tell me," she said as Isobel looked across to her, "how can I bring the sparkle into your eyes on this beautiful day?"

But Isobel's reflections had darkened her mood, and she was not ready to come back to the light. "I just want things to go back to the way they were," she said, emphatic in her weakness.

"To a life with love and caring but no passion? Can you really go back to that, now you know what true passion is?"

"Maybe I will just have to settle for less than everything," she replied with a bitter laugh.

"And look for more passion elsewhere?" asked Maria sceptically.

"No, not me. I thought I could do that, have Peter for love and Jay for passion. But now I know I can't. So I will just have to go back to Peter, if he still wants me, and just accept him as he is."

"And why would he not want you?" Maria looked at her in exasperation.

"There's something I haven't told you," said Isobel quietly. "Peter has an assistant in his office who follows his every move with her tongue hanging out. I have seen how she looks at him, like a puppy wanting to be stroked. She's quite pretty, in a petite way, and much younger than me."

"But Peter is devoted to you, he doesn't notice other women," said Maria impatiently. "Of this you were sure, more sure than anything else. Am I not correct?"

"I sometimes doubt every belief I once held. I think that if I were to give him some reason to doubt me…and if *she* ever found out that I was not the perfect wife that Peter must tell her I am, well, he would have to be very strong, because I think she would stop at nothing if she saw real opportunity."

Maria reached out to her friend and took her hands.

"Isobel, if I say something to you, will you promise not to take it the wrong way, and not hate me?"

"You mean I deserve everything I get," said Isobel, trying to make light of it and afraid of how earnest her friend looked.

Maria squeezed her hands tightly. "Have you thought that with you and Peter, that you are perhaps getting back what you give out? That you love him and care for him and do everything for him, but that you don't make him feel special. Not like a man wants to feel special."

"What do you mean?" said Isobel, already flinching in expectation.

"Well, for Peter, he looks to his work to make his chest puff out, yet he has a beautiful wife. Why does it not puff out for you, like it does with Arnie for me? You told me about the time in Bangkok. Maybe Peter has needs too, but he loves and respects you too much to express those needs, as he perhaps tried to on your honeymoon. And maybe now, it is simply that you are both in a rut, and one of you must take the lead out of it. And if you do not, well, then maybe you create opportunity."

"And you think I am responsible for creating this…opportunity?" asked Isobel timidly.

"Not creating it, no, but perhaps contributing to it. If this woman is clever, she will see what you are not giving Peter and she will smell opportunity. And then some day, maybe not far off, perhaps Peter will have some great victory, and she will be there watching, waiting, and she will throw her arms around him in celebration. And she will look into his eyes like she believes he is a god, knowing that men believe themselves gods in moments of triumph, and at that moment he would need to be very strong not to take the gift that is being offered up to him."

Isobel stared past her as the image flashed before her like a premonition. Maria left her to think, saying nothing more for a long time before leaping up to rouse her from her thoughts.

"Now it is time to enjoy the beach," she declared. "Let us splash our feet through the sea and show off like we are as vain as the Italians."

She strutted out to the water's edge, absorbing and pointedly ignoring the admiring eyes, her beauty untouchable and infallible, almost other-worldly.

Isobel stared after her as she stood up to follow, feeling the hot sand on her feet and the spray on her face. She knew she could never be Maria, and a chill ran over her skin as she remembered his hands upon her again, as dread cast its shadow over the sun.

Forty-three

Isobel stood in the blank expanse of Florence airport waiting for Peter's flight to disembark, her inner turmoil contrasting with the organised rush all about her. Peter had agreed to meet Andy at the airport to discuss investing in Castello di Capadelli and Isobel invited herself along, puzzled and disappointed that her husband had not thought to ask her. It was to be a fleeting visit on his part — his flight home being only six hours later — but her pleas that he stay over had fallen on deaf ears, he had things to do in London. Nevertheless, she sent the briefest of texts to Jay, saying that Peter was in Florence till the morning, grateful for a plausible reason to stay out of Jay's bed. As she waited there alone she wondered when the lies would end, if they would ever end.

She flopped down with a thud, feeling sick with the fear that now resided in every corner of her life. She took out a magazine, convincing herself it was important to read a little Italian every day, but soon found herself going back over the same sections, taking nothing in, and growing increasingly uneasy. Maria's words of the previous day echoed in her mind, stamping themselves over the magazine in great cruel letters — "it only takes one wagging tongue."

She knew her behaviour since her arrival had been faultless; she had not spoken to or seen Jay, even though her phone had several messages and unanswered calls. Yet still she fidgeted as she waited, feeling that her very appearance might somehow betray her, if it had not already. The consequences of discovery did not bear thinking about, yet she thought of little else; the tears, the hurt, the slamming of doors, and the nightmare of taking apart in days what twenty years had put together. Where would she live? Back in the Cotswolds with an infirm mother or in an empty flat in town perhaps? She could always stay in Capadelli, in her new romantic hideaway, she thought bitterly.

The automatic arrivals door parted as the first of the passengers made their way through the unmanned customs area. Peter would be one of the first out, Isobel was confident of that. He believed in travelling light. She glanced through the doors at the narrow line of approaching passengers who straggled out like ants with their baggage trailing behind them.

After what seemed a lifetime of looking for her husband, she did not immediately recognise him. The school boyish side parting that had been his signature haircut since childhood, and to which he had clung despite the slight thinning and backward progression of his hairline, was gone. A much shorter, almost crew cut, style was in its place; he looked years younger and somehow sharper, less bland. His clothing too was markedly different, complementing the look perfectly with expensive, smart, casual attire that would not have been out of place on Bond Street. As Isobel stared at him in astonishment, her mind went back to the day of his return from Paris, when she found his blue silk boxers in the laundry basket, at first thinking they were her own French knickers, because Peter only ever bought multi-packs of sensible cotton Y-fronts from department stores. She had immediately known that Rachel had bought them and, despite herself, examined them for any trace of excitement, but found nothing. She had despised herself for even thinking of suspecting him, because if he had anything to hide he would surely have thrown them away. Because that is what she would have done.

"Wow, Peter," she said, banishing her thoughts as she reached up to kiss him, "you've had a make-over. What brought this on?"

"Nothing," he said with a casual shrug. "The hairdresser suggested the cut, and I just thought I'd freshen things up a bit."

"You look great, you really do," she said, her voice becoming slightly false as a sliver of doubt entered her mind. Peter had been going to the same hairdresser for five years; why the change, and why now? And the casual outfit had not been thrown together; it had been *put* together, right down to the suede loafers. It was all so unlike him.

Isobel took the plastic bag that he was carrying and put her arm through his. As they walked the long white corridors to meet Andy she grew gradually more uneasy, feeling a stiffness in his arm as if he were suffering her attention, as one suffers the hold of a grumpy old relative. But his smile and his tone were natural enough, so perhaps she imagined it; certainly she was unable to remember the last time she had given real thought to any part of Peter's body.

They took a window seat in the corner of a lounge with a view across the runway. Peter was not hungry and Isobel professed the same even though nothing had passed her lips all day. She told Peter she did not want a coffee, but he arrived nevertheless with a large latte and her favourite cake, a blueberry muffin, and a green tea for himself.

"There really was no need for you to come across," said Peter as he watched her pluck a blueberry from the muffin.

"I wanted to see you," she said with a warm smile, adding, "I'm missing you," but not quite believing she was. He touched her hand but did not respond in kind, so she continued. "I would like you to stay tonight, if you can."

"I need to get back, but I thought when we're finished with Skinner, we could pop into Florence. It beats kicking around the airport for five hours."

Isobel's jaw dropped open. Kicking around airports was what Peter did; preparing for calls, making calls, checking mails, working on presentations. It was the first time she could remember him not relishing the prospect.

"So things are quiet?" she asked, recovering her composure.

"No, surprisingly, they're not. Aside from this circus with these clowns in Tuscany, I seem to be in more demand than ever." He sat back in satisfaction and took a sip of tea. "Head-hunters every day, a couple of old clients have been on the phone wanting me to help out, and the Telecommunications crowd have a position for me. Not something I'd be interested in, but nice to be asked."

"Word's out then," said Isobel with a nervous smile, not wanting to elicit too much business conversation.

"Yep, seems so, and without me making a single call. Other than fixing our man Brooke, I was planning to take it easy, maybe pop down to the boat for a few days. But looks like that might be difficult."

Isobel nodded as she rustled through the carrier bag she had relieved him of, pulling forth an inconspicuous airport paperback.

"Why thank you, darling, that's very thoughtful of you." She had already turned to the back cover. "A crime thriller?"

Peter leant across and took the book. "Sorry, it's actually for me." He winced apologetically, tucking it into his case.

"You are reading a *book*? Not emails, not airport billboards?"

"I've just finished one, as it happens, one of yours that was knocking about, but I thought the crime thriller might be more in keeping with the job at hand, you know with Skinner and Brooke." He laughed as he spoke, pronouncing their names like some low-budget TV thriller.

She laughed in return, bemused by her own pleasure. "So you want to go into Florence? You weren't that enraptured last time as I recall. You have a restaurant in mind?"

"I thought we might do a gallery, the Uffizi maybe."

Isobel almost fell off her chair. "Nice idea, but no chance," she said ruefully, "the queue will be half way to Pisa this time of year. Remember, we had to skip it last time."

"I've got VIP passes," he said with a grin.

Isobel was almost speechless. "You mean you've actually arranged something. I thought that was my job, or, or Rachel's." The laughter died from her eyes as she said the name.

"Well, right now I don't have an assistant, so I called the concierge service you use, and they sorted it all out."

Isobel choked on the last blueberry in reply, but before she could ask how Peter even knew she used a concierge service, Andy arrived. He rushed up, spluttering an apology about his driver, red faced and flustered.

"No worries, no worries," said Peter, with a warmth and friendliness that Isobel wasn't expecting. "Ok if we talk here?"

Andy nodded and Peter signalled for a coffee as the other man rummaged frantically through his things, his breathing jagged and fast.

"Take a breath for a minute or two, Andy, there's no rush," said Peter benevolently. "Ok if Isobel sits in?"

As Andy nodded and sought to compose himself, Peter calmly and neatly laid out two files, a notebook, and a pen — he did not arrive at business meetings half prepared.

"Ok if we get straight down to it?" asked Peter, with no sign of waiting for, or needing, an answer.

"Sure," said Andy, still catching his breath and fumbling in his briefcase.

"Firstly, Andy, I must congratulate you on the quality of the prospectus, and for all the supporting information; it's great when things are done so professionally."

Andy had his doubts about that; quick and dirty was Jay's style, but he withheld any assumption and latched his eyes onto Peter, buoyed by the eagerness in his eyes.

Peter's intonation was enthusiastic as he continued. "The reality is that I was sceptical about this opportunity when Jay asked me to look at it. So initially I thought of it as a desk exercise, a favour to Jay mainly, perhaps something I might be able to recommend to one or two of my contacts that are active property investors. Which I am not, by the way, I hardly know a brick from a budgerigar, let alone the business you guys are in."

Andy nodded; he found Peter's manner perplexing and took his self-effacement at face value, sounding almost patronising in his reply.

"I'm happy to explain anything that wasn't clear in the prospectus."

Peter did not even glance at him and continued as if he had not spoken.

"Anyway I'm now thinking that this is something that I might want to invest in myself, subject to what I hear back from my advisors, but everything they've told me so far is most encouraging." He turned to Isobel and put his arm round her shoulder. "And Isobel just loves the place. And she's the foremost expert in spending my money," he said with a smile.

Andy nodded understanding. "Yep, I've got a wife like that too," he replied. Both men laughed, and some of the tension was released. Andy gave her a furtive look as Peter rifled through his papers; she looked too classy for the rumours to be true, but if they were he certainly approved of Jay's taste.

"The advice I have," continued Peter, "is that any decision will hinge on what the property is worth now, as future income is uncertain."

Andy frowned and shook his head a little. "Unfortunately, Peter, I don't think I could countenance a transaction based on simple property values."

"Of course, of course, I understand that. But supposing we were looking at just the underlying property values, what figure would you have in mind?"

Andy hesitated.

"Just a ball park," said Peter with an encouraging smile.

"I would need an updated valuation, of course. But, just as an initial number, around thirty million. Pounds, that is," added Andy, suppressing a lump in his throat at the gravity of the figure. But Peter, who was used to advising on investments of hundreds of millions for clients, did not blink.

"Well, that's something we can work around then."

Andy rushed headlong for the light at the end of the torture, seeing his salvation miraculously materialise before him.

"When would you be able to get back to me? It's just that I have a couple of other investors looking at this too."

"That really depends on you. The bank wants to have a look around — due diligence and all that malarkey — just routine I expect."

"I'd need time to arrange it, set it all up," said Andy, his eyebrows narrowing. "And I have to think about the staff, this could all be very unsettling to them."

"No need for that," said Peter, brisk and authoritative. "I expect these guys do it all the time. Just tell whomever you need to that the taxman is auditing you, and you need to review the accounts. Shall we say tomorrow? Just tell your guys in Capadelli to expect some whippersnappers in suits to poke around for a day or two."

"A day or two?" said Andy in alarm.

"Beats me too." Peter gave him a comradely smile. "But I guess they have to spin it out to justify those mind-boggling fees."

"Which you're picking up?" said Andy.

"But of course." Peter turned to Isobel. "If you've got nothing else on, darling, maybe you could pop into Capadelli this week, say hello to the team on my behalf. That would be all right, wouldn't it, Andy?"

He nodded as Peter swivelled one of the files around to face Andy, and offered him a pen. "Now all I need is your signature on a few authorisations; the accountants won't lift a pebble without permission." Peter stood up, looking down on him like an examiner.

Andy studied the documents for a long time, but finally signed as Peter silently hovered.

"So tomorrow then," said Peter cheerfully, "and I will have a definite answer for you in five days. How does that sound?"

Isobel almost ran to keep pace with Peter as they left the airport, desperate to convey her admiration at how well he handled Andy, how he'd reduced a wily businessman to rubble before him.

"It was all so fast, Peter," she said, full of excitement as they pulled out of the car park. "I don't think Andy even knew what hit him."

"Preparation, speed, and surprise. It's the only way to do it," said Peter, his professional manner betrayed by the spark of triumph in his eyes.

"Yes, but I mean, you hardly gave him time to think, and he didn't even realise he was being railroaded into letting the accountants in tomorrow."

"Oh, I think he did. But as soon as he pushed me on timescales, I knew I had him."

"Do you think he really believed that you were as keen as you said?"

"That's what he wants to believe, that I'm his golden goose," said Peter, with a derisory, almost pitying, laugh.

Isobel raised the corners of her mouth but her stomach started to churn when the implications of his victory became clear. She was now expected to be in the lion's den the very next day. There could be no hiding away now.

"So the show's on the road," said Peter. "Sorry to spring tomorrow on you, but you are ok with going to Capadelli, aren't you?"

"Of course, why wouldn't I be?" said Isobel quickly, worry rapidly rising up inside her. Peter glanced at her and ignored the question.

"It's a great opportunity for you to be nosing around."

Isobel half-nodded before pausing and turning it into a shake, belatedly realising she had no idea what was going on.

"What are the accountants actually going to be doing?"

"It's going to be a drains up review. The whole lot, so we see what's in the sewer."

"But I thought you'd already got most of what you needed?" she asked tentatively, worried she was being sent back for Peter to feed his ego, or perhaps even for his revenge.

"A lot of it, yes, but there will be gaps, intentional gaps. We need access to their computers."

"But will…will Brooke agree?" She cringed at the loudness of her voice in the confines of the car, too afraid of it being quiet.

"Brooke doesn't have a say, Skinner is in charge now," said Peter confidently.

Isobel wasn't so sure. "I don't know, he's still the boss around Capadelli," she said, turning her face to look at the passing countryside, wanting to avoid his gaze.

"Not for long, if I have my way. And get this; I'm using the outfit Brooke used to work for, BB&T — that will be poetic justice. They are the best in the business, so we get the true financial position. And I've also got their legal people involved. Scams are one thing, but if there has been any criminality in the way things have been done, we need to know about it before Brooke has disappeared into his bolt hole."

"Do you really think it's that serious, that Brooke is a crook?" Isobel didn't want to believe it, but Peter's authority was almost omnipotent.

"I think it's a possibility, but that would be for others to decide. But it's a fine line between a scam and a crime, and Brooke will know where that line is, and think he is just the right side of it. Well, maybe he is and maybe he isn't."

"But Brooke will want to know what's going on, if you are bringing people in, he's going to want to obstruct things, isn't he?" She didn't want to press Peter further but fear gripped her judgement in a vice.

"We need to ensure the accountants get to the documents before Brooke gets to the shredder. So that's why you need to be with the accountants as early as you can."

"But won't Jay be there?" she insisted, flinching at her stupidity.

"How the hell would I know?" snapped Peter, as if the name touched a nerve. "But maybe you can think of something to make sure he's not."

Isobel tried to keep a poker face. She had no difficulty thinking of something to keep Jay away, but she was determined to avoid it at all costs.

As she stared at Peter, his eyes on the road, it occurred to her that they had been together for over an hour and she hadn't seen the infernal phone to his ear.

"You haven't forgotten your mobile, have you, darling?"

Peter reached into his pocket with one hand as he held the wheel with the other.

"It's been switched off."

Peter and Isobel had not even reached the car park before Andy called Jay, all but jumping up and down in the lounge to contain his ecstasy.

"I've got some good news at last," he said with delight, not even waiting for Jay to speak.

"The cancer is in remission?" asked Jay.

"If my only problem was cancer, I'd be smiling. You sitting down?"

"I am now," said Jay, as he hit the golf ball down the 18th fairway at Castelafi Golf course. "What's the scoop?"

"Peter Roberts has bought your proposal." He announced the news syllable-by-syllable, eking out his pleasure piece by piece.

"Now you are joking?" Jay's voice resonated from the earpiece, its shock hanging almost visibly in the air.

"I kid you not. I just came out of meeting with him, he's eager as a virgin in an Amsterdam whorehouse." Andy was only driven to crudity when his emotions reached points of extremity. Jay felt almost fond of him as he replied.

"An apt metaphor perhaps."

"Anyway," continued Andy, "guess who we have to thank?"

"Err, give me a second to think, the man that wrote the prospectus maybe?"

"Invented it more like," shot back Andy cheerfully. "No, seems like the lovely Isobel is driving it. She's fallen in love with the place, you could almost say she, how shall I put this, she can't get enough of it…" He left the innuendo hanging there, but Jay seemed oblivious to it.

"So you've agreed money?"

"We've talked money, and he didn't even flinch when I told him how much the site alone was worth. So, seeing as I'd give the place away if I could, I reckon a deal can be struck."

"Let's not get ahead of ourselves, Andy; deals like this aren't done in a heartbeat."

"Which is the other thing I need to tell you about. His bankers are involved. They want to kick over the stones around Capadelli, and they want to start tomorrow. So I need some adult supervision on site, other than the ridiculous Irishman. You need to be there, that ok?" The only emotion in Andy's voice was derision for Eamon; he could see no reason why Jay wouldn't drop everything and save them both.

Jay envisaged his plans for tomorrow, they primarily involved Isobel and a blindfold, and he had no plans to change them and babysit accountants.

"I'll make sure it's covered off."

"I don't have anything to worry about on this, do I, Jay?"

"The books are cleaner than a dentist's teeth. At least the books they'll see."

"Good. I don't need to tell you how much we need this."

"Sure, Andy, I get it," said Jay, hitting the off button as he rooted around for his lost ball in the rough.

Forty-four

Peter's footsteps echoed with a sort of hallowed menace as he paced the marble foyer of BB&T, the company he had enlisted to find out exactly what was happening at Castello di Capadelli. He was due to meet with Toby Brougham, a senior partner, and the rest of his team in mere moments — only a forbidding oak door stood between him and the truth. As his name was called and the door swung open his heart lifted with the prospect of retribution and, as he walked in to see a formidable semi-circle of experts, waiting to deliver their verdicts on the ill-fated venture, he felt all-powerful again.

At the centre sat Toby, crisp and polished in his black suit. He had the appearance of wisdom; he was silver haired, and every feature on his face was outlined by a series of faint wrinkles, extending outwards like ripples on water. A thick-rimmed pair of spectacles rested majestically on his nose and when he looked down to read his notes — intertwining his long fingers in meditative thought — they slid down to the end, giving every impression of condescending severity. A lesser man would have been cowed in his presence but Peter was clad in the iron armour of his business persona and had been in the game long enough to recognise Toby as a softly spoken philosopher beneath a granite shell.

Toby gave Peter a curt nod before he began, his voice ringing out emotionless and authoritative.

"We have completed our initial review of the company, though we must stress that we do not yet know everything, and that further work is needed."

"Of course," said Peter; the necessity of further investigation was a phrase he had used with clients a thousand times.

"The financial situation, Mr. Roberts, is critical." Toby looked down gravely to the figures at his fingertips, his glasses sliding ominously downwards. "The company is, we believe, insolvent. I am sorry to be the bearer of bad news." He paused to let the message sink in, his studied countenance inviting some form of reaction from Peter, whose face was serious but otherwise blank, a studied mask to hide his satisfaction from the room.

"So, there's no possibility of them turning the situation around?"

"No possibility at all as we see it," said Toby, his mouth a straight, thin, and unchangeable line. "They owe twenty million Euros to creditors alone."

"So they're in a bit of a fix then?" asked Peter, controlling a twitch of laughter with iron will. Toby narrowed his eyes and looked hard at Peter, focusing his gaze through the lenses like beams of light.

"I'm afraid so, Mr. Roberts. I'm sorry we can't be more encouraging with this opportunity."

Peter nodded, his face set in disappointment. "You say that millions are owed to creditors, is there any possibility this is a case of fraud?"

Toby looked to his right and motioned for a young woman with a pinstriped trouser suit and apricot lips to speak. She rose from her seat and adjusted her glasses, her voice loud but pleasant.

"Certainly the case has many of the characteristics of what most people might consider a fraud, but it is a complex area."

Peter nodded impatiently, hastening her on with an almost imperceptible cough.

"What we do believe," she continued, "is that Mr. Brooke, unknown to Mr. Skinner, has used the venture to divert funds to his own companies, principally through commissions and expenses."

"So that is fraud then?"

The smart young woman removed her designer glasses for dramatic effect. "That's potentially a valid conclusion. But there's nothing that he's done that is, strictly speaking, illegal."

Toby broke in to offer his words of wisdom. "What I can say is that we have seen cases like this before. Often you will hear plausible sounding explanations for what has been done. So then it becomes a matter of who you believe, really."

Peter nodded, his chin set hard, and stood up to leave. "Toby, your guys have done excellent work, thank you."

"But we have other matters to discuss," he said, anxious perhaps to keep the many meters in the room ticking, while also rising to meet Peter's eyes.

"As I can imagine. But I can read faster than even you guys can talk, so I'll settle for the report."

The older man nodded with the faintest semblance of a smile, and the respectful bearing of a man who knows he has met his equal, and led Peter out of the conference room and to his office. It was like walking into open air; the room was situated on a corner and both outer walls were made of glass. The Thames ran beneath, docile and green, straddled by the imposing London Bridge, which sat to the left of the window like office art.

"This is the dossier you asked for, Peter," said Toby, now opting for the familiar address, as he passed across a sealed red envelope with 'secret' marked in black letters across its surface. "I'm afraid it doesn't make for pleasant reading. I say that with particular regret because, as you know, Mr. Brooke — or Brookes as he was then — qualified with us and worked here in this building. Many people here still remember him, which might tell you something also."

"So I heard," said Peter, leaning forwards in interest. The wrinkles around Toby's mouth contracted in response, scoring deep into his face like scars.

"It is a long story, Peter, and I'd rather not bore you with it."

"I'm curious. How about the short version?"

Toby leant back in his chair and stared out the window, as if seeking the past in the murky waters below. "Ah," he sighed, "what might have been. Julian was very gifted and very popular — he had a generosity of spirit that drew people to him. But he was unorthodox in his methods. A maverick you might say. Some of the old guard disliked that; they looked at Julian and saw the future, and felt threatened by it. His maverick methods, you see, brought in a lot of business. He was, as we say, a rainmaker. Someone destined for the top."

"So they ganged up and got rid of him?"

The lines grew deeper around the old man's mouth, closing up into terrible blackness. "Not exactly. Julian's unconventional approach extended to his personal expenses. Maybe we should leave it at that?"

Peter shook his head in refusal and incredulity. "You fired him over a few dodgy receipts? I've not come across that before. Why didn't you just warn him, put him on the straight and narrow? Give him a second chance, or a last chance?"

"There were those that wanted to," said Toby, sage-like and wistful, "because the tragedy of it was that Julian was not lining his own pockets. His mantra was to give clients what they wanted, everything they wanted, you know, the whole fleshpot-demimonde of city-player schmooze." Peter nodded with a grimace, acknowledging a method that had never been his own. "So Julian covered himself by submitting spurious receipts — quite a lot of them."

"Sounds a bit harsh," said Peter with a frown. "How many in this building haven't slipped through a receipt or two that they shouldn't have?"

"Quite so. Unfortunately for Julian, someone had taken an intense dislike to him. She's still with us in fact. Sara Golding. A bit of a ball-breaker."

"The woman who runs the TMI account?" asked Peter in shock, his brain kicking into overdrive.

Toby raised his eyebrows in admiration. "My, my, Peter, you have been busy. Anyway, when the expenses irregularity blew up, she went after him, and got the support of a few of the old guard."

"And it was goodbye Mr. Brooke?"

"Precisely. Though of course the record shows he resigned, which he did, but with a gun to his head," he turned away, looking mournfully into the waters once more, "a gun in Sara's hand."

Peter nodded, his eyes too on the water as the old man continued.

"I saw Julian a couple of times after that; I could see the experience had changed him, scarred him even, he was somehow harder, more ruthless, and of course bitter. I think it was the injustice, or perhaps I should say the double standards, that really got to him."

Peter was satisfied, everything fitted. "Ok, let's move on. What has he been up to since he left you?"

Toby reverted to a more formal air, as if leaving a trance. "Mr. Brooke is a clever man. Over the last eight years he has used that knowledge most effectively in a succession of business ventures, most of which have ultimately failed, sometimes at significant cost to others. I think you know the most recent example."

"I do, the Malaga scam."

"The document we have prepared sets out the history of Julian's companies over that time. He has registered and folded over fifty businesses in the UK alone during that time, but none of the fallout has ever stuck to him personally. The dossier is purely factual. It makes no judgements; we are after all not the police. You must draw your own conclusions." He looked Peter straight in the eyes, showing his own decision in the fond light at their centre.

"So how has he got away with it for all these years?"

Toby laced his fingers with an almost dreamlike fluidity as he gave his reply, admiration faint behind his words. "What we can say is that Mr. Brooke has been particularly astute. Most of the ventures were set up in other people's names. And it is perfectly possible, if you are clever and cynical and, yes, even perhaps thick skinned enough, to go from one failed venture to another, while personally profiting in the process."

"And without doing *anything* dishonest and illegal?" asked Peter with scepticism.

"Let us be realistic," said Toby, swivelling to face the window and delivering each word with the distant assuredness of a deity. "The business world is full of chicanery. If you are motivated by high moral principles, it is perhaps better to pursue a career in the church than in the City. So frustrating as it may be, using the rules to your own advantage is not a crime."

Forty-five

As Andy strode along to his meeting with Peter he went with the urgency and expectancy of a bookie on his way to the racetrack. He was looking almost unrecognisable from the flustered man at the airport. He was translucently pale, an almost monochrome figure in his black suit. Everything about his appearance suggested precise control, from the meticulously flattened hair to the mirror-shined shoes, and the pedestrians milling about on Tottenham Court Road subconsciously moved aside as they met his path, thin and determined. Jay had called him a few days earlier, incandescently angry after being alerted to the accountant's microscopic activities at Capadelli, and the conversation still rung in Andy's mind, echoing over and over again like thunder in a storm.

"You said Peter Roberts was just going to have a look at a few things, now I'm being told it's a full-blown tax audit? What the fuck are you up to?"

"What the fuck am I up to?" Andy had replied in exasperation. "What the fuck are you up to, more like. We agreed you were going to be on site to supervise things!"

"Something came up," Jay had said casually as Andy tore at his hair.

"I can imagine," he said with a heavy sigh. "The tax story is just a cover so the staff isn't alarmed."

"You and Roberts aren't up to something, trying to cut me out or stitch me up, are you?"

Andy had exhaled in loud frustration, "I assure you this is something that I reluctantly agreed to. But as Roberts is paying, and as it's been forced on me, it may be no bad thing to get a full accounting update. I'm the principal investor. So please don't tell me what I can and can't do. If you suffered disruption to day-to-day operations then I apologise. Goodbye."

He smiled at the recollection of his victory, but it was cold comfort in the face of whatever Peter's investigators might have found out. Although, Andy thought to himself as he reached the door of the office Peter had hired, it had taken him two years to properly understand what was going on in Tuscany; how much could they really have learnt in a few days?

But as he walked through the door and sat down opposite Peter, his quiet confidence was shattered with the first blow.

"Before we talk about what each of us want, I have a few things I need you to know," Peter said with the gravity of a doctor about to diagnose a terminal condition. "Almost nothing about your company in Italy is legal. You're running a hotel without the proper licences; that in itself might be a police matter."

Andy straightened himself in his seat at the mention of the law but fought to retain a sphinx-like expression.

"You are also trading while insolvent, which, in case you don't know, is viewed much more seriously in Italy than the UK. Without wishing to be melodramatic, you might be looking at a significant term of imprisonment."

Andy laughed nervously, sure that Peter was overplaying his hand.

"Imprisonment? Be serious. I've done nothing wrong."

Peter continued with his deadpan delivery. "That would be for the court to decide."

Andy rose slightly from his seat and then set himself back down in agitation. "I have no idea where you think you are going with this nonsense, but even if you possessed a shred of evidence for what you are claiming, I am just one director, and my company in Italy is only a small part of a much larger operation."

"Yes," said Peter with all the humour of a hangman, "but one of the many problems you have is that the company shares are registered in your name; you are the only named director. So it's you alone who is legally accountable."

Andy rose fully now, hardly able to believe what he was hearing. "But—" he began and then stopped as realisation hit home like a hammerhead — why Jay had made him sole director, why all the money travelled to Jay's companies and not his own. He was the fall guy. The thought of Interpol and an international arrest warrant with his name on it flashed through his mind. He fell back into the seat like lead but mastered his fear and resolved to be lectured no longer.

"Let's cut the crap here. You obviously have no interest in Jay's proposal, and probably never did, so what *do* you want?"

"I want Brooke hung out to dry," said Peter with venom in his voice, "like he's hung you out. It's that, or my file goes to the Italian police and the UK serious fraud office."

Andy narrowed his eyes and looked at Peter intently, wondering if he had heard the rumours too.

"And what's in it for me, supposing I had an interest in doing that?" he asked, sick and tired of being the victim.

"Stop fucking with me, Andy," said Peter, unwilling to consider negotiation. "You tried to screw me over for thirty million and you can't even pay this month's wages. If you do what I want then I'll protect you until you've spoken to your advisors and sorted this mess out."

"I want to see some evidence—"

"I have the evidence," Peter interrupted, "on BB&T headed paper no less." He thumped down a file as thick as Andy's briefcase. "I can let you have some of this. A redacted version, as the spooks call it."

Andy knew when to quit. "Jay's not an idiot," he sighed, "he's not going to just roll over and let us do this. How am I supposed to get him to play ball if, as you say, he's insulated himself better than Al Capone?"

"Didn't they get Al Capone for tax dodging?" said Peter with a sombre smile. "Anyway, it's your problem now, you've got three days to get back to me, or the shit hits the fantasy."

As the days passed, Andy's rage and indignation flared and flickered with his mood. He felt a marionette in Peter's hands and he hated it, but nothing could conceal that —regardless of his motives — Peter had done him a favour. Legal and financial advice had confirmed that he was but a phone call away from a prison cell — only one path lay before him and to either side was an abyss, each crafted by the two men that pulled him in grotesque puppetry.

And so it was with resolve — the iron resolve of a man crushed by ultimatum — that Andy flew out to Tuscany to meet with Jay, convinced that he was at least siding with the lesser evil, and ready to announce the closure of Castello di Capadelli.

As Andy sat in Jay's office, looking out at the clean bright courtyard with its closely pruned plants and immaculate stonework, he could not quite believe what he was to say, or that so idyllic an image could be so false.

"What's on your mind, Jay?" he asked, determined at least to be human.

"Well, for one thing I was hoping for an update on the Roberts proposal. It all seems to have gone quiet."

"No, it all seems to be proceeding to plan."

"So that review didn't turn up any show-stoppers?"

"A few difficult questions, but nothing I couldn't handle." Andy flopped his arm causally over the studded armrest. "Frankly, I think the man is out of his depth. I expect to hear something next week."

"That's good," said Jay, running his finger along his lower lip. "I had him down as a smart cookie though. You don't get to where he is without knowing your onions."

Andy faltered for a split second. "Well, I expect so, but then again he has no direct experience of our industry." He let the briefest hint of a smile light his eyes. "What else is on your mind?"

"Come on, Andy, we've known each other too long, you know what's on my mind," Jay snapped.

"No announcement yet then?"

"No." He bored deep into Andy's eyes, as if holding him accountable.

"And your instincts tell you what?"

"Everything says we've won it, but—"

"But a call might help?" Andy interrupted, the smile growing within him.

"No one else can get to Epstein but you, and the file's sitting in his in-tray."

"Hum. I'd love to make the call, Jay, but you see the thing is I'm in a bit of a bind myself. In fact, it's lucky you're here, because the police could knock on that door any minute. Take a look through this while I get us both a coffee." Andy pushed across a file, and rose to his feet.

The blood had drained from Jay's face when Andy returned, but the fire in his belly was far from extinguished.

"I'll need time to go through this, but the conclusions are flawed, it's all supposition," said Jay. "If you let me—"

Andy held up the palm of his hand as he cut Jay short. "Don't even go there. I'm done with your spin. You can't talk your way out of what you've behaved yourself into, not this time."

"Who pulled this shit together?" Jay had to struggle to not shout and Andy drew strength from his lack of composure.

"I've had my accountants and lawyers on it for the last month. Obviously, I'm shocked. All I asked for was a standard risk assessment. The operation here will have to close, before someone else shuts it down. And anyway, as you can see from the figures, the business in Capadelli is totally bust. But it seems your operations in the UK are, well, armour plated."

"But what about the Roberts proposal?" asked Jay, confused but resilient.

"He wins," said Andy with a theatrical sigh, "I'm going to sell, but it will be a fire sale."

"I thought you said he was out of his depth?"

"That was before you asked me to make a phone call."

"And I'm the villain of the piece?"

"I think that puts it rather well," said Andy with an exaggerated grimace. "But here's what I propose. You resign all your positions and interests in what we have here, and I will make the call."

"No fucking way, Andy," said Jay vehemently. "Fire sale or not, this place is still worth millions of anybody's money, and I'm entitled to twenty-five percent of whatever it realises."

"Which won't cover your unpaid tax," said Andy with an ominous raise of his eyebrows.

"What's the taxman got to do with this?" shouted Jay, exasperated and wrong-footed by Andy's change of tack.

"Quite a lot actually, my dear Julian. You've been routing all your sales and commissions and other revenues to offshore accounts.

I have all the records. That is tax evasion, which last I heard was a crime. Unless, of course, you've been declaring the money transfers…"

Jay stood up and made towards him, angry not at the prospect of ruin, but the shift in control. Andy rose to meet him and for a second it seemed the two men might come to blows. But Jay's dependency on Andy's goodwill demanded conciliation.

"You can't unload all this on me now and expect me to give you an answer," he said, hoping for some miracle, thinking Andy too moral, too judicious, to play tough and dirty.

"That's up to you, but the clock is ticking on your deal, and it could be called at any time." Andy looked at his watch. "Think about what I've said. You can keep the file — I've got copies. I'll set up a contract signing ceremony in London on Monday, which I believe is the deadline Epstein is working to. You sign over what I want, and I sign over what Roberts wants. That's the deal."

And with that he strode out, feeling the master once more.

Andy called Peter as soon as he got to the car, standing in the shade of a crumbling church that shed its dust onto his shoulders with no regard for his feelings of triumph.

"No promises — he's thinking about it — but I think he will play ball. He walks away with no compensation — that's several million at the least. That enough of a roasting for you?"

"And you'll block his music deal?"

"How come you know about that?" said Andy, taken aback at Peter's inside knowledge, and wondering again about the rumours.

"No mystery," said Peter casually, "he mentioned it over dinner."

"The music deal is the only leverage I've got. I'm the turkey here remember, not Jay. Anyway, there's a lot of people involved in that deal, people who have done me no wrong."

"So you'd be happy to see Jay make millions on a deal you've set up, when he's cost you millions, and damn near put you behind bars?" Peter's tone was provocative, challenging Andy to take from the taker. "Maybe that's a scenario you might want to ponder."

Andy bridled at being patronised. "A pound of flesh not enough for you?"

It wasn't. Peter continued to turn the screw without mercy or regret. "What's more important here, Andy, your principles or a lifetime living with Kate's wrath?"

"I've delivered on my part of the deal; Jay will be at the meeting to sign the papers, so back fucking off," said Andy, testosterone rising within him like mercury in a blast furnace.

Peter duly backed off, but with a parting shot. "Ok, Andy, but just ask yourself this. If it were the other way round, would Jay leave you a lifeline?"

Forty-six

The conference room at BB&T might have been designed to intimidate. It boasted high ceilings, a plate glass wall to the river side, and an array of imposing oil paintings, the paint and board images of the firm's finest men, each staring down in hallowed superiority. As Isobel walked in, two paces behind her husband, she marvelled at his confidence — a titan with the stage presence of a master of his craft. Only two figures awaited them, standing the other side of a twenty-foot teak conference table. They were Sara Golding and Brandon Colville, the head of the UK firm and a man of considerable fame.

"You've twenty minutes to make your pitch," said Brandon after the briefest of pleasantries, as if Peter were selling double-glazing. "It's been a long day."

Peter ignored the slight and went straight for the jugular. "You guys are dead in the water on the TMI deal. Which is the only reason you took this meeting. I can change that."

"Our business affairs are confidential, Mr. Roberts," said Sara Golding coldly, "and as far as I know you have no mandate from TMI."

Peter directed his gaze at her boss. "You said we've got twenty minutes. Do you want to spend it posturing, or talking business?"

Brandon let out a short laugh, but raised a hand in Sara's direction to signal silence. "Go on."

It had taken Peter less than two minutes to wrest control of the meeting; Isobel was frozen with shock and awe.

"You know that they've already decided in favour of your opposition," said Peter, daring them to contradict him.

Sara bit back, "Rick Epstein's going to make the call on this deal," only to receive a withering look from Colville.

"Epstein doesn't know the difference between a back office and a post office; he's going to rubber stamp this deal...unless someone gets to him. I can give him the reason he needs." Peter looked from one to the other, letting the implication sink in.

"Which is?" Colville asked.

"My business affairs are confidential."

The old man laughed again. "Touché. What are you proposing?"

"That I call Epstein on your behalf, and give him that reason. The reason to override the steering committee."

"That's some call," said Colville, his body leaning forward towards Peter as Sara Golding sat bolt upright. "And, if we were interested, what would be your fee?"

"Two million...plus expenses. No win, no fee. And your man Toby that's been doing some due diligence for me, he writes off his bill."

Colville drew his fingers down the corner of his mouth. "Two million for a phone call? Even if what you propose is of interest, my firm is a partnership, I can't agree to something like this on the hoof; I must consult investment committees and so on."

Peter looked at his watch and held his hand out towards Isobel; she passed across a thin file and Peter pushed it across the desk.

"You've got an hour," said Peter, "fax a signed copy of this to me by 5pm."

Sara Golding could contain herself no longer. "You are pretty sure of yourself, aren't you, swaggering in here like you own the place? What if we take our chances with Epstein?"

Peter gave a suppressed laugh as Isobel shifted behind him, unable to keep her nerve.

"Then I make the same offer to the little guys. I guess they might be faster on their feet."

Peter walked out with great, firm footsteps, leaving the imprints of his soles in the pile of the carpet.

"You were brilliant," said Isobel, as soon as they were beyond the revolving doors. "Sara Golding had a face like a frying pan, and as for Colville, I think he actually enjoyed it, the sheer nerve, right in his inner sanctum."

"It won't count for much unless Skinner calls Epstein," said Peter, tempering his wife's elation, "and I reckon that's in the balance."

Peter didn't need to wait for the fax. Thirty minutes later, Colville phoned. It seemed he had spent most of the time checking out Peter's credentials. Whatever Colville had learnt, it was enough to upgrade their embryonic relationship to first name terms.

"The two million won't fly, Peter. Here's the best I can do. A one million success fee, if we win, and a one hundred and fifty thousand pounds retainer a month, for six months, win or lose."

"And you write off Toby's fees?" said Peter, more in assurance than question.

"Of course. I'm standing by the fax machine. Do we have a deal?"

"We do."

"Welcome to BB&T, Peter."

Isobel held her palms to her breasts then pinched her nipples before emerging from the bathroom feigning nonchalance, thankful that Peter could not see the fluttering fingers inside her stomach. She glided across to the dresser in all her grace and beauty, youthful and lissom in a satin top and red silk shorts. She pretended not to notice her husband's eyes on her smooth, svelte legs, no doubt puzzled to see her displaying them. She stood before the dresser, leaning her face close into the mirror, her arched back emphasizing her pert, round derriere, as she dabbed around her eyes with a wipe as if to remove some final trace of make-up, imagining his gaze burning in to her. When she could sustain the charade no longer, she discarded the wipe, and turned towards the bed, throwing Peter a half smile. She lay next to him, his eyes now fixed on the ceiling, his hands behind his head, and she imagined the excitement of the meeting still running through his veins, as it ran through hers. She wanted to take him, to pleasure him in the way she pleasured Jay, in the way he once craved for her to pleasure him. But fear and guilt forced her to lie still and wait for him, knowing that her wantonness would surely fuel his suspicions, if not confirm her betrayal.

He stayed silent and made no move to touch her and eventually she was compelled to follow her urges, and she turned to him, her fingers raking his chest under his pyjamas, as she kissed him on the shoulder. "I was so proud of you today," she whispered, clawing at his chest, want burning inside her. But still he lay passive, so she gently nuzzled her head against his neck and pressed her breasts into him, bringing her leg up to rest across his thighs.

She thought she sensed his body tense, but he remained motionless on his back. "I'm pretty shattered," he finally said, as he took her wrist and lifted her hand from him, kissing her on the brow, before pulling the sheet up over him, as he silently turned his body away.

Forty-seven

Even before Isobel entered what she feared might be a coliseum of woe, emotions were high and division was in the air. Sheltered from the sun under a faded parasol as they pulled on their cigarettes, a huddled group with gravelled Glaswegian voices was marking out the field of battle.

"I'm telling you now, Kenny, it's a den of thieves that we walked into like babes in the wood, and worse is yet to come, mark my words," said the man in the waxed green jacket.

In between hurried puffs of smoke, his companion, a man short in stature with a pinched face and a head as smooth as an eggshell, did not agree. "And I'm telling you, you are wrong. Andy Skinner is an honourable man, of that I am sure. If it weren't for him I'd be sleeping under an olive tree tonight while that rogue Devlin was laying out sleeping bags for a caravan of Irish tinkers to throw their heads down in my apartment. It's the devious Dubliner that should be hanging from the Capadelli clock tower, with 'abandon all hope ye who dealt with me' branded on his bull shitting arse."

Isobel skirted round the swirling tobacco cloud above the Scotsmen with head down, not wishing to disturb the debate, and slipped into the humble but high-ceilinged Capadelli village hall by a side door; as she did so she was hit by a wall of noise like a kindergarten playroom. The room was crammed like a commuter train with anxious looking holiday-home owners, their sunburn and agitation glowing red despite the respite provided by the coolness from the morning heat. Isobel stole along the aisle at the side, her large sunglasses and a fashionable sun hat offering some disguise against the few eyes that flicked her way as she sought out a seat. She could see Rosie Barker's worried face through the largely white-haired heads that obscured her view of the stage and she automatically shirked away from its gaze; for although she bore no ill will towards the hapless British owners, she had heard the rumours at Castello di Capadelli that she was the cuckoo in the nest, some even saying she was Jay Brooke's lover. Should they recognise her, she expected that she too might be hung by her heels from the clock tower alongside the already indicted Eamon. She knew only too well she was risking confrontation, and possible humiliation, to discover whether the tale of misfortune she endured from Geoff Barker was as common amongst the British owners as the poor man would have her believe.

It appeared from the crowd that some twenty owners and their spouses had responded to Rosie Barker's email and Isobel was shocked that so many had flown to Tuscany at such short notice. Their attendance made her stomach contort with foreboding as she imagined what horrors could have compelled them to travel all this way for the sake of an hour's discussion. Her fears were confirmed even before the meeting began as she listened in on the discussion of two, clearly newly acquainted, women to her left. They both told heart-rending stories of shattered dreams and unfulfilled promises; the more bitter of the two now having to re-mortgage her home, the other unable to pay for her daughter's wedding.

As their lamentations grew more intense and each shared in the others misery, they grew close to tears and would surely have succumbed to them if Geoff Barker had not elicited the room's attention in the only means at hand, by thumping out a Beethoven theme from the piano that dominated the stage. His objective achieved, he let out a hollow and humble cough to signal that it was time for shared sorrow to give way to measured debate. He began with a personal account of his own situation, and the painful financial circumstances he and Rosie now found themselves in. As he recounted the way he felt he had been strung along for nine months by Eamon, there were murmurings of assent around the room.

"Both Rosie and I feel desperately let down by people we trusted," Geoff continued as the murmurs died down. "What hurts most of all is that we have been lied to." A look of pained indignation was pasted across his pallid face and the wrinkles around his mouth sagged with its downturn in a veritable portrait of wretchedness.

The solemnity was broken by a reedy voice that piped up directly in front of Isobel, as a heavy set woman with sallow skin and bulging eyes made herself heard.

"You are placing the blame on the wrong person," she claimed. "I have spoken to Eamon, and I know he wouldn't lie to *me*, and he assures me that the problems we have been hearing about are the fault of Andy Skinner. He is the multi-millionaire that funds the development, and he hasn't been paying what he's supposed to."

"Fiddlesticks, woman!" shouted a Glaswegian voice. "Is it that you are besotted with the Irish buffoon or what? Can you nay see Devlin is no better than a snake oil salesman, and his master and mentor Mister Brooke likely as slippery."

The woman leapt to her feet in outrage, but her protestations were drowned in a crescendo of voices, as each in the room voiced their view as to where guilt belonged, though no one in the room suggested they might be the victims of their own folly. It seemed to Isobel that Eamon's defenders were carrying the day at the expense of Andy, with hardly a single shot fired in the direction of the miraculously immune managing director himself, Mr. Jay Brooke.

Isobel looked on in outrage and longed to raise her voice with the others now erupting into argument about her, to tell them who the real villain was. But as she listened, the certainty with which she entered the meeting was ebbing away. For all were either saints or sinners, depending on which voice was loudest. During the next thirty minutes her uncertainty was only increased as the room heard a catalogue of complaints, broken promises, and unfulfilled expectations — from kitchens being charged but not supplied to the removal of the Armani toiletries from the bathrooms. And to most in the room, the tight-fisted Andy was emerging as the prime suspect for turning the dream into a nightmare. It seemed the list of Andy's crimes would never end, until an Indian man ascended the platform and silenced the room with a disappointed stare.

"All these problems are no doubt valid," he said, his voice pleasant and melodic, "but the issue is not who makes the shampoo that is in the bathrooms; the issue is that individually and collectively we are owed a lot of money, and we need to agree what, if anything, we plan to do about it."

The room fell silent in deference to his succinct wisdom and he continued with his speech. "Now if, as Mr. Barker suggests, we are not going to be paid the money we are owed, then we have been swindled. And if that is the case the people who have been feeding us false hope and lies for the last year or more are nothing better than cheap charlatans."

"You are not seriously suggesting that the whole thing is a fraud?" cried the sallow-skinned lady. "Because Eamon has explained it all to me. He and his company are only intermediaries, agents really, doing what they are told to do by Skinner. Eamon is as upset about it as we are. He would never—"

"I'm not sure we know enough to say that it is a fraud," continued the wise man, trying hard to disguise his irritation with the woman's objections, "but I am confident that at some point we've all been cheated and lied to. I propose we withdraw our properties from the scheme that allows the company to rent them out when we don't use them; that might bring them to their senses, and understand we will not be trifled with."

There were murmurings of disquiet amongst some in the room at the thought of taking such decisive action, but Isobel was buoyed by his suggestion and tried to instil courage in the orator with her gaze as he was drowned out by a cacophony of arguments. Fortunately, he did not seem defeated and he raised his voice to continue.

"You do understand the law in Italy regarding property debts?"

From the silence that greeted this question it was clear that no one in the audience did.

"Well, in Italy, the law is different from the UK, but it is also clear. The owner of a property pays all its charges, regardless of whether it is being rented or not. In addition to service charges and utility bills, many other charges come with owning a property in Italy. You must even pay for rubbish collection." Jaws were dropping as the man spoke. "And of course you have the annual property tax, plus several local taxes. And then again, even if you do not rent out your holiday property in Italy, the State assumes that you do, so you must also pay Italian income tax on the assumed rental income."

Stunned silence swept the room. The decision whether to declare their Italian rental income — if they ever received it — to the UK tax man was worry enough; to know that they must also deal with the Italian tax authorities sent a shiver down the spine.

"So, if Mr. Skinner's company has not been footing the charges — which I think we can safely assume they haven't — then we are each liable for thousands of pounds worth of bills."

A deadly silence fell over the room as the truth sank in. Several ladies in the audience began to quietly cry and Rosie Barker broke into a flood of noisy tears. Only one pallid face remained unaltered and it belonged to the bulging-eyed woman.

"It's not true. It can't be true. Eamon would never do this to me!"

The Indian gentleman's face drooped in despair and he made his way silently back into the crowd with the slow and heavy footsteps of a father following the coffin of his only son. In his place rose an elderly lady with a spring in her step and blue eye shadow up to her eyebrows. Isobel's heart leapt; it was Eileen Carragher who, regardless of her fondness for Eamon, would surely engender good sense and unity into the divided crowd.

"Hello everybody, I am Eileen Carragher from apartment sixty-nine. Can I speak for a minute? I really don't know what to make of everything I have heard today and I don't understand a lot of what you have been saying, it all sounds like the movies to me. But I do have a suggestion, and I am sorry because it will probably sound silly to most of you."

Isobel's body relaxed as she saw how easily the woman won over the assembled owners. "Until we are sure of the situation," she continued, "I think it would be wise to not be rash. And we must remember that three hundred members rent our apartments, and they have done nothing wrong, so it doesn't seem right to spoil their holidays. Wouldn't it be better if we just sat down with Mr. Skinner and listened to his explanation?"

Isobel had to restrain herself from running to the front as the old lady's speech concluded. She wanted to scream, to yell at the top of her voice, "How can you do nothing?" But Geoff gave her no opportunity to do so. He jumped on Eileen's suggestion, keen to have reached some resolution by the end of the meeting, and backed it wholeheartedly.

"It has been a long meeting but I hope you will agree worthwhile. I believe as a group we are all now much better informed on the situation at Capadelli." The room nodded as he bumbled on. "Mrs. Carragher's idea is a good one. If we are all in agreement, I will take responsibility for organising the meeting she has proposed. I will write to everyone, including to all the many owners who, unfortunately, couldn't be here today in person. Is that ok with everyone?"

Isobel could have cried as she looked at person after person indicating their consent, their faces radiating temporary happiness and confidence in the knowledge that something was being done, and someone else was doing it.

"As regards the rental scheme," Geoff concluded over the rising noise, "I will leave what people want to do as a personal decision. Rosie and I have made up our minds; we are particularly disappointed with some of the visitors who are being allowed to rent our apartment — not our type of people at all. So on Monday we will be writing to formally withdraw our apartment from the scheme. I personally encourage others to do the same, but that is your choice."

"Yes, yes, that is what you all must do!" screamed Isobel, but it was only the voice in her head and even that seemed drowned out as the owners left the hall in noisy confusion, not much wiser than when they arrived, and she had no choice but to follow them. She glanced at her phone as she stood outside the hall to find seven missed calls — two from Peter and five from Jay. How she wished Peter were here to help now; to be cool and clearheaded, to see a solution without being blinded by the aura of emotions — pity, sadness, and fear — that lingered from the meeting.

She had been dreading her next encounter with Jay, and wracking her brains how best to avoid it. But now she was torn between anger and fear; the only right thing to do seemed to be to confront him with the litany of charges that had been laid against him and his cohorts. She needed to find out for herself whether he was the callous con man that some in the room alleged, or whether some case for the defence existed, that he was a victim as much as the rest, exploited by the miserly and ruthless moneyman Skinner, as the sallow-skinned lady from south London claimed. Whatever his other faults, she was certain that a streak of generosity ran through Jay as surely as the colours in a stick of candy. She imagined herself confronting him: she would hear him out, but if he was guilty as charged, she feared she would be unable to contain her anger, let alone feel his touch on her skin. And as she imagined the scene, of being again at the mercy of his powerful hands and hypnotic gaze, her resolve to confront him weakened.

Out of the corner of her eye she spotted Mrs. Carragher walking towards the square where the taxis gathered, and on a whim of mercy ran after her, intent on saving at least one innocent. But as Isobel closed in behind her and reached out her arm to say hello, the old woman held her phone to her ear. "Hello, Eamon dear," she sang into the mouthpiece, "I do believe you will have to get me another bottle of your champagne, because you won't believe what I've got to tell you."

Isobel shrank back in shock. Was there no limit to the duplicity that she was caught up in like a fish in a net? She so wanted to call Peter, to hear his reassuring voice, and to ask to be allowed to free herself from the miserable task he had set her. But what reason could she give, that her detective work was exceeding his expectations? She looked again at the list of missed calls, hesitated, and then hit the speed dial button.

Forty-eight

Isobel had already tried Peter's mobile three times without success. "Please, please, please answer," she said aloud, desperate to speak with him, to share her news from the owners' meeting, but more importantly to have him resolve her dilemma, whether to see Jay or to continue to evade him. It would be so much easier to have Peter make the decision for her.

"Damn you," she exclaimed as the automated message kicked in. She looked at her watch and began to wonder where on earth Peter could be. His phone was always with him, clipped to his belt like some miniature life-support machine when it was not being nursed in his hand or pressed to his ear. Exasperated and confused, she called the home number but with little expectation. Peter routinely let it go to voice message, as the calls were invariably for her. Just as despair took hold, the phone was answered. It was a woman's halting voice.

"Hello?"

"Who is this?" demanded Isobel, half thinking she had somehow hit the wrong button, but trapped in the terrible knowledge that she hadn't.

"Oh, I'm sorry, Isobel, it's Rachel." A discomforting silence followed as neither woman seemed to know what to say next; Isobel's heart and mind raced, she saw her sprawled on her sofa across Peter in ownership. She sought to recover her composure; whatever was the shameless wretch doing in her home, answering her phone? She didn't even work for Peter anymore. It was the younger woman who spoke next, offering no explanation for her presence.

"I suppose you're after Peter, I'll just get him."

You suppose! And who the hell else do you suppose I could be after, the window cleaner? Isobel was ready to explode. *And you will get him? Get him from where? From what?* But she was unable to bring the avalanche of questions from her mind and into her mouth, and before she could say anything, she heard a tap as the handset hit the table. More questions flooded in. Why didn't Peter just pick up another phone, why didn't she take the handset and deliver it to wherever he was? What were the two doing, she wondered as she waited for what seemed an eternity, imagining them conspiring across the handset, their lips shaped like love and deception.

She wrestled her imagination under control, knowing it to be fed by her own guilt. Peter came to the phone. She searched his voice for some inflection, some nuance, some difference, but could detect nothing, only the bland, almost business-like tone in which he so often spoke to her on the phone.

"Sorry, darling, I was just in the bathroom. Everything ok?"

Isobel's imagination immediately flew back into overdrive. Was Peter now in the habit of going to the bathroom without his trousers, without his belt that held his precious machine, and in the middle of the day? Isobel tensed herself as she sought to appear calm, unable to hold back the obvious question.

"Why didn't you answer your phone?"

"Oh, that, I had it switched off."

Isobel's mind went to Florence airport, and her confusion that Peter had switched off his phone, and her pleasure that he had done so. It seemed wonderful then but was hollow now.

"And why is Rachel there?"

"I thought I mentioned it. She's helping me organise the leaving do, and we're just going over a few things together. Everything ok your side?"

She listened intently to every aspect of his speech, his tone seemed deadened, and she wanted to pounce on the inflection like a cat, to force him to unveil himself. She was becoming something of an expert in recognising such signs, but normally in her own voice. The thought struck her that Rachel might well be listening on the other line, that she in all probability was listening, if she were not lying next to Peter, tickling his privates and daring him to laugh, as she had once done when Jay had taken a call from Rusty.

"Everything's fine," she said, the lie falling from her lips both fluid and natural. "The horses and everything ok?" He told here they were. "Peter," she said with emphasis, seeking to alert him to the possibility that they were being listened to, "is this a good time to talk about what's happening?"

He seemed to understand her question; he was good at reading signals, when he was minded to.

"Don't worry, Rachel's in the kitchen, making some coffee."

"Make sure she uses fresh water," said Isobel with malice, determined not to surrender the rights of her domain to the usurper.

Peter laughed. "Tell me how things went in Capadelli."

She pushed from her mind as best she could the image of Rachel lying spread-eagled in her marital bed, and relayed the events of the morning. Peter listened with great interest, an interest that she had not sensed in him for years. He made sounds of encouragement at all the right times, asked questions when something was unclear, and was genuinely touched by her account of personal suffering. His response was lightening her mood, and easing her fears for what the afternoon held, when she was pulled back to reality with a bump, as Peter thanked Rachel for the coffee. She gritted her teeth remembering every time she had placed a coffee on Peter's desk only for him to continue writing as if she were invisible to him.

Isobel's temporary calm was destroyed when Peter took over the conversation. "There's still some information I need, so I've had to send the accountants back in to Capadelli. I need you to go in this afternoon and see them."

"This afternoon?" she said, desperately trying to master all emotion in her voice. "I really don't think I can do that. Brooke will almost certainly be around, and me being there will only raise his suspicions."

She bit at her thumb while Peter was silent in thought. "Do you know where Brooke lives?" he asked.

She heard her own intake of breath and belatedly clapped her hand to her mouth to muffle it. He gave no sign of having heard it. Isobel pulled her hand away, letting lies pour in a torrent from her mouth. "I'm not sure. Maybe San Miniato. Yes, I think Gina mentioned it."

"San Miniato?"

"Yes, you remember, we had lunch there. A charming place on a hill. It's about half an hour from Capadelli."

"Couldn't you call Brooke and ask to meet him there? That will keep him away if he's at home, and if he's already at Capadelli then he will probably pack up for the day and not return, leaving the accountants a free hand to dig around."

"But if I did that, and I don't know why he would agree, then it would tie me up too—" Isobel's mind momentarily returned to the last time she was tied up with Jay, or rather by Jay "—so then I wouldn't be able to see the accountants."

Peter had already solved that problem in his head and he relayed the answer in triumph. "You are in Capadelli now but Jay doesn't know it, right? Arrange to meet him in San Miniato for a late lunch, and slip in to the development behind his back when he leaves, and then shoot down to meet him!"

"This is not some west-end farce, Peter," Isobel exclaimed, trying to channel her fear into anger, "anything could go wrong. Why can't I just stay where I am, check-in with Gina every so often, and whenever Jay does leave, go in and see the guys from BB&T?"

She heard an impatient sigh on the other end of the line. "But I need you to see Brooke too; you've got to find out if he's planning to do a runner, and if so, when. Now be a good girl, and give him a call."

Forty-nine

The morning sun had given way to dark clouds, and rain began to fall as Isobel turned off the main road and began the long ascent to Castello di Capadelli. The rain soon became relentless in its dullness, a grey drizzle that added no drama or poignancy to her mission. Everything seemed to droop beneath a film of moisture, not a single person was to be seen, and the white umbrellas outside the bars and cafés sagged in misery. The roads too were deserted and Isobel turned on the wipers, which rhythmically revealed the landscape and hid it again as she drove slowly and unwillingly towards her destination.

As she entered Capadelli village itself she pulled over onto the dark wet cobblestones, brought to a halt by a strange mix of fear and nostalgia. She pressed herself against the seat and took in the scene, almost alien in the greyness, with all its dirt and colours washing into the overflowing drains. Her eyes rested unconsciously on the local bar and she became lost in crushing and unforgiving memory of when she and Jay had stolen into the back room and he had kissed her and run his hands over her body, and she had enjoyed letting him. Isobel screwed her eyes tightly shut, fighting off the images, but they were unyielding. She saw him daring her to follow him into the toilet, and saw her laughter — so hard that she felt she would explode — when he reappeared after waiting for ages, convinced she would follow him. Isobel gripped the wheel until her hands lost all colour, as if forcing the memory from her body, but it was pointless. She saw him feign sadness and demand she go into the bathroom and remove her panties in punishment; she saw herself disappear and coyly re-emerge, letting him caress her under the table with reckless abandon. Tears fell into her lap as she saw him drive home, the panties on his head in retribution for his forwardness. She restarted the engine and shattered the silence, wanting to break it and unable to bear the memory of her own happiness.

The rain grew heavier as Castello di Capadelli came into view and, to her surprise, Isobel started to notice people on the side of the roads, a slow trickle at first but quickly turning into groups then crowds as she neared the gates. They all trudged doggedly through the rain, their heads bent beneath hoods and heavy hats. A white van screeched up behind the car and Isobel pulled over to let it pass; the letters on its side seemed familiar but she could not place them. As she turned the final bend, driving at a snail's pace for fear she might hit someone, the lines became a crowd and she saw the familiar iron gates above their heads, swamped in a black mass of human beings.

Isobel peered through the mist at them, her windscreen fogged by the anxiety of her quick breath. The degree of the chaos became apparent as she wiped it aside; people shouting and holding placards, standing in regimented lines outside the gate whilst many others stood and watched. Isobel leant forward and squinted to read a sign. The words 'ENGLISH PIGS OUT' were blazoned across the cardboard in a bloody red. Anxiety now seized her and she tried to reverse but it was impossible, so she started to turn as the spectators shuffled grudgingly out of her way and the people with signs turned, moving in unison to converge on her car. Their faces were ugly with anger, the water sliding from their grimaces like sweat, and genuine fear gripped Isobel as they advanced. She turned towards the white van, her eyes drawn to its paleness amongst the mess of limbs and leering faces, and as her survival instinct took over her she recognised the painted letters — it was the TV station. She steered towards it as an attractive young woman brandishing a microphone ran towards her, hoping to be safe from harm beneath the camera's lens. But she was overtaken by two hooded figures that rushed at the car, wielding their placards like staves. The first, a heavily built man with rabid eyes, struck his sign against the windscreen as Isobel screamed, desperately wrenching the steering wheel to complete the turn. An angry looking young woman, her hair bedraggled from the wet and her face contorted with contempt, was pulling at the door handle next to her. But Isobel accelerated and the woman let go, mouthing curses, as she sped off into the rain.

The car lurched and roared as Isobel tore down the winding roads, her legs and arms shaking as she struggled to hold the wheel steady. As soon as the last walker was out of sight she pulled over and threw herself from the car. She landed on her hands and knees on the verge, took a deep breath, and then vomited violently as her whole body contorted into inhuman shapes. She crouched on the grass for a moment, cold and shaking, before scrambling back into the car. She leant for a long time against the seat, waiting for the nausea to release its grip on mind and body and for her heart to stop racing. When some semblance of calmness finally returned to her she took out her phone and called Peter. She held on, imploring him to pick up, but the call went to voice message and she threw the phone at the back seat in terrified rage and cursed him for her aloneness. But as the rage subsided and Isobel dwelt on the owners' meeting, an entire room full of useless wrath and worry, her spirit and courage seemed to rise up in her, and she was overcome by indignation and the injustice of everything. Resolution grew within her and she flung herself onto the back seat, scooped up the phone and rang reception, hoping to get hold of her old ally. When no one answered she left a message, asking Gina to meet her at the back entrance, hoping and praying that she received it in time.

Isobel put her foot down and carved a frantic and inefficient path through the side roads and their bewildering confliction of signposts. She had only been through the back gates once and that was in the dark, with Jay guiding her, his hand tight round hers as he led her into depravity beneath the stars. She shook him from her mind and drove by instinct, cautiously navigating the maze of roads until trial and error delivered her to her destination. She edged up stealthily, trying to appear innocuous in front of the few locals that milled around with their hands in their pockets, and they made no move to stop her.

But, as she approached the final few yards to the gates, a man in a hooded anorak stepped out before her, the palm of his dirty hand held towards her. He was wearing some kind of plastic ID badge in an attempt to convey authority, but his shabby dress belied the effort and she wound down the car window with confidence, looking down her nose imperiously with a condescending 'yes?'

"Who are you?" he demanded, pushing his stubbled face almost into Isobel's.

"I beg your pardon," said Isobel, startled and pulling back from the smell of alcohol and garlic.

"Who is she?" someone shouted from the rag-tag onlookers behind.

"Are you Italian?" asked the man. "Media?"

"It's none of your business who I am," said Isobel, "now let me pass."

"You are a very pretty lady, but I am an official from the workers council, and we are checking everyone before they go through," he said. His eyes raked over her body as he spoke.

"My name is Isobel Roberts, now *kindly* let me pass."

The man stood his ground, his elbow pressing down on the open car window. "You must wait," he said drawing on all his assumed authority and without explanation, turning to his friend. "Signora Isobel Roberts, English I think," he shouted over his shoulder. "Is she on the list?"

The list? thought Isobel, fear and fury building within her. *Am I to be put against a wall and shot like Mussolini and his mistress?* A man with a clipboard stepped forward and pressed a phone to his ear.

Isobel's heart raced as she waited; the atmosphere of intimidation was overwhelming and it was taking all her self-control not to drive away. She slipped the car into reverse, ready to shoot back at the first sight of a placard, or a firing squad.

The young man with the clipboard came off the phone, and let out a gruff sounding laugh.

"It is only the English meretrice, let her through."

The dialect was strong, but Isobel was sure she understood it. The man pressing down on the window leant in and took her cheek between his thumb and forefinger, squeezing it hard.

"My name is Gianni, you ask for me in Capadelli, when you want a *big* man." He cupped his crotch and leered at her. Isobel pulled in her elbow and struck him a fierce blow on his arm with all her force.

The man stepped back laughing and waved her through. "The meretrice has balls!" he shouted to his friend, who guffawed like a donkey in response.

Isobel sped through the gates as Gina opened them, and pulled to a shuddering halt, spraying gravel behind her into the rain-filled air. She slumped over the wheel, pressing her fists into her eyes to hold back the tears. *Is this what its come to?* she asked herself silently. *The English whore?*

Gina pulled open the car door and, almost kneeling, extended an arm around her, her face full of worry and pity.

"Do not be upset, Isobel, it means nothing, what they say, they are *feccia*; I'm sorry I do not know the English word."

"Scum," said Isobel with a poor attempt at a smile.

"Yes, scum, they are scum." Gina nodded vigorously. "Today I am ashamed to be Italian. They said the same to me when I arrived. Please, I apologise for them. We are safe in here; security men are inside, and they have guns. No one will come past the gates. Mr. Skinner arranged it."

Isobel's anger at the physical assault, and the insult, was subsiding. But she was not sure she believed Gina, that her looks alone provoked the goading. The taunt was too specific, too direct. She sensed something spiteful in the way it was gleefully uttered.

"What is going on, Gina?" she asked, dropping her voice to a low whisper as they began to walk.

"You do not know? It is very bad, Signora. Yesterday appeared a story in the local paper that the English developers have been operating here illegally. The picture of Signor Skinner was in the paper. The one on the brochure. The police were here earlier too. They asked for Signor Skinner. They said they would be back later. I think they plan to arrest him."

Isobel had never seen Gina so ill-composed, her eyes were wild and a smudge of her carefully applied lipstick faded into her cheek.

"What else did the newspaper say?" Isobel asked, trying to control her own nerves.

"That the English have no money to pay anyone. Signor Mancini is speaking several times in the story. And now this morning the staff has learnt that they have not received their salary. They believe it is because of Signor Skinner, and they have been told that today he will sack everyone."

"Who has told them?" asked Isobel, wondering if this was yet one more charge to put at Jay's feet.

"The workers council. They are the people outside. I think they are trying to make trouble for Signor Skinner, and his wife too, because she is on the brochure. I think perhaps, Isobel, they mistook you for her; the staff have been listening to the workers council, who are all communists and troublemakers—"

"And *feccia*?" said Isobel with a smile, drawing strength and composure from Gina's hysteria.

Gina smiled. "Yes, that too, but you must not say that word. But what the council say has made many people angry. They are waiting to hear from Mr. Skinner, or Mr. Brooke." Gina lowered her eyes as she said Jay's name.

"So is Jay here?"

"He was. But he left earlier. He took a call and he went off straight away; maybe he heard the people from the workers council were marching here from Capadelli."

Gina put an arm around Isobel, and the two walked towards the courtyard in silence, both deep in their own thoughts. To Isobel, her mission now seemed irrelevant. She did not care about getting information anymore. She wanted to see Jay, to confront him, to shame him, no matter what the cost to herself. But first she would do what Peter had asked; that would cost her nothing.

As she entered the inner courtyard she was acutely aware of being watched; it seemed like faces were at every window, each full of questions. But no one approached her. Was it fear that kept them silent, she wondered, fear of the power her husband now wielded, or was it contempt? She walked on with Gina by her side, forcing herself to hold her head high. She knew she had harmed no one, only herself. And Peter.

Gina led her into the offices where the accountants were busy, swarming around a hopeless looking Davide, clutching papers and talking hurriedly as he watched in despair. He approached Isobel, fearing for his livelihood like all the rest. "Are they closing us, like the rumours say?" he asked her.

"I'm sorry, Davide, you must talk to Mr. Brooke," she said, not meeting his eyes.

"I am worried, Signora. I have been an accountant for many years. I fear these people are here to do more than they say. But I am powerless. They have signed authorisations from Mr. Skinner."

"Then you must ask your questions to Mr. Skinner," snapped Isobel, without meaning to and immediately regretted it. She touched Davide's shoulder and looked at him apologetically. He seemed to understand that she did not want his questions, and he sloped away to the cubbyhole of an office that was his only kingdom. She introduced herself to the closest of the investigative team, a bright-eyed young trainee that wore his First in computer science like a medal. He reached into his case and gave her a package.

"This is for your husband." He gave a furtive look in Davide's direction, but his door was closed. She gave him a sealed envelope in return.

"My husband needs something else. This note will explain."

The young man read the note and seemed to immediately understand.

"If it's anywhere on a hard disk, I'll find it," he said, "and I'll leave it on a memory stick for you to collect…if I don't see you first," he added with a wink.

"I need it today. You've got an hour," she said sternly, feeling every male glance as a rumour-fuelled slight on her morality.

Isobel went to the cold and empty Visconti suite and called Peter again. The last of her composure rested on him answering and she sighed in audible relief as he picked up the phone. She refrained from relaying the day's drama to him, saying only that things were going to plan and that she had the information he wanted.

"And Brooke?" he asked in curt response.

"I'm still trying to track him down."

"You and a few others I should think," he said with a barking laugh. But Isobel did not linger on his victory; she did not want to talk about Jay or about great plans and devious schemes. She wanted to escape from the whole world of deceit and deception, to get back to the world she knew. So she asked him about the horses, the farm, what he ate for breakfast, whether he'd remembered to put out the bins, anything to lose herself in the mundane world she had been so desperate to escape, and which now seemed so inviting. And he told her about mundane things, and asked her about mundane things, and she was happy again, for a while.

Fifty

She was late at the cafeteria that Jay had nominated, just around the corner from his apartment. They had enjoyed a nightcap there once before, in happier times. It looked onto a narrow and curving street, quiet and shady despite the bustle in the surrounding roads. The few customers present were idling away the late afternoon, most sipping a drink, one playing on the fruit machine in the corner. Isobel searched the room but saw no sign of Jay — another game perhaps. If so she didn't need it, her stomach was churning and her hands were trembling. She went to the counter and ordered a coffee with a brandy, pouring the spirit into the coffee before ordering another, which she threw down her throat as the assistant looked at her, wide-eyed and open mouthed. "Prostrovia," said Isobel, in invented Russian, as she banged down the glass, returning the woman's stare.

She made her way onto the back terrace that boasted a panoramic view over the valley; the last of the afternoon's sunlight dancing on the green fields below, it could have been a scene from her imagination, months before, as she dreamt of a cinematic love affair in the hills of Tuscany. How empty that dream felt now. She sipped from her coffee and steeled herself for the ordeal ahead, feeling the onset of a headache with the creeping nausea.

Jay eventually made a hurried arrival onto the terrace, apologising as he walked towards her. He bent to kiss her but she offered only her cheek.

"You are angry with me," he said, uttering possibly the greatest understatement ever to have entered her ears. He cupped her hands before she could withdraw them, and held them tightly, pulling them to him and kissing them slowly and fervently.

"Please, Jay," she said, looking around for justification, but they were alone on the terrace and she had nothing else to say.

Isobel's heart had raced when he walked in, but now it seemed to be running slower, the brandy taking hold, she hoped — the other explanation, that he could calm her after all he had done, was too awful to even contemplate. Yet she had expected to be repulsed by him, and wasn't at all; she had no idea what she felt. But she had come to hear him out and she would do so, feeling that, at least, she owed him.

"Why have you been avoiding me?" he said. "Hiding up in Lucca when you have an apartment in Capadelli?"

"Two apartments," she reminded him, though both were awaiting the new furnishings she now wished she never ordered.

"And you have not been returning my calls, till this afternoon. Have I done something wrong?" She looked down and did not reply, fearing his gaze. "Because I hope not. Andy has told me that Peter is interested in a deal with him, so this is something for us to celebrate." His eyes never left her. She pulled her hands from him and hid them on her lap. The woman arrived with a coffee for Jay. "Would you like something?" he asked Isobel. She shook her head, but the waitress was not so easily deterred.

"*Another* brandy perhaps, madam?' she asked in Italian. Isobel's face reddened as Jay got the gist of the question, and seized on it.

"Yes, two large brandies, please." The woman gave Isobel what she took to be a disapproving look, before retiring. "A brandy will warm our hearts," said Jay, "and today I want them to be warm, because we're together." He smiled a small and hopeful smile at her.

"You are talking like a lovesick teenager," she said, without any of the warmth he begged of her. She thought she saw hurt in his eyes, but she continued in the same cold fashion. "You wanted to see me?"

Jay had heard enough; he had his pride after all. "Isobel, if you have something to say, please say it. If I've done something wrong, I apologise. Ok?"

She had prepared for confrontation, but did not seek it, not yet anyway.

"I'm sorry. It's just that I am falling to pieces this last week. Whispers at Capadelli that I am your whore." She spat the word out in self-disgust. "And I am sure Peter has noticed something, even if he hasn't heard anything. And then there are these rumours about you... there was a meeting in Capadelli—"

"Stop it." He seized her behind the elbows and pulled her arms from under the table, grasping her hands in his again. "Listen to me, you are no one's anything, and whatever anyone is saying about us, let them go to hell. I wanted to see you to give you something, and to tell you something. And anything you've seen or heard since we last made love doesn't change what I want to do or say."

She felt herself go limp, now wishing to stand up and leave, without hearing or saying anything. But she was powerless to lift herself, in the same way she had been powerless to resist his darkest desires.

He eased his hold of her hands and gently laid them on the table with a final caress. He produced a gift-wrapped, oblong package from his pocket. "I'm going to give you something today and you are going to accept it, or it will stay here on this table when we leave." She stayed silent, neither agreeing nor disagreeing with his terms. "And after I've given it to you, I'm going to tell you something. And no matter what you think of me when I'm finished, what I give you stays with you, or it stays here." She felt herself nodding without wanting to, a strange listlessness seeming to have come over her, a stoical acceptance that whatever was happening was meant to happen.

Jay passed the package over and she removed the wrapping with hands shaking and tears in her eyes. She felt like she was unwrapping a final memory, one last placebo amongst all the lies and the deception. She sat staring at the oblong jewellery box, not wishing to open it. "It's beautiful," was all she could say. And it was. An eighteen carat solid gold necklace.

"I'm sorry Jay, I can't—"

"Just put it on, please. I want to see it on you, if only once."

She put it to her neck but she was unable to manage, such was the trembling in her fingers. He leapt up and helped her, securing the clasp behind her neck, before sitting back in front of her. She ran her fingers along the precious metal, feeling it cool against her skin. The waitress arrived with the brandies and put them down in front of her, her hands taut around the glasses with wonder and envy.

"I'm sorry, it's what delayed me. I had it specially made, and they needed to adjust the clasp."

"You wanted to tell me something." Her hands fell slowly from the necklace and she let him take them again in his, because it was easier than resisting.

He looked into her watery eyes and squeezed her hands in a reassuring way; his voice was low and confessional.

"You said you wanted me for yourself, remember? That you couldn't bear the thought of me touching anyone else like I touch you?"

She hung her head. *So this is what it is all about*, she thought, *he wants to tell me he's leaving Rusty or, more likely, that she's left him.* "It wasn't about Rusty…" she managed to say, choking back sad indignation.

"And I'm not talking about Rusty. I'm talking about someone else." Isobel's stomach churned faster, her head aching from the brandy and her own confusion.

"You remember the girl you asked about, from the Cobham evening?" He seemed to brace himself and inhaled a long breath. "Well, her name's Lucy, and she's been my mistress for the past two years." She looked up at him, seeing only sincerity in his eyes. She wanted to believe him but wasn't sure she could.

"I've been looking to end the relationship since before we met. We don't see each other that often, sometimes less than once a month. I'm all over the place and she's an air stewardess. I was very fond of her, I am very fond of her, but I don't love her, and I never have."

Isobel was struggling with the shock of his unexpected revelation, trying to make sense of it, trying to see through it.

"But she loves you?"

"She has a boyfriend, and has had since before she met me, who dotes on her. But she's an ambitious girl — in a good way — and, yes, maybe she loves me, or thinks she does, but I can't help that."

"So you have just used her for sex — like you've used me?" She pulled away her hands again, sure that she knew him now. She saw immediately that her words had shocked him, hurt him, that after all he had vulnerability within him. In spite of herself she felt sorry for him, and in that sorrow was again drawn to him. She wanted to touch him, to make the pain go away, but she held still, sensing that the fight was going out of him.

"If that's what you think," he said, now seeming crushed, "then maybe there's nothing more to say." He leant back in his seat as he said it, abject resignation on his face.

But now that Isobel's emotion was stirred, she could not take the exit he was offering. "But why have you not ended it? Why haven't you just said 'I don't love you, it's over, goodbye?'"

"Like you came here to say to me?"

His words burnt into her. It was as if he could see through her like glass. She had not done it, she castigated herself, because she was using him, using him to draw out the secrets that she would give Peter to damn him to his doom. And as the words burnt deeper, she was seized by guilt.

"When did you last see…Lucy?" she asked, wanting him to save himself.

"After I saw you in the Savoy; it was the reason I couldn't stay over, even though I wanted to. I had promised to take her to a wedding and I couldn't bring myself to let her down."

"Where was this wedding?" said Isobel, her eyes narrowing.

"Here in Tuscany, Florence of all places, I'd promised to take her. It was all planned to fly out from Gatwick; then you called and I didn't want to disappoint you either." He was holding her hand again, running his fingers over her white knuckles, the tips of his fingers seeking out her slim wrist under her cuff. And she let him, her mind swimming in conflicting thoughts, her skin tingling to his touch, her body beginning to feel for him. "But it is all over now, and I am going to tell her this weekend and that's a pledge I've made to myself, because of you."

Isobel didn't know whether to laugh or cry, to hug him or run. Jay took the decision away from her, moving around beside her and pulling her into him.

She tried to remain limp but she could not, and as he forced his mouth on hers, she returned his embrace, but, with a final effort of will, pushed him away.

"I'm sorry, Jay, this is just too much for me to cope with right now. I need time to think."

He clasped her chin and looked into her eyes and she saw he was smiling, his old self-assurance radiating from him. "Take all the time you need, I will go and get us two more brandies."

She went to the bathroom while he was gone and sat in the narrow cubicle, letting the tears flood out, pulling sheet after sheet from the roll and wiping her tears away. When the tears stopped she went to the mirror, white specks of tissue were stuck to her wet make-up. She washed her face in cold water. The dispenser was out of paper so she lifted the hem of the dress to dry her face, and reapplied her make-up, a battle raging within her. She ran her fingers along the necklace as she admired its beauty, then took it off and returned it to its box; she would slip it into his pocket.

Isobel checked her phone, but found no message or missed call. Peter's lack of concern worried her, though perhaps he was too busy with Rachel to think of her. She felt pangs of guilt for mistrusting Peter, yet she could not push the thought fully from her consciousness.

Jay was waiting with the drinks, but she did not want to sit down again. "I'm sorry, I need to go. Peter is due to call any minute. And I really can't handle my emotions right now." He followed her to the door; his apartment was to the left, her car to the right. She was glad of the rapidly descending darkness and the emptiness of the street. She stretched up to kiss him goodbye, her hand searching for his jacket pocket, but he sensed her intent and seized her wrist, pulling her body violently into his, and, in one swivel of his large frame, they disappeared into a doorway, his back to the street. She struggled against him, but he held her to him effortlessly. She tossed her head from side to side to avoid his lips, but he took her face in his free hand and held it forcefully as he pressed his mouth to hers, and soon she gave up her efforts to stop her lips being forced apart. In one swift movement he swept his hand under her dress and forced it between the tops of her thighs, his mouth still locked on hers. Again she resisted, clamping her legs to restrain him, but he would not be stopped, and took hold of her panties and tore them from her. And as the skimpy material floated to the ground, she felt her resistance go with it. She knew he sensed it too, perhaps it was the quiver in her thighs that gave her away; he eased his vice-like hold on her, his other hand grasped her shaven mound and began exploring her, her knees weakening as he did so. Isobel knew she needed him with the same intensity as the first time. She reached out her hand and felt the same urgency in him, unchanged from their tryst in the woods. Finally, she pulled her mouth from his. "Please Jay, not here, not in the street." But she held his body close to hers as she spoke, her nails digging into his back. Jay eased away from her, and she bent to one knee before him to pick up her torn panties and the fallen jewellery box; he gazed into her eyes before she dropped her head in submission, and silently took the hand that he offered.

Fifty-one

They reached the door to Jay's apartment without saying a word, her trailing a step behind him, her hand stretched out to his, like a wayward child brought to heel. He opened the door before turning to her, whisking her up in his arms and carrying her over the threshold.

Standing next to the bed they both began to undress, she slowly undoing the buttons on the front of her long black dress, not to rouse him, for she knew it was not necessary, but deep in thought as she sought to push the returning feelings of guilt from her mind.

"Is your phone off?" he asked, finally breaking the silence, and she nodded, saying nothing. They stood a foot apart, facing each other, naked, she struggling to hold his gaze. Jay reached behind her to the dresser, and she felt their bodies touch as he did so, and he gave her a smile, but she did not reach for him as she often did. He stepped back, the box in his hand and she watched transfixed as he opened it. He put the golden chain to her neck and she pushed her hair back to help him, and able to bear it no more she pulled him to her. Jay leant behind her again and Isobel saw the torn panties in his hand and he gently wiped himself with them and finally she giggled, but nervously, before putting her hand to the panties and finishing the task.

He laid her on the bed, and neither spoke. He did not explore her in his usual way but simply put himself above her and she opened her body up for him because she knew he was ready, and that she was ready, and he made love to her slowly and gently, and she took him slowly and gently, and when it was over he fell beside her, and still he had not spoken. And after a while he spoke. "I love you, Isobel." And it was the first time he had said it, or anything near to it, and she was pleased that he had waited, that he had not said it in the throes of his own passion, or as she had cried out his name in her own fulfillment, and she thought that she believed him. But she knew that with Jay she would never be sure, totally sure, in the way that she was with Peter. She stayed silent and said nothing, much as she knew he wanted to hear her say she loved him.

When he fell asleep she rose from the bed and went to the bathroom to phone Peter. Her call went unanswered, yet somehow she did not mind. If he was with Rachel she knew she could not blame him because, perhaps, he knew or suspected she had someone, even if he did not suspect it was Jay. She was sure he had known ever since they had driven into Cobham and he had asked, "what made you have a full wax?" and she blushed scarlet because they had not made love and he had not seen her naked, and she knew he must have touched her, when she was sleeping. He had bided his time, she was sure, to see how she would explain herself. And she had stammered out some explanation in reply, knowing that he saw the lie, even though he said nothing.

Her phone vibrated to interrupt her thoughts and she saw it was the house phone. This time Isobel did not ask why he had not answered and he did not ask her where she was or what she was doing, only if she was ok. She was pleased that his voice was normal, with no hint of suspicion, and a brief wave of calm washed over her.

"I'm sorry," she said. "I left your note with the accountants and they promised to do their best. But I couldn't get hold of Brooke until much later, and he was too busy to meet this afternoon so we agreed to have dinner. I hope that's ok?"

"Maybe even better. He's more likely to drink and that will loosen his tongue for you."

If you only knew how loose that tongue already is for me, thought Isobel with another rush of guilt. "Everything ok your end? Rachel get back ok?"

He said that she did and she said she'd call in the morning, hoping he would not suggest they speak again later.

Jay came to the bathroom and asked if everything was ok, and she said that it was. He relieved himself in front of her, as Peter never would, and she watched him, unsure of everything again.

She did not want to go back to bed and suggested they go out to eat, but he just shook his head and left the room, returning with a tray of strawberries and ice cream and a silver bucket with ice and champagne. He had found a wilted yellow flower and put it on the tray, saying, "I'm fresh out of roses," as he poured two glasses and looped his arm through hers so they were coupled as they sipped it. She laughed, and he took a spoon and began to feed her the ice cream and strawberries, putting a scoop on her nipple before licking it off, laughing as she shivered.

Isobel stayed silent through it all, sensing he wanted to speak, and fearing the intensity in his eyes.

"I don't think I'll have much more need to come out to Tuscany," he began, his face deadly serious, "except to see you. Andy's going to be taking over things here. What happens in Italy now is up to him."

"So you'll be spending more time in London, on the music project?"

He had already told her pieces of it, and now he told her the rest.

"One way or another, I will hear the decision next week. Win or lose, I've hired a boat on the Thames and I'm going to be thanking the team for all their work and, hopefully, celebrating. I was thinking you might join me…but if you think it's too public, I'll understand."

"But won't Rusty be there?"

"She's in Texas, looking at schools for the boys. She's probably going to go back in October."

"But your work's here, in London, I mean."

He shrugged his shoulders. "I told you I was waiting to be served the papers, remember? We'll probably sell up in Cheshire and I will get a place in London."

"Even if…things don't work out on the music project?"

"London is where the action is. And I'm nothing if not a survivor. If the music deal doesn't happen then something else will. I'll just make it happen, and I will bounce back." Isobel knew that he would. He was that type, the sort that you couldn't keep down with a sledgehammer. "So will you come on the boat?" he asked tentatively, almost pleading.

"I'll check Peter's schedule. I think he's going to Brussels, so maybe I could just stay in the background."

She fed him a spoon of ice cream. "The owners' meeting in Capadelli. I was there."

"Yes, I know."

She was startled that after all her subterfuge, he knew, like sometimes he seemed to know everything, and to be able to see into her soul. She thought about the hapless Barkers, who had closed by swearing the assembly to secrecy, and she fought tears from her eyes at their vulnerability, lambs among lions.

"There were a lot of distressed people in that—"

"Listen, Isobel, I do what I have to. That's how I survive. No one has ever looked out for me, until now." He leant over and kissed her, pushing a dollop of ice cream from his mouth to hers as he did so. "Everyone in that room got what they paid for, a holiday home in Tuscany at a price they were happy with when they bought it. Did Eamon spin things a bit? Well sure, he's paid to sell. But as for a dream under the Tuscan sun, dreams are what you make them. They need to stop feeling sorry for themselves. They need to start living their dream, and stop looking to others to make it for them. Because everyone else is too busy with their own dream."

His words fell into her heart like stones, all the dreams it held now brittle as glass.

"I don't know, Jay, that seems a harsh way to see the world."

"If I'd had someone alongside me like you these past years, someone who looks to what they can give, not what they can take, maybe I'd think differently. So there's hope for me yet." He refilled her glass and she was starting to feel lightheaded, having eaten nothing all day except the strawberries and ice cream.

"And the new Jay starts this weekend, when you have your heart to heart with Lucy?"

"I don't want to hurt Lucy. She's done me no wrong, and she's just a girl who's trying to pull herself up in life by her bra-straps. But it's not going to be easy to tell her, or else I would have done it a long time ago."

"But we all get hurt in relationships, women at least, if not you, you heartless sod. What else has stopped you?"

"Lucy's been getting really unpredictable. I do fear for what she's capable of."

"You mean hurting herself?"

"I don't know about that, she's got a lot of fight that girl. But the way she's been talking she might do anything. She turned up at our school sports day a few weeks back, damn near brought the event to a standstill the way she was dressed; she got an inch away from clawing Rusty's eyes out, even went up to the boys, just to make sure I knew what the stakes were."

To Isobel, this sounded like Jay looking to his own survival rather than protecting Lucy from hurt, but maybe that was how life was after all, at least in Jay's world. "So how are you going to tell her?"

"This Saturday. She's coming to Tuscany."

"So one final romantic weekend?"

"That's what I'm determined to avoid. We are going out, but I've invited Eamon and Gina along. At the end of the evening I will tell her."

"Gina? So does Gina love you too?"

Jay let out a long laugh. "She's working for Mancini. Just someone else trying to stitch me up." Isobel looked away, guilt rushing back into her. "Gina is being used. But she's playing way out of her league; I saw through it pretty much the first hand she dealt me, but I went along with it because it suited me to."

"But you can't be sure, that's just your instincts."

"Oh, I'm sure, all right. I've got my ways. I'm not as stupid as Mancini thinks; one of the Italians let me in on the scheme over a bottle of wine. I almost laughed, in fact I would have done if the wine hadn't cost so much."

Isobel had always liked his dry humour, and she laughed in spite of herself. There were no questions left, and he seemed to sense it. He took a sip more of champagne, put his lips to hers, and passed it into her mouth. He waited till she had swallowed, and gently pushed her back on the bed. He took a longer drink, emptying the glass, and leant over her belly, and slowly dribbled a line of champagne down to the top of her thighs. She laid back and closed her eyes. *Just one more time*, she said to herself, as she felt his tongue retrace the line of his lips. *Just one last time.*

Fifty-two

The hot summer evening had given way to humid darkness and the white halogen headlights of Maria's car illuminated the dancing moths as they batted their paper wings against the windscreen. "You are sure this is the place?" asked Maria.

"Yes, the concierge let it slip; he booked the arrangements for Jay."

She and Isobel sat motionless in the car, engaged in low, hurried conversation as they peered single-mindedly into the blackness. "It is the right thing to do," said Maria for the hundredth time since they left the restaurant. "Your future is in your own hands, and you must be sure that Jay is not deceiving you." Isobel gestured her assent, allowing Maria to finally turn into the large parking area of Club Nero, which beamed its searchlights into the night sky, flickering and criss-crossing as the two women sat still and watchful beneath.

"You got your gun with you?" said Maria, as she switched off the engine, unable to share in the indecision that possessed her friend and sure that she already knew what to expect — a neon spectacle of Jay's duplicity and Isobel's naivety.

"Please," Isobel implored her. "I'm a bag of nerves already."

She stared again into the darkness, amazed that such expansive nocturnal activity could be found in the backwaters of Tuscany. Her ignorance made her only more nervous and she turned to Maria in fear again. "We'll never find them, even if they are here."

Maria snorted with amused impatience. "I've been here a zillion times, we'll definitely find them."

"But what if we just stumble upon them…and they see us?"

"Then we will play innocent," Maria shrugged, "we have as much right to be here as they do."

"But Jay will know I'm *stalking* him." Isobel spat out the word, hitting the dashboard for emphasis.

"Calm down," said Maria, "it is nearly eleven. By now they will have moved to the dance area, and we can see everything from the mezzanine bar, which should be almost deserted. If they are here, we'll see them."

Maria was proved right. The two women slipped up to the mezzanine bar, lit by table lanterns and inhabited only by shadows, and soon spotted Jay, a handsome and strangely still figure amongst the rippling, twisting dancers. The two women hovered above him, visible from the dance floor only as faceless silhouettes.

It was Isobel who broke their vigil with a squeak, "that's her!" she mouthed, pointing into the writhing mass of people. Maria leant over the barrier in anticipation as Lucy pushed through the crowds towards Jay; a rushing, smouldering temptress with long brown limbs held together by the tiniest black dress.

"What's going on down there?" asked Isobel, leaning to join Maria as she edged out of sight.

"She's playing some sort of drinking game with that Irishman from Capadelli," said Maria, curled like an acrobat over the edge.

"And Jay?" asked Isobel apprehensively.

"He's sitting down, talking to Gina."

They watched with anxious fascination as the night unfolded, with Eamon refilling Lucy's glass at every opportunity; she became increasingly erratic, draping herself erotically over Eamon and talking excitedly in his ear, flicking her eyes back to Jay with increasing frequency as he ignored her.

"Slut," said Isobel vehemently as Maria hushed her in glee.

"Look," said Maria, pointing down, "the Irishman is making progress."

They watched as Eamon pulled Lucy to him and beckoned her to the dance floor; Lucy tried to coax Gina to join them, but Gina refused and let them run off together into the crush of the floor.

"I'm going down there," shouted Maria, the music reverberating over her voice. "We won't see anything once they're lost in the crowd. You stay here and keep an eye on Jay. It's maybe not Lucy you need to be worrying about."

She hurtled off into the light and sound and Isobel refocused on Jay, studying his body language as he sat with Gina, he mostly watching the dance floor and only occasionally responding to her attempts at conversation.

Out of the darkness Maria returned, her eyes full of excitement and her voice urgent. "She's going completely crazy down there. I'm not sure she even knows where she is, she's that spaced out. She was gyrating like a belly dancer in the middle of a circle, with everyone egging her on, and when I left, the Irishman had his hands all over her...and I mean everywhere, and she was letting him. Beauty or not, she's a complete man-eater of a tart. No class at all. I don't know what Jay must have been thinking when he got mixed up with her."

"She's a gold-digger too," said Isobel, self-righteousness boiling within her as she imagined Lucy's bloodstained claws in his flesh. Maria hushed her again, more insistently this time, and grabbed her arm.

"Quick, it looks like they're getting ready to leave!" Isobel jumped into action, snatching up her bag from the chair. "Wait, no, they've sat back down again." Maria craned her neck as she bent over the rail once more. "I think the tart's going to the loo...yes, she definitely is, they're round the back, behind the kitchens."

They moved along the rail, echoing Lucy's footsteps as she made her way unsteadily along the wall below them, swaying and wobbling as she leant against it for support.

"I know it's strange, but I'm worried for her," said Isobel, turning to Maria with concern as Lucy almost fell.

Maria laughed almost cruelly. "This is the real world, Isobel; go down any high street this time of night, and you'll see girls in a much worse state than her. You try and help them and they gouge your eyes out."

Lucy lost her footing and toppled over, collapsing awkwardly on the ground with her long legs splayed beneath her like some fallen antelope.

"I'm going to help," said Isobel instinctively, pulling her arm from Maria's hold and rushing forward before her friend had the chance to restrain her.

She arrived to find Lucy on all fours, trying to get to her feet but unable to, one broken shoe in her hand. Isobel halted, fearful of discovery, but she knew she couldn't just leave her half-prostrate on the ground.

Lucy turned her head towards the figure above her, losing her balance and tumbling onto her backside. "Pull me up, Gina," said the girl, as she stared up at Isobel. "I'm a bit tipsy."

Isobel grimaced and hauled her to her feet. "I'll help you to the bathroom, Jay sent me to check you were ok."

At the sound of his name Lucy smiled and pushed back her golden hair, looking Isobel in the eyes with gratitude. Isobel flinched at her gaze, shocked to find warmth and vulnerability where she had expected to see ruthless avarice and naked wantonness. She was inexplicably filled with compassion for her fallen rival.

"Come on, give me your arm, and your shoes."

"But you're not Gina," said Lucy in confusion.

"I'm just a friend, Jay sent me, ok?"

Lucy nodded and did as she was told, clinging to Isobel like a child as she supported her to the toilets like the walking wounded.

"Please wait for me," said Lucy as Isobel deposited her outside an open toilet door. "I don't want to get lost."

Isobel glanced furtively over her shoulder, aware that Gina might arrive at any moment. In a flash of inspiration she led Lucy into the disabled cubicle, bolting them safely inside together. She appraised the bedraggled seductress as the sheer surreality of the situation hit home; for a moment she was tempted to leave her, to punish her somehow for who she was. But Isobel dismissed the thought almost instantaneously, that wasn't who she was. Instead she grabbed and dampened some towels, cleaning the grass and dirt from the girl's hands and knees, as Lucy stood passive, smiling like a sad circus clown.

"There, good as new," said Isobel with an almost maternal tone.

"I wish I talked posh like you," said Lucy, sniffling with gratitude. "Jay likes girls who talk posh."

"You talk lovely," said Isobel, brushing the last blades of grass from Lucy's dress as the girl looked up at her with warmth and curiosity, as if trying to place her in the fog of her memory.

"Is it ok if I take a pee?" asked Lucy sheepishly.

"I will turn my back and cover my ears," said Isobel, again both surprised and touched by the young beauty's humility.

"Can I tell you a secret?" she whispered.

Isobel nodded conspiratorially, a million possibilities exploding in her mind.

Lucy looked up at her solemnly and then broke into a giggle. "I'm not wearing any panties."

Isobel wanted to judge her but burst into laughter, completely charmed by her forthright allure.

"I'm ok now, you can turn around," said Lucy, staggering to full height and kissing Isobel on the cheek in childlike gratefulness.

"Don't forget your shoes," said Isobel, resisting a strange urge to give Lucy a reassuring hug; she held them out as Lucy fought to open the door, her mouth bright and vague. Isobel pulled back the bolt, giving Lucy a final pat on the bottom as she encouraged her on her way.

Isobel sat in the car, entangled in a swirling mass of contradictory emotions, as she and Maria watched the taxi pull up outside Eamon's apartment. They strained to see through the blackness and Isobel's stomach lurched as Eamon emerged from the cab, pulling Lucy from the back seat as she tried to tug her dress back down.

"I bet he was really glad she wasn't wearing any knickers," snorted Maria, as they watched Lucy bear his caresses with oblivious resignation as she followed Jay and Gina up the steps and into the building.

"She's just a lost soul," said Isobel, with a faraway look in her eyes.

Maria rolled her eyes upwards. "I say we give it fifteen minutes," she said, full of certainty. "If Jay is not back down by then, you will know everything you need to know. Because that girl is only good for her bed, and there's no mistake about that."

Eamon's apartment had the unkempt look of temporary accommodation; bare and unloved with empty bottles on the table and discarded clothes draped haphazardly on the furniture. As Gina and Jay sank into the sofa, Eamon opened a bottle of wine and filled a glass to the brim, handing it to Lucy with a flourish. She looked timidly into the redness and took an unladylike gulp, before pulling Gina up from her seat as Eamon flicked on the music.

"Come on, Gina, let's dance for the boys."

Lucy put her arms around Gina's neck and began to swing her hips. Gina stared helplessly at Jay but allowed Lucy to grind against her body as she swayed passively in the centre of the room.

"Come on, Jay, join the party," said Lucy, meaning to seem casual but unable to disguise the sound of her pleading.

"I'm about danced out tonight," he said, looking into his lap.

She broke off from Gina and tried to pull him to his feet, desperate for affection and reassurance. But he resisted and she, recoiling in rejection, reached for Eamon, swirling herself around him in manic, hysterical sadness. And as Lucy spun she began to feel the room spin; Eamon grabbed her as spinning turned into falling and she landed on the sofa, staring blankly at the faces above her.

"I think you're about done in, Lucy," said Jay, "it's time to call it a night."

"I'm fine, I'm fine," she insisted, slurring her words as the room spun. "Just give me a few minutes, and I'll be fine." She closed her eyes, shutting the room out as nausea washed over her.

Gina clasped Jay's hand between hers. "I think I should go now, Jay. Will you take me back, please?"

Jay hesitated. He had encouraged Lucy into Eamon's eyes with relief, even pleasure, but to leave her in her current state seemed a step too far. Gina pulled at his arm again, silently imploring him to leave and sure that, if what they witnessed in the car was any indication, this was where Lucy wanted to be. But he couldn't convince himself that was the truth and he bent over Lucy's lifeless form, patting her on each cheek as he spoke.

"Lucy, it's Jay. We need to get you home. You need to get up, ok?"

Her eyelids fluttered but she only groaned, a green pallor glistening beneath the sweat of her brow. Jay was preparing to lift her when Eamon appeared carrying a blanket. He placed it over Lucy and turned to Jay, his face full of promises and boundaries.

"It will be the devil of a job getting her down those stairs, boss. She might be better sleeping it off where she is."

Jay looked down at Lucy who seemed to have fallen asleep, her thumb crammed into her mouth like a baby.

"She'll be sound where she is, boss. Here, take my keys, I'll get a cab in the morning."

Again Jay held firm but Gina squeezed his hand, nodding reassurance.

"Maybe you're right," he conceded. "I'll wheel by in the morning with her suitcase."

Gina pulled him gently to the door and shut it before he could look again, ushering him out and to the car. Eamon watched them, not moving from the window until the headlights were a distant orb of light in the winding streets. As the glow faded altogether, he strode over to Lucy and pulled the blanket from her body. He surveyed her for a moment before hauling her up and tugging off her dress, already engorged by the mere thought of what he was about to do.

Isobel allowed herself a sigh of relief as Jay and Gina appeared on the steps.

"Looks like you were wrong, Maria, no night of debauchery after all," she said triumphantly, grinning with the beginnings of elation. Maria shook her head, a grim smile on her face, looking hard at Gina. "The real test is still to come; mark my words, that young woman wants more than a peck on the cheek tonight."

Isobel said nothing, her eyes now fixed on Jay who was glancing nervously along the deserted road. He looked straight at their BMW and, if it were not for the heavy black tint of the windows, would have met Isobel's gaze.

"Do you think he suspects anything?" she asked Maria quietly, as if afraid Jay might hear her.

"No, impossible," said Maria, as she hit the ignition and followed the car. "What man would suspect you of following him in a car?" Isobel conceded with a laugh. "Besides," said Maria, interrupting her mirth with scathing honesty, "if Jay did think he was being followed, then there's probably at least one hundred other people that it's more likely to be — if he's as much of a rogue as some say."

They pulled in at a safe distance as the car stopped. Jay got out and looked back at the BMW again before helping Gina from her seat.

"Shall we have a coffee now Jay?" she said, leaning towards him until her breasts brushed his chest.

"I'm sorry, Gina, tonight it is I who lacks the courage."

Gina laughed automatically, convinced he would not refuse her, and pulled at his arm. Isobel held her breath as he relented, and joined her on the doorstep, as she searched in her bag for her keys. She dangled them before him smiling, but he took hold of her and gave her a polite kiss on the cheek, before jumping back in the car and speeding off.

Isobel and Maria watched in amused shock as Gina threw down her pashmina, and stood staring down the street after the taillights of Jay's car.

"Looks like he got cold feet," was all Maria could offer as she waited for Isobel's gloating victory speech.

But Isobel's mind was now swimming in doubt, all her uncertainties returning as she thought of Lucy and Gina, of Jay's calm magnificence amongst the bedlam of the evening, and of his cool indifference as he left Eamon's apartment.

"Let's go home, Maria," she said, her voice low and weary, as she fought back her tears.

As cool, faint rain washed away the excesses of the night from the streets of Capadelli, Lucy awoke alone and naked in Eamon's living room. A bucket sat amidst a puddle of vomit on the stone floor and her face and hair were matted with stickiness. She reached shakily for her phone and called Jay, barely managing to ask to be picked up before she threw up whatever dregs were left inside her. She stumbled to the bathroom to clean herself up and, as the cold, clear water rushed over her hands, tried to piece the night together.

She looked at her face; the stickiness was not vomit and she knew all too well what it was, she could still smell it — even above the odour of sickness. Lucy tried desperately to remember whose it was as she rubbed at her face. She looked down at her body and followed the trail of stickiness with a flannel. Out of the blur of her memory an image hit her and she almost cried out at its vividness. Eamon's face looming, dark and ravenous with bulging eyes above her bare breasts as he entered her again, as she pulled him to her, desperate to make him finish as the room spun around her.

Tears ran down her face as she realised what she'd done, but she had no time to ascertain her own guilt before Jay arrived with her suitcase. Lucy watched him carefully as he entered; she saw no anger in his face — perhaps it was not as bad as she feared.

She smiled bravely, not wanting to let him know how clouded and confused was her memory of the night before, that she was so drunk she didn't know who she had slept with, how many people she had slept with, or what they had done with her.

"I'm sorry, Jay. I really am sorry. The state I am in and everything. I just lost track of how much I was drinking." Black mascara began to stain her face as she spoke.

Jay surveyed her with concern. Her dishevelled state did not match well with the version of events he'd received earlier from Eamon: that he had woken to find Lucy in the bedroom, asking where the loo was. That she had emerged from the bathroom naked, and climbed into his bed complaining she was cold, and that things had gone from there.

"Do you remember what happened last night?" he asked, compassion in his voice. "In which bed you slept?"

"I didn't know what I was doing last night," she babbled. "If I was hitting on Eamon it was to get your blood up, that's all. Maybe I did want to party when we got back, with the four of us, I just don't know. I really can't remember anything after we left the nightclub. You have to believe me, Jay."

Jay hesitated, trapped between conscience and opportunity, all his plans and all his fears whirring through his mind; this was the perfect moment to end things. He was confident that he could spin Lucy any version of the night's events and she would have no way of separating fact from fiction. She would be gone forever, driven away by her own irreparable guilt and shame.

She broke his silence with a sob. "I'm really, really sorry. Whatever happened last night I didn't want to cheat on you, please believe me."

She was at his mercy but he couldn't bring himself to see her hurt anymore.

"Listen, Lucy, you've nothing to be sorry for. Nothing happened last night, ok? You were just not feeling well, that's all. And you were sick in the night. That's all. Everything is ok."

He held her tightly, feeling the tears on his cheek. They stood there for a long time, taking solace from their sins in each other's arms. Finally Lucy spoke.

"What happens now?"

Jay saw Lucy as far as the departure gate. She was quietly crying as he handed her the boarding pass.

"Please, Jay, don't let me leave like this. I'm begging you. I made a stupid mistake, that's all."

Jay put his arm around her.

"It's ok, Lucy, there's no harm done. I just need some space. Some time to think about things. Don't feel bad about anything that's happened this weekend. Let's just remember the good times we had. You will be all right, you've got Rob, remember? Now you need to move or you will miss your flight."

"But you will call me?" He flinched at the helpless pleading in Lucy's voice, and for a second he was tempted to say he would.

Fifty-three

Isobel stopped as she crossed London Bridge and leant against the grey stone balustrade looking into the forbidding waters below, the sins of her summer of love wreaking her body and eating her soul. The noon-day striking of the great bell of Westminster pulled her from her thoughts. Somewhere in the bowels of the BB&T offices her husband and her lover were crossing swords, playing out the final act in the charade that was the contract signing ceremony, Jay wanting nothing more than to get away, Peter wanting nothing more than a decision on the music deal arriving before he did so. She had told Peter she was lunching with Maria in Cobham, and had promised Jay to be on the boat before twelve; if either looked out from the towering plate glass offices onto the bridge below, they would know she had lied. Well, she would lie no more.

As she entered the marbled foyer of BB&T, her stomach knotted from tension; she felt insignificant, lost in its cavernous emptiness, a vast atrium stretching above her. The cold iridescence of the walls sent shivers through her blood, and the enquiring gaze of the immaculately groomed receptionist only served to increase her anxiety. She took a seat but her restlessness forced her back to her feet, and she gravitated towards a shimmering brass plaque on the far wall, wishing she were invisible. From a distance it dazzled in the artificial light but as she grew closer the shining expanse formed into words, engraved deep in the glossy metal. They were the BB&T partners' names and she looked up at them through sad and tired eyes; she knew if Jay had played his hand differently ten years earlier, his name would, in all probability, be in front of her.

As she searched inside herself, hoping to find courage and strength for what lay ahead, hurried footsteps broke the sacrosanct silence of the marble, and she turned to see Jay.

They stood transfixed, staring at each other, his eyes glassy and awash with pain, defeat etched into every line of his face. He all but ran to her as she moved forwards. But as he went to embrace her she froze, staring over his shoulder in fear and consternation. Peter was lurking in an alcove, tall and triumphant, watching and waiting. Everything swirled around her in his shadow, fifteen years of marriage and all the life before it — everything she had and everything she wanted. Jay smiled as she stared deep into his eyes and held his arms open again in a gesture of vulnerable love. She clenched her fists in determination, the shadow of Peter ever in her mind, and embraced him.

"I'm sorry, I couldn't wait," she said. He held her for a long moment, as she let her arms fall limp, before she broke from him. He seemed to her dazed and shaken from the meeting and she saw he did not want to let go.

"The other night. I was there. I saw what happened to Lucy."

She saw him search behind her eyes before he spoke. "The white BMW?"

She nodded. He grasped her forearms pulling her back into him. "It was the only way," he said.

"No Jay, it was *your* way. And your way will never be my way." She pulled her right arm from him, and reached into her bag, and pushed the jewellery box into his palm. "It's Lucy who deserves this necklace, not me." She stepped back from him, out of his spell, and was free. "Goodbye Jay."

Isobel turned from him as he shrank away, and shuffled towards Peter, numb with pain, regret, and relief.

"I'm so, so, sorry," she said, hanging her head and afraid to touch him.

But he pulled up her chin to look into her eyes, and drew her to him, holding her into his warmth.

" I forgive you," he said simply.

She stepped away from him, and took his hands from her. "But I didn't come here to ask forgiveness. And I do not seek it." She squeezed his arm. "Everything that I have done was a choice, my choice.

Forgiveness won't change that." She saw bewilderment in his eyes. She slipped off her wedding ring and pressed it into his hand, and closed his fingers around it. "I thought I'd found what I was after, but instead I found myself." She held his gaze in silence as understanding slowly displaced confusion. She kissed his hand. "It's the right thing to do Peter; we both deserve better than…than insipid contentment." She gave his hand a final squeeze, released it, and turned towards the door.

Miles away Lucy admired the diamond on her finger as she waited for the phone to answer. The ringing stopped, and she sucked in a deep breath.

"I'm just leaving, Jay," said a cold and harried female voice.

"It's not Jay, it's Lucy Baker."

"I'm sorry honey, do I *know* you?"

"You saw me at sports day. I'm the slut with the long legs and tight arse."

Acknowledgements

I am grateful to many gifted professionals for reading earlier drafts and for their candid comments and suggestions. Most notably, Rebekah (Becky) Brown for her scrupulous editing, to Stephanie Hale of the Oxford Literary Consultancy for expert advice, to the authors Matthew Branton, Tom Fuller and Ré Ó Laighléis, for their guidance and support, to Nasrin Sharifi for her inspirational cover concepts, to my friends in the Cobham Book Club who served as a literary focus group, and to the community of talented writers and aspiring authors to be found at www.youwriteon.com who generously provided written reviews.